The Promised Land

Roberta Kagan

Other Books by Roberta Kagan on Amazon:

All My Love, Detrick

Detrick is born with every quality that will ensure his destiny as a leader of Adolph Hitler's coveted Aryan race. But on his seventh birthday, an unexpected event changes the course of his destiny forever. As the Nazis rise to power, Detrick is swept into a life filled with secrets, enemies, betrayals, friendships, and most of all, everlasting love.

You Are My Sunshine: A Novel of The Holocaust
The Companion Novel to *All My Love, Detrick*

A golden child is engineered to become a perfect specimen of Hitler's master race. But plans can change. Alliances can be broken. Love and trust can be destroyed in an instant when people are not what they seem. In a time when the dark evil forces of the Third Reich hang like a black umbrella of doom over Europe, a little girl will be forced into a world that is spiraling out of control, a world where the very people sworn to protect her cannot be trusted.

The Voyage: A Historical Novel Set during the Holocaust, Inspired by True Events

On May 13, 1939, five strangers board the MS *St. Louis*. Promised a future of safety away from Nazi Germany and Hitler's Third Reich, unbeknownst to them, they are about to embark on a voyage built on secrets, lies, and treachery. Sacrifice, love, life, and death hang in the balance as each fight against fate, but the voyage is just the beginning.

A Flicker of Light

Hitler's Master Plan was devastating. In 1935, the Nazis established a program called "The Lebensborn." Their agenda: to genetically engineer perfect Aryan children. These children were to be the new master race once Hitler had cleared all undesirable elements out of Europe. Within a year, the home for the Lebensborn was built. These institutions were designed to give the appearance of comfortable homes where the expectant mothers were provided the finest food and care. However, the homes for the Lebensborn were in fact glorified prisons where the women, who were doing their patriotic duty by having a child for Hitler, were prevented from leaving by armed guards and barbed-wire fences. Even if a mother changed her mind and asked to keep her child, it was impossible without the consent of the father, who must be willing to adopt the baby. It was not until the papers were signed that the mothers learned that any child born with even the slightest defect would be immediately euthanized. This was a terrifying discovery for the women, as they were now powerless to protect their offspring. After the child was born, the mother was forced to leave the institution and any further knowledge of her child's future was never revealed to her.

The year is 1943. The forests of Munich are crawling with danger under the rule of the Third Reich, but in order to save the life of her unborn child, Petra Jorgenson must escape from the Lebensborn Institute. Alone, seven months pregnant, and penniless, avoiding the watchful eyes of the armed guards in the overhead towers, she waits until the dead of night. Then Petra climbs under the flesh-shredding barbed wire surrounding the institute and, at risk of being captured and murdered, she runs headlong into the terrifyingly desolate woods.

Even during one of the darkest periods in the history of mankind, when horrific acts of cruelty became commonplace and Germany seems to have gone crazy under the direction of a madman, unexpected heroes come to light. And although there are those who would try to destroy it, true love prevails. Here, in this lost land ruled by human monsters, Petra learns that even when one faces what appears to be the end of the world, if one looks hard enough, one will find that there is always "A Flicker Of Light."

The Heart of a Gypsy

If you liked *Inglorious Basterds*, *Pulp Fiction*, *Django Unchained*, you'll love *The Heart of a Gypsy*!

During the Nazi occupation, bands of freedom fighters roamed the forests of Eastern Europe. They hid, while waging their own private war against Hitler's tyrannical and murderous reign. Among these Resistance Fighters, there were several groups of Romany people (Gypsies). *The Heart of a Gypsy* is a spellbinding love story. It is a tale of a man with remarkable courage and the woman who loved him more than life itself. This historical novel is filled with romance and spiced with the beauty of the Gypsy culture. Within these pages lies a tale of a people who would rather die than surrender their freedom. Come. Enter their little-known world . . . the world of the Romany. If you enjoy love, romance, secret magical traditions, and riveting action, you will love *The Heart of A Gypsy*.

Please be forewarned that this book contains explicit scenes of a sexual nature.

"A Nazi on Trial in God's Court"

Himmler, Hitler's right hand man, has committed suicide to escape persecution after the fall of the Third Reich. What he doesn't realize is he must now face a higher court: God's court. In this story, he meets Jesus and is tried in heaven for crimes against humanity, and the final judgment may surprise you.

The Promised Land

Roberta Kagan

Please visit www.RobertaKagan.com for news and upcoming releases by Roberta Kagan. Join the email list and have a free short story emailed to you!

A note from the author:

I always enjoy hearing from my readers. Your feelings about my work are very important to me. Please contact me via Facebook or at www.RobertaKagan.com. All emails are answered personally, and I would love to hear from you.

Foreword

In 1917, many years before the Nazis terrorized the world, Great Britain made a promise to the Jews in Palestine and the Zionist Federation. The British vowed that if the Jews would support the Allied efforts in World War I, the British would "use their best endeavours to facilitate the achievement of . . . a national home for the Jewish people" in the country of Palestine. It was the dream of this homeland that kept many Jews alive while they suffered in concentration camps.

The Balfour Agreement

From the Jewish Virtual Library

The British government decided to endorse the establishment of a Jewish home in Palestine. After discussions within the cabinet and consultations with Jewish leaders, the decision was made public in a letter from British Foreign Secretary Lord Arthur James Balfour to Lord Rothschild. The contents of this letter became known as the Balfour Declaration.

Foreign Office

November 2nd, 1917

Dear Lord Rothschild,

I have much pleasure in conveying to you, on behalf of His Majesty's Government, the following declaration of sympathy with Jewish Zionist aspirations which has been submitted to, and approved by, the Cabinet.

His Majesty's Government view with favour the establishment in Palestine of a national home for the Jewish people, and will use their best endeavors to facilitate the achievement of this object, it being clearly understood that nothing shall be done which may prejudice the civil and religious rights of existing non-Jewish communities in

Palestine or the rights and political status enjoyed by Jews in any other country.

I should be grateful if you would bring this declaration to the knowledge of the Zionist Federation.

Yours,

Arthur James Balfour

When World War II ended, the world gasped in horror at the atrocities that the Third Reich left behind. They were so appalled at the massive piles of dead bodies and emaciated survivors that they began hunting for Nazi war criminals. A military tribunal was formed with representatives from the United States, Russia, France, and Great Britain, and trials began for the Nazi criminals in Nuremburg, Germany. Several of Hitler's elite could not face persecution and committed suicide while awaiting trial.

However, not all of the Nazis were caught. Before the war ended, the Third Reich had secured friendships with several South American countries. These countries offered safe harbor to those Nazis able to escape justice.

When Hitler was sure that his regime was lost, he went to his underground bunker with his longtime girlfriend Eva Braun, as well as Dr. Joseph Goebbels, Mrs. Goebbels, and the six Goebbels children to commit suicide. When the bodies were found, the six children lay on a bed asleep for eternity. Eva Braun, Dr., and Mrs. Goebbels lay dead as well. Even the lifeless body of Hitler's beloved German shepherd was found. All of them had taken cyanide capsules. However, Adolf Hitler's body was not with them. There has always been speculation that he may have escaped. On the other hand, what if we entertained the idea that in a secret mission, the Führer had been kidnapped and murdered?

Meanwhile, the broken and tortured Jews were liberated from their persecutors. Now they were free, but everything that they had had before the war was gone. They found themselves without homes, and most of them ended up in displaced persons camps. What suffering under Hitler had taught them was that the Jews needed a homeland, a safe place where they could go when the rest of the world turned their backs on them. So, remembering the promise that the British had made in 1917, the Chosen People turned to the United Kingdom and asked the British government for the land of Palestine. Arab resistance to a Jewish homeland in Palestine was strong. Seeking good relations with Palestinian Arabs in the hopes of retaining critical political and economic interests in the area, Great Britain failed to keep its promise.

Chapter 1

Spandau Prison, 1947

At six a.m., a loud alarm sounded to awaken the prisoners, the captured notorious Nazis housed in the fortress known as Spandau Prison. The once highly respected Work Detail Führer, Manfred Blau, stretched.

It was the first of the month, and on the first of each month, the prison patrol changed hands. Each of four world powers took turns protecting the world one month at a time by lording over the Nazis serving time in Spandau. Today, the Americans assumed control. They were the best wardens; the food and treatment were humane under the US, unlike the month-long terms under the Russians. They were savages. Having fought the Germans on the battlefield, the Russians poured their remaining aggressions on this handful of Hitler's top men. The Brits and the French were not as bad. Manfred wondered why the British didn't engage in torturing the prisoners. After all, Germany had bombed the hell out Britain. Well, if you really gave it some thought, the Nazis had massacred the Americans in Normandy, too. There was really no rhyme or reason to their callousness; the Russians were just more brutal.

He quickly made his bed, if you could call it a bed. It was really no more than a simple iron army cot with a wooden board beneath the mattress. The board was placed there in a futile attempt to give the lumpy mattress some shape, but instead, it felt as hard as the black cement floor.

When the Nazis had controlled this prison, they'd painted the walls a dark forest green, causing the cell to feel as if it were closing in on its inmate. That was one of the Nazis' means of extreme torture. Hitler's henchmen had other methods, too, many of them even worse. But the Germans only used Spandau for political prisoners. Once the concentration camps were running, the Nazis began to employ even more vile methods of torment.

Manfred sighed. If he had to be incarcerated, at least it was never under the rule of the Third Reich. If he found the Russians brutal, he knew that they would appear like angels compared to his own party.

He knew how heartless the Nazis were. They were trained to be that way. Any sign of weakness was not only frowned upon by the party, but it could cost the weakling his life. Weakness was considered a sign of inferiority and would not be tolerated in a member of Hitler's superior race.

Manfred had not started out as a violent man, but he'd adapted. He had to in order to survive, to be accepted, to stay above scrutiny. So, he'd been brutal to the Jews that he had been forced to control at the two camps where he'd been stationed. His rough treatment toward them came from his disgust at having been forced to work in the camps in the first place. He was an artist. If his damn father-in-law had kept his nose clean, Manfred would never have been subjected to the vile conditions in the camps in the first place.

The guards would be coming to open Manfred's cell any minute, but before they did, he wanted to take a look out the small barred window above his bed. He stood on the cot and gazed out, as he did every morning. The peacefulness of the dawn always seemed to calm him.

"Blau. 63927," the guard said, banging his stick across the cell bars. "Let's go. Get in line. Breakfast."

Manfred left his cell and got into the procession of men. It always amazed him that the prison was so well guarded. There were more personnel than he could count: guards, medical staff, cooks. Outside, the walls were ten feet high and covered with broken glass and barbed wire. They'd certainly made sure that the seven prisoners, eight including Manfred, would never escape.

Manfred smiled to himself. This was evidence that his jailers were still afraid of the Nazis. They knew that Germans were born smarter. That was why they had better be sure to take severe precautions to contain them. Deep down in their small minds, these Americans, French, British, and Russians knew that the Aryans were the superior race. And they also knew that the Nazi party would rise again.

As he did every morning, Manfred got in line behind Walther Funk, nodding to him as he did. Then behind Manfred was Albert Speer. He was the only man there whose company Manfred enjoyed. The men marched through a cafeteria line where their trays were filled. Then they proceeded to the long wooden table to take their seats. On the other side of the table sat Baldur von Schirach, Konstantin von Neurath, Karl Dönitz, and Erich Raeder. All the way down at the end, always alone, never associating with the others was the most important prisoner of all, Rudolf Hess.

In better times, when the Germans were winning the war, Manfred had seen Hess at parties. They had never spoken; Hess was a loner, always at Hitler's side with Göring, Himmler, Eichmann, and Manfred's best friend and mentor, Dr. Joseph Goebbels. Now they were all dead, except for Hess and the handful of men in Spandau Prison. Manfred had heard rumors that Eichmann had escaped, but he was not sure if they were true. He'd never known Eichmann very well. Once or twice, he'd seen him at meetings. Eichmann always gave Manfred a chill. His head was always cocked to one side, with that lazy eye, which seemed to be passing judgment on anyone who came under its glassy scrutiny.

The prisoners sat quietly eating their breakfast of two hard-boiled eggs, a slice of toast with butter, and a small bowl of applesauce. When the Russians were in charge, there was never any butter or applesauce and only one egg was served. Manfred looked at his plate and decided that it was good to have the Americans back. There would be strudel after dinner again. *Yes, America prided itself on being humane even to the inhumane*, Manfred thought, as he shook his head smiling. *Foolish Americans*. They reminded him of big St. Bernard dogs with wagging tails.

Just then, a male voice speaking in broken German with a strong American accent came over the loudspeaker. He began reciting the rules. Each time the controlling country changed, some jerk felt it necessary to announce the regulations again. Manfred could almost recite them verbatim. No talking with fellow prisoners, no newspapers allowed, no diaries or memoirs of any kind, family visits limited to fifteen minutes every two months. Not that it mattered much to Manfred since he had no family left anyway. The worst thing of all was the nighttime flashing of the lights. Every fifteen minutes a guard came around flashing a light in his face to be sure he had not committed suicide. If he hadn't already considered killing himself, this continuous disruption of his sleep could certainly influence him in that direction.

With a sideways glance, Manfred quickly looked over at Hess, wondering what the man might be thinking. He was certainly handsome with his wavy, coal-black hair and dark, brooding eyes. All of the guards, from every one of the countries, kept a heavy watch on Hess. The rest of the prisoners were not so important, and the guards never paid much attention to them. Except perhaps Speer. He had been one of Hitler's favorites. In fact, he was Hitler's architect.

Here at Spandau the prisoners were referred to by their numbers rather than their names. Manfred knew that this was just another method of dehumanizing and humiliating the prisoners. The Nazis had used the same method on the concentration camp victims.

Manfred kept an eye on his jailers. He could see that they were far too busy arranging their own lives to waste their time getting to know a bunch of Nazis. Well, it was their loss. *They certainly could have learned a lot from their captives*, Manfred thought. To the guards, this was just a duty, and the only job that they were told to perform was to be sure that no one escaped. They executed the task with diligence.

After the Germans finished eating, they were escorted outside, where each of them had been given a small plot of land to garden. The Americans, the French, and the British allowed them to grow whatever they chose, but the Russians insisted that they grow only vegetables, no flowers. This disappointed Speer. Many times Speer had told Manfred how much joy he found in the beauty of his flower garden. He'd taken great care to arrange it just the way he felt it should be, with the colors complementing each other, the shapes and sizes of the plants coordinating so as not to overwhelm. Manfred had to admit it was lovely before the Russians discovered what Speer was growing and pulled everything out of the ground. Personally, Manfred didn't care about the flowers. He didn't care about the vegetables either. He was just glad to be outside of the stone, blood-colored walls, out in the fresh air, far away from the smells of disinfectant and death that hung inside the prison.

The sun began to grow brighter as the dawn turned to late morning.

Manfred Blau leaned back on his haunches and smoothed the soil around the slender green sprout. It always amazed him when the earth gave birth to that first tender shoot. How strange that from a tiny seed a life could be born. Miraculous! And he had to admit, he did enjoy having the fresh vegetables harvested and used in the prison kitchen.

He gazed across his plot and saw Rudolf Hess kneeling as he carefully planted a seedling into the earth. What had become of them? How had this all happened to his precious Third Reich? He had blindly believed the Führer when he had promised the German people that the Reich would last for a thousand years, pledging his allegiance to the party and allowing the doctrine to penetrate his mind and soul until it became a part of him. And now, everything had gone bad. Darkness had enveloped his beloved Third Reich, and here he was in Spandau Prison. Adolf Hitler had ended his life, but more importantly, Manfred's dear friend and mentor, Joseph Goebbels, had also committed suicide.

Then to make matters worse, after Manfred had been imprisoned for three months, he'd received a letter informing him that his wife, his only love, Christa, had died. She'd been ill for a long time, and although he expected the news, when it came, it shot through him like a cannon tearing through his belly, leaving a gap that he felt could never again be filled. Even if he ever left this place alive, he would never see her again. Just the knowledge of that was enough to drive him into a deep depression.

Before she'd died, Christa had sent a letter that seemed to say good-bye. She'd informed Manfred that she'd given their adopted daughter, Katja, away to a friend who had agreed to take care of her. She said she felt it was best not to disclose in a letter the name of the friend in case someone was monitoring his mail. This news unnerved Manfred, not because he cared so much for the little girl. He'd been too busy with his work at the concentration camps to spend much time with the child, but he knew how much Christa loved Katja. When Christa gave Katja to someone else, that indicated to Manfred that Christa knew she was dying and that her time would come soon.

Manfred assumed that Christa had taken the child to her birth mother. That would have been the logical thing to do. After all, Christa had all the paper work telling her the name of Katja's mother. They'd received all of the documents guaranteeing them that the child they were adopting was of pure Aryan blood. In fact, the Lebensborn Institute had assured them that the child had been checked thoroughly, and she was not tainted with any unsatisfactory characteristics.

That was such a happy time for the couple, filled with love and the promise of a wonderful future. Manfred sighed with bittersweet pain as he recalled that visit they'd made to Steinhöring, the home for the Lebensborn, in Munich. It had almost been like reliving their honeymoon, which had also been in Munich, courtesy of the Reich. In his mind's eye, he could still see Christa on that day when they had gone together to collect the child. She had smiled at him. She was so happy. Seeing her this way made his heart melt. Then she took the child into her arms for the very first time and he saw the tears roll down her cheeks. The love he felt for her swelled inside of him, and he was afraid he might cry, too. He hadn't cared about being a parent, but he knew she did, and because he adored her, her joy was all that mattered.

For a while, their lives seemed perfect. Manfred was on his way to becoming a success with the party. He was working directly with Goebbels, Hitler's Minster of Propaganda, who had become like a father to him. He was married to the girl of his dreams, and their small family was thriving. They had plenty of food, and he was making a good salary. He and Christa were invited to the most exclusive parties, and they had been accepted into the highest circles. It seemed as if nothing could ever go wrong.

Then, on Katja's third birthday, Christa's father, Dr. Henenker, shot a hole right through Manfred's idyllic life. Dr. Henenker had been caught hiding Jews. The Reich turned an angry eye on Manfred. After all, this was his wife's father. How could he not have been connected to the crime in some way? Christa foolishly begged him to intervene on her father's behalf. Manfred assured her that he had no control over what happened to Dr. Henenker. He told her to forget her father, that her father would pay the penalty of death and there was no changing that.

Now Manfred had to prove himself, or not only would the doctor pay the penalty of death but so would Manfred, Christa, Katja, and Christa's mother. All night long, Manfred had agonized over what to do about the situation. It was then that his friend Dr. Goebbels had come up with a solution. In order to demonstrate that he had no prior knowledge of his father-in-law's crime, and to prove that his allegiance was to Hitler and the party, Manfred agreed to shoot and kill Dr. Henenker while Christa and her mother were made to watch. He didn't want to do this, but it was the only way that he could show them that he put nothing above his loyalty to the party.

So, in one dark moment, everything Manfred had spent his life carefully building vanished. The Reich accepted his act of devotion by allowing him and his family to live and also by permitting him to remain a member of the party. However, there had to be punishment, and so, Manfred lost his prestigious office job and was sent to work as an officer in a concentration camp.

Thus began the curse, a dark shadow that continued to follow him. It was at that first camp that he'd met the devil. He could still remember her face. Zofia, the Jewess, the one who had tempted and taunted him with her wild eyes. Everything that he did to her was her doing; her evil powers had forced him to lose self-control. She was not human, she was an evil spirit; he had no doubt about that.

When he received the letter from his dying wife, Manfred had held the letter to his chest. While sitting in his cell, alone, he had cried. Then, with trembling hands, he had asked the guard for a pen. The guard had been reluctant at first, but Manfred gave him a package of cigarettes, and the guard gave him ten minutes to use the writing implement.

He was rushed. He would have liked to take more time, to contemplate his words, but since there was no leeway, he quickly answered that letter from Christa. Manfred wrote his heartfelt apologies for everything he'd done over the years that he and his wife were together. These were confessions he'd wanted to say so many times but was unable to speak the words. Now, alone in his cell, with ten minutes to apologize for a lifetime of mistakes, he began, "My darling, My Christa, I have never, nor will I ever, stop loving you. You may find it hard to believe, but you are my reason for living. You were the reason that I did what I did . . ." He spoke of the regret he had for what had happened with her father, with the child, with the party, between the two of them. "If I knew that you had found it in your heart to forgive me, I could go to my death in peace. When I am executed, it will be your face that I will envision, and if I have your forgiveness, then it will be my memories of you that will lighten my load. I will eagerly await a response from you. Your husband and the man who will love you even in death, Manfred."

That was how he'd ended the letter, the ink smeared slightly from a single teardrop that fell as he carefully folded the toilet paper he was forced to use for his letters. But he'd never received an answer. The next time he heard news of Christa, it was in a letter that came from the hospital informing him that his wife was dead. He'd never recovered from the loss; not fully anyway. He accepted the knowledge because he had no other choice, but he knew he would never again be happy. So, when Hess came one afternoon and told him that Manfred's escape was planned by ODESSA, he could find no enthusiasm in the knowledge. He agreed to do what was asked of him.

Manfred knew that ODESSA was using him to test the waters. They wanted to see how difficult it would be to liberate a prisoner from Spandau before they attempted an escape for Hess. But Manfred didn't care; it didn't much matter to him if he lived or died. He had nothing left to live for anyway.

Now, in the prison yard, Manfred looked across the plots of land and watched the prisoners as they raked and hoed the soil. So, this was what had become of the beloved Third Reich, the Reich Hitler had promised them would last for a thousand years. Albert Speer, Erich Raeder, Funk, and others were locked up like animals. He'd heard whispers that Eichmann, Mengele, and perhaps more had escaped to South America, but no one knew if this was fact or just hopeful speculation. If all went as planned, he would soon be in South America as well. If there were other Nazis who had escaped, he would join them and help plan a rebirth of the Reich.

He should be excited, but without Christa it all seemed pointless. The bright sunlight stung his eyes like tiny pinpricks. He squeezed his eyes shut. And then he saw them again, those black onyx eyes that haunted him. The eyes of the Jewess, Zofia. She'd cast a spell on him; he was sure of it. He could not rid himself of her memory. He should never have taken her into his house, never have touched her body in that dirty way. Hitler had forbidden sex between Aryans and Jews, and now he knew why. If you took a Jewess to your bed, she would possess you like a demon. That Zofia woman had not wanted him, and he knew it, but he could not help himself. Sometimes he'd gotten rough, he had lost control, but even so, her life was not nearly as bad as it would have been if she'd remained living in the barracks with the other prisoners. Manfred had been kind to her, kinder than he'd been to any of the others. Then, after all that he'd done for her, giving her the opportunity to escape the starvation, disease, and filth of the barracks, bringing her to live with him and his family, the ungrateful bitch had turned on him. She had sat in front of the tribunal in Nuremburg telling them what a monster he was. In fact, she was probably a good part of the reason that he was convicted.

He knew Jews were dangerous, extensions of pure evil. In fact, he had heard that they ate something called matzo, a bread made from flour mixed with the blood of Christian babies. And he also knew that Zofia hated him. When he'd forced her to lie with him, it had given her the opportunity to penetrate his soul and curse him for all time.

Manfred's eyes stung from the light of the sun. Lately he'd developed terrible feelings of panic, of loss of control. He gasped for breath and then fell back on his buttocks, his heart pounding wildly. *I should have killed that Jewess while I had the chance, should have broken the spell before it took hold. As long as that woman lives, I am in danger*, he said to himself.

"Manfred Blau, you have a visitor." It was Mitchells, the guard who had been paid off by ODESSA. Manfred had been expecting the visitor. But this was not a good time.

The sun's rays pierced his eyes. He squeezed them shut and then opened them again. There was only darkness, with just a hint of light at the periphery of his vision. He closed his eyes hard again, trying to make the darkness disappear, to make his vision normal. Nausea brought a stream of vomit into his throat. He did not want anyone to see him puke, so he swallowed. For a while, it had seemed as if these incidents had stopped, but now, clearly, the dizzy spells were returning.

"Blau?" Mitchells was getting impatient.

"Yes, I'm coming," Manfred croaked.

Manfred swallowed hard, the vomit kept creeping back up. He was trying to regain composure. His mouth felt like a desert at noon, but he forced himself to stand on his shaky legs. Then, slowly, Manfred followed the guard inside the prison.

They sat with a wall between them, Manfred and the visitor. The visitor was a very thin man in a dark blue suit with a crisp white shirt and a matching navy blue tie. His eyes were so small that it was difficult to determine their color. He was bald on the top of his head, but the perimeter was surrounded by thick coarse white tufts cut very short.

"My name is of no concern to you. All you need know is that I am with ODESSA, and I have the plan for your escape from Spandau. If all goes well with you, next we will go forth with our rescue efforts for Rudolf Hess."

Manfred nodded.

"Now, listen closely and I will tell you the plan . . ."

Chapter 2

Koppel Bergman packed his cardboard valise with the few items he'd acquired while in the DP camp, then he tightened his belt. His pants were so big on him that they seemed like an inflated balloon. The previous night, he'd said good-bye to the Americans who had helped him in the DP camp and then had checked into a cheap hotel where he would prepare for his journey. He wanted to get far away from the watchful eyes of the other Jewish survivors, studying him and wondering where he was going. The DP camp had not been a welcoming atmosphere for Koppel because so many of the Jewish refugees remembered him as a member of the Judenrat in the Warsaw Ghetto. The Jews had not forgotten his face. They knew him well. Under German orders, they had selected him to join this Jewish council, but as the war wore on, Koppel had cooperated with the Nazis.

When he'd first become a Judenrat, he felt guilty. But his mother had insisted he take the role to which he was appointed, even that he work with the Nazis rather than against them. She wanted the additional ration cards. And since his father had died many years ago when he was only eleven, she'd leaned heavily on him always. He wanted to please her; she knew him well, and she had the power to make him feel like a king or like a worthless nobody. Because of her, he had never married. Instead, before the war, he'd spent his years devoted to the Jewish community. When it all began he was close to forty, and she was already an old woman. Although sometimes he wished he could abandon or kill her, he knew he would do neither. He both loved and hated her.

Each day, it was Koppel's job to choose which of his fellow Jews would be next to go on the trains to the camps. The Nazis gave him a quota that he had to meet. So he'd walk through the streets scribbling names to fill the next boxcar.

For a while, it had made his life easier. He had access to food and luxuries the others could only remember from before the Nazis came to power. Because he had the power to be generous and so few had anything at all, he'd had his choice of women, all except one. Zofia. Zofia, that bitch. He had been so generous to her. He had even given extra food to the two old lesbians she lived with. And how had she thanked him? She'd spurned him, giving her affections freely to another man.

Koppel rubbed his rheumy hazel eyes with his thumb and forefinger. He'd never had good vision, and it seemed to be getting worse.

Zofia. He hated to think about her. And he hated the shame he felt when he remembered the time he'd spent in the ghetto. There was no doubt that he'd done things that he should feel guilty for, but times were bad. It was every man for himself. He had done what he had to do to survive.

Once the Nazis had had no more use for him as a Judenrat, he had been loaded onto a boxcar. He'd respected the guards, treated them like friends, but in the end, Koppel was still a Jew. Even now he could remember that train stinking of shit, vomit, and death. He had known that the Nazis didn't really care for him, but he had expected better treatment than the others. He'd helped the Nazis, worked beside them, sacrificed his own people for their cause. And, for as long as it had lasted, his life as a Judenrat had been good.

On the train, he'd been spurned by the other Jewish prisoners, called names. They'd even spat at him. But he hadn't cared. He was too busy contemplating the scheme he'd already put into motion, and trying to figure out what he would do to survive once he arrived at his final destination. As a Judenrat, he knew better than the others what was in store at the end of the journey. So, he knew that he had to find a way to save himself. Koppel was aware that they were on their way to Treblinka, and Treblinka was a death camp.

At a death camp his chances of survival were slim. So, although he'd been unable to find any way to escape, he'd done the next best thing. As a Judenrat he had become friendly with one of the guards in the ghetto. Not a true friend, Koppel didn't delude himself into believing that the bastard was sincere. Koppel was too smart for that. But at least he and the Nazi were on speaking terms, familiar enough for Koppel to use his wits to convince the Nazi to have him transferred to Auschwitz instead of Treblinka.

It all began late one night when one of the Judenrats was sent by the guards to leave with the rest of the Jews on a transport to Treblinka. Koppel saw that happen and decided that he must do something to save himself quickly. Until one of his peers had been included in the transport, Koppel had hoped that his work for the Nazis would save him from sharing the fate of the other Jews. Now he knew better.

With his heart pounding out of his chest, Koppel had searched the entire ghetto, then waited until one of the other Nazis left and the guard he knew well was walking alone. Koppel called to the Nazi from an alleyway between two buildings. The guard gave him a puzzled look, but he walked over. That was when Koppel sprung the trap. Koppel told the Nazi that he had buried a two karat diamond ring somewhere in the ghetto. First Koppel tried to offer the ring as a bribe for his escape, but the Nazi refused.

"Sorry Koppel," the guard said, smiling. "They know how many of you Jews are left here in the ghetto. I cannot let you go because it could cost me my job. But about that ring." The guard lit a cigarette. "I could torture you and make you give me that ring. You realize that don't you?"

"I realize that, but you still would not have the ring because I would die before I gave it to you," Koppel said, trembling as he stood in front of the man who would decide his fate. Koppel's mind was like a runaway freight train moving at one hundred miles per hour. His heart had leapt out of his chest and was threatening to pound right out of his throat. This was his only chance. He had to come up with something quickly, before the moment passed.

"If you send me to Auschwitz instead of Treblinka, I will tell you where to find the ring."

The guard smiled and took another puff of his cigarette. "Of course, I will have it arranged for you. So, now that we have gotten that out of the way, tell me. Where is the ring?"

"Not now, not until I arrive at Auschwitz safely."

"And how will I get the information from you then?" the guard asked, raising his eyebrow.

"Send one of your friends to find me," said Koppel. "Someone you can trust."

The guard bit his lower lip. "What a fool you are Jew to challenge me," the guard said, shaking his head.

But Koppel had expected this, and his answer to the Nazi was simply, "I am worth more to you alive than I would be dead. If I am dead, you will never have the diamond. It is worth a lot of reichsmarks.

What difference does it make to you where I go, or what happens to me once I am gone from here? Think it over. If you can arrange for me to be taken to Auschwitz instead of Treblinka, I will direct you to where the jewel is buried."

Koppel had more inside information than most Jews, and he knew that if he could not escape his fate altogether, Auschwitz was still a better option than Treblinka. At least at Auschwitz, if he was strong enough and lucky enough, he might be used for slave labor. Laborers had a better chance of survival than those who served no purpose to the Nazis.

The guard studied Koppel for several moments without speaking. Then Koppel saw a quick flash in the guard's eyes. Koppel recognized the flash, it was *pure greed*. Taking a deep breath, Koppel knew that he had hit his mark.

"Very well. I will have someone meet you at the end of the line in Treblinka and send you on your way to Auschwitz. You will find that it is not much better there, but who knows, maybe you'll survive. I don't care what happens to you as long as you live long enough to give the information about the ring to my friend. And know this, Jew; if you are lying and there is no diamond, I will see to it that you meet a more horrible death than you can ever imagine."

"You will have the diamond," Koppel said.

So after the train arrived at Treblinka and the other prisoners were herded like cattle from the train into the camp, Koppel was pulled away and taken by one of the guards who said that he had been instructed to meet Koppel at the train. Koppel felt a glimmer of hope that maybe things really had gone his way when he was taken to the Lodz ghetto, but that hope was smashed immediately when he was shuffled on to another train. This time he was fairly sure that he was on his way to Auschwitz. Well, at least the Nazi had not lied to him, yet.

He knew if he survived the transport, at some point he would be approached by an arranged connection and forced to divulge where to find the ring. Then, once he'd given up his hold on the diamond, if the guard threatened him, he would explain that he had buried jewelry all over the ghetto and that this was only one of many pieces. If need be, he would use the rest slowly to entice them for as long as he could to stay alive. These heirlooms and expensive trinkets were pieces that he'd received in exchange for bits of food, and now they were his only hope.

The train he was now riding to Auschwitz had the same horrific conditions as the one he'd taken to Treblinka. He'd escaped certain death, but from what he understood about his new destination, Koppel knew that he must appear healthy when he arrived. He knew Dr. Mengele would be standing at the station, as the train was unloaded, pointing at each person, directing each one to the left or to the right. Those headed left were destined to live, but those going right would die. It was as simple as that. If a prisoner looked as if he could work, he would be sent to live; if he were too weak or too old, he would be sent to the gas chamber right away, the same day he arrived.

Koppel had stepped off the train, and from where he stood he could see Mengele's white coat and the two lines forming. His heart pounded in his chest. He began to pray, but secretly he feared that God was angry with him for everything he'd done to the others in the ghetto. Still, he begged and pleaded.

After he had gotten closer, he felt as if his heart would burst through his chest, shooting his blood all over Mengele's starched white coat. Koppel's vision had clouded and the earth began to spin, but he had willed himself not to pass out. As he had approached the Nazi who would decide if he would live or die, he could not help but plead with God for forgiveness for all that he'd done to his fellow Jews. Then, by some miracle, he'd been sent to the left.

When he heard the words, "To the left," and saw Mengele's long gloved finger pointing to the line for the living, he almost fell to his knees with gratitude. But he knew he must resist. At any moment, and for any reason, Mengele could change his mind. Instead, Koppel had thanked God silently and repeatedly for sparing his life. His mother had not been as fortunate. He had watched helplessly as she was sent away to the gas chamber. His heart and mind conflicted, he had felt a strange mixture of pain and relief.

Once he'd made it through the initial ordeal of changing into a gray striped uniform and endured the shaving of his head, his forearm had been tattooed with a number. The needle and ink burned as they entered his flesh. For the rest of his life, this number would serve as a reminder of where he'd been, what he'd endured, and also what he had done. In those first days, his fingers had grazed the angry red skin surrounding the tattoo often.

It was a week later that he was approached about the ring by a Nazi officer who was visiting the camp. Koppel gave the officer the location of the diamond. Although until the day he was liberated, Koppel feared that the Nazi officer would return, Koppel never saw him again.

Now in his hotel room he looked at the numbers on his arm. Because of them, even in the heat of summer, he wore a long-sleeved shirt.

In the camp, Koppel knew he had to keep a level head if he was going to survive. He had to make himself useful. After he had been branded like an animal, he'd studied the workings of the place, carefully watching until he found a way to make himself indispensable to the Nazis.

Then, like in the ghetto, he had begun to work for the Third Reich, this time as a kapo. The kapos were the Jews that had been assigned to keep the other prisoners in line for the Nazi guards. Once again, he had traded his fellow Jews for a few extra crumbs of bread. And of course, once again, he had been hated, had been branded as a traitor, a brand even stronger than the tattoo on his arm. Everyone saw Koppel as the Jew who had helped the Nazis kill his own people.

Well, it had not been easy, but at least he'd survived. Not only had he survived, but he'd earned the trust of the guards also. This had given him the opportunity to steal some tiny pieces of gold that he'd found among the ashes of the burnt Jewish bodies. In the teeth of prisoners, it was gold that had been overlooked as the Jews had been sent into the gas chambers or burned in the crematoriums. Once even, he had found a ring.

These treasures had not been easy to acquire. He'd taken a huge risk going out in the dark of night and sifting through the gray mass of ash, stumbling upon bones and other human matter. His hands had trembled. He'd gagged, but he had continued lying face down in the pile of human residue, holding up to the light of the moon anything that looked as if it might be of value. There had not been a lot, but there had been enough . . . just enough for him to keep hidden until now, just enough for him to start his life over. What good would that gold have been to a dead man? They were just small pieces he'd stolen and had stuffed up into his anus, in case he had been caught on his way back to the barracks. He'd lain on the floor removing them quietly, had hidden them under a broken floorboard under his cot. Then, when nobody was around on another night, he'd gone out behind the barracks, had dug a hole, and had buried his treasure.

During the day, he'd watched that space constantly. His eyes darting as the prisoners had been lined up for roll call each day. If his treasure had been discovered the guards would have taken it. Then they would have killed the prisoners one at a time until someone had admitted to having stolen it.

He'd seen this happen once.

Two guards had found a half loaf of bread under a mattress. While the roll call was being read, one of the guards had held up the bread, demanding to know the name of the thief. Nobody would come forward and admit that they had stolen the loaf. So the guards had gone down the line shooting each prisoner who shook his head denying that the bread had been his until they had come to a young man, no more than seventeen.

They had held the bread in front of him. From where Koppel stood, he had seen the boy trembling. The adolescent had been about to deny that the bread belonged to him. Everyone had known that he would be shot, but before the boy had spoken a voice came from the end of the line. It had been that of a middle-aged man, perhaps forty. He had called out, "It is mine. I stole the bread."

Koppel had heard a whisper from one of the prisoners: "That is the boy's father."

The guard had walked over to the older man and had called him out of the line. "No Papa," the boy had cried out. "NO."

"You say that you stole this bread?" the guard had asked the older man.

"Yes. I did," the man had said. Everyone had known that he would protect his son with his own life.

"NO!" Again the son had wailed.

Koppel had wished this business finished. Koppel had reasoned, *If they killed the older man, I will be safe. That will be the end of it. But if they don't, there are only five more prisoners before the guards get to me.*

"I stole it," the father had said.

"Get down on your knees." The guard had kicked the older man in the back while he was kneeling, causing him to fall forward. "Get back on your knees, swine. Now put your hands behind your head."

The man had done as he had been told.

The son had rushed out of the line and had run to his father. "Please, it was mine. I stole it."

The guard had turned on the boy, shooting him.

A wail had come from the father. Then the guard had turned the gun on the older man, shooting him in the back of his head, too. Blood poured from the two bodies and mingled on the cement.

"Let this be a lesson to all of you not to steal from the Reich," the guard had said. Then the guard had pointed his gun at two prisoners, one of them Koppel. "Clean up this filthy mess," he'd said.

As Koppel had wiped the blood off the ground, his eyes had never left the spot where he had buried the gold.

Well, that was behind him now. He'd sold enough of the gold to have what he needed to leave Germany forever. The rest was sewn into his coat, to be sold piecemeal. Koppel had paid his way, with the blood money, and soon he would board the ship *Exodus* and be on his way to Palestine. There he would do his best to shed the stigma of his past and become a part of the Jewish community. But, this was just a stepping-stone. He had bigger plans. As soon as it was possible, he would apply for a visa to the United States of America where he would go to start his real life. There he could disappear into the crowds and truly leave everything he'd done behind him.

He combed his thinning hair as he looked into the cracked mirror. He felt like a very old man. His fingers trembled, and he'd developed a condition whereby he produced too much saliva; often it dribbled down his chin. Above his left eye, he wore an angry red scar to remind him of the time a guard at the camp had hit him with his rifle butt.

So much had happened. He'd witnessed such atrocities, and his participation in many things still haunted him. But the memory that bothered him the most was sending the woman Zofia on the train to Treblinka. When he'd written her name and those of the two lesbians she lived with on the list of those being sent to the camp, he'd done so in anger. He remembered her turning to look back at him; her soft black curls cascading down her back. Their eyes had met, but only for a moment. He had been sitting at the table assigning the next group of Jews to be taken, and she and the two old women were being shoved into a boxcar. The strangest thing about it all was that he loved her, but because she loved another man, had taken that man to her bed, Koppel had needed to make her pay. When the door to the train car had slammed shut, it had struck such fear and pain in his heart that he had gone to the bathroom and washed the sweat from his face with cold water. By the time he'd returned, the train had been on its way out of the station to the dreaded camp.

Koppel doubted that Zofia or either of her friends had survived. Very few did. Very few were capable of doing what it took to make it through. Koppel knew how to stay alive. He survived because he traded everyone and everything to save his own life.

He clicked the closures on the suitcase shut. No use thinking about the past. It was time for him to start over. What he had done, he'd done because he had no other choice. Koppel stretched his back and heard the bones crack. A crash of thunder startled him and he jumped. Looking out the window Koppel saw that the sky had turned the color of burnt ashes and was streaked with silver flames of lightening. A storm had sprung to life out of nowhere.

It was time to go. Koppel had no umbrella, but he did have a raincoat. Slipping the slicker out of his suitcase, he threw it on. Then he picked up his bag, turned off the light in the dirty hotel room, and walked out, closing the door on Germany and all he'd witnessed there forever. Koppel had at least a day's train ride to Marseilles. Then from Marseilles, he would have to travel by bus to the port of Sète where finally he would board *Exodus* and be on his way to Palestine. The Promised Land.

Chapter 3

Shlomie Katz knew that the time had come to leave the DP camp. He'd been wasting away long enough. It was certainly no paradise, dirty and overflowing with sick and grief-stricken refugees. Everyday more poured in . . . these poor, tortured souls were all that was left of Hitler's plan for mass eradication of the Jews.

Even though Shlomie was at the camp day in and day out, the smell still bothered him, and the stories from those who'd traveled to this German DP camp from camps in Poland horrified him. They'd come to Germany because here they would be under the protection of the Americans who seemed to want to help them make their way to Palestine. Even though the Jews had been liberated, feelings of anti-Semitism in Europe had not decreased at all. One of the arrivals at the camp told a story of a small village in Poland where, following the liberation, the Jews who were still alive had returned to their homes. There they were subjected to a pogrom where they were murdered by their former neighbors.

Perhaps Zofia and Isaac were right when they said that the only choice for Jews was a homeland of their own, a Jewish state in Palestine. Shlomie would have preferred to go to America, however securing visas was almost impossible. Not that getting to Palestine was much easier. The British had promised the land to the Jews, but now Bevin, the prime minister of Britain was reneging on his word. It seemed that the Chosen People would never be at peace.

Shlomie washed his face with a bucket of cold water and thought about Zofia. He knew why she'd left early that morning before he'd awakened. He'd asked her to marry him, thinking that with Isaac missing, she might consider it. He had always loved her, from the first moment he saw her. But, she did not love him; she would never love him. Even when Isaac was gone, Zofia did not turn to him, a fact he had to come to terms with.

When Isaac had gone out to the forest to find food for the three of them, it had been just Shlomie and Zofia. In his mind he'd created a fantasy. He'd made believe that the two of them had fallen in love and planned to marry. Then, when the Americans had picked them up and taken them to the Germany DP camp, it had been the two of them again. Shlomie had accompanied Zofia to see her daughter Eidel. He'd held Zofia as she cried when she had decided that it was best to leave Eidel with Helen, the woman who had taken Eidel and raised her as her own while Zofia had been locked in the Warsaw Ghetto. It had been plain to see that Eidel thought of Helen as her mother and Zofia as a stranger. Shlomie had been proud of Zofia when she put her child's feelings before her own and left Helen's home without Eidel. He'd held her as she cried; he'd comforted her. Then he told her of his feelings, confessed his love, proposed marriage, but she'd refused him.

A short while later, she had left the DP camp early in the morning while he was still asleep. She'd left forever without saying goodbye. He'd awakened as he did every morning, looking for Zofia. When he'd turned over, he saw her empty cot. The pain he felt in his heart had been so great that he could not cry. Maybe it was just that he had been through so much since the beginning of the Nazi takeover. He'd endured the loss of his family, his friends, and his home. Then he'd suffered unfathomable cruelty in the camp, only to escape and live in constant fear while hiding in the forest. Perhaps he'd forgotten how to cry.

Well, no matter, the time had come for him to put in a request to the Americans to help him find a way to Palestine. It might take a while, but then again, he had time. In fact, he had nothing but time. If he could just get out of Europe, leave the memories behind, perhaps he would find a wife to care for. And if he were fortunate, perhaps he might even find it in his empty heart to love again. And then maybe, just maybe, by some magical stroke of luck, this imaginary woman might just learn to love him, too. Yes the time had come. Shlomie must put one foot in front of the other, take one breath at a time, and slowly start living again.

Chapter 4

"Katja, come here sweetheart," Zofia Weiss called. "You should have a little something to eat before bed; we have a long trip in the morning." Zofia knew that Katja had been too excited to eat her supper, and she would not eat much when she awoke. Katja had no appetite in the early morning.

"We are going all the way from England to France, right?"

"Yes, Sunshine, that's right." Zofia got up and took Katja's hand, leading her to the kitchen. "How does some bread with jam sound?" She knew that Katja would eat bread with jam even if she refused anything else. Over the years, Zofia had come to know this child very well.

"And once we get to France, we are going for a long boat ride all the way to the Jewish homeland, right Mama?"

"You are a very smart little girl. And that is why you are my sunshine." Zofia said, and she kissed the golden blond locks on top of Katja's head. God, how she loved that child.

Zofia had worked and saved every penny to make this dream of finding her way to Palestine come true. But it was with a heavy heart that she would sail toward the Promised Land, because this dream was a dream she'd shared with the only man she had ever loved, Isaac Zuckerman, and he was gone. She had lost him when she, Isaac, and their friend Shlomie had escaped from the Nazis. They had been hiding in the forest. Isaac had gone out to find food and had not returned. Zofia knew that if he had not been killed or captured, he would surely have come back. She and Shlomie had searched for Isaac for several days, but he was nowhere to be found.

How can it be that life goes on even when a part of you has died? she thought while spreading strawberry jam on the thick slice of bread.

"Mama?" Katja was tugging at her arm.

"Yes, my sweet Sunshine."

"Look, Ethel is wearing the new dress that you made for her. She wants to look her best for the trip." Katja held Ethel, the rag doll, up in the air. Ethel was the only toy she owned. Zofia had made the doll for Katja using buttons and yarn to create a face and hair. "When we get to Palestine will you teach me to sew? I'd like to make doll clothes," Katja said, her bright blue eyes shining with interest.

Zofia knelt down and hugged the little girl. "You are only seven. I am not sure you are old enough to work with a needle. You could hurt yourself." This child was all she had in the world, and although she'd not been her birth mother, Zofia felt as if she were her true mother.

"I promise to be careful. You said we would try to buy a sewing machine of our own and that maybe you would start a business as a dressmaker. Remember?"

"I do remember. And I would love to do that, but why don't we wait and see what life is like in Palestine."

"Mama," Katja looked up at Zofia. Zofia could see the storm brewing behind her daughter's gaze. "I am sad."

"But why are you unhappy? You were so excited to go on the boat and to see Palestine."

"I am going to miss Elizabeth, and all my other friends at school, too."

"I know, but you will make new ones. Come sit beside me and I'll read to you."

Katja cuddled up to Zofia as Zofia began to read.

That night after Zofia had bathed Katja and put her to bed, she began to pack their things. There was not much, just a few dresses. Two of Katja's and two of Zofia's, their underclothing, and toothbrushes. Once the suitcase was filled, she locked her bedroom door. Then she unlocked the bottom drawer to her desk and took out a long fat envelope stuffed with papers. She listened at the doorway to the bedroom to assure herself that Katja was asleep. Then she opened the envelope.

The last time she'd looked at these papers had been when Christa had brought the child to her. The words that were written within these documents told the story of Katja's beginnings. Her mother, Helga Haswell, had given birth to her at Steinhöring, the home of the Lebensborn Institute, and a year later she had been adopted by Christa and Manfred Blau. Zofia had known the Blaus very well. Manfred had been the Work Detail Führer at the camp where Zofia, a Jew, had been imprisoned. He'd chosen her to come and live with his family in order to help his wife, Christa, who was sickly, care for the child.

As Zofia had come to know Christa and Katja, she had learned to love them. However, Manfred's tortured mind had caused him to inflict terrible acts of cruelty upon Zofia, as well as upon his own wife, who had born the scars of both the physical and mental injures in silence. The longer Zofia knew Manfred, the more she had come to despise him.

Once the war had ended and Manfred had been arrested, Christa feared that she was too ill to care for Katja alone and so had come to Zofia. Christa had seen Zofia at the trial where Zofia had testified against Manfred. That night Christa had gone to Zofia's hotel room and had begged her to take Katja and care for her. Christa had told Zofia that she knew how much Zofia loved Katja, and if Zofia would take the child then Christa could die in peace, knowing that child would be safe in Zofia's care. Zofia had agreed. She did love Katja and was happy to have her.

Now that several years had passed, that love had become even stronger, and she and Katja had grown inseparable.

Zofia bit her lower lip; the feeling of the envelope in her hand burned her fingers. She tucked the papers into the bottom of the suitcase. Several times, she'd considered burning them, but she couldn't be sure whether someday Katja might need information on her medical background. But unless that happened, it was best that the papers remain hidden. The words on those documents would only scare and confuse the child. Zofia covered them with the clothing. Next, she tucked the Star of David necklace that she'd given Katja for her last birthday into the side pocket. Then Zofia closed the suitcase and lay down beside her daughter to try to sleep for a few hours before the ordeal began.

In the morning, Zofia prepared a light breakfast of bread and cheese. Then she quietly entered Katja's room. For a moment, in the stillness of the morning, Zofia watched Katja sleep, marveling at the sweet little miracle she'd been blessed with. Katja lay on her side, her thumb in her mouth. Just a hint of shadow from her eyelashes was cast upon her cheek as the morning light began peeking through the window.

"Katja," Zofia whispered, gently rubbing the child's soft ivory cheek with her forefinger. "Sunshine, it's time to get up," Zofia said, leaning down and kissing Katja's forehead ever so lightly.

The little girl stirred and looked up at Zofia, blinking and rubbing her eyes.

"Good Morning, Sunshine." Zofia said. During the last six months when they had lived in Great Britain, Zofia had learned to speak the language very well, and she only spoke to Katja in English or Yiddish, never in German. Secretly, Zofia feared that hearing the German language might bring back painful memories for her daughter.

Katja smiled.

"I have some breakfast ready for you."

"I'm not hungry."

"I know that, Sunshine. I know you hate to eat first thing in the morning, but we have a long trip and I think you should try."

"All right," Katja said. Zofia smiled. Katja was such an agreeable child. As Zofia watched Katja get out of bed, her small delicate feet bare against the wood floor, Zofia's heart hurt with the depth of the emotion she felt toward this little one.

Zofia had insisted that Katja always wash her face and brush her teeth upon rising. It had become a habit. So, before she went to the table, Katja engaged in her morning routine.

With Katja at the table picking at the bread and cheese her mother had prepared for her, Zofia finished adding the final items to their suitcase; toothbrushes, soap, and washcloths. When Katja could eat no more, Zofia wrapped what was left of the breakfast in a white towel that she placed in her handbag. She knew from experience that Katja would be famished at about ten a.m.

"All right now, go on and get dressed. I laid your clothes out on the bed for you," Zofia said.

"Yes, Mama."

They walked to the train station, Katja with her doll in one hand, wearing a light blue summer dress, her blond curls bouncing as she walked. Zofia, with her slim figure and long dark hair, was carrying the suitcase in one hand and holding the child's hand with the other.

As they waited to board, Zofia thought about Isaac. He had had golden hair; he could have easily passed for Katja's father. How she missed him. She'd shut away the dreams they had for a life together when he'd disappeared that day in the forest. All she had left of him were the wonderful dreams and the beautiful memories.

Zofia helped Katja up the steps and onto the train. They found two seats together. "Can I sit by the window, Mama?" Katja asked. "Ethel has never been on a train, and she would like to look out the window." Katja held the doll up toward the glass.

Zofia smiled and nodded. "Of course you and Ethel can sit by the window."

Katja sat down but got up immediately.

"It's hot." Katja said, and Zofia realized that the leather seat would burn Katja's legs so she took one of her dresses out of the suitcase and laid it on the seat. Then she lifted Katja and put her on top of the fabric.

"Better?" Zofia asked.

"Yes, thank you, Mama," Katja said. Zofia leaned down to kiss the top of Katja's golden head, and then she sat down beside her.

An older woman with graying hair and matching skin sat across from them. "What a lovely child," she said as she looked at Katja.

Katja eyed the woman suspiciously and leaned in closer to Zofia. *She is so shy,* Zofia thought. *I hope she will be able to make new friends in Palestine.*

"Thank you," Zofia said turning to the woman.

Katja watched intently out the window as they passed through the English countryside, but after a while the motion of the train rocked her to sleep, her head on Zofia's shoulder.

The ride from London to Dover took approximately two hours. Katja slept on and off, sweating, her face flushed with the heat. She complained when she woke that her legs and back hurt from sitting. Zofia felt bad for the child. She realized that such a grueling trip would be exhausting for Katja, no matter how much she slept. The heat of the summer in early July made the journey uncomfortable. However, had it been winter, the trip would have been far more perilous.

In Dover, they boarded a crowded ferry that reeked of garlic from sausages and salami. It was hard to find a seat that was not in direct sunlight. Zofia feared that the hot rays would make Katja ill, so Zofia took Katja downstairs where she laid her dress down on the cool floor and told Katja to sit on it. They were headed across the English Channel to Calais. The boat ride would take no more than two hours; if all went well, they might make it in an hour and a half.

When they finally left the boat, Katja complained of a headache. Zofia wet a cloth with the small canteen of water she'd brought and held it against her daughter's forehead.

"We are in France now, Sunshine." Zofia knelt so that she would be on the same level as Katja. Then she smiled at Katja and wiped her face with the towel.

Next, they would have to take a train to Marseilles. If only she'd had the money to purchase a berth, it would have been easier to make Katja comfortable. Well, she didn't have the funds, and there was nothing she could do now. All she could do was make Katja as happy as possible. This was a lot of traveling for a child. In fact, once they arrived in Marseilles, they had to take another train for over two hours to Sète, where they would board *Exodus* and be on their way to Palestine.

By the time they were seated on the train in Marseilles, Katja was hungry. She ate far too quickly. The gobbling of her food and the motion of the train upset her stomach, and she began vomiting. Zofia kept her daughter close. She pulled Katja's hair back and held a paper bag for her as she retched. Once Katja was finished, Zofia wet the cloth again and wiped Katja's forehead.

Then Katja began to cry.

"Shhh, you're going to be fine. You're just not used to all of this traveling. It's all right. Shhh. It's going to be just fine," Zofia cooed softly as she wrapped a trembling Katja in her arms.

"My stomach hurts, and I'm scared," Katja said

"Don't be afraid, my darling, my Sunshine. I will never let anything happen to you. Do you believe me?"

Katja nodded.

"Do you know how much I love you?"

"Tell me again," Katja said, smiling slyly. This was an ongoing jest between them.

"I love you with all my heart," Zofia said. Zofia was comforted by Katja's smile. It told her that Katja had begun to feel better.

"Sing my song, Mama?" Katja asked.

Zofia gently squeezed Katja's shoulder. Then she began to sing softly as the train rolled along the track.

"Good morning merry sunshine, How did you wake so soon? You've scared the little stars away"

Katja joined in. She knew this American song very well. Zofia had sung it to her for as long as she could remember.

"When skies are gray," they sang together, mother and daughter. A heavyset woman with several ample chins in a pink flowered housedress beamed at them from across the aisle.

"You'll never know, dear, how much I love you." As they sang "I love you," mother and daughter, as had become their custom over the last few years, pointed at each other, and then laughed.

Chapter 5

"It has all been arranged. You will go to the dock at Sète in France, and be taken by U-boat to Argentina. Once you are there, a car will be waiting to take you to a remote village in the countryside. No one there will know you or care about your past. A small villa on the outskirts will be provided for you with everything that you will need. Once you are moved in, you will stay inside your house and make contact with no one. Then you must wait until a man comes to your door. He will tell you that the mynah bird sings one thousand songs. That phrase is the password. That is how you will know that he is your contact. This man is a trusted officer of the Third Reich. His name is Konrad Klausen. Commit this name and the phrase to memory, because you must not write it down anywhere. Do you understand everything I am telling you?" the Odessa agent asked.

Manfred nodded.

"There is no room for error."

Again, Manfred nodded.

"What was the password?" the agent asked.

"The mynah bird sings one thousand songs," Manfred said.

"And the man's name?"

"Konrad Klausen."

"Good, very good."

"But how am I to get out of this prison?"

"Listen carefully. I will tell you what is to be done. Now, my directions must be followed exactly, do you understand?"

"Yes." Manfred nodded.

"Good, then I shall tell you all that you need to know."

Manfred felt a bead of sweat tickle his chest beneath his shirt. His eyes were locked on the goat-like eyes of the slender man from Odessa.

"In a few days, Manfred Blau, you shall be joined by a cell mate. His name is Dolf Sprecht . . . That will signal the beginning of your escape."

Chapter 6

The SS *Exodus* was originally a US-owned coastal passenger ship called *President Warfield*. Zofia looked at *Exodus* and her heart sank. Could this old battered vessel make it across the Mediterranean Sea with all of these people on board? She bit her lower lip and looked down at the top of Katja's blond hair with worry. What if the ship sank? What was she thinking? How could she have taken her child on such a dangerous journey? *I must not think about the risks or we will never get to Palestine. Katja and I have waited so long to be on our way to the Promised Land. This is our only chance.* Zofia had worked hard to make this dream a reality; she had scrimped and saved. During the day, she took in work as a seamstress, sewing ornate gowns by hand. Then three nights a week, she cleaned factories. Her sleep suffered, but she was young and strong, and she wanted more than anything to leave Europe and find her way to a land where Jews were safe.

In order to work at night, Zofia had arranged for Katja to stay in the care of the downstairs neighbor, Joanne. Joanne had a daughter Elizabeth, who was only a year older then Katja. Zofia had paid Elizabeth's mother to watch Katja and that was how the two little girls had become best friends. Now, Zofia wondered if she was making a mistake taking Katja away from the life she had come to know. This child had been through so much already, and Zofia's only consolation was that she hoped that Katja didn't remember most of her time in Germany.

"Mama!" Katja said, alarmed, tugging hard on Zofia's sleeve. "I think I left Ethel on the train. We have to go back and get her."

Oh no, Zofia thought. She took a deep breath. "I'm sorry, Sunshine, we can't go back now. I wish we could, but even if we tried, the train has already left the station. We have to get in line so that we can board the ship."

Zofia's heart hurt as she saw Katja's eyes fill with tears.

Zofia knelt down level with Katja: "How about this? I promise that when we get to Palestine, I will teach you and you can make your own doll. What do you think? That would be fun, wouldn't it?" Zofia asked, running her hand over Katja's hair. It was obvious to her that her daughter was tired. The trip had made her irritable, and now she'd lost her doll.

"I wish we could get Ethel. She was looking forward to going to Palestine."

"I know, but we can't. But I promise you, Ethel will be just fine in France. When we make your new doll, you can learn to make clothes for her as well." Zofia knew how much Katja longed to learn to sew. She'd wanted to wait until Katja was a little older, but she decided that this was the only way to make Katja feel a little better.

"You promise?" Katja said, rubbing her eyes, which had turned red with exhaustion.

"I promise, I'll teach you. You'll have to be very careful of the needle. You will be careful won't you?"

"Yes, of course, Mama." Katja smiled, and Zofia felt a little better.

"Come here let me hug you." Zofia could feel Katja was clammy and sweaty. Her dress clung to her small frame. It was July 11th, a sizzling summer day.

Zofia hugged Katja and held her for a moment, feeling the tiny heartbeat against her own.

"Let's keep the line moving," said an angry, wrinkled old man standing behind them and wearing a tattered brown suit far too big for his skeletal body.

"Mama, I'm so warm. It's so hot outside." Katja's face was flushed and her brow wet with sweat. Zofia's eyelids felt heavy from the harsh rays of the sun and the relentless heat.

"Do you want a drink of water?" Zofia asked Katja. There was not much water left, but she'd saved as much as she could for the child.

Katja nodded "Yes, Mama, I'm very thirsty."

Zofia put the suitcase down on the ground beside her and reached into her handbag bag to search for the canteen she had packed. As her fingers navigated through the contents (her wallet, their papers, and several handkerchiefs) in an effort to find the water, Katja spotted a man walking a small black and white dog. Without warning Katja turned and ran after the man. Zofia called her name, "Katja, come back here right now!"

When Katja continued after the man, Zofia called out frantically, "Katja come back!" Zofia knew that if she moved, she would surely lose her place in line. As it was, they had at least two hours to wait before boarding.

"Katja," Zofia cried. But Katja was out of sight. Zofia could not run while carrying her heavy valise, so she left her suitcase and went dashing after Katja. Pushing through crowds of people in a panic, Zofia began to feel the perspiration trickle down her brow and moisten the armpits of her dress. She looked everywhere, but she could not see Katja. Zofia cried out again, her voice hoarse with fear. So many people, anything could happen. Katja could even have fallen in the water. "No God. Please . . ." Zofia was crying, her head spinning around, looking in every direction. Finally, Zofia spotted a little girl with curls the color of daffodils on the other side of the dock. She ran as fast as she could.

"Katja . . . don't run away like that," Zofia said hardly able to catch her breath. "What were you thinking?" Zofia grabbed the little girl and wrapped her in her arms.

"Look, Mama. Look at the puppy."

Zofia was suddenly angry. "I see the puppy. But, you cannot leave my side. Do you understand me? What you did was so dangerous." Zofia didn't realize how harsh her tone of voice had become until she saw that Katja was crying. Then Zofia's shoulders slumped, the anger dissipated, and she broke down.

"I'm sorry, Sunshine. I know it has been a long hard day for you. But please don't leave my side again. Someone could take you, or you could have been hurt. You must stay with me at all times. Now let's get back in line before we lose our suitcase, if we haven't already. I'm sure we have lost our place." Zofia shook her head, exasperated. She took Katja's hand and began to lead her back to the line. Then she saw a familiar face.

"YOU!"

"Zofia!"

"Koppel."

He nodded. His expression was a mixture of fear, anger, and joy.

"Mama, when we get to Palestine can I have a dog?"

"We'll see." Zofia could not take her eyes from Koppel's face. Her voice was a deep, menacing growl. "Do you know what happened to my friends and me after you sent us to the camp?"

Koppel swallowed hard. His hands trembled so greatly that they looked as if they were going to detach from his arms. A thin line of drool began dripping from his mouth.

"Fruma and Gitel, the two ladies I lived with. Remember them? I know you must. Those two ladies who were so kind to you, I'm sure you can't have forgotten? Well, Koppel, because of what you did, they were taken to the gas chambers; sent to their deaths right away, as soon as they got off the train. Their blood is on your hands. YOUR HANDS, KOPPEL! And me? I suffered plenty, too. Plenty. Now, after all you did to the Jews, you would dare to go to Palestine? To the Jewish homeland? How could you?"

Koppel tried to push her out of the way.

"Don't you touch me, you dirty pig," Zofia said, shaking herself back.

Koppel pushed her harder and she fell to her knees on the cement floor.

"Mama!" Katja cried out in terror.

Then Koppel turned to walk towards the line to board the boat. But, just as he did, a man came out of nowhere. A tall, strong, and muscular man. His fist caught Koppel in the mouth, blood shooting out like a torpedo, as Koppel fell to the ground.

Zofia's hand went to her throat. Could it be? Could this be true? Was it a vision? Was it possible? Dear God, am I hallucinating from the sun? "Isaac?" she said, her voice barely a whisper.

"Zofia, thanks be to God. You are here. I thought you were dead. I cannot believe it's you." His blond hair glistened in the sunlight.

"Mama, who are these people?"

Zofia could hardly breathe.

Isaac helped her to her feet. His hand traced the line of her face. His eyes were deep azure pools of emotion. "My Zofia . . . you are here. This is like a dream. When I was captured, all I could think of was you. Every day that I was in the camp, I worried and prayed that somehow you would get by, somehow God would find a way and you would live. I searched and searched for you after the war. Then I went to a DP camp. When I got out, I looked again. But I couldn't find you anywhere." Isaac said, embracing her tightly.

Katja pulled at Zofia's skirt. "Mama? Mama, who are these people?" she asked.

"Eidel?" Isaac said, nodding his head towards Katja.

"No, Katja."

He looked at her puzzled. "Later," she said "I will explain."

Koppel's eyes darted around. He was getting up from the ground slowly. His nose was still bleeding, but he seemed to be trying to slip away unnoticed.

"This man—" Zofia saw him slinking off and she pointed to Koppel. "—this man was the Judenrat that sent me and my friends to the concentration camp."

Koppel fell back down when Isaac's eyes trapped him, holding him fast to the ground.

Isaac stood like a mountain over Koppel. "Listen to me. We are going to Palestine. If you are on this boat, make sure I never see your sorry face again, because next time, if the child is not present, I might just kill you."

Koppel's face was pale. His hands trembled even more than usual as he lay on the ground. Who was this giant, this Goliath of a man with the heart of King David? Koppel was terrified of him.

"Get out of here. I feel sick to my stomach when I look at you," Isaac said.

Koppel gladly got up. He grabbed his bag and ran into the crowd.

"Mama? You still haven't told me what's going on here."

"I know, Sunshine, I will. Just give me a little time. Right now we must hurry. I left our suitcase behind when I came looking for you. I pray that no one has stolen it." Zofia took Isaac's hand on one side and Katja's on the other and began to walk very quickly back toward the boarding line. Her palms were damp and itchy, worrying about her belongings. If the suitcase was gone, so were the papers with the facts about Katja's birth in the home for the Lebensborn. That would not be so terrible, except whoever might take those papers would know that Katja was not born Jewish. In fact, she was a child engineered by Hitler to be the perfect specimen of an Aryan. Katja was a combination of a blond, full-blooded, German mother and a father who was an officer in the SS. This knowledge could cost Katja dearly in her later years.

A shiver ran up Zofia's spine. She should have destroyed those papers. She should have destroyed the past before it destroyed them.

Chapter 7

"I'm Dolf Sprecht," said a young, blond man who resembled Manfred. Dolf extended his hand.

Manfred nodded as he studied the man who had just become his cell mate. "Manfred Blau." Manfred shook his hand.

Amazing how effective ODESSA was. Sprecht could have passed for his double. *Did anyone else in the prison notice that? Could the guards be that stupid?* The man from ODESSA who'd come to him with the directions for his escape had told him that he doubted anyone would pay any attention at all. Manfred Blau, the ODESSA officer said, was little more than the number on his uniform. To the prison guards, he did not have a name or a face. Not like Hess.

What had this man, this Sprecht, done to be brought to Spandau? Had he been a Nazi guard somewhere? Manfred had been warned not to ask any questions, but he longed to know. What had the spider network arranged in order to have this man placed in his cell? What had Dolf been promised? It was obvious that Dolf did not know the entire plan. He must not have been told that they planned to kill him.

"How long is your sentence?" Sprecht asked.

"Hmm? I'm sorry I didn't hear you." Manfred said. He'd been too lost in thought to listen.

"Your sentence. How long are you serving?"

"Oh, life, I am here on a life sentence. You?" Manfred just had to ask in spite of his directions not to ask questions.

"I've served most of my time. I have only three months left." Sprecht said. "I have heard of you. You are rather famous, you know?"

"Me? Famous?" Manfred chuckled.

"You are a war criminal, aren't you?"

"That is a term that has been used to describe me. However, I don't see myself as a criminal at all. I am a soldier, a man who followed his heart in a quest to build a better world. We lost the war, but that doesn't make me a criminal. I am loyal to my chosen party. To the Reich, to the building of the Aryan race, to a greater good.

"Yes, well . . ."

"Are you German?"

"Yes, I am."

"And did you not support the Fatherland, support our Führer?"

"I did and I do, more than you know. I believed that what our Führer had been trying to accomplish was the making of a world far better than the one we live in. But I cannot see how he could have just abandoned us, leaving us to the mercy of our enemies. How could he have committed suicide when we need him more now than ever? Unless, by some miracle, he is alive. Have you ever thought about that? Have you ever considered that possibility?"

"I have thought of it, certainly, but it is believed that he and several other high officials were found in his underground bunker, dead."

"Ahhh, but Hitler's body was not found."

"Are you sure of this?" Manfred sat up straight, listening intently.

"I am." Dolf said, smiling. "And that is why, whatever sacrifice is asked of us, we must all do our part to keep the Third Reich going. That is the only way we will rise again."

Manfred nodded, studying his idealistic cell mate's open smile and honest eyes. In a few days, Manfred would kill this man. That was the arrangement. He must murder this man called Dolf Sprecht. It made Manfred a little sad. He could learn to like him. The two had a lot in common. Nonetheless, this was part of the escape plan.

Outside his cell, Manfred could hear the echo of Rudolf Hess calling for the guards, complaining of stomach pain again.

Chapter 8

Zofia felt as if she had been swept up in a tornado of emotions; immense joy to be reunited with Isaac, and at the same time, gripping fear that someone had come upon the suitcase with the papers tucked deep inside and taken it. People were poor, they had nothing. It was doubtful that the suitcase would still be there. She moved as quickly as she could, keeping a grip on Isaac and Katja until she got back to the line. Over the half hour she'd been gone, the line had grown in length. It took several suspenseful moments until she recognized the crusty old man who had stood behind her and Katja, complaining. Beside him rested their suitcase. If need be, Zofia knew that Isaac would defend her.

"Mister, this is my suitcase," Zofia said, her voice as strong and authoritative as she could muster.

"I know that. I was watching it for you, holding your place in line. Now, get in line and keep moving," he said, a small smile creeping over his weathered face.

The old fellow had surprised Zofia. She thought he was ornery, but in fact, he was actually a kind person. Just weary. Weren't they all?

As they stood in line, Isaac held Zofia's hand. In his other hand, he carried their suitcases. Her suitcase tucked beneath his arm, his own in his hand. The three of them actually looked like a family. Katja had blond hair like Isaac, but she had a small delicate build like Zofia. Zofia observed all of this, and breathed a sigh of relief. Once she explained everything to Isaac, the two of them would marry and Katja would carry his name. Nobody would ever know Katja's real background. In fact, she would start calling her Kayla. At first, it would sound like an affectionate derivative of her name, but little by little, it would become her name. Then Zofia would change it legally.

Finally, they climbed the gangplank and boarded the *Exodus*.

Row upon row of bunk beds filled the deck of the boat. There was no privacy anywhere to be found. Zofia could see by the way Isaac looked at her that he too longed to be alone with her, if only for a few minutes. To hold her in his arms, to tell her all that he'd been through, and to listen as she told him everything that had happened since they were last together. She wanted to tell him everything about Katja, and then the painful events concerning Eidel. But she couldn't. Not while anyone, especially Katja could hear. For now, she must be satisfied just holding Isaac's hand and looking into his eyes, thanking God that he was still alive. It truly was a miracle.

They chose two bunks. One Isaac would share with another man, and the other Katja would share with Zofia. A look passed between Zofia and Isaac, a look only the two of them understood. Their eyes met, for only a second, but each of them knew the longing to lie together, to feel their skin against one another, to listen to their hearts beat, and to share all of their thoughts, their fears, and their desires. *This is what is meant by being in love,* Zofia thought. She'd never wanted anyone as much. A smile of understanding crept across Isaac's face. He felt the same. But he also knew that for the sake of the child, they must maintain a respectful distance.

"Welcome, my Jewish brothers and sisters." A booming male voice came over the loudspeaker. My name is Yitzhak Ike Ahronovitch, but you can call me Ike. I am the captain of this ship. If my calculations are correct, there are 4,515 of you brave souls on your way to Palestine. Like all of you, this voyage has been a dream of mine for a long time. As you can see, I can't offer you a luxury vessel for the journey."

There was laughter from the crowd

"But, we do have a ship, we have hope, and we have a dream. So without wasting any more time, God willing, let's get this vessel moving and be on our way to Palestine, our homeland."

The crowd applauded.

"To the Promised Land."

Everyone stood and cheered. Then the boat began to rock to life. A loud horn bellowed a warning as the ship of tattered people who'd survived unspeakable horrors moved slowly away from the dock and all of the memories of Nazi-occupied Europe. A slight drizzle fell from the sky, but the sun burnt brightly from behind the clouds and Katja pointed to a rainbow.

"Look, Mama, it's a rainbow."

"Yes, Sunshine, so it is," Zofia said, as she kissed the top of Katja's head, and then looked at Isaac. He sat straight and tall, the large muscles in his arms flexed as he squeezed her hand. There were tears in his eyes.

"Isaac," she said, her voice barely above a whisper.

"We are finally on our way home." He swallowed hard and looked at her, his eyes glossed over with tears.

She nodded. "Yes . . ." But she thought, *God only knows what we will find when we get to Palestine.*

Chapter 9

Dolf Sprecht snored lightly in a steady rhythm. Manfred watched him from his bunk on the other side of the cell. It was time. If all went well with Manfred's escape, then the spiders would work on Hess's, and if Hess were freed it would be a huge victory for the Nazi party. Manfred reached under his pillow where he hid the small bag he'd been given. Although the dark room did not allow him to see the contents, he knew that inside the fabric sack rested the tiny pill that would end Dolf's life and, in turn, would end Manfred's existence as Manfred Blau. For once Dolf was dead, Manfred would steal his identity. Manfred would become Dolf Sprecht. The body that would be found dead in that prison cell the following morning would be wearing the number and clothing of Manfred Blau. The guards would believe that Manfred had bitten into the cyanide capsule and committed suicide. Since Dolf had almost fully served his sentence, Manfred was about to be a free man.

Earlier that night, Manfred and Dolf had shared half of a bottle of schnapps that ODESSA had given him. However, as Manfred was instructed to do, he pretended to sip, while giving most of the drink to Dolf. Manfred had been told that the liquor contained a drug that would put Dolf into a deep sleep, making the job much easier.

Quietly, Manfred rose from his cot and walked over to where Dolf slept, the capsule feeling sticky in his hand. Manfred felt his heart racing. What if somehow Dolf awakened before it was over? Would he struggle? Manfred was not sure that he was strong enough to overtake Dolf in a fight.

Dolf snored, his mouth slightly agape. Gently, Manfred lifted Dolf's lip and carefully arranged the pill between his back teeth. Then, placing his hand under Dolf's chin, Manfred pushed hard enough to crush the pill in Dolf's mouth. Dolf's eyes flew open for a moment with lack of understanding, and shock. He stared at Manfred, as if to ask *why?* Then Dolf's body twitched and a strong odor of feces permeated the air. Manfred looked away. He couldn't bear to be so close to Dolf's face while he was dying.

It was only a few seconds that Dolf twitched and writhed, and then he was still. Manfred shuddered, and then quickly exchanged shirts with Dolf. Now Manfred wore Dolf's shirt with Dolf's number and Dolf wore Manfred's. From this moment on Manfred would be known as Dolf Sprecht. And since Dolf Sprecht would have been done with his sentence in three months, Manfred would be a free man in less than half a year.

When he got out, ODESSA would arrange for him to be transported to South America to meet a group of escaped Nazis who had found refuge there. And from there . . . well, who could say what the future might bring? For the first time since his notification of Christa's death, Manfred felt a tingle of excitement. Perhaps something wonderful might be on the horizon.

Chapter 10

Katja had made a friend, a little girl a few years older than her, who had come aboard with only her older sister. Her name was Rachel. Zofia overheard them as they sat on the ground, twisting a piece of string with their hands. Rachel was as dark as Katja was blond. Her long black curls hung down her back, her olive skin was browned to a creamy tan, and she had laughing almond-shaped black eyes.

Zofia knew Katja was shy. It had taken a long time for Katja to make friends with Elizabeth. However, this little girl was so endearing that Katja took to her almost immediately.

Zofia breathed a sigh of relief as she watched the two of them playing. She had felt terribly guilty pulling Katja away from the life to which she'd adjusted. After all, Katja had been tossed about far too much already.

Isaac sat beside Zofia on the deck of the ship. A breeze came off the Mediterranean, floating through her long dark hair.

Zofia could not yet believe that Isaac had returned. She had dreamed of this moment for years. She would daydream about it when she was awake, but when she dreamed at night, her experience was so real that she resented waking. She'd resigned herself to the knowledge that Isaac was gone forever.

But he wasn't gone; he was alive, he was here, right here beside her. She thanked God again for the thousandth time for the blessing of returning her beloved. Zofia smiled at Isaac then gently caressed his thumb with her own.

"I thought of you every day . . ." He moved very close to her ear and whispered so that only she could hear him. A shiver of desire tingled through her. She looked into his eyes and felt that she could easily lose herself there forever. He reached up and touched her face. Then she heard Rachel laugh and remembered that they were in public view, and the children were playing only a few feet away. Zofia composed herself.

"What happened after you left Shlomie and me in the forest when you went hunting for food?"

"I was captured at gunpoint by four SS officers. They were having a picnic with their girlfriends, but still had time to stop and force me into an automobile. Then I was taken to their headquarters and from there to Treblinka," he said. Then, for the first time, she noticed the dark blue tattoo of numbers that looked as if it had bled into his arm. She turned to him and gently ran her fingers over the tattoo.

"They did this?" she asked.

He nodded.

"Did it hurt?" she whispered, feeling foolish, not knowing what else to say.

He shook his head. "It hurt me much more that I couldn't see you, that I couldn't be with you, that I couldn't take care of you. I didn't know how you would manage. I didn't know if you would be able to manage. Every day, I prayed that you would find food, that you would not be captured . . ."

"Isaac . . ."

"I want to hold you in my arms. Zofia, for so long that dream was all I had to keep me alive."

Zofia heard the two little girls giggling, and she saw Rachel's sister pull a handmade doll out of her bag.

"When the army came and liberated us, everyone around me was so frail, but I was still pretty strong. Perhaps because I was captured so close to the end of the war, the Nazis hadn't had the chance to starve me to the point of weakness."

She nodded.

"Then I traveled from DP camp to DP camp looking for you. In one of those camps, I even slept in the barracks where the Nazi officers had slept. I still smelled the smell of their cologne and it made me want to vomit. After that, I left the DP camps and I went back to the forest, the forest where we had met and lived. I roamed like a nomad. I was still searching everywhere for you, praying every day. I wondered if you were wandering somewhere in the forest, unaware that the war had ended."

"I thought of you every day, as well. After the war, Shlomie and I were rescued, but we had no place to go and no money, so we were staying in an American DP camp. I began helping the Red Cross reunite people with their lost loved ones. The lists of people who were searching for their families came in every day. I was hoping that somehow, some way, I would find you." She wiped her eyes before the tears could spill onto her cheeks.

"Shhh, my darling, my only love . . . shhh. It will be all right now. As soon as we get settled in Palestine, we'll get married and then we can leave all of this behind us and begin our lives."

She nodded. "Yes, Palestine."

He swallowed hard. "Yes, the Promised Land. Finally Jews will have a homeland, a place of our own."

"I've heard it's little more than a strip of desert. They say that nothing will grow there." She smiled at him.

"Could very well be, but it will be our strip of desert. We will find a way to make it fertile. No matter what, no Jew will ever be without a place to go. When the Nazis took over, we had no one to turn to and the entire world turned their back on us. Now we will have Palestine."

She smiled at him. "Yes," she agreed.

"Mama . . ." Katja said.

Zofia turned as Katja walked over to her. "This is Rachel, my new friend, and her sister Shana."

"Hello Rachel and Shana. I am Katja's mother, Zofia, and this is my soon-to-be husband, Isaac."

Chapter 11

Had it really been so easy? Manfred marveled as they took the dead body of Dolf Sprecht away. No one, not one guard questioned Manfred's identity. They accepted him as Dolf Sprecht, and the dead body as Manfred Blau. *Amazing*, Manfred thought. *Could they really be so stupid, so dim?*

"This is what the Nazis do. They somehow get hold of a cyanide capsule and *bam*. They take themselves out," an American guard said as he placed the body onto the stretcher. "We should have watched Blau more closely."

"Yeah, I know they kill themselves. They'd rather die than face the loss of their precious Reich. All the big shots bit cyanide. Himmler, Goebbels, all of 'em," a tall American with broad shoulders and a slender waist added, as he tossed his cigarette to the ground and extinguished it with the toe of his boot. Then he took the other side of the stretcher and the two guards began to carry the corpse away.

"Well, goodbye Manfred Blau. Another dead Nazi, huh? Let's throw him in the morgue and get some lunch," the first American said.

It had worked. Manfred was now Dolf Sprecht. He would be released from prison in less than three months. Leaning back against the wall as he sat on his cot, he wished that his wife, Christa, would be waiting for him. But he knew that he had to accept that that part of his life had ended forever. So many mistakes he'd made, so much had gone sour between him and Christa. The sad part was that he would never have a chance to apologize. He thought of Christa's cornflower eyes and her wheat-colored hair. Then he thought of that little girl, Katja, who Christa had loved so much. Christa, my Christa. Everything I did was for you . . .

"Sprecht, get up . . . time to go outside and do your work in the garden." At first Manfred had ignored the guard. He didn't realize that the guard was speaking to him. Then it dawned on him; he was Sprecht. It would take some getting used to, this new name, this new identity.

Manfred stood and stretched. He leaned back and the bones in his back cracked slightly. Then he followed the guard outside. Manfred was led to Dolf's plot. He hoped they would not ask what he had planted, because he had no idea what kind of seeds Dolf had placed into the earth. It would be a surprise for all of them, most of all Manfred. From across the yard, Manfred saw Rudolf Hess. Hess nodded and smiled. All was going as planned.

Chapter 12

Shana was wonderful with the two little girls. Often she sat playing with Katja and Rachel on the floor of the deck. It amazed Zofia how strong their imaginations were. They played with toys made out of the smallest, most insignificant objects. Zofia worried about the name Katja, but she decided that it was too late to change Katja's name, even after all her intentions to change it. The child had already made friends and been introduced to others on the boat as Katja before Zofia had had the chance to intervene. So Katja would enter Palestine with the name given to her at her Nazi christening, which was held at the home for the Lebensborn.

Once Zofia felt confident that she could trust Shana to watch the girls, Zofia and Isaac slipped off to find a place to be alone on the lower deck. Under the stairs was a small unnoticed space, covered over by the staircase. It was just large enough for them to lie down Isaac took Zofia's hand and pulled her into the space. After they were sure no one was anywhere around, they fell into each other's arms. The feeling of Isaac's heart so close to her own brought tears to Zofia's eyes and the water from those tears stained her face as she held fast to him. She pulled back, their eyes locked. She leaned up to him and their lips met. When their skin touched again for the first time after so long, it took Zofia's breath away. For Isaac, it was the closest he had ever felt to God.

"I love you, with all my heart . . ." Isaac whispered in her ear after they had made love. "I still can't believe this is real. You are here with me, in my arms . . ."

She nodded, too choked up to answer.

"I will take care of you Zofia, and I'll take care of Katja, too. I will adopt her, raise her as my own."

There was an unanswered question that lay between them. Zofia knew she must tell him. "I saw Eidel."

"She is alive?" he stammered. Looking away, she knew he had been afraid to ask what had happened to her daughter. She knew she assumed that Eidel must be dead.

"Yes, she is alive. When I sent her away to live with my gentile friend Helen, I was in the ghetto, and very uncertain as to what the future would bring. I wanted her to survive. She was just a tiny baby.

"After the war was over, I went to find her. Shlomie went with me. I had planned to take her with me. But when I saw her, Isaac . . ." She felt the words catch in her throat.

"When I saw her with Helen, I knew that the baby I had sent away from the ghetto was not the same person as this little girl who loved Helen as a mother. Helen loved her, too. To take Eidel away would have been selfish. It would have hurt her deeply. She didn't know me; she would have felt that she'd been ripped from her mother's arms.

"Helen had renamed her. Her name is now Ellen. I watched through the window as little Ellen played outside with her friends. And it was then that I realized that Eidel was gone. This child that I was watching was Ellen and she was Helen's daughter. So I left, with my arms and my heart empty."

For a while there was silence. He stroked her hair and held her close to him.

"You are probably wondering who Katja is?"

"I assumed you would tell me when you were ready," Isaac said.

"It's a long and very complicated story."

"Go ahead. I am listening."

"It's strange. I'm not sure how you are going to feel about it, but I will tell you."

He did not speak. He just continued to rhythmically stroke her hair.

"When I was a prisoner in the concentration camp, I was selected to be sent to the home of one of the SS Officers. He had a sick wife and wanted a female prisoner to take care of his home and their daughter. His name was Manfred Blau. Do you know this name?"

"Nu? Doesn't everybody know the name of such a terrible man?" he seethed.

"He was a terrible man, but his wife, Christa, was not terrible. In fact, she was very kind to me. Katja . . . she was the little girl that

Manfred and his wife Christa had adopted from the home for the Lebensborn. You know what the Lebensborn is?"

"No."

"It was a program where the Nazis were trying to make perfect Aryan children. They would mate a German woman with an SS officer. Then, when the baby was born, unless the father wanted the child, the Lebensborn took the baby. When a German couple could not have children, and the father was in the SS, they were given permission to adopt one of these babies. Katja was one of the babies born in the Lebensborn. Manfred and his wife Christa could not have children, so they had adopted her."

"Oh, my dear God! They thought that they could build a race of people the way that dogs are bred."

"That is exactly right. Anyway, the Blau's adopted Katja. But when I met her, Christa was sick. Very sick. It was heart disease. She was always weak and tired. I spent most of my time taking care of Katja. I practically raised her."

"This was before we met? Before you escaped?"

"Yes. I loved Katja like she was my own. I missed my Eidel so much, it was good to have another child to nurture. I have come to regret being involved with Eidel's father, and I will be forever sad that my mother would not support me during my pregnancy, but Fruma and Gitel showed me I could endure anything. Never did I regret having my baby. I can say the same about the Blaus; working for Manfred Blau, having to submit to his whims for my own preservation, was awful, but being in the position to care for Katja was never a hardship. When I escaped Treblinka, I assumed my time with the Blaus had ended. But it hadn't."

"So, how did you find Katja again?"

"I went to the trial for Manfred, the trial in Nuremberg. I testified against him."

Isaac took her hand and nodded his head. "That must have been very hard for you."

"It was terrible. The entire time I was there, I had to look at his face. I had to remember the terrible things he did to me, to the others;

it was like reliving the nightmare all over again. But once I'd finished telling my story, I finally felt free. It was strange. It was as if I'd let go of the past and could finally live my life without thinking about what happened."

"I understand," he said.

"Anyway, I was staying in a hotel in Nuremburg for the trial. The night after I had testified, Christa came to my hotel room. She begged me to take Katja. She said she knew that she was dying and did not have much more time. She said she would not feel good about leaving the child with Manfred, even if he was acquitted, but we both knew Manfred would be convicted."

"So you agreed to take Katja?"

"I agreed."

They were both silent. Isaac squeezed Zofia's hand. "She is a pure Aryan. She has the blood of the Nazis running through her veins. You know that?"

"She is a child, an innocent child, which is all that I know. She is not a Nazi. She doesn't even know what the word Nazi means."

"You love her?" He asked.

"Very much. She is like my own daughter, my own blood."

For a long time he said nothing. The old ship rocked forward and back, in conjunction with the waves. Then Isaac lifted Zofia's chin and looked into her eyes. "If you love Katja, then I, too, will love her. We will raise her as our own child. We will raise her as a Jew in the Covenant of Abraham."

"And after we have our own children, what then?" Zofia asked. After the miscarriage in the woods, Zofia was not sure that she could bear children, but she wanted to hear Isaac's answer.

"Then Katja will have a brother or a sister."

Her heart swelled with such love for him that she felt it might burst. "Isaac, what a good man you are. And how I love you."

He leaned over and kissed her.

Often at night, screams could be heard echoing through the ship, as some of the refugees awakened with nightmares. No one mentioned these things, but they all knew that the dreams were of the horrors that the survivors had endured, terrors that would haunt them forever.

Katja and Rachel had become good friends. They spent their days together, and seeing them at play gave Zofia peace of mind that she'd made the right choice for Katja.

One afternoon as Isaac took a nap, Zofia watched Rachel and Katja as they played with three boys: Mendel, who was Rachel's age, and two others who were a few years older.

"I am the king," Rachel said "Everyone will do as I say."

"You can't be king," Abe, one of the boys, said. "You are a girl."

"So what?" Rachel answered. "I can be whatever I want to be, and if you try to stop me, I'll bop you in the nose."

Katja laughed.

"A girl who is a king? That's silly," Abe said.

"No, it's not. She can be queen with the powers of the king," Katja said.

Abe laughed. "She has no powers; she's just a girl."

"Don't laugh at her." Rachel said, "Katja will be a knight in my court."

"This is a stupid game," Mendel, another of the boys, said. "Girls being kings and knights. You should be our queens and princesses. We should be the kings and knights. Then, when we go off to battle you can give us a handkerchief as a token of your love."

"That's the way you see it, Mendel. I am going to be the newly appointed king of Germany." Rachel stood tall. "And you know why? Because I will be the knight who killed Hitler. That will be the reason I am appointed king."

"I'm not playing if you are a king," Abe said "Besides, you can't kill Hitler. He killed himself."

"Well, in my game, I killed him."

Katja smiled. "I'll be a princess. I don't mind."

"You don't have to be. You can be whatever you want," Rachel said. "I say so."

"I want to be a princess," Katja said.

Mendel smiled at her. "You can be the princess that I am going to marry. I will rescue you from the tower. How does that sound?"

Katja smiled back. "All right."

"Rachel?" Mendel questioned. "If you aren't going to be a princess, then how can we rescue you?"

"I don't need anyone to rescue me. I can rescue myself. And . . . I am not going to be a princess."

"Fine, have it your way," Mendel said and smiled at Katja, who was standing behind Rachel.

Katja lowered her eyes.

Rachel stood up with her legs spread apart and her hands on her hips. "So, here is how it's going to go. We are each going to be rulers of our own countries. And we are all going to go to war. All except Katja. Are you sure, Katja, that you just want to be a princess?"

"Yes, very sure."

"Because you can be or do anything you want to. I won't let these boys tell you what to do."

"I know." Katja got up and squeezed Rachel's shoulder. "I want to be the princess."

"Fine, it's your choice." Rachel said.

"I want to be the ruler of Palestine." Abe said.

Rachel cocked her head. "I should have chosen that. But all right. You be the ruler of Palestine."

Isaac came walking up on deck. Zofia turned to look at him. The sun burned brightly behind his back illuminating his golden hair. *He is so handsome,* she thought. *And God has blessed us. We are both alive. We are here, and we have found each other again. I will miss Eidel for the rest of my life. But . . . Katja needs me. No matter where she came from, she is just a child. She loves me like a mother, and I love her, too. I will care for her, and I will be the best mother that I can be.*

Isaac leaned down and kissed Zofia. All of the children started laughing. "Go on, you silly pumpkins," Isaac said to the children, pretending to be angry. "Go on with your game and don't pay attention to things that don't concern you."

Zofia patted the bench next to her. "Sit," she invited. "It's a beautiful day. There is such a nice breeze off the water."

"Yes, so there is."

They sat holding hands and looking out over the aquamarine-colored waters. Soon, very soon, they would be in Palestine. Neither of them knew what to expect, only what they had heard. But no matter, whatever waited for them in Palestine, it had to be better than the memories they had left behind, the memories of Nazi-occupied Europe.

The sun burned brightly during the days, and because of the relentless heat most of the men had discarded their shirts. The women had rolled up their sleeves and removed their stockings. However, at night a cool breeze swept through the dilapidated vessel, bringing relief from the sizzling afternoons. Because the ship had far more passengers than it was built to carry, the toilets had begun to overflow. The nauseating smell flooded the boat, and the clean sea air did nothing to dispel it. In the heat of the day, the odors were the worst, and often Zofia felt as if she might be sick. It had become a regular sight to see one of the passengers vomiting over the side of the boat. The overcrowding also affected the sleeping arrangements. Everyone slept in rows on the deck, and privacy was difficult to find.

However, even with all the problems on the ship, the passengers were filled with joy, hope, and expectation. Talk could be heard among the broken and torn refugees, talk of a force that had grown within them as a result of all they'd endured. A force declaring that nothing would stop them from building their homeland. And . . . soon, they would arrive in a land that, until now, had existed only in their hopes, in their prayers. The vision of a land of their own had carried them through the horrors of the camps, the deaths of their loved ones, the illnesses, and the loss of everything they owned. The dreams of a real Jewish homeland had kept them alive against unfathomable odds, and now these dreams were about to become a reality.

Or so they believed . . .

Chapter 13

"Dolf Sprecht, you are free to go."

Manfred stared at the French prison official. Over the past three months, he'd grown used to being called Dolf Sprecht. To the world, Manfred Blau was dead, and that was as it must be in order for Manfred to escape Spandau and help the Reich rise again.

What amazed Manfred most was that none of the guards had noticed the switch. They read the number on his uniform and just assumed he was Dolf Sprecht. Of course, ODESSA had arranged Dolf's murder on the eve of the first of the month, just before the countries in control of the prison changed hands. He had executed ODESSA's plan under the change from American to British control. And it had gone incredibly smoothly.

Manfred should not be surprised. How many of the prisoners in the concentration camps had he recognized by anything but name or number? After a while, their suffering faces had looked all the same. They all seemed to be masses of bones, bones that jutted against the skin so sharply it seemed as if they would cut right through. All of those terrible faces had become a blurry vision that haunted him late at night when he tried to sleep. He had nightmares of the lines and lines of stinking, walking corpses on their way to the gas chambers, limping slowly and staring at him. He could smell their unwashed flesh, as the foul odor of their burning bodies poured like the rapids of a wild river right out of the smokestacks of the crematorium.

If only Christa's father had not tried to hide his Jewish friends. As hard as Manfred tried to forget the past, to release the thoughts concerning his father-in-law and how the old man had ruined his life, everything bad always reverted back to that stupid old bastard. If not for Dr. Henenker, Manfred would have worked in the offices of Dr. Goebbels, comfortable and safe, throughout the entire war. What a wonderful job he'd had, what a wonderful time it had been in his life. Manfred had won the friendship of the powerful and respected Dr. Goebbels, Hitler's Minister of Propaganda. Goebbels had mentored Manfred, treated him like a son. And every day Manfred had made connections, rising rapidly in the party. What a bright future he'd believed awaited him. Damn his father-in-law.

"Here are your release papers, Sprecht." The French guard handed Manfred a pile of documents.

Manfred took the papers. Then silently, he turned and headed out the door of the Spandau Prison . . . a free man.

Over the course of the last three months, he'd received instructions as to what he must do as soon as he was released. These directives had been carefully smuggled in to him, and he'd memorized them and then chewed and swallowed the paper.

Manfred would miss Albert Speer. They had become friends. Speer was a man of honor. To Manfred, he represented a perfect example of a man of the superior race. Speer made it clear to all of the other prisoners that after the war had ended, he had refused to run or commit suicide. Speer said that he was no coward and that if he had not believed that what he was doing was best for the Fatherland, he would not have been a part of the Nazi party. Therefore, he would not run. He would stand up for what he knew to be right. Speer, a talented architect who had become Hitler's Minister of Wartime Production, was a man who had won Manfred's admiration. However, emotions must not cloud Manfred's judgment. There was no time for sentimentality, so Manfred Blau, now known as Dolf Sprecht, left the prison without saying good-bye to his only friend.

He only had a few hours to meet his contact at the train station in Berlin, from which he would travel to Hamburg. Apparently, his departure location had been changed at the last minute. He'd only received the information the previous night. That was probably done intentionally to keep anyone from trailing him. Manfred would be leaving out of Hamburg the following night on his way to Argentina. Before the war had ended, the Perón government had made agreements with Hitler and ODESSA that if the Nazis lost the war, they would be welcomed into Argentina. From what Manfred understood, several of the high- ranking officials of the party were already living in South America. Adolf Eichmann and Dr. Mengele were there. So was Konrad Klausen, the man who would contact him within a few days of his arrival in South America with further instructions.

Chapter 14

Shana and Zofia became friends. They sat on the deck watching the children play one hot afternoon a few days after the ship had set sail.

"Where are you from, Shana?"

"We came from Romania, my sister and I. We had two brothers and our parents. They were all killed."

Zofia nodded, not wanting to continue questioning.

Shana wiped the sweat from her brow. "We lived on a farm. Rachel and I were fortunate. Our neighbor had agreed to hide my sister and me. My parents had arranged it by offering them money and crops before things got out of hand. But, even though Rachel and I were not killed, we saw it all. We saw everything, including the murder of our family."

Again, Zofia nodded. She took a handkerchief from her bra and wiped her face.

"Rachel and I were in the barn just across the field from our home. That's where the neighbors kept us. Inside the barn was a cellar. During the day, we often stayed down there. But one afternoon, we needed to see the sunlight. The darkness of the cellar had become unbearable. I told Rachel that we could spend a couple of hours upstairs but then we must return. It was dangerous for us and for the neighbor. We were sitting quietly, enjoying the light when we saw the soldiers come riding in on a truck. There were maybe six or seven of them. I don't remember. I wanted to run out and warn my parents. But I couldn't. If I had left Rachel she would have run right after me and then . . . well . . ."

"Yes," Zofia said. There was silence for a few moments. "You did the right thing."

"Dear God, the guilt I feel . . . I hope I did the right thing. The first thing we saw was the Nazis shooting our cows. I was shaking. Rachel was standing beside me. Her little heart was beating so hard that I was sure I could feel it against the side of my body, but she didn't say a word."

From across the deck Shana and Zofia heard Rachel say, "No, Mendel, this is how you play this game." The other children sat watching. Shana gazed upon her sister.

"She is such a strong little girl." Tears came to Shana's eyes.

"That's good. Especially with everything she has been through." Zofia said.

"We were still watching out the window, Rachel and I. As you know, barns do not have glass windows like in the city. The windows are just openings in the walls."

"Yes, I know." Zofia said.

"Then two Nazis pulled my mother out of the house. She screamed and screamed. Sometimes at night I can still hear her screaming. My father came running from the field with my two brothers. The boys were only nine and ten. But one of them rushed to the Nazi who held my mother and tried to fight him. My brother was shot and killed instantly. Then one of the other Nazis shot my other brother and my father. I heard Rachel gasp. I knew we were too far away for them to hear us, but still, I put my hand over her mouth so she would not cry out. Then all of them . . . all of them . . . they raped my mother . . . they raped her until she stopped screaming. She just lay there.

I felt the tears from Rachel's eyes fall on my hand that still covered her mouth. My throat was as dry as sandpaper. I wanted to look away, but I could not. This was my family. These people were all that Rachel and I had in the whole world. The Nazis were laughing, whooping and hollering. Rachel trembled in my arms. I knew we both wondered the same thing. Was our mother alive? Then we got our answer. One of the Nazis, a tall one with very short, blond hair, shot my mother. I could not see his face, but I heard the gun shot. She never made a sound. By now Rachel's whole body was trembling so hard that I felt she might have a seizure or something. I turned her away from the window, and held her in my arms as the Nazis got into their car and rode away.

Once we were sure that they were gone, we both ran outside to see if anyone from our family was still alive. My mother's housedress was pushed up immodestly to her waist. She was naked. I saw the horror in Rachel's eyes. I pulled my mother's dress down covering her nakedness in an attempt to preserve whatever dignity she had left. Then I checked each of them. They were all dead. I turned away from the terrible scene to look at my little sister. She was vomiting profusely; her face flushed red and covered with tears and sweat. She was all I had left in the world. I went to her and held her while she emptied the contents of her small stomach. Then I took her in my arms and we both wept. From that day 'til now, I have been her mother as well as her best friend, and she has been mine."

Zofia had heard horror stories before. Everyone had one in the DP camp. But each person's experience still shocked her as much as the first. There was nothing to say. There was never anything to say to the survivor. "I'm sorry," was all Zofia could muster. Her comment seemed so trivial, she felt ashamed.

"Children are remarkable," Shana said, smiling as she patted Zofia's hand. She seemed to know how inept Zofia felt at that moment. "Look at how she can laugh and play and go on living. I thank God for that every day."

Zofia nodded. "Yes, children heal very well. They seem to recover faster than we do." Zofia thought about Katja.

"Perhaps they forget." Shana said.

"We can only hope that they do." Zofia answered. She was glad that Shana did not ask for her story. She had not yet made one up that included Katja and she was not going to tell Shana the truth about Katja. She was never going to tell anyone. Katja would have a new start as a Jewish girl in Palestine.

For a while, they sat silently, side by side, their hands folded neatly in their laps, looking like twin tattered dolls, both of them lost in thought, caught in a web of memories. Then Rachel came running over to Shana. "We want to go to the captain's station, where they steer the boat. The captain said it would be all right with him," Rachel pleaded with Shana. "Can we?"

Shana's shoulders dropped. She didn't want to discourage Rachel's natural curiosity, but the boat was so crowed, and she wanted to keep a close eye on her sister.

"I'll be with them," Mendel said. "I'll watch out for them. I'm ten, I'm older."

"I'm older than you. I turned thirteen two months ago, so I am pretty grown up, and I will make sure that both Katja and Rachel are safe." Abe said.

Zofia sighed. She was not keen on letting Katja out of her sight either.

"Please, Mama?" Katja pleaded. "We'll be right back. I promise."

"Why don't I go with you?" Zofia suggested.

"No, Mama, I'm not a baby. Please. You're embarrassing me."

Zofia looked at Shana. Shana shrugged her shoulders.

Just then Yossi Harel walked by. Everyone knew that he was a member of the Mossad, the Israeli secret service. Yossi attracted their attention with his air of confidence as well as the fact that he was handsome, muscular, and incredibly sexy. Yossi walked up and smiled at the children.

"Mr. Harel," Rachel said, "Will you please take us to see the place where the captain steers the boat? I know if you are with us, our families will let us go."

Shana's mouth fell open. Her little sister certainly had some nerve.

Yossi let out a laugh. "You are one bold little girl," he said, smiling. "All right, I'll escort you and your friends to the wheelhouse, but we must be quick. I have things to do."

Rachel's face broke into a huge smile. "Can we meet the captain?"

"If he is there of course you will meet him," Yossi said.

"Now may I go?" Rachel asked, her long black curls flipping as she turned to look at her sister.

Shana just shrugged. "I suppose," she said.

"Mama? Can I go with them?" Katja asked.

Zofia nodded. "Please be careful." she said.

"No need to worry. I'll have them all back here in fifteen minutes," Yossi reassured her. "Come on all of you . . . So, what are your names?"

"I'm Rachel."

"Abe."

"Mendel."

"Katja," she said, as she followed right behind Rachel and then turned to glance back at Zofia, who smiled and nodded at her.

"You are the future of our Jewish race." Harel smiled, patting Abe's back. "Come on then, all of you; let me introduce you to our captain. Do you know his name?"

"No, what is it?" said Rachel.

"I know." Abe smiled.

"You do? Huh? Nu, what is it?" Yossi said.

"Ahronovitch," Abe answered. "I heard him say his name when he made an announcement."

"You're right. His name is Yitzhak Ahronovitch, and he is a very good friend of mine," Yossi confirmed.

Zofia watched as Yossi led the children, answering their questions with patience.

"He's very handsome, isn't he?" Shana mused aloud.

"That he is," Zofia answered. She noticed that a slight pink blush had come over Shana's cheeks. Zofia smiled. "He certainly is."

Chapter 15

Although the ship had just set sail, two children had already been born on board, and even with the poor living conditions and lack of adequate food, everyone rejoiced. New life was surely a good omen. However, later that week, Zofia heard the hush of whispers circulate amongst the passengers.

She had fallen asleep on the deck from the heat of the mid-afternoon sun. Isaac and Katja had fallen asleep, too. Isaac and Katja remained sleeping, but the buzz had stirred Zofia awake. She rose and went to find Shana to see what was going on. Before she left, Zofia turned and took a last look at her little family. A smile crept over her face, all the way from her heart. Isaac and Katja were growing closer every day. Everything would be all right; they would be a family, safe together for the rest of their lives, in Palestine.

Shana was sitting on the edge of the cot she shared with Rachel, who was also asleep.

"Is something going on here or am I imagining things?" Zofia asked Shana.

"A woman died in childbirth earlier this afternoon. A lot of the passengers are saying that it is a bad sign."

Zofia raised her eyebrows. "It's terrible, that's for sure. But, sadly, women die in childbirth quite often. So, I don't believe that this tragedy is in any way a foreshadowing of our journey."

"I wish I could be as optimistic as you are," Shana said. "I am afraid all the time."

"I am afraid too," Zofia agreed, as she sat down beside Shana, careful not to wake Rachel, "but we can't let old superstitions get in the way of our future."

"Then how do you do it? I don't even know half of what you have seen and experienced, but I know it has been hard. How do you smile and laugh and go on even with everything that you have been through. I am only asking because I want to know your secret. I want to do the same thing, but my life stopped that day when I saw my family killed. Yes, I go on living and I try for Rachel's sake, but inside I am dead."

"You are not dead. You are alive. That is the gift. Don't you see?"

"I see, but I feel so depressed and guilty that I survived while the rest of my family died."

"You must not feel that way. Your family would want you to go on, to live, and to bring children into the world. They would want that."

Shana nodded. "I suppose."

"Do you want to know how I know you are still alive?" Zofia said, massaging Shana's upper arm. Shana shrugged.

"Do you remember the other day when that handsome Mr. Harel came over to us and took the children to see the wheel house?"

"Yes, I remember."

"Your face, when you looked at him, your face told me you are not dead. You are hurt, I know, but you are not dead, Shana. You must pick up the pieces of the past, and for the sake of your dead loved ones, you must live. You must bear children and name them for your family members so that those that you have lost will have a namesake in the new Jewish homeland."

A tear fell from Shana's eye. Zofia reached up and wiped it away.

"Shanala, mine kind, my sweet child. Live . . . You must live," Zofia whispered.

"My mother called me Shanala." Shana smiled through her tears at Zofia. "Even though you're far too young to be my mother, Zofia, you are like a mother to me."

"Let us just say I am an old soul," Zofia said.

Shana laid her head on Zofia's shoulder. "I will try, Zofia. I will try to start living again."

Chapter 16

"It is imperative that you leave Europe as quickly as possible. We found it rather simple to pay the jailers to overlook your true identity. However, now that you are out of prison and visible to the world, it will not be so easy to keep you safe. There are people who will remember your face, Manfred Blau. People who will want to see you dead. If you are recognized as Manfred Blau rather than Dolf Sprecht, you will be back in prison before you can blink an eye. And perhaps you will be executed for your attempted escape. Therefore, you will leave Europe as quickly and quietly as possible. Be prepared to leave Berlin for Hamburg tonight. Once you arrive at the port, you will be traveling by U-boat to South America."

"I thought I would be leaving from France," Manfred pressed.

"As I told you, there has been a change of plans."

"Any reason?"

"We have our reasons. It's none of your concern. Just be ready to go when it gets dark. A car will come for you. You won't be seeing me again. So, best of luck to you. Heil Hitler."

"Heil Hitler," Manfred echoed, wondering if Hitler were actually dead.

It took Manfred almost no time at all to pack. He only had a few possessions, and whatever he needed would be provided by the party once he arrived at his destination. During better times, when the party was flourishing, he'd heard Himmler and some of the other officials talking about Argentina. He recalled them saying that it was a lot like the Swiss Alps. When Manfred thought about the Alps, his mind went immediately to Christa and to their honeymoon. Christa, his one true love, so long ago. Manfred sighed. It was time to stop reliving the past, time to move forward. Christa was dead, he would never see her again, and that way of life was over. Now he must start anew.

Chapter 17

Descending upon each rung of the wrought iron ladder felt like climbing deeper and deeper into a coffin. Manfred did not dare look any of the other men in the eyes for fear they would see the terror he felt being enclosed within this vessel that would soon slide deeper and deeper into what felt like a grave under the sea.

Manfred had never been in a submarine, and until now, he'd never known that he had claustrophobia. As the vessel submerged deeper, his ears rang with a low constant din, and then they felt as if a needle was being shot through them. The rooms surrounding him had been painted a pea-soup green color, and that added to the dizzying nausea he already felt.

His bunk was so small that it would fit inside a closet.

Days became nights and nights became days, and because there were no windows and no natural light, it was hard to tell them apart. Manfred lost track of time. He slept and awoke without knowing what day or what time it was. All he knew was that it seemed as if he'd been aboard this ship for a lifetime.

The other men kept their distance, hardly speaking to him other than to bring him his food, all of which was dried or canned. He wondered how these sailors lived like this for years, moving like sharks beneath the depths of the waves, never seeing sunlight.

Being alone in this capsule gave him far too much time to think . . . to remember. Sometimes he would close his eyes and remember his beautiful wife dancing with Himmler at one of the galas they'd attended. His mind ran away with him, and he wondered if Christa and Himmler had slept together. Himmler had been so helpful in securing the adoption of the little girl from the Lebensborn for Christa. Manfred sighed. His heart hurt him when he thought about how much Christa had loved that child. He had no idea what had even happened to the little girl, little Katja. Well, no matter. Perhaps she'd gone back to her birth mother. That would be the best thing for her. Manfred knew he could not take care of a child, nor would he want that responsibility. Katja. Why could he not forget the little girl?

Manfred's nightmares became more frequent. He would close his eyes and awaken in a cold sweat thinking that he'd died and gone to hell. His heart would palpitate, and it would take several minutes for him to realize that he'd been asleep. The faces of the Jews he'd murdered would not let him rest, and he began to dread closing his eyes.

Soon he would be in South America, where he would find a whole community of like-minded people. Perhaps he would begin to feel more at peace when he had others around him who understood what the Third Reich was trying to achieve. What the rest of the world refused to understand was that in order to create a perfect world, first there had to be an ethnic cleansing. In order to build fresh, the old must first be destroyed. It was hard work—dirty, messy, disgusting work—but in the end if the Reich had achieved what they set out to do, a race of superior men would have ruled the earth. Superior Aryans without tainted blood, without handicaps and diseases. Only the strong and healthy would have been bred to create a race that was invincible in body and mind.

Manfred was to meet with Konrad Klausen when he arrived. He'd been given a little background on Konrad. He was told that Konrad had worked on the punch card system and then had been transferred to work on the "Final Solution." Manfred had listened, but he didn't care much about Konrad's past. Konrad was nobody to him. However, he did have a secret wish that Dr. Goebbels had not really committed suicide with his entire family. If only somehow Goebbels had escaped from the bunker and the bodies that were found had been substitutes, fakes placed there by ODESSA so that Goebbels and his family could escape. How wonderful it would be if he got to Argentina and found out that Goebbels was still alive. He'd heard rumors when he was in Spandau that Hitler and Eva Braun had escaped to South America by a U-boat that was probably very similar to the one he was on right now. Perhaps it was true. Perhaps it was the same boat. Maybe Hitler had slept in this very bunk. Even better, maybe Joseph Goebbels had slept here . . . What a splendid thought.

Chapter 18

Although *Exodus* had undeniable problems, the broken-down vessel was a ship of hope. It had been a week since the boat had set sail. Because of lack of private space, and Katja's presence, they had only made love once. Since that time under the stairwell, they could only exchange brief kisses, brushes of hands, and looks of longing. However, one night as the passengers sat on deck singing along with a guitar player, Shana offered to watch Katja so that Zofia and Isaac could take a walk alone. Zofia accepted gratefully. She was glad that Katja was comfortable with Shana and Rachel. And she was relieved that she could trust Shana to take care of her child.

Zofia and Isaac left the crowd quietly. They slipped down the stairs and ducked under the stairwell to their secret hiding place, where they could embrace and kiss freely.

"Zofia, my love . . ." he whispered, his voice hoarse in her ear. Then he gently kissed her cheek. "Can you believe it? We're almost there. I heard the Captain say that we are about 20 miles off the southern coast of Palestine. Soon, my darling, we will see the land that we have dreamed of for so long."

She nodded. "I can't believe that it is all really happening. I remember when we were in the forest, you and I and Shlomie, and we used to talk about Palestine. Then, it was nothing more than a fantasy. But it did keep us going. Do you remember?"

"Of course, I do. How could I ever forget? I used to wonder what Palestine was like. I'd heard so many different stories about the place, ever since I was a little boy."
"Yes, me too. I heard that it is a desert; that the climate is hostile. It's very hot and dry, and nothing grows. At least that is what I've heard."

"It won't matter. We will find a way to survive. Now, we are finally safe. We will be a family, you and little Katja and me. Together we'll build a life in our Jewish homeland."

"I am glad that you and Katja get along so well," Zofia said

"I am, too. I was afraid she would resent me coming into your lives."

"So you made an extra special effort to make her feel important and loved. Oh, Isaac, you always know what to do."

"I don't know if that's all true. I mean, I did everything I could do to let Katja know that she is loved. I wanted her to know that she was not going to lose you, but she was going to have two parents instead of one. I am glad it worked, but I don't always know what to do. I've made plenty of mistakes in my life," Isaac confessed.

"You know what to do for me. You know what to do for me, always." She smiled. "Remember when we were in the forest, and all we could get was that raw meat and I couldn't eat it; it made me sick? But you knew what to do. You helped me by telling me a story that reminded me of your mother's bakery. And because of your story I was able to swallow that nasty meat."

"Yes, I do." He smiled. "I also recall the fat little boy I was growing up. I remember how I'd sit in the back of my mother's bakery watching you when you came in to buy bread. I was so shy. I couldn't get over how pretty you were. You never noticed me then."

"Isaac, I was just a child myself. I didn't notice much at that time in my life."

He laughed. "It doesn't matter. You're mine now, and until my dying day I will do everything I can to make you the happiest woman in the world for having chosen me as your husband." Gently he let his lips brush hers and she felt her entire body tingle with desire.

Isaac took off his shirt and rolled it into a pillow. Then he gently lifted her head and placed the pillow beneath it. He began to unbutton the top of her dress. She reached up and touched his face. "Isaac . . ." she whispered.

He took her in his arms. No matter how many times they made love, the magic of their bodies coming together, the ecstasy of his body against hers never failed to amaze her. When they had been separated, the memory of their moments together sustained her. But the reality far surpassed the memory. Isaac made love to Zofia, slowly, tenderly, holding back in order to savor every precious second. His desire was as strong as the current of a wild river. She felt the power of his yearning and her own need for him possessed her. And once again, as it was the first time in the forest, and every time since, she felt the electric spark of the union of their souls as their bodies became one.

They lay together for a long time, just holding each other and reveling in the miracle of being together again. Zofia lay with her head on Isaac's chest, and he ran his hand through her hair.

As the music began to die down upstairs, Isaac said, "We should get back. I don't want Katja to worry or to come looking for us."

"Yes, I suppose we should," She agreed.

As they dressed, they could not help but smile at each other.

When they returned to the deck, nobody seemed to have noticed that they had been gone.

Isaac and Zofia sat side by side on their small cot while Katja sat in front of them in a circle with Rachel, Mendel, and Abe. The crowd was clapping and singing a song in Yiddish. Even though the ship had only been at sea for a week, everyone seemed to be getting to know each other and there was a feeling of family amongst the passengers.

Then a slender man with a long, pointed nose and dark hair, stood up. Zofia thought he must be in his early thirties. His face and body indicated as much, but his eyes, his eyes were ageless. He turned to the guitar player and requested a song. Then, in a haunting tenor voice, he began to sing. It was a song that told the story of the Jews, of their plight throughout history, and of their endless wandering in search of a homeland. When he finished, Zofia felt a tear fall upon her cheek. She turned to Isaac. He looked at her, his face wrinkled in thought. Neither said a word. He just took her in his arms and held her tightly.

That night as Zofia slept, a cool breeze danced up from the emerald waters of the Mediterranean. She cuddled deeper into the crook of Isaac's arm as Katja spooned into her stomach. The water gently rocked the boat while the sound of the waves played a soothing melody. The sky was a black silk blanket filled with sparkling crystal stars.

Then a thunderous crash came out of nowhere. Zofia jumped up to a sitting position, followed by Isaac who awoke immediately. Katja opened her eyes but did not move. She looked around her still groggy with sleep.

"What was that?" Zofia asked Isaac.

He shook his head, "I don't know."

On July 19th, 1947, a Friday morning at two a.m., Exodus 1947 *was attacked by the British. It was 20 miles off the coast of southern Palestine. The old worn-out vessel carried more than 4,500 souls who thought they had finally seen the end of Jewish persecution. Little did they know that their battle had just begun.*

Chapter 19

A loud voice came from out of the darkness. "You are in territorial waters. Stop your ship immediately; we are going to board you."

Zofia grabbed Isaac's hand.

"What is going on?" She said, her voice hoarse. "Oh my God, we've been boarded!"

"This is the last chance you have to stop this vessel and turn back. The passengers onboard are attempting to enter Palestine illegally. This is the British Navy. We must have your word that you will turn your ship around or we intend to board you."

Lit firecrackers were being hurled onto the ship's deck, exploding in a burst of fire and smoke. Someone screamed.

"Watch out, come here, stay close," Isaac said to Zofia.

"This ship has no intention of turning around. We are going forward to Palestine," a man's voice from the loudspeaker of the boat answered.

Then it happened. Something rammed into the boat, catching it on a wave and suspending it in mid air. The force of the impact jolted Zofia off her cot and onto the floor. She shielded Katja so the child would not fall also. The ship, trying to right itself, wobbled unsteadily in the water. People were wandering the deck, some panicked, others still groggy with sleep. The old vessel swayed, listing heavily to one side. Then, Zofia saw that a large group of English sailors had boarded the ship. The sailors kept coming, more and more of them. To Zofia, it seemed as if there might be a thousand. She looked out across the sea and saw the British flag flying from the bow of the attacking ship. Before anyone had a chance to move, *Exodus* was flooded with tear gas. Katja awakened, disoriented, and gasping for breath. Men wearing Royal Navy uniforms and carrying guns were all around the deck, forcing people out of their beds at gunpoint and pushing them into a line.

"You will do as we say," one of the Navy men demanded. "Get into this line, and prepare to leave this ship."

People began to rush about gathering their families close to them in panic. The tear gas burned Zofia's eyes, and she had trouble staying focused, her nose was running profusely. Katja was choking and vomiting on the ground. Only Isaac remained somewhat in control of himself.

The Royal Navy began to threaten the passengers with thick wooden clubs. "Get in line," they shouted. "Get in line now."

Zofia could not move. She felt as if she were glued to her cot. Then, across the deck, Zofia saw a young boy of about ten years old throw an orange at one of the sailors. The fruit hit the man in the face, wetting his cheek and his uniform with juice. The sailor pulled a gun and shot the boy. Zofia gasped and grabbed Katja, holding her close and covering Katja's eyes with her hand. The child who'd been shot fell to the ground. The gun blast only caused greater panic amongst the passengers. People were crying. Some were jumping overboard. They were screaming and shaking their fists.

However, some of the refugees who had survived the concentration camps were not willing to take orders without question. They had done that in the past and it had cost them dearly. Now they would fight. Several men began to charge at the sailors using anything they could find as weapons: pieces of wood, knives, broken bottles. In turn, the sailors began to hit several of the resisters with clubs.

Zofia saw Yossi Harel's large frame reach down and lift a young boy as if the child were weightless. Then in one swoop, Harel spirited the boy out of harm's way. Zofia recognized the child. It was Mendel, one of the boys who had become friends with Katja. Harel put the boy down in a corner where he would be safe.

The shrieks of the women pierced the night air. Isaac pulled Zofia and Katja up and began pushing them toward the stairwell where he and Zofia had hidden when they needed privacy. Katja gripped Zofia's skirt with one hand. Tears filled the child's eyes as she sucked her thumb. Zofia tried to comfort Katja by smoothing her hair. But Isaac insisted that they move quickly. He reached down and lifted Katja, carrying her in his arms as he led them away. He needed time to think, time to figure out what to do. Everything was happening so fast. More shots rang out, followed by louder hollering. Zofia stood still, frozen, unable to move. Blood covered the deck. She looked at Isaac, but her eyes did not comprehend.

"Come, hurry . . ." Isaac said, as he shook Zofia's arm. "Stop watching what is happening, it will only terrify you. We must act quickly. Follow me . . ."

Zofia gave Isaac her hand and he led her down the stairs and under the stairwell. From where they were, they could hear the chaos but could not see anything. Both Zofia and Katja tucked their faces into Isaac's chest. He held them close to him. In a soft voice cracking with pain Zofia said "We were almost there, just a few more miles, almost . . ."

Isaac nodded and he squeezed Zofia's hand.

Zofia was sure the ship was sinking. Water had begun to seep into the belly of the boat and fill the small space where the family had gone to take refuge.

A loud crash of glass shattering somewhere upstairs pierced the screams of the passengers and the shouting of the sailors. Katja covered her ears. Zofia gave Isaac a worried look. The water began to surround them and grow deeper by the minute. Isaac knew he would have to take them all back upstairs. The ship was sinking. If they stayed below, they would drown. But before he could move, four sailors came rushing down the stairs. Zofia felt her heart pumping in her throat and ears. She could hardly contain her fear as the British came around the corner and discovered them.

"Get up. Everyone is leaving this ship." One of the sailors said, grabbing Zofia's arm.

Isaac stood and moved to attack the man, but the three other sailors held him back. The one who was not restraining Isaac hit him in the mouth. Isaac struggled to escape their hold.

"You are all coming with us. And believe me . . . if you cause a problem we will shoot you on the spot."

Isaac knew they had to leave the ship. But he could not think clearly. He wanted to fight these men, wanted to kill them.

"Please, Isaac . . . we must leave here. The ship is sinking. Don't fight with him. If he kills you, I will die, too," Zofia said, her eyes meeting Isaacs'. She saw that her pleading had reached him. His body went limp with surrender.

"We'll follow you. Please, I beg you; just don't hurt any of us," Zofia said as she helped Katja to her feet. The entire bottom of Katja's dress was wet with seawater. Katja's eyes were large with terror as she stared at the sailor, sucking her thumb frantically. Isaac gave the sailor a menacing stare. Then he lifted Katja into his arms and took Zofia's hand, and the three of them climbed the stairs to join the other passengers in a line that had been formed to exit the ship.

"Come on, let's hurry this up." One of the Navy officers pushed Zofia a little with his rifle butt. Immediately Isaac handed Katja to Zofia, then he stepped forward, his chest out, unafraid of the sailor or his gun.

"Don't you ever touch her again," Isaac said, his English rusty but his eyes piercing the soldier with a threatening stare.

"Please, it's all right. I'm not hurt," Zofia said and she grabbed Isaac's arm, afraid that the sailor would shoot him.

Isaac shrugged her off and stood between Zofia and the sailor, still staring at him, challenging him.

The sailor looked at Zofia holding the little girl, and then he glanced at Isaac. The sailor was a big man, tall and well-built, in his early twenties. He sighed. Zofia saw his eyes soften. He seemed to have a certain respect for Isaac. She wondered if he had a wife and child of his own.

"I'm sorry," The sailor said.

Isaac nodded, and gently guided Zofia and Katja into the line of terrified passengers.

As Zofia and her family stood on the deck, one of the Navy men jumped over the side of the craft. Zofia turned to Isaac. "Did you see that? That sailor just committed suicide."

Isaac shrugged. He put Katja down between the two of them.

Across the way, Zofia saw Shana and Rachel. They were being forced into the line to disembark. Rachel shrugged the sailor's hand off of her shoulder. Then she proudly took her sister's arm and the two of them walked together. Once again, Zofia was amazed at Rachel's courage. *What a fearless little girl Rachel is*, Zofia thought.

Unexpectedly, Katja let out a piercing scream. Zofia was afraid that something or someone in the crowd had hurt her. Immediately both Zofia and Isaac bent down to see Katja crying and pointing to a child's body that lay in a pool of dark blood, an orange in his hand.

"That's Abe . . ." Katja said. "That's my friend."

Zofia lifted Katja and held her in her arms, turning her child's face away from the murder of the young boy.

Isaac gave Zofia a worried stare. She nodded in agreement as the line continued to move forward. "Where do you think they are sending us?" Zofia asked Isaac.

He shrugged. "I don't know. But I do know one thing. Remember that fellow who had thrown you to the ground when I first saw you on the dock?"

"You mean Koppel?"

"I believe that was his name," Isaac said.

"Of course, how could I ever forget him? He caused me so much grief," Zofia said.

Isaac motioned with his head to a spot on the deck. "Look over there."

Zofia turned her head and there she saw Koppel on the ground, blood pooling all around his head.

"At least he won't be bothering us anymore." Isaac said.

Zofia stared at Koppel. That man had caused her such heartache, such misery. He'd sent her dear friends Fruma and Gitel to the concentration camp where they had died. She'd spent years hating him, and yet, looking at him now, all she could feel was pity. Zofia turned her head sharply away as the vomit rose in her throat. She glanced out at the vast body of water surrounding them; the dark waves rocked the boat. Then an idea came into her mind. She looked around her, feeling her heart race. Then she turned to Isaac.

"Isaac, Koppel was in the Judenrat. He probably has quite a bit of money or valuables on him. We need everything that we can get our hands on to help us get back to Palestine."

Isaac nodded. "You're right."

"Katja, don't move. Stay right here. I will be right back. Do you understand me?" Zofia said, as she bent down eye level with the child.

Katja nodded. "Mama, don't go away." Katja held fast to Zofia's dress. Then she turned to Isaac. "Will you stay with me?" she asked Isaac.

"All right Katja, you come with us, but don't ever tell anyone what you are about to see today. Nod your head if you understand me."

Katja nodded. "I'm scared, Mama."

"I know, Sunshine. But you must be brave," Zofia said, and she kissed Katja's forehead.

"Come now, both of you. Let's hurry," Zofia said. "We're going to take whatever valuables he has on him that might be of use to us later."

Isaac nodded.

"You keep watch; I'll go through his pockets," Isaac said to Zofia as they made their way across the deck.

"Don't forget to check the lining of his coat. He may have sewn some things inside," Zofia said. Then she turned to Katja "Turn your head away. It is better you shouldn't see this."

"God forgive me," Isaac whispered. He looked around him and then took a deep breath. Kneeling beside Koppel, Isaac searched the Judenrat member's pockets. Inside he found several pieces of gold jewelry, some of it half melted. Then, inside Koppel's breast pocket, Isaac found a small diamond ring. Isaac ran his hands over Koppel's jacket and the legs of his pants to see if he could find any bumps where something might have been hidden, but there were none. Then he checked Koppel's pants pockets. Nothing was inside. Meanwhile Zofia knelt beside him, watching in all directions. In all of the commotion, no one noticed as Isaac shoved Koppel's possessions into his pocket.

"All finished?" Zofia asked.

"Yes, hurry, let's get back to Katja," Isaac said.

They arrived back in line where Katja waited, sucking her thumb. A few tears had fallen down her cheeks and Zofia gently wiped them away. Then she kissed the child and held her close.

"You have blood on your hand," Katja said to Isaac.

He cringed and wiped the blood on his pants leg.

"It's all right, Isaac. We did what needed to be done," Zofia said.

"I feel sick about robbing a dead man," Isaac said.

"Never mind that, don't think about it. What did you find?" Zofia whispered.

"Jewelry, gold, and a diamond ring. I took everything. These were probably things Koppel stole from other Jews."

"Yes, they probably were. But we can't help that now. I know you feel badly but please don't. The money we get from selling these things will help us. Hide them well. We don't want the British to find them and take them away."

"I will," Isaac said, his fingers folding over the valuables. Then with his other hand he removed his cap and tucked the jewels into a panel just above the brim. With great care he adjusted the fabric so that there was no bludge where the stolen goods were hidden. "They should be safe here," he whispered to Zofia.

For a few minutes neither of them spoke. They were lost in thought. The noise on the ship seemed far away.

"Isaac," Zofia said, her voice barely above a whisper, "where do you think they are taking us?"

He didn't answer, and she wondered if he had heard her at all.

Zofia could see several of the passengers dropping lifeboats onto the Navy ship in an effort to damage and possibly sink her. A passenger came rushing at one of the sailors wielding an ax, but was brutally beaten with the butt of a rifle and subdued.

Even amidst all of the chaos and destruction, the Captain of *Exodus* and his crew still put up a hell of a fight to bring the ship into the port in Haifa. Many of the passengers continued to resist, and as they did, more people were injured. From where she stood, Zofia could see several of the crew members in a huddle on the deck. Then the crew dispersed and a voice came over the loudspeaker.

"My friends. This is Yossi Harel. I regret to inform you that the *Exodus* must surrender. There are too many passengers who are in need of medical care. If we agree to surrender, the British promise to bring doctors and nurses aboard. Therefore, I must announce that *Exodus* surrenders."

There was a gasp from the crowd. Some of the passengers cried out in angry protest.

Rachel gripped her sister's hand and pulled her forward as they both came running up to Katja.

"Did you see? Abe is dead."

"I know." Katja had tears in her eyes, but Rachel looked angry, her black eyes glaring.

"Bastards, all of them," Rachel said.

Katja had never heard anyone use that word before and it shocked her.

"Do you think they are going to kill us, too?" Katja asked.

"I don't know. I hate them. I hate them as much as the Germans," Rachel said. "And as long as we live, we will fight until we have a Jewish homeland, no matter what anyone tries to do to stop us."

"Shhh," Shana whispered. "Quiet, Rachel."

"I will not be quiet. I am not afraid."

"You should be," Shana said.

"But I am not."

Katja whimpered softly and tucked her head into Zofia's skirt. The voice of an officer of the British Navy came over the loudspeaker.

"You may sit. However, you must remain in line. Anyone who disobeys will be dealt with severely. If you need to use the facilities, you must request permission from one of the guards."

Doctors, nurses, and naval men carrying first aid kits had begun to board *Exodus* and tend to the injured.

Isaac squeezed Zofia's shoulder in reassurance. She looked up at him. The sun had just begun to peek through the clouds and its bright glare burned her eyes. The compassion in his gaze made her afraid she might cry. Neither said a word, but the glance that passed between them bound them in emotion.

It was an extremely hot day. The sweat trickled down Zofia's back as they waited under the rays of the glaring sun to see what the British had in store.

***

Late that afternoon, Zofia assumed it was somewhere around four o'clock, *Exodus* pulled into port in Haifa.

"Stand up, all of you. Rise, please, and prepare to disembark." An announcer with a proper English accent said over the loudspeaker.

Katja had fallen asleep with her head on Zofia's lap. Gently, Zofia rubbed Katja's back and whispered, "Wake up, Sunshine." Katja was clammy with sweat, her face flushed from the heat.

"It's all right, let her sleep. I'll carry her," Isaac said.

Rachel had fallen asleep as well, but when her sister nudged her, Rachel stirred awake. Her long dark hair was stuck to her neck with perspiration, but her dark eyes were alert with malice.

Zofia, Isaac, Katja, Rachel, and her sister Shana were pushed into a line to board a waiting ship. The waiting boat had a large metal cage installed on the deck to contain the Jewish refugees. When the cage was loaded—beyond capacity—a British sailor slammed and then locked the steel door. Then the rest of the passengers were led to another ship that had a cage just like the first one.

The children were awake now. They all stood huddled together.

"I wish I had my doll, Ethel," Katja told Rachel. "I miss her so much."

"I don't care about dolls. They are just toys. Toys are silly. I wish I had a gun and I could kill all of these sailors."

"Ethel was not silly. She was my friend. She talked to me and she understood when I talked to her."

"No, she didn't. Dolls are not real. They are only bits of cloth or whatever they are made of. They don't talk and they can't answer. And they can't help you when you're in trouble."

Katja began to cry.

"I'm sorry. I didn't mean to be so cruel to you." Rachel shook her head, and then she said, "Come here," and put her arm around Katja's shoulder.

Rachel smoothed Katja's blond curls and began to sing her a song in Yiddish.

"I can't believe Rachel still remembers that song. Our mother sang it to her when she was very young," Shana said to Zofia.

"It worries me to think just how much of this they will remember," Zofia said.

"All of these children have seen so many horrible things, and they are only children. No child should go through what they have been through," Shana said.

"Yes, they have witnessed far too many terrible things," Zofia said, biting her lower lip as she watched the children.

Chapter 20

When Zofia, Katja, Isaac, Rachel, Mendel, and Shana got to the front of the line, they saw the three prison boats lined up and being filled with passengers.

"Mama, those things look like the cages that we saw when we went to the zoo, the ones where the animals live," Katja said, her eyes wide with fear.

"It will be all right," Zofia said as they watched the other passengers being led to cages on two other ships.

As they got closer, they could see and hear the imprisoned passengers. Some were crying, others were pleading to know what fate had in store for them, and some were praying.

Two young boys who'd been locked into the wire cage on one of the ships were pleading for help.

"Please, can I have some water for me and my brother?" One of the boys reached his hand through the bars, trying to grab one of the British officers in charge.

The officer ignored the child.

Isaac was so moved by the boy that he halted in front of the cage.

"Don't stop. We have to keep this line moving," a guard said while pushing Isaac with his rifle butt.

"Don't touch me," Isaac spat, his eyes glaring at the man.

"Please, Isaac, please. I don't want you to get hurt."

The sailor, a double-chinned, red-faced man with beady eyes, challenged Isaac. Zofia could see that he wanted to fight. She knew that Isaac was strong and that he could take the gun away from the guard. But there were so many guards and so many British sailors, it would only be a matter of time before one of them killed him.

Isaac was so angry that he stood staring intently at the guard.

"Isaac," Zofia pulled his shirtsleeve. "Isaac, please!" her voice was louder, cracking with fear. It broke the spell of Isaac's anger. He turned to look at Zofia.

"Please, don't get yourself killed. I love you. I need you . . ."

Katja began to cry softly.

Isaac nodded. Then he turned to the guard one last time. His eyes told the man that he was only backing down for his wife's sake. How many times would he have to swallow his pride, his sense of manhood? As they approached the front of the line to board the ship, the children—Katja, Mendel, and Rachel—walked ahead.

"We are cutting the line off here. You, start going to the next ship," ordered a young sailorwith a thick cockney accent.

"No, please," Shana said. "I must go with my sister." Her English was broken and sprinkled with Polish, but because of the way she held her sister, the soldier seemed to understand what she was trying to say.

"My husband and I must go with our daughter," Zofia said.

The sailor was no more than nineteen. He had pumpkin-colored hair, a full face of brown freckles, and a warm smile. He looked at Shana.

"Please . . ." Shana said, her eyes filling with tears.

The boy in the Navy uniform nodded.

"The three of you go on together. We'll cut it off after you."

Shana breathed a sigh of relief. She quickly glanced at Zofia, who shared her feelings. Then Isaac, Shana, and Zofia followed the children on to the ship *Empire Rival*. The deck was nothing more than an iron pen, with a wooden latrine containing five holes. The Empire Rival would hold over a thousand prisoners.

Zofia, Isaac, Shana, and the children found a corner and huddled together. Zofia held Katja in her arms and secretly wondered if she had made a mistake taking the child out of her secure life in London. Then she glanced over at Isaac, who looked angry and frustrated at the situation. A deep wrinkle had burrowed between his eyes as he looked out over the water.

If she had not followed her dreams, had not taken this risk and packed up her life to board *Exodus*, she would never have found Isaac again. She would have lived the rest of her days thinking that he had died in the forests or concentration camps in Poland. Zofia reached over and tenderly touched Isaac's shoulder. The furrow of anger left his brow as he turned to look at her, his eyes glossed over with love. No matter what happened, it was all worthwhile, just to be here sitting beside each other, knowing that whatever they would face in the future, the three of them would be together.

***

No one knew where the ship was headed. From the deck, Zofia could see the two other ships, *Runnymede Park* and *Ocean Vigour*, that carried the other refugees from *Exodus*. They were docked in a row under the relentless heat of the summer sun. Once, Rachel tried to ask one of the sailors where they were going, but he threatened her and so Shana immediately grabbed her bold little sister and pulled her away.

"Don't bother them." Shana warned Rachel. "You must remember that you are only a little girl. You could get hurt."

"I am only a little girl right now, but someday, I am going to kill all of them: the British who are keeping us prisoners and the Nazis who killed our family."

"Don't talk about such things. Sit down and be quiet before the wrong person hears you." Shana pulled Rachel over to sit down, but Rachel shrugged her off.

"I will kill them someday . . . I will!" Her eyes were filled with tears and her little body shook with anger, but she sat down between Mendel and Katja.

Katja didn't say a word; she just rubbed Rachel's back.

"They had better let us out of here," Rachel shouted, getting up and walking to the bars of the cage.

"Hush, before you get hurt." Shana shook her sister's arm.

"How can they do this to us? I just will not stand for it. I won't," Rachel fumed.

"You will sit down and be quiet for now." Shana said.

"Come and sit by me." Katja patted the ground beside her and Rachel sat down.

"The three of us should form some kind of an army and fight these sailors," Rachel said to Katja and Mendel.

"Rachel, Abe is dead. These men shot him. They could shoot us, too. We had better do what they tell us to do."

"All right, I guess I have no choice, but only for now. One day I am going to do something. When I am older and I can get a gun, I won't let them get away with this," Rachel said, tears of anger glistening in her eyes.

"Shhh, I know how you feel." Katja said and she put her arm around her friends' shoulder.

Mendel looked at Katja. She shook her head. He reached behind Rachel and squeezed Katja's hand.

"I am so angry," Rachel said. "We had to go through the 'Bricha' to get here. We had to do so much and now this."

"What is the 'Bricha'?" Katja asked, still rubbing Rachel's shoulder.

"It's the underground for illegal immigration to Palestine."

"What does that mean?"

"It means that they helped us get here. They gave us money, too, and now we can't even get in to Palestine. I don't know what these dirty pigs are going to do with us, but I can tell you that it won't be good," Rachel seethed, pointing to one of the sailors.

"Rachel, try to calm down. It doesn't help when you make the sailors angry," Mendel soothed.

"I just hope they don't keep us in this prison until we die, or they kill us" Rachel said.

"Could they do that?" Katja shivered.

"I don't know. All I know is they shot people on the ship, and some of those people were children, so they could do anything. I am afraid they might be as bad as the Nazis."

Katja looked at her friend. "I'm scared, Rachel. I am so scared."

"I know. Me too, but we have to be brave. We have to make a plan for the future. Someday we have to pay them all back for this," Rachel said.

"It's going to be all right," Mendel said. "Nobody is going to kill us." He rubbed Katja's forearm. "Don't be afraid."

"They might try," Rachel said.

"We will be all right," Mendel repeated.

Isaac and Zofia sat in silence, watching the children and listening. A single tear fell down Zofia's cheek. She quickly wiped it with her fist. Isaac leaned over and kissed her.

"At least we are together," he whispered. "And, I love you . . ."

They had each received a dirty, threadbare blanket on which they were to sit, sleep, and eat. Katja held her blanket in her arms and sucked her thumb.

"What would happen if we tried to escape? We could climb over the top of this cage, then steal guns and start shooting," Rachel suggested.

"That's barbed wire," Mendel said, pointing to the wire at the top of the cage.

"It looks sharp," Rachel said, her hands balled up into fists.

"It *is* sharp. It will cut your hand off if you grab it and try to climb out of here," Mendel warned.

"I'd like to get some kind of a cutter and cut it," Rachel said.

"Where are we going to get a cutter, Rachel?"

Katja wasn't listening. She was tired, hungry, and thirsty. She leaned against Mendel and he put his arm around her shoulder. Then Katja balled up her blanket and laid her head on Mendel's lap.

Zofia looked across the Mediterranean Sea. She had been so hopeful, so close to her dream. Now, it was hard to say what would happen to her family.

"Look, over there," Isaac said, pointing to a group that had been imprisoned in a cage on shore. "Is that Shlomie?"

Zofia stood up to get a better look. The sun was blindingly bright, and it was hard to see clearly, especially long distance. "I think so, but I can't be sure."

"Shlomie . . . Shlomie . . ." Isaac began to call out. "Shlomie Katz, is that you?"

"Isaac? Isaac Zuckerman? My God! It is you!" Shlomie ran to the fence surrounding him. Isaac ran as close as he could within the enclosure on the ship to where Shlomie was imprisoned on land.

"Zofia is here, too," Isaac said.

Zofia walked up to the fence. For just an instant, she saw a grimace of pain cross over Shlomie's face. Then it was gone.

"Zofia, Isaac, my dear friends. It is so good to see you both. Safe. Alive."

"You were not aboard *Exodus*, were you?"

"No, I was aboard another ship. We were captured a week ago," Shlomie said.

"Do you know where they are going to send us?" Zofia asked.

"I don't know. I don't know what is going to happen. All I know is that somehow, some way, I am going to get to Palestine," Shlomie shouted.

"I don't know where this ship is headed, but until we meet again, God bless you and keep you safe," Isaac said.

"And God be with you, and Zofia, too."

"Who is that, Mama?" Katja asked.

"An old friend," Zofia answered, wringing the skirt of her dress in her hands.

Chapter 21

For three days, the refugees sat imprisoned on the stationary vessel, broiling in the hot sun. Their bodies were covered in sweat and filth, their minds clouded with worry. They didn't know what was to become of them. Many of them had borrowed money from various Jewish organizations to pay their fare on *Exodus*, such as the International Refugee Organization, the American Joint Distribution Committee, or the Bricha. Now those resources were exhausted, and without them it would be impossible to find another way to get back to Palestine. The refugees, many of whom had survived the horrors of the Nazi concentration camps, were now imprisoned again, this time under British rule.

Then, on the morning of the third day, the engine of the boat rocked to life and the ship set sail. Several hours after the voyage had begun, an announcement came over the loudspeaker. Gasps could be heard from within the enclosure. The fears of the refugees had been realized; the Captain announced that they were on their way back to Europe, back to where they started.

***

One morning Zofia felt a change in the motion of the boat. She awakened to find that the ship had docked just outside of the Port-de-Bouc in Toulon, France. From her place on the deck, she could see that the other two ships had docked at the French port as well. So, they were going to France? Zofia shook her head as she looked across the water. The sun had just begun to peek through the clouds, and the cool morning air felt good on her face.

"Zofia," Shana had come up behind her.

Zofia turned. "Can you see that sign? We are in France."

Shana nodded. "Do you think we will ever get to Palestine?"

Zofia shrugged. "I don't know. I hope so. I cannot believe that we were so close, and now we are back in Europe."

"Before we got on *Exodus*, I was trying to get a visa for Rachel and me to go into the United States. It was nearly impossible."

"We are Jews, and the sad truth is that nobody wants us," Zofia said, shrugging her shoulders.

"What is it that makes everyone think we are so different?"

"Who knows? All I know is that it has made my life very tough."

"Mine too. And, little Rachel, my gosh, she is like an angry old woman, and she is just a child. It frightens me to see how filled with hatred she has become. I am frightened that her outspokenness will get her hurt or, God forbid, even killed. I shiver to think what could happen . . ."

Zofia nodded. "It is true that Rachel is direct, and unafraid." Then Zofia put her arm around Shana's shoulder. "But in a way, I really admire her. She is so young, but she is already so strong."

"Or so foolish?" Shana said, sighing. "As only the young can be."

Chapter 22

A restless energy shot like a bolt of lightning through the enclosure as the prisoners awoke to find they were docked. Several people tried to ask the guards questions:

"Are we getting off the ship, here at the dock in France?"

"What is the plan? What are you going to do with us?"

Unfortunately, they were ignored.

Zofia's lower back and legs ached from sitting on the ground in the same position for so many hours. The cage was over-crowded and the smell of unwashed bodies and urine had gotten so strong that even the sea air could not dilute them. *If only I could jump off the side of this boat and feel the water on my skin, in my hair*, she thought. People were all around her; she felt as if she were suffocating. Zofia had to get up and stretch.

Careful not to step on anyone, she stood. Her limbs tingled from lack of movement. She reached down and tried to massage them. Then she looked across the water at the port. What are we going to do now? She sighed; it would be so easy to just give up, to just stay in Europe. But if all the Jews stopped fighting there would never be a homeland. Her eyes burned and her head ached.

***

It was early afternoon before the Captain's voice came over the loudspeaker.

"In an hour, you will begin to disembark."

"We will not go." A male voice rose loud above the crowd. "We will not go on land here in France. Take us back to Palestine."

The crowd cheered, and others chimed in with similar sentiments.

Then a chant began, "Justice for the Jewish people."

Zofia remembered that slogan from a sign that had been posted in the DP camp. Louder and louder, the crowd's angry voices chanted the words. "Justice, Justice, Justice."

Then the loudspeaker was overtaken by one of the leaders of the Jewish refugees. "We will stage a hunger strike, now, while the world is watching, the press is watching. We will not eat or drink until this ship is on her way to Palestine. The British promised that we would have that country as our own, and we will have it, one way or another. NOW . . . Chant with me. 'Justice for the Jewish People.'"

And the chanting continued.

A swastika was emblazoned onto the British flag, and it was raised as someone cried out, "The British are as bad as the Nazis."

Katja cuddled under Zofia's arm. Isaac stood, his voice loud and angry as he chanted with the others, his fist raised high in the air.

If the French had agreed to force the passengers off the ship and on to French soil, they would have been taken from the ship in France. However, the French did not want the Jews either.

A sign was posted where all of the prisoners could see it. It read: "If you do not agree to disembark by tomorrow evening, August 22, you will be taken to Hamburg, Germany. Signed: 'On Behalf of the British Government.'"

One of the passengers yelled, "They want to take us back to Hitler, back to Germany. We cannot go; we must continue our hunger strike."

So for twenty-four hours the already-dehydrated and emaciated Jews, both children, and adults, fasted. The world watched in horror as the photographs of the tortured refugees appeared in the news. The media attention was just what the Jews were hoping for, and on the second day, when the ship set sail, they prayed that they were on their way back to the Promised Land. However, they feared that they were headed straight to Hamburg.

Zofia had never experienced a headache like the one she had now. The blood pounded behind her eyes. The heat, the fasting, and the worry was more than she could bear. She lay on the deck holding Katja, who had fallen asleep in her arms. Isaac watched her with genuine worry. Now that the hunger strike was over, he gave her his share of the food and water. She didn't want to take it. She knew he needed it just as much as she did, but he insisted. Zofia sat up sipping the water. She felt as if she might vomit. Shana and Rachel sat on the other side of her, and for once, Rachel was quiet. Even she was apprehensive that Katja might lose her mother.

"Eat a little bit more," Isaac gently coaxed Zofia, touching her cheek, but she couldn't.

"I'm sorry, Isaac. I'm so tired. I just need to rest."

"Come then, rest." Isaac took off his shirt and made a pillow for her, which he laid on his lap. Gently, he helped her lay down. Katja was still huddled into her arms. "Sleep my darling, my love," he whispered.

Zofia could hear the worry in his voice and feel the gentle rhythm of his hand gently massaging her shoulder as she drifted off to sleep.

When she awoke during the night, everyone had fallen asleep except Isaac. He still held her gently as she lay upon his lap. When she opened her eyes she smiled at him, and she saw that a furrow of concern had deepened between his brows.

"How do you feel?" He whispered.

"A little better," she said. It was true. She did feel a little better, but still so tired and weak.

"I've been worried."

"I know. I'm sorry to have upset you," Zofia said.

Gently, Isaac took Katja off of Zofia and laid her down beside him. "Here stretch a little. Your legs must be stiff."

"Yes, they are stiff. My legs are cramping," she said.

"I know. It's from the lack of water."

She nodded.

"Can you stand up and stretch them?"

"I'll try."

He stood first, and then helped her to her feet. Zofia's legs ached and felt like jelly. She could hardly stand. Isaac held her in his arms.

"Stretch, my love; come on, let me help you," Isaac said. He held her as he tenderly massaged and stretched each of her legs and arms. "Let's try to walk a few steps," he said, holding her tightly around the waist so she would not fall. Carefully he guided her through the maze of sleeping bodies on the deck of the ship.

"My legs feel a little better."

"That's good, now sit down, and wait." He helped her to sit beside the sleeping Katja.

"Where are you going?"

"Just wait. I'll be right back."

For about fifteen minutes, Zofia gazed up at the dark, star-filled sky. Finally, Isaac returned carrying a flask.

"Drink," he whispered.

"Isaac? Where did you get this?"

"Never mind, just drink."

"Is this someone else's water? Did you steal it?"

"Don't ask me, just drink. You must drink Zofia. Do as I ask. Please. No questions."

She nodded, her head tipped to the side as she studied him.

"Please, drink . . ." he said again, "please . . ." He put the flask in her hand.

"But it's funny; I'm not even thirsty anymore."

"Zofia, when you aren't thirsty any more, that is when you really must drink. Don't ask me anything else; just please, this once, listen to me and do as I say. Drink."

She raised the flask to her lips and drank.

Zofia felt a little better, but her headache persisted, accompanied by nausea as the boat rolled along the waves.

When they arrived in the port at Hamburg, Zofia shook her head, tears threatening to fall as she frowned at Isaac.

"It's funny how sometimes you just want to believe something so badly that you refuse to accept the facts that are right in front of you."

"What do you mean?"

"Somehow, I knew that we wouldn't get to Palestine. We're Jews. Nobody wants us. I had hoped that they would relent and take us back to Palestine. Of course, I knew it would never happen. We're Jews. The world doesn't do nice things for Jews." She was trembling, her face had fallen, and she was fighting against a flood of tears.

Zofia could not miss the concern in Isaac's eyes.

"How are you feeling?" He asked.

"Not so well," she said. "I'm still very nauseated, and my headache comes and goes. Sometimes it's worse than other times."

He nodded. "No matter what happens I will find a way to take care of you."

"I know," she said, but she could not hide the loss of heart from her voice.

For eighteen days the passengers had baked in the hot sun, and now once again, they were rounded up like animals.

Isaac helped Zofia to her feet and held her up as they were ushered out of the cage and off the boat. He kept a close eye on Katja as she walked a little ahead, holding hands with Rachel and Mendel.

Once they were on land, they were loaded onto open trucks at gunpoint, and then transported to a British-controlled DP camp in Germany. The bouncing of the vehicle made Zofia so sick that she vomited over the side.

Katja turned white as she watched Zofia. Her small fist went into her mouth and she began biting on it. "Is mama going to be all right?" She asked Isaac.

"She will be all right." Isaac said. He cuddled Katja's head against his side.

"Are you sure?" Katja had begun to cry.

"I'm sure."

"Your mother will be fine," Rachel assured her.

Mendel took Katja's hand and held it tightly. She looked at him, her face scrunched up with fear.

Chapter 23

As soon as they arrived at the DP camp, Zofia was taken to the camp hospital. Isaac and Katja went with her. Shana, Rachel, and Mendel followed. They watched as the doctors and nurses began working on her.

"Can you watch Katja?" Isaac asked Shana. "I'll be right back."

"Of course," Shana said.

Isaac went over to the group of busy medical professionals who were rushing about between patients. "Please, I am her husband, can I talk to someone?" He was speaking Yiddish, peppered with the broken English that he'd acquired from the Americans while in the DP camp after his release from the concentration camp.

At first they ignored him, far too busy to be bothered. Then a young nurse with bright eyes and a soft, ivory complexion saw the desperation on his face. "Excuse me, doctor. I'll be right back."

"I'm Jane." She spoke with a thick British accent. "How can I help you?"

"She," Isaac indicated Zofia, "she is my wife. Please, is she okay?"

"She is badly dehydrated, and she is quite run-down. However, she is young and strong and I believe she will make it through. She just needs food, water, and rest."

"Can I help?"

"No, just stay out of the way. We are a little overwhelmed here. A lot of the people who came to the camp today are very ill."

"Can I come back to check?"

"Of course you can, just, as I said before, try to stay out of the way."

"Thank you," Isaac said.

"She will be all right. She needs care," Isaac said to Shana when he returned. "Would you mind taking Katja and trying to find an open bunk in one of the tents surrounding the medical tent? I know there is not much space, but do what you can. She needs to get some rest. I am going to camp outside the hospital tent so that I can be right here if Zofia needs me."

"Please, papa. Let me stay." Katja said. "I promise I won't be any trouble."

Isaac looked at the child, her blond curls knotted, and her face dirty. He felt sorry for her. She had just turned seven years old and she had to bear so much on her tiny shoulders.

"Come here, Katja." He held out his arms for her.

She went to him. He hugged her.

"Of course, you can stay with me."

Tears rolled down her cheeks.

"You are a good papa," She said.

He nodded "I will take care of you. And soon mama will be well, and we'll all be together again."

Isaac felt the tears well up in his eyes, but he fought them. "Let's sit down under the tree. Come." He took her small hand in his own. He would do his best to take care of her.

Zofia slept, her eyes opening occasionally, but her limbs were far too weak to move. She would gaze at Isaac and Katja, not comprehending who they were or where she was. Her eyes would focus for a moment, and then she would drift off into restless sleep again. Her dreams were fitful. Sometimes she dreamt of Manfred. She would hear his voice as he roared orders at her. Then, even worse, she would feel his cold, clammy hands upon her body. This recurring dream caused her to awaken bathed in sweat, crying. But she was oblivious to the comfort that Isaac tried to bestow upon her.

Other times she dreamed of the forest, where she and Isaac had been hiding and how they'd fallen in love. She could see his eyes, as blue as the sky above her, laughing eyes, gentle, loving. She heard his laughter, and in her dream she laughed, too. Oh, the joy and bliss she always knew in his arms. And, she dreamed of Eidel, Fruma, Gitel, Christa, and the baby she'd miscarried in the woods. She spoke to Fruma, told Fruma how sorry she was that what had happened between herself and Koppel had cost Fruma and Gitel their lives, and even though Fruma was dead she answered "I forgive you. You didn't know, you couldn't know."

It could have been weeks that she slept, even months. Zofia lost track of time. But one morning, just as the sun rose in the late summer sky, she awakened as if God himself had touched her with his hand and sent her back to the land of the living. For the first time, she was able to fill her lungs fully with air and sit up without falling back in exhaustion. Isaac, who had been resting on the ground just outside the hospital tent, he saw movement through the tent opening. Since Zofia had become ill, he hadn't been able to sleep deeply. Isaac was always aware of Zofia, always checking to see if she needed anything. He left Katja asleep on the ground, with his shirt rolled beneath her head for a pillow and went inside.

"You're awake? I sawyou." He knelt beside Zofia's bed.

"You must have been sleeping with one eye open." She laughed.

"I've been so worried. I guess I have been listening for every sound, watching for every movement. The nurses and doctors are so busy, and I was afraid they wouldn't hear you if you called for them."

"I'm so hungry."

"That's good."

"Doctors? Nurses? Am I in a hospital?" Zofia asked, puzzled.

"Yes, in the DP camp under British rule in Germany."

"Are we prisoners?"

"No, we can leave any time; we just need to decide what we want to do. I haven't given the future much thought. All I could think of was you. Right now, you need to eat so that you can grow stronger. Let me see if I can get you some food."

"Will the English give you food?"

"Yes, they are in no way as bad as the Germans. They just broke their promise to us about Palestine. But let's not think about all of that just yet. We have plenty of time to figure it all out when you are stronger. I can get you some food. And for right now, that is what you need."

She nodded. "Where is Katja?"

"She is asleep right outside the tent."

"Do you think she is safe out there all alone?"

"The camp appears to be quite safe. But I will wake her up and send her in here to stay with you while I go and get you something to eat."

A few minutes later Katja, still sleepy, came in to the hospital tent with uncertainty in her eyes. "Mama, are you feeling better?"

"Yes, Sunshine, I am doing much better."

Katja ran to Zofia and climbed up on the bed. She laid her head on Zofia's breasts. "I was so afraid you would die. I was so afraid." Katja was crying.

"Shhh, Sunshine. I am going to be just fine. Don't cry. Everything is all right."

Zofia ran her fingers through Katja's tangled hair. "Shhh . . ." she whispered again.

Katja grew quiet, content to lay with the only mother she could remember. She had not slept well since Zofia had been hospitalized. Now with her head on Zofia's chest, the gentle rhythm of Zofia's heartbeat coaxed her to sleep like a lullaby.

Every day Zofia was getting stronger until finally the doctors felt she could be released. One of the nurses gave her a sponge bath, and she felt clean for the first time since she'd left London.

That night Zofia sat with her family and friends while some of the other residents of the DP camp put on a play. They sang and danced and told jokes. Zofia smiled as she thought about how much her people had been through, and yet they still found such joy in life. Some of the performers had once been professionals on the European stage, and their talent still had the power to stun the audience. The play brought back memories of all of the artists who had created cultural communities even under the oppression of the Nazis in the Warsaw Ghetto.

After the show, Shana offered to watch Katja for the night. She would take Katja back to the tent where she and Rachel were staying, so that Zofia and Isaac could go off away from the others, somewhere under a tree and have some time alone together.

"Would you like to go and stay with Rachel for the night?" Zofia asked Katja.

"Are you sure you are better? You promise you won't get sick like that again?" Katja asked. Zofia saw the fear in Katja's eyes.

"I am fine. I will be right here to have breakfast with you in the morning."

"Do you promise?"

"I do, and I have never broken a promise to you, have I?"

"No Mama, you haven't."

"So, would you like to go then? You and Rachel could have a nice sleepover."

"Yes," Katja giggled.

"Katja slept over once before when you were in the hospital and we talked all night," Rachel said.

"That's fine, but you will have to whisper. You don't want to disturb the other people in the tent. And you will have to promise me that you will listen to Shana and do what she tells you."

"I promise," Katja said.

Once Zofia and Isaac were alone, they went off to a secluded part at the edge of the DP camp. They sat down under a tree and Isaac took Zofia in his arms.

"I was so worried . . ." He whispered in her ear. "I was so afraid that I had finally found you only to lose you again."

"I'm right here, beside you. I will always be beside you, Isaac."

"I want to get married. There has to be a Rabbi here."

"Yes, there are probably several."

"All we need is one," he said, smiling at her. "I will ask around in the morning. By the way, does that mean that you will marry me?"

"Of course I will marry you."

"I knew you would. I just wanted to hear you say it again." He smiled. "Zofia, I love you with all my heart. I never thought I could love anyone or anything this much."

"I feel the same, Isaac. I feel like no matter what life brings I can face it as long as we are together."

He took her in his arms and their lips met, warm and familiar. Then tenderly, with his fingers trembling with emotion, he began to unbutton her blouse.

Chapter 24

Zofia awoke at dawn to find Isaac already awake. They lay wrapped in each other's arms watching the sunrise.

"Today I am going to ask everyone here in the camp if they know of a Rabbi."

Zofia laughed a little.

"Why do you laugh?"

"Because you are so persistent. I didn't think that marriage would still be on your mind this morning."

"You don't want to marry me?"

"I do. I want to marry you more than anything."

"Marrying you has been on my mind from the day I first saw you. You were just a little girl coming in to buy bread, and I was the little fat boy sitting on the wooden pallet in the back of my mama's bakery. How could I be anything but a chubby child with lots of dreams, with the way that my mother baked that bread I ate constantly?" he wondered aloud with a laugh. "You are my true love, my best friend, and the person who I want to spend the rest of my life with."

"And you are mine.

Chapter 25

"Nu? Who could imagine such a mitzvah would happen right here in this DP camp?" Shana said, smiling as she helped Zofia dress for the wedding.

The dress had been loaned to her by one of the British nurses. It was a simple cream-colored dress made of heavy cotton, a little too large for Zofia's tiny frame. However, when Zofia saw how she looked, she could not contain the smile that came over her pretty features. Shana had taken Zofia's long black curls and pulled them back from her face with a tortoise shell comb, a gift from one of the prisoners (for whom Isaac had helped build a cot large enough for she and her husband to sleep on). Another of the nurses gave Zofia a nearly empty tube of cherry red lipstick, which Zofia smeared lightly upon her cheeks and full lips.

"You look beautiful," Shana gushed.

Zofia gazed at Shana, tears tickling her eyelids. "Thank you for all of your help getting ready for the wedding."

"It was nothing, I enjoyed every minute of it." Shana assured her. "I think Katja's dress is dry. I washed it and wrapped her in a sheet until it was done. She and Rachel have been playing cards with Mendel. I'm so glad that the three of them can keep each other entertained. It's good that they have each other."

The wedding began at sundown.

Several of the men had gathered to build a chuppah out of tree branches and leaves. They held the four posts up high enough so that the bride, the groom, and the rabbi, along with a small table (on which stood a glass of wine), could fit beneath the canopy.

The Rabbi entered the chuppah and the crowd grew silent.

One of the men, who had a long gray beard, played guitar. A singing group had been formed; their voices were exquisite and melodious. As the services began, the singers joined in harmony to create a haunting melody of traditional Yiddish music. Shana and Katja walked down an aisle carved into the dirt then lined with wild flowers and dandelions.

Next, Isaac walked alone. He waited beside the Rabbi.

Then there was a moment of silence.

The singers began again, their voices filling the air as Zofia walked forward carrying a small bouquet of wild flowers that Katja, Mendel, and Rachel had gathered. Some of the crowd gasped, others had tears in their eyes. She came forward to the entrance of the canopy. Isaac's eyes never left his bride as she circled the chuppah seven times. Then, once she'd finished, Zofia came to stand beside him.

The Rabbi said the prayers, and then the couple made their vows. Isaac placed the ring he'd taken from Koppel's pocket on Zofia's first finger. He knew the ring had once belonged to a woman who died in one of the camps. That bothered him in a way, but in another way, he wanted to honor the previous owner, whoever she was, with the love that he and Zofia shared. Somehow he believed that the woman who had once worn that ring was watching and smiling, knowing that her legacy lived on through the two of them. Each of them took a sip of the wine. Then the glass was placed on the ground. Isaac raised his foot and stomped on the glass. The gathering of people cried out "Mazel tov" and "L'chaim."

And here—on German soil that had once been ruled by the cruelest madman of all time—Zofia and Isaac were joined together under God, in marriage. And, once again, against all odds, the Jews celebrated the joys of life.

Chapter 26

"I'm going to find a job. We'll leave the camp and begin our days together as husband and wife. We can't live like this forever," Isaac said the morning after their wedding.

"Here in Germany?" Zofia asked.

"For now, until we have plenty of money. Then we can try to go to America."

"You don't think we can ever get into Palestine, do you?"

"I don't know. I would hate for us to save all of our money only to have our hopes squashed again."

She nodded. "A Jewish homeland; perhaps it's nothing but a dream."

"Besides, I want to earn some money. I had mixed feelings about putting that ring that I took from Koppel on your finger. I want to buy you a ring of your own, not one that was stolen from someone who was murdered. The only thing that made it easier to use that ring was that I felt that the dead woman's legacy lived on through our love and our marriage"

"Isaac, I feel that way too. I believe that the woman who owned this ring would want me to wear it rather than for the Nazis or the British to have found it. I will cherish it because it represents the love I have for you. If she, whoever she was, can no longer wear this precious band to represent the feelings she shared with her beloved, at least wherever she is she will know it is still a symbol of true love and marriage . . . it has not been melted down to serve a terrible cause like Hitler's Third Reich."

"My darling, my love," he laughed, shaking his head. "You have such a way of rationalizing everything."

Later that afternoon Isaac left the camp to look for work. While he was gone, Zofia and Shana washed clothes, while Rachel, Katja, and Mendel played tag.

"Children are wonderful. They have a way of healing," Shana said.

"Yes they do, but I wonder how much of what happened stays with them, buried deep in their hearts only to come out later when they grow up."

"I've often wondered that as well. But, after all, aren't we the lucky ones? We survived," Shana said, but her eyes were dull and did not have the spark a girl her age should have.

"We are fortunate to be alive," Zofia said, rubbing Shana's shoulder as she hung a threadbare shirt of Isaac's on a clothesline to dry.

For a few minutes, the women worked in silence.

"Do you ever feel guilty about living while the people you love are dead? I know this sounds crazy, but sometimes I think about my family and I wish I could have died with them."

"Then who would take care of your sister? Would you have Rachel die, too? She is so young, so full of life, and so spirited."

"I can't imagine her dying. The thought is terrifying to me. I'll tell you a secret, if you want to know."

"If you want to tell me," Zofia said.

"Sometimes, when everyone is asleep, I still pray. Even with everything that I've seen, I still believe. Silly, I guess, but I ask God 'please take me first, before Rachel.' I couldn't bear to lose her."

"I understand. It's not silly, I still believe, too. And, I feel that way about Isaac and Katja."

Shana hung her head. "Do you think we will ever get out of Europe? Do you think that Palestine will ever be our homeland?"

Zofia shrugged. "I don't know, but I hope so."

Chapter 27

"Anti-Semitism is alive and well and living all around us. There are former Nazis walking the streets. Nobody would hire me. Not one person would give me a chance, because I am a Jew. Hitler is dead but nothing has really changed." Isaac threw his hat down on the cot. "I'm tired, Zofia. I'm tired of fighting."

"Isaac, we can never stop fighting. If we do, then the Nazis have won. Tomorrow I'll try to find work. Maybe it will be easier for a woman. I am less threatening."

"No. I don't want you to have a job while I sit here in this camp depending upon the charity of the British, who for all intents and purposes are our enemies."

"Enemy is a strong word. They just don't want to give us their land," she said, smoothing the golden curls out of his eyes.

"They promised us that land and now they refuse to make good on that promise." He shook his head. "So we sit here, valued less than humans, waiting for them to give us a crust of bread. I don't want this, Zofia. I am young, I am strong. I can work and make my own way. If I can just find a job, we can save money and then decide where we want to live. I still say we should try to go to America"

"America." She shot him a glance "They don't want us. It's almost impossible to get in. You know that we have talked about this so many times before."

"Still, if I can find work, if we have a little money . . ."

"We still have the jewelry that we took from Koppel. We can sell that if you think it will help. I'm willing to try to go to America if that's what you want," she said.

"Yes, we can sell it, but how long do you think the money will last if I don't have a way of earning more?"

She shook her head. "I don't know. For now, Isaac, I think we should both keep on looking for work and stay here until we find a way to bring in some steady income."

He reached up and put his hands to his temples squeezing as if he wanted to push every memory from his mind. "I don't know if you have heard this story, but it haunts me, so I'll tell you. After the war, a group of Jews were released from one of the death camps. I don't remember which one it was. But anyway, they got out and went back to the old village where they had lived before there were Nazis, and do you know what happened?"

She shrugged. She could see by the anger in his eyes that the rest of the story would not be good.

"All of their old neighbors were there. People they'd known their entire lives."

Again, she nodded. His eyes blazed dark and ominous.

"All of their friends and neighbors started a pogrom and killed them. They gathered them together and stuffed them into a barn. Then they lit the barn on fire. Do you want to know why, Zofia? Do you want to know?" He didn't wait for her answer. "Because they didn't want to give up the land and possessions that had belonged to the Jews; the stuff the Nazis gave them when they rounded up their Jewish neighbors and their friends. These people who they knew; the doctors who delivered their children and then treated them when they got whooping cough. The bakers, who baked their bread, like my parents. We, Jews, are worth less to them than the horses in their barns. Our lives mean nothing. To the gentiles outside of this DP camp, this prison without bars, we are nothing but a threat. They don't want us. The British won't help us, and we're stuck here living like animals."

"Isaac," She whispered. "Isaac, let me get you some water."

He shook his head. "I don't know what to do? I've heard that many people are posing as gentiles, but I won't do that. I won't cover up who and what I am. Too many Jews have died because they were Jews. I won't disgrace their memory. I'd rather go back to living in the forest, to living off the land the way we did when we were hiding from the Nazis, than to deny my birthright."

"I would never want you to pose as a gentile. Never! I am not ashamed that we are Jews." She put her arms around him, but he shrugged her off, got up, and walked away.

"You don't know what it is like to be a man."

"No, I am afraid I don't," she said, getting up and going to him.

"I feel like a failure. My responsibility as your husband is to take care of you, to give you a good life. And how can I do that? I have nothing to give you. I can't take care of you. I am worthless. You are my wife, the love of my life, the only woman who has ever touched my heart, and in turn, all I can give you is a home in this depressing, pathetic place. My father would be ashamed." He shook his head.

She turned him toward her. His brow was deeply furrowed. Sympathy for him began to creep over her as she looked into his eyes.

"Zofia, Zofia," he whispered. "What will become of us?"

"Please, for now, just try to be calm. We'll find a way. We are Jews. It's part of our makeup to find a way to survive when it seems impossible. Haven't we done that all throughout history?" She smiled and winked at him.

He looked at her and she saw the anger fade from his handsome face. Then he laughed, throwing up his hands. "It's no wonder I love you. You know how to make me feel better no matter what we have to face. You are my light in the darkness." But even as he embraced her, she felt a tear slip down his cheek.

Zofia held Isaac for several minutes in silence as she ran her fingers through his soft blond curls. Then she looked up into his eyes, and a bolt of overwhelming sadness shot through her heart as she noticed that a web of wrinkles had begun to form around his eyes. Her hand went to his face, and then, as if she had the power to take his pain, she gently tried to smooth the wrinkles away. He smiled at her. It was a sad, defeated smile that hurt all the way through her. Zofia took Isaac's hand in both of hers. The skin was coarse and callused. She raised it to her lips and tenderly kissed his palm. She felt the tears begin to take form in the back of her eyes. He reached up with his free hand and caressed her chin.

"We will find a way to get through this," she whispered. "You'll get work. It will take some time, perhaps, but you will. And we will be a family."

"Have I ever told you that you are beautiful?" he asked.

She looked away. It had been a long time since Zofia felt beautiful. From the sun, her skin, which had once been soft, milky, and white, was now rough and the color of cinnamon. It had been a very long time since her eyes sparkled with the innocence of youth, but they did shine with the wisdom of age. And although her body was strong, the bones of her rib cage were visible. A long time ago, she'd believed she was beautiful, but now she knew that Isaac only saw her that way because he loved her.

It made her happy and sad at the same time. He loved her and she rejoiced for the wonderful gift of his love. But she lamented the loss of her youth.

The wind kicked up and a bouquet of multi-colored dried leaves danced across the yellowing grass of the open field.

He touched her face. "You are beautiful, Zofia. Don't ever doubt that," he said, as if he were reading her mind.

She smiled a wry smile at him. "I love you, Isaac."

"We'll find our way," he said and he took her in his arms. "Together, we'll find our way . . ."

Chapter 28

The winter rushed in on the coattails of a blizzard. Wind and snow danced through the DP camp. The British handed out used coats and sweaters that had been donated by Jewish organizations to shield the survivors against the cold. Zofia and Shana volunteered to help in the kitchen while the children played on the floor of the dining area. Mendel, Rachel, and Katja had become inseparable. The three were together all the time. They had no toys, so they fashioned games out of sticks and rocks. The two women watched as the children played.

"I'm glad they have each other. It is hard for us as adults to live in this camp; can you imagine how difficult it must be for a child?" Shana said.

Zofia nodded, but she didn't agree. From what she could see, the children were quite content with their surroundings. And for that, she was happy.

Outside, an army truck came barreling through the storm, covered with snow. It slid on the ice as it came to a stop.

"Look at that truck," Zofia said. "Can you see the small flag with the stripes and the stars?" Zofia smiled at Shana, "Look, do you see it? It's right by the driver, over there by the window."

"I see it," Shana said.

"They are Americans."

The vehicle held two men and a pile of boxes.

"I think they are bringing supplies," Shana said.

"Thank God; we're running low on food."

The men got out of the truck and began to unload the cargo at the back of the kitchen. From where Zofia and Shana were working they could see them clearly.

"Look at the one with the thick dark hair. He is so handsome," Shana said.

"Yes, he is," Zofia said.

"I wish I had a better dress."

"Don't be silly. You are a lovely girl," Zofia said, casting a sidelong glance at Shana. How selfish she had been. She had never even thought about how Shana must feel. Shana was still a young woman; she should be out dancing and not stuck in a DP camp. Zofia remembered how she'd felt when she was imprisoned in the Warsaw Ghetto. She had been about Shana's age then. She was angry every day because she felt that her youth had been stolen.

Shana was talking about the American, but Zofia was not listening. Her mind was flashing back to the Warsaw Ghetto. She remembered standing with her friend Fruma in the dark alleyway. Her daughter, her baby Eidel, was asleep in her arms. She knew that this was the last time she would hold Eidel as a baby. Her hands were cold, her body shivering, as she handed the child to a man who worked with the black market. To this day, she remembered the kindness in his eyes, the gentle way he took Eidel in his arms. He was such a strong man, yet so very tender, very much like her Isaac. She even remembered his name, Karl Abdensern. She never knew what became of him, but he was the man who would save her daughter's life.

Zofia could still feel her body swaying as she was standing there, leaning against Fruma, who held her tightly. Zofia could hardly breathe and she was afraid she might faint. He took the child, and as he did, she felt an icy, cold fist shoot through her breast. Her arms were empty, helpless, hanging at her sides, without purpose, and she was yearning for the weight of her baby to fill them. Her eyes followed Karl as he nimbly climbed over the rooftop carrying her child. For an instant, she caught a glimpse of Eidel's face in the moonlight, and then Eidel was spirited over the top of the building and she was gone. Her daughter, her Eidel, went over the wall, out of the ghetto, and to the safety of her dear friend Helen.

As Zofia and Fruma walked back to their apartment, she felt as if her heart would never mend. At that moment in time, she believed that her life had ended. How wrong she had been. God sent a light into the darkness of her life, the light of true love. When she looked into Isaac's eyes and felt completion in his arms as they made love, she knew that whatever she had been through was all worth the suffering because it had ultimately brought her to him. Every day that Zofia had suffered under the sadistic torture of Manfred Blau, the Work-Detail Führer, when she was in Treblinka, she had thought of Eidel. That was the only thing that had kept her from committing suicide. The only way Zofia could fall asleep was to think about the day when she would hold Eidel in her arms again. Sadly, this did not come to pass, but God had seen her through. He had sent her Katja.

Katja, who filled her need for a child; Katja, who became her heart and soul. She thought that with Katja in her heart, she had no room left to love anyone or anything else. But then God had been even kinder, for then there was Isaac, alive. And now, even though she was here in this DP camp, with an uncertain future, she was filled with happiness, more happiness then she could ever have imagined. She had Isaac and Katja, and she knew Eidel was where she belonged. Zofia's life was not perfect but it was very good. She took a deep breath. Yes, it was very good.

"Zofia, he's looking over here," Shana said. Her face glossed over with a pretty peach blush. "What should I do?"

Zofia smiled, drawn back to the present time by Shana's words. "Nothing. Just smile at him."

Shana smiled and then looked away quickly. She whispered to Zofia, "Is he smiling?"

"Yes," Zofia whispered back.

"I gotta say, boing," the other soldier said, nudging his companion with his elbow. "That gal across the way that you're staring at . . . She's one gorgeous dame."

"Shut up," the soldier with the wavy dark hair answered. "Act like a gentleman. You're embarrassing me."

"Hubba, Hubba! Leblanc, you sure got good taste," the other soldier answered, laughing and pushing his dark-haired friend.

"Get outta here." The dark-haired man called Leblanc answered, shoving his friend.

A few minutes later, LeBlanc walked over to where Zofia and Shana sat. He carried two oranges, a rare treat.

"Good afternoon, ladies," he said with a smile. Zofia saw how white his teeth were, his skin was clear, and he looked healthier than anyone she had seen in a long time. "My name is Larry Leblanc, but my buddies call me Lucky. I brought these for you . . ."

Lucky handed each of them an orange.

Shana had become almost fluent in English.

"I hope I'm not being too bold, but may I ask your names?"

Shana cleared her throat. Zofia could see that her young friend was tongue-tied. "I'm Zofia and this is Shana."

"Nice to meet both of you. May I sit down?" he asked.

"Hey Romeo, get over here and help me. Who made you Sergeant today?" the other American said with an easy laugh.

"Excuse me. I have to help my fellow soldier, then, if it'd be all right with you, I'd love to come back and talk. Would that be all right with you?"

Shana nodded.

"Okey dokey, then," Lucky smiled.

Shana and Zofia watched Lucky as he sauntered back to his counterpart.

"Okey dokey?" Zofia repeated. "What does that mean?"

"I have no idea," Shana said and they both giggled.

When Lucky returned to find Shana, Zofia got up and left with the excuse that she needed to find and speak with Isaac about something. She asked the children to accompany her, leaving Shana to talk to Lucky privately.

Chapter 29

Several days passed and the Americans were still at the camp. Zofia could not miss the glow on Shana's face. It was as bright as the sun on a summer day. Shana had always been a pretty girl, but now she was truly beautiful. She could be seen walking with the American, both of them whispering, sometimes her arm tucked into his.

Zofia was happy for her friend. Perhaps Shana would marry this boy and move to America. That would be such a blessing for Shana and Rachel. America, everyone wanted to go to America. Everyone but Zofia and Isaac. They still dreamed of Palestine.

One morning Zofia awoke early. When she turned over, she felt that Isaac had left the bed. She watched as he stood before the mirror. He did not know she was awake. Slowly he removed his yarmulke and the mezuzah that he wore around his neck. Even from where she lay quietly on the cot, Zofia could see that he had tears in his eyes. He was still unaware that she watched him. He carefully folded the articles he treasured, the articles that defined him as a Jew. He slid the small cardboard suitcase out from under the bed that contained his tefillin and his bible. He picked up the book and tenderly kissed it, and then he placed all of the items in the suitcase and whispered under his breath. "God, please forgive me. I must deny the blood of my ancestors so that I may find work in order to feed the ones I love."

Zofia gasped and stuffed her fist into her mouth so that Isaac would not hear her. She knew how much Isaac's Jewish heritage meant to him. She longed to go to him, to put her arms around him and tell him that he needn't do this. But she knew that if they were ever to leave this camp, then Isaac had to find work, and she had to find work as well. And if that meant posing as a gentile, than that is what had to be done. Zofia had learned that sometimes it was necessary to do things that one hated in order to survive. Biting her knuckle, Zofia moved deeper under the covers so that Isaac would not know that she had seen him. She did not want him to know that she had witnessed his shame.

After he left the barracks to go out into the world, Zofia got up and watched him through the window. Her heart ached as she saw his strong back, filled with determination, walking toward their future. Leaving what he felt was his integrity behind. She remembered the small pouch of gold that they had taken from Koppel. It was now hidden under their thin mattress. Perhaps she should sell the jewels; but they would still need work. The money would only last so long, and then…if any opportunity ever came their way to go to Palestine, they would not have the funds. No, she would keep that small pile of treasure hidden, lest it be stolen. She would wait, at least for now.

Once she could no longer see him, Zofia broke into tears.

When he returned that evening, he returned with money.

Isaac did not know that Zofia knew that he went out to work posing as a gentile. He thought she believed he'd found work as a Jew. Either way, as time went on, it mattered less and less how he acquired the jobs, it mattered only that he did. Isaac was strong and as a gentile, he found work easily enough. There were reconstruction jobs all over Germany due to the destruction caused by all the bombing. The money was not good, but at least he had funds coming in, and he saved every penny, planning to find a place to live for Zofia and Katja, far away from the DP camp. The more productive he felt, the better his mood. Zofia wished he would talk to her, that he would tell her the truth. She would never have judged him. But he didn't. Perhaps he couldn't, and she didn't push him.

Chapter 30

"Give me your finger," Rachel said, after she had cut her own finger with a piece of broken glass. Blood spurted from the slash and began dripping on the ground.

"I can't," Katja grimaced.

"Then do it yourself, Katja. Don't you want to be bound to us by blood?"

"I do, but I'm afraid to cut myself," Katja said. "And the sight of the blood is making me dizzy."

"Here, Mendel, you do it next."

Mendel took the piece of broken glass and cut his finger.

"You're the only one left," Rachel said.

"You do it for me. I can't do it," Katja said, looking away with her eyes scrunched shut tightly and her finger stuck out.

Rachel made a small, quick cut. Katja winced.

"Now, let's all put our fingers together so that our blood gets all mixed up. That way we will always have each other's blood running through our veins."

The three friends put their fingers together, their blood blending.

"As of this day, I hereby declare that we three will always be bound together by blood. This will be our secret society. No one must ever know. We will watch out for each other and take care of each other forever because we are brother and sisters. The oath that we are taking is a vow that we will never lie to each other and we will be friends forever, no matter what happens. Does everyone agree?"

Mendel and Katja nodded.

"Does anyone have anything else they want to say," Rachel said. No one said anything. "Then as of this moment, I, Rachel Perloff, make this promise," Rachel said. "Katja do you take this vow?"

"I do," Katja said.

"Say it then," Rachel said.

"I, Katja Zuckerman, take this vow."

"Mendel, do you?"

"I do. I, Mendel Zaltstein, take this vow."

"Then as of this day, April 24, 1948, we three are a secret family of friends bound by blood," Rachel said.

"Should we have a name for our group?" Mendel asked.

"That's a good idea. Any suggestions?"

"How about 'Friends for Life'?" Katja said.

"That's good," Rachel said.

"How about 'The Jewish Brigade'?" Mendel said.

"What about 'Our Jewish Army Bound by Blood'? We could call ourselves JABB?"

"I like that," Mendel said.

"Me, too," Katja nodded. "It sounds so strong and powerful."

"We will be strong and powerful someday, watch and see," Rachel said.

Chapter 31

Meanwhile, in Palestine there was unrest, not only between the British and the Jews, and between the Arabs and the Jews, but also within the Jewish population itself. Militant Jewish groups had formed years earlier. As time went by, these rebel Jewish groups grew stronger and began to engage in attacks on the British. These acts of violence against the British were openly disapproved of by The Jewish Agency for Israel, an organization started in 1929 to found, build, and maintain a strong and vibrant Israeli state.

For Shana, the days were a little brighter as the green grasses began to sprout their slender green tendrils, breaking through the last of the winter snow. She could not remember ever feeling so glad to be alive. For as long as she could remember, the only purpose she had had for living was Rachel. The rest of their family was gone, and everything she'd known before the Nazis took over had changed. All of her friends had disappeared or died and she had been forced to stop her education. Unlike girls her age before the war, Shana had no pretty clothes or boyfriends. In fact, her existence had been reduced to the very basics, food and shelter.

Now, for the first time, she had begun to feel what it meant to be young and alive. Every night, Shana met Lucky outside of the hospital building, and they walked or went into the closed cafeteria and sat talking in the darkness. The only light visible was the glowing red light from the tip of his cigarette. At first, she'd been shy, clumsy, and awkward. She had never even been on a date before. But Lucky's easy laugh and funny jokes had slowly coaxed her out of her shell.

"Where are you from?" Shana asked him one night as they walked under the stars. It was strange how the DP camp no longer looked like an ugly concentration camp to Shana. In fact, it began to feel like Shana had always imagined attending the university would have felt.

"A little town in Louisiana, just outside of Baton Rouge," he said.

"Louisiana?"

"Yeah, it's in the southern United States."

"What is it like there?"

"Heck, it's a lot different from here."

"Tell me all about it. I really want to know," she said.

He took her hand. "May I hold your hand?" he asked.

She nodded.

"All right then, I'll tell you. It's beautiful. We have these magnolia trees that smell so good you'd think there was perfume in the air, especially when it gets real hot in the summer. On Sunday, my mom, my brother, and I used to get all dressed up and go to church right down the road. Then afterwards we had lunch at our house. All of the relatives came. It was like our Sunday ritual."

"Your father?"

"He died when I was little. I never knew him. I lived with my grandparents until they passed. They left the house to my mom. She was their only child."

"So you lived in their house?"

"Yeah, they weren't rich, but they did okay. They left my mom a little money and we got along."

"And your brother?"

"He was killed in the Pacific. He was a pilot in the air force."

"I'm sorry."

"Yeah. Me, too. I miss the kid. He was my little brother. We grew up doing everything together. I'm the older one; by right, I should have gone first."

She squeezed his hand.

"Rachel is your sister?"

"Yes. She is all I have left. My family is all dead."

"Geez, that's tough. I'm sorry," he said, taking another cigarette out of the package.

They walked for a while in silence. He stopped for a minute to light the cigarette. She waited quietly, not knowing what to say.

"Hey, I've got an idea. How would you like to go dancing?" Lucky asked.

"Dancing, where? I don't even know how to dance."

"We could go into town. And don't worry, I'm a great dancer. You just follow my lead, and in a few minutes, you'll catch on."

"I don't know."

"Come on; you could use a little fun."

She looked away. "I don't think so."

"Hey, what is it? What's the matter?" He gently turned her around to face him.

"This is the only dress I have."

"Is that all?" He laughed and his laughter made her angry.

"It may not seem like anything to you, but to me, well, I look a mess." She folded her arms over her chest. "I think it is time for me to say goodnight." She began to walk away.

"Hey, wait a minute. Don't get all huffy. How about I get you a pretty dress, and then we go dancing? What do you say?"

"I say that I could not accept a dress from you."

"Even if I said, 'Please'? I want to get out of here, too. You'd actually be doing it for me. It'd be like a favor."

She looked at him; his eyes were dancing in the moonlight. "Please?" He said again.

"Well, I don't know."

"Come on, say yes," he said. "Come on." He nudged her gently. And she nodded.

"Yes, all right. I'll go." She smiled

The following night, after dinner, he brought her a large white box with a red bow.

"Come into the cafeteria and open it," he said, taking her hand and leading her, knowing that nobody would be in the cafeteria and they could talk privately. "I hope you like it."

Once they were inside, he took her to the back, by the only window in the room. The moonlight lit the area just enough for her to see.

"Well, come on, open it," he said, smiling.

She nodded, a little nervous, her hands trembling as she took the top off the box. She gasped when she saw the dress. It was black silk with a lace overlay. There were matching black pumps with a small heel and a pair of silk stockings. Carefully, she lifted the dress. In the moonlight she could see that it had been adorned with tiny pearls that sparkled.

"This is so beautiful," she said, her voice hoarse.

"I sorta guessed on the size. I had the sales gal help me. I hope it fits."

"It looks right. The shoes look like they will fit as well," Shana said, thinking that the pumps looked a little too big, but she could stuff the toes with paper.

"So, you will go dancing with me, Cinderella?"

"Who?" Shana asked, her head tilting to one side.

"Cinderella. You know, Cinderella?"

She shook her head.

"Never mind; it's just a fairy tale."

She nodded. "I'd love to hear the story, the fairy tale. Sometime." She sighed.

"You want me to tell it to you?" He smiled.

"Would you?"

"Yeah, why not," he said, and he told her the story of Cinderella. When he was finished, she had tears in her eyes.

"That's a beautiful story. I think I remember my mother telling me that story long ago, but I cannot be sure."

He smiled. "So, what is the verdict, will you go dancing with me?"

"I will."

"That's great!" He said. She could see the delight in his full, bright smile.

"I will be like Cinderella," she giggled.

"And I will be your handsome prince."

That night, as she lay on her cot, Shana laughed. When had she ever heard someone use an expression like *that's great*, or *okay*? Or *okey dokey*? He was so American, she thought, so exuberant. So damn wonderful.

Chapter 32

"I'm in love, Zofia," Shana declared, as she and Zofia were walking toward the children's schoolhouse.

"Lucky?"

"Yes, Lucky!"

"Does he know?"

"Not yet, but he will tonight. I am going to tell him. The Americans are leaving in the morning, and I want him to know how I feel before he goes."

"I don't know what to say. Only that I am happy for you," Zofia said. She was skeptical. She wanted to tell Shana that one mistake could change your life forever. When Shana told Lucky how she felt about him, would he say that he loved her, too? Would he take her to America? Or would he walk away? Zofia knew the pain of unrequited love.

"I feel so good. For the last week, every night, we have been sneaking out and going dancing."

A few months earlier, Rachel had begun to share a cot with Katja, freeing Shana at night to do as she pleased. Because the two girls slept right next to Zofia and Isaac, Shana knew that Rachel would be safe. Most nights, the two little girls giggled until they fell asleep or someone in the barracks complained. Then, once everyone was asleep, Shana got up quietly and dressed. Then she went out to meet Lucky, careful to return before anyone awakened.

"I never even realized that you were gone during the night." Zofia laughed. "You certainly had me fooled. Tell me about him," Zofia said as she arranged a pile of books into a stack on the table. Taking a rag, she washed a glob of glue and several pencil marks off the desk. Then she wiped her hands on her apron and sat down beside her friend. "Go on, I'm listening," Zofia said, turning to face Shana head on. "I want to hear all about him."

"He is the most incredible person I have ever known. He comes from a town near New Orleans. His family is French, but they are not from France. They are from some strange and exciting place that is very far north. From what he says, his ancestors came down a river from this place called Quebec, a long time before he was born and settled in Louisiana. His father was a lawyer just starting out when he died suddenly, and he calls his mother a society lady." She giggled. "I am afraid that he isn't Jewish, but I don't care. I have never felt this way about anyone before, and I want to hold on to this feeling forever. If he asked me to, I would convert."

"Yes, I know how you feel. It's wonderful to be in love," Zofia said, and she thought about Isaac. If Isaac had been gentile, she would probably have done whatever he asked, even convert. Then Zofia fixed her eyes on Shana. "Have you two discussed the future?"

"You mean getting married? No, never. But I am sure he will ask me to marry him once he knows how I feel about him."

Zofia looked down at the box of pencils in front of her. A few of them had bite marks. Some of the children liked to chew on the wooden pencils. Zofia moved the box to the center of the table. It was an absentminded gesture. One she performed because she could not think of the right words to say. Zofia knew that soon Shana's American would be returning to his home. Would he take Shana with him? Zofia would miss her friend, but if Shana were happy then she would be happy for her. But what if Lucky chose not to take Shana back with him? How would Shana cope?

"He says that where he lives, there are swamps that have snakes and alligators just a few miles from his house."

"Really? I once saw an alligator in a zoo in Poland," Zofia said. "It was a very long time ago. They look very similar to crocodiles and they are quite dangerous."

"He says that the creatures almost never leave the swamps."

"Well, that's a good thing," Zofia nodded.

Shana got up and took out a small pile of paper and laid it on the desk. Zofia watched her. She couldn't help but remember how she'd felt when she thought she was in love with her teacher. That was when she'd gotten pregnant with Eidel. Mr. Taylor. She'd never forget him. He'd dismissed her feelings as if they were just child's play, and he'd broken her heart. Zofia watched Shana, her face glowing, her feet light as air. She was so in love and so optimistic.

"What a silly conversation we are having," Shana laughed. "All about alligators." Shana was putting graded papers in front of each chair; papers that Zofia had worked on the previous day. "Larry wants to go back to school when he gets back home. He plans to get his degree in law and then follow in his father's footsteps."

"That's a good career," Zofia said, still watching her friend.

"I told him I want to go to school, too. I explained that I had been forced to stop my education because of the laws forbidding Jews to go to school."

"What did he say?"

"He thought it was a good idea that I go back and finish." Shana smiled.

"I couldn't agree more," Zofia said, smiling. "You would make a wonderful teacher."

"Do you think so, really?" Shana said

"I do. You are very good with the children and you have such patience."

"Do you want to know a secret?"

"If you would like to tell me."

"I think that once Lucky knows that I am in love with him, he will start making plans to take Rachel and me to America."

"Would you like that?"

"Of course I would, wouldn't everyone?"

"I suppose," Zofia said. "America. From what I have heard, life is good in America. Personally, I would rather go to Palestine. I think Isaac would prefer Palestine, too. But, I must say that it would probably be wonderful to live in America. Like a dream. I've met a lot of Americans since the war ended. Since they all seem so carefree, I have a feeling that the country must be as rich as everyone claims."

"Yes, they all look well fed, and they do have a certain ease about them. It's as if they don't comprehend real cruelty. Which is strange, considering that most of them are soldiers and they have suffered a great deal in the war," Shana added.

"I know what you mean. They seem to be easy with the world, and somehow, regardless of what they have been exposed to, they have this attitude that things should be fair. In a way, they are almost like children."

"Lucky said he couldn't believe how barbaric the Nazis were. He was one of the soldiers who liberated several of the concentration camps. He said he would never forget what he saw there. It still makes him sick."

"Yes, it was so horrible that it was unbelievable, even for those of us who were tortured. But the difference is that we saw it all first hand, we lived through it. I don't think America has ever known anything like that."

"Lucky told me that there was a time that Americans kept people with black skin as slaves."

"Really?"

"Yes. Lucky said that they were once slaves working on these big farms called plantations. And from what I understand, the owners of the plantations could be very cruel."

"I never knew. You wouldn't think that the Americans would do something like that. It sounds like Nazi behavior."

"There is a lot we don't know about that goes on all over the world, just like there was a lot that the Allies didn't know was happening to us here during the war," Shana said.

"I believe that some of them knew, they had to, but they didn't want to know. They turned away. It was easier not to face the truth."

"You think so?"

"Who knows? I can't believe that so many people were murdered, and nobody was aware that it was happening. But, I can't be sure."

"Oh Zofia, every survivor will carry these dreadful memories for the rest of our lives, even little Rachel. She was so young, but she saw the death of her family. She saw it with her own eyes. And, I know that no matter what I do, she will always hold that anger inside of her. It scares me. I am afraid sometimes that it is eating away at her."

Zofia nodded. "I know. I understand what you mean. We survived. But we will never forget."

Chapter 33

Lucky whistled softly as he approached the gate where he saw Shana leaning against the fence, her arms behind her back, waiting. She watched his broad shoulders and easy stride. There was something about the Americans; they were different from the British or the Russians, and definitely nothing like the Germans. Somehow, Shana thought, it seemed as if they saw the world through different colored lenses. They'd witnessed the suffering, but imbedded somewhere deep inside them, there was this knowledge that things ought to be better and human life had great worth. She treasured that clean, direct American way of thinking. And she loved Lucky, loved his sexy, relaxed way of being.

"How's my pretty angel tonight?" he said, reaching up and caressing her cheek.

"I'm fine." Shana blushed. "How are you?"

"Swell as always, except I have a little bit of bad news."

"Oh?"

"I'm not sure if I told you, I think I might have. But I wanted to let you know that my buddy and I are shipping out in the morning."

She knew they were leaving, but hearing the words spoken aloud stung her.

"When will you be back?" She felt her heart drop in her chest.

"Don't know for sure. I'm headed home on leave."

"Home to America?" Of course, she thought, feeling stupid for even asking. Where else would he be going home to?

"Yep. Home to Louisiana. And I sure as hell am looking forward to it. I can almost taste Mama's jambalaya. And hot corn bread with melted butter." He was smiling and licking his lips.

"Will I ever see you again?" She could not look at him. Tears had begun to well up in her eyes; her mouth was dry as sandpaper. She had to tell him. Why was it suddenly so difficult?

"I hope so. I'll try and come back here and visit you."

"Oh . . ." The single syllable caught in her throat.

"Heck, we had some laughs, right?"

She nodded, unable to speak because of the tears breaking through, running down her cheeks against her will.

"Hey, peaches, don't cry . . ."

"I'm sorry," she said, her voice cracking. Why was she so emotional? She knew he would be going, but somehow she thought that he would make some plans to return . . . something solid, something concrete. Perhaps he would feel differently once he knew how she felt about him. Shana inhaled deeply. TELL HIM. She coughed and turned away, looking out at the street. It was difficult to voice her feelings out loud, to bare her soul, to be so vulnerable. "Thank you for all of the kind things you've done for me," she said, cringing at how stupid she thought that sounded.

"You don't have to thank me. I like you a lot, you're a great gal," he said, squeezing her shoulder. "Come on now, don't cry."

"Lucky . . ." she said, swallowing the thick lump that had formed in her throat. Then, biting her lower lip she added, "Larry . . . I love you."

He didn't speak. She didn't know what to do, what to say. She wanted to run away, run back to the barracks; hide in the darkness of her room.

But she couldn't; she had to see his eyes. His eyes would tell her everything she needed desperately to know.

She turned her head to look at him. He looked genuinely confused, sad, filled with regret.

"Whoa . . . love? Shana, sweetheart, I don't know what to say," Lucky said, throwing his arms in the air.

"How do you feel about me?"

"Like I said, you're a great kid. I like you a lot. But, Shana, I got a girl back home waiting on me. She and I have been together since high school. We're engaged; we're supposed to get married when I get back."

"Oh? And what were you doing with me then?"

"We were just spending time. You know . . . both of us were lonely, and I thought that maybe we could make each other happy for a while."

"Oh, I thought . . ." she turned away, her face in her hands. She couldn't bear to meet his eyes. Shana felt like a fool, and she was sure that her heart would never be whole again. "I was a virgin, Lucky. You were my first man," she whispered.

"Geez, I had no idea," he said, taking a cigarette from his breast pocket and lighting it. "I'm sorry, kid. I didn't mean for you to get hurt."

She looked at him. He did look truly sorry, and that made her feel worse. There was nothing more to say. She wanted to be as far away from him as she could get. Shana didn't answer. She turned and ran back to the barracks. Still wearing her dress, she threw herself upon her cot and wept.

Chapter 34

The Americans rolled away in their army truck the following morning, waving goodbye out of the windows as their small flag fluttered in the spring breeze. Shana was nowhere to be found. Zofia looked everywhere for her. She had not shown up at breakfast, and Rachel had come to Zofia asking if she'd seen her sister. This was not like Shana, and although Zofia did not let on to Rachel, she was worried. However, Rachel, even at her young age, was no stranger to tragedy. Instead of playing with Katja and Mendel, she lay on her cot gazing out the window.

For a while, Katja and Mendel played outside the barracks while Zofia stayed inside with Rachel, neither of them speaking. But it was not long before Katja and Mendel came inside. Katja quietly lay beside her friend, and Mendel sat next to Katja. None of them were speaking as Katja smoothed Rachel's hair.

As always, regardless of the hardships he faced when leaving the camp to find work, Isaac returned with a smile on his face. He vowed to shelter Zofia as much as possible from facing any more hardship. He walked into the barracks with his well-worn gray pants and stained cotton shirt, smelling of springtime.

"My sweetheart, why are all of you here in the barracks? Are the children ill?" Isaac said to Zofia, as he looked over at Rachel and Katja lying on their cot. Mendel was sitting beside them holding Katja's hand. He had a worried look on his face. As he spoke, Isaac walked over and felt each child's cheek to check for fever.

"How are you, Sunshine?" he asked Katja. "Are any of you feeling sick?"

"We are all right, papa." Isaac's loving and caring ways had won Katja over. It warmed Zofia's heart to see them so close.

"So why are the three of you here in the dark bedroom on this lovely day? You should be out playing. You were always playing in the snow."

"Come outside with me, Isaac," Zofia said. "I want to talk to you."

He looked at her then back at the girls. Zofia nodded to him, "Come," she said again.

They walked outside.

"Shana is missing."

"Missing?"

"Yes, I don't know where she's gone. I'm sure that you saw the American boys who were staying here in the camp. You know who I mean; the American soldiers?"

"Yes, two of them were here, I think."

"Correct, there were two. Well, one of them had been seeing Shana romantically."

"Yes. And?"

"They left today."

"Do you think he took her with him?" Isaac asked. "Would she leave Rachel behind?"

"No, he didn't take her. I saw him leave. He was with the other soldier. There was no one else in the army truck."

"So where do you think she went?"

"I don't know. Yesterday she told me that she was going to tell him that she loved him. She thought he would marry her and take her and Rachel to America."

"And he left without her?" Isaac repeated, more to himself than as a question.

"Yes."

He slumped against the wall of the room. "I hope he didn't break her heart."

"I'm sure he did," Zofia said. "I just hope she is all right. That she hasn't done something foolish."

"Let me go and see if I can find her," Isaac said.

"I tried earlier," Zofia said. "I looked everywhere."

"Well, it doesn't hurt to look again," he said.

"Go ahead. Try," she said, lifting her hands in defeat.

Isaac kissed Zofia's forehead. "I'll be back soon."

Chapter 35

Isaac walked for nearly a half hour, combing the camp. He found Shana sitting among the garbage cans behind the kitchen.

He walked over to her quietly.

"Hello, Shana."

She nodded.

"It certainly smells terrible back here. Can I sit down and talk to you for a minute?" Isaac asked.

She nodded again.

"Everyone is worried about you. Zofia has been looking for you all morning and your sister is distraught."

"I'm sorry. I just needed some time alone," she said.

"I understand." He sat beside her without speaking for a few minutes. "Do you want to tell me what happened?"

"No," she said. Then she hesitated. "Lucky left. He left and he said he never cared about me anyway." She started crying. "I was in love with him and to him I was just a plaything."

Isaac sat, drawing his knees to his chest, listening.

"I had our whole future planned. We were going to get away from this terrible place and all of the horrible memories. He was going to take Rachel and me to America. I even thought that we would get married. What a stupid fool I am. I am so ashamed."

"It's all right," he said. "Don't feel foolish. I know that love can be the most wonderful thing in the entire world, but because it has the power to be so wonderful, it also has the power to hurt you deeply."

"Yes. It sure does."

"I know you don't believe me right now. And I know you feel like giving up, but you are young, Shana. You will find love again."

"I will never trust another man. NEVER!"

"Not all men are bad. Look at me and Zofia."

"I wish I could find a love like you two have for each other. I doubt something so good could ever happen to me. I always seem to find heartache and suffering, in every aspect of my life."

"You never know what the future will bring. We have all been through a lot of horrible things. Zofia and I were lost to each other for a long time. I thought that she was dead. The pain was so intense that I wanted to die, too. Every night I would ask God to take me, but every morning I would wake up and force myself out of bed. I believed that God had a purpose for me, something I had to do before I could die. And . . . I thought that purpose was to keep living and get to Palestine. Perhaps there I could do some good for our people.

The morning that I left the DP camp where I was staying in order to board *Exodus*, my heart was heavy. All I could think about was how Zofia and I had shared this dream, and now I was going to Palestine alone, without her, in hope of working to build a Jewish state. I had given up on love. I'd even cursed God for taking the only thing in my life that mattered. I cried, I considered suicide, but in the end I bent my head and bowed to God's will.

And do you know what happened? As I stood in line waiting to board the ship, God blessed me with the most wonderful, unexpected gift. I found Zofia again. It's true; we did not get to Palestine. But can you imagine the joy I felt when I saw her alive? It was something that I never thought, never dreamed, could happen."

She nodded.

"There IS a point to this long-winded story," he said, smiling at her. "Right now, you think that you have no reason to go on. But you do. God has something in store for you. I don't know what it might be, but I do know that if you allow God to take care of you, he will. And you must also think of Rachel, and follow your dream of going to the Promised Land. Keep that dream in your heart. Then let God bring you the love you long for; you'll see. Trust him. Believe me, he will deliver."

"Do you really think I will ever find real love? Someone who will care for me, who will share my life?" she asked.

"I know it. You just have to believe. Put your trust in God, swallow your pride, and swallow your pain. For now, go back and take care of your sister. And I will tell you a secret." He winked. "I still believe that somehow, some day we will all go to Palestine. And, somewhere, I don't know where, but your one true love, your destiny; your *beshert* is waiting. You must live so that you can be there and be ready when he appears."

"Isaac, you are so wise."

"Ech, I'm not wise, I just know what I believe, and I know what I have witnessed. I have seen many things. I've seen pain and suffering, but Shana, I have also seen love and miracles. Trust God, Shana . . . trust God."

Chapter 36

Ships of illegal immigrants came flooding the shores in an attempt to enter Palestine. Some came in secret at night, others in the light of day. The British stopped them and forced the passengers into camps in Cyprus. These camps were filthy, with inadequate food and water. They had no sanitation and were far too small to accommodate the never-ending flow of Jewish refugees. But buried within the hearts of the prisoners in these sordid camps lay the seed of hope, hope that someday the Jews would have a homeland.

Shlomie rubbed the bottoms of his sun-scorched feet. Somehow he would have to acquire some shoes, but he would not steal them the way that his were stolen at night as he slept. He crossed his legs and watched the other prisoners in the Cyprus DP camp as they danced traditional Jewish folk dances while others sang, clapping their hands. The sun was setting and the cool night air descended upon the desert.

He still could not believe that he'd seen Isaac and Zofia. He had thought that Isaac was dead, and as jealous as he was of Zofia's love for Isaac, he had still mourned for his friend. For Shlomie and Isaac had grown to be best friends, like brothers, during their time as partisans in the forest. Shlomie was happy to see Zofia and Isaac alive, even though they had been on *Exodus* and, therefore, were on their way back to Europe.

Shlomie had come to Palestine another way. He'd been smuggled in on a boat filled with Jewish scientists; he'd befriended them in the DP camp after Zofia had left. They'd planned the mission well, but not well enough. The boat they had chartered made it all the way to the other side of the world only to be apprehended by the British when it arrived. Because they were illegal, they'd all been imprisoned on the island of Cyprus. The climate was harsh. Clean water was a rare commodity, food was scarce, and the smell was a nagging, nauseating reminder of the germs that were always spreading from the continuous arrival of people and overflowing latrines. However, regardless of the conditions, the Jewish people on Cyprus had not lost optimism.

When he arrived, a friend had told Shlomie about an underground tunnel that some of the prisoners were digging at night as they'd planned their escape. Shlomie had not given it a second thought. He immediately offered to help. It was grueling labor that had to be done well after dark for two reasons: one, the heat of the day would have made the strenuous labor impossible; and more importantly, two, the tunnel was an escape route that had to be kept top secret, even amongst the others in the camp. Shlomie had never been strong like Isaac; he'd been more of an intellectual, but this was a cause he believed in and so he would work until his back broke to achieve his goal.

"Come, dance with us," one of the female scientists said.

Shlomie shook his head. "Not now. Maybe later."

Chapter 37

Her name was Esther, and she'd just had a baby in the Jewish wing of the British Military Hospital. Her husband, Lazer, sat holding the child while she danced with the women. Lazer smiled across the field at Shlomie. Shlomie returned the smile, lost in thought. He would like to have a family someday. It was said, and he agreed, that the Jews who'd survived the Holocaust had the responsibility of rebuilding the race by having as many children as possible. Someday he'd like to have a large family living in Palestine. Most of the people in the camp were young, Shlomie thought. That might be because very few of the old people were strong enough to survive the Nazis. Although the Jews were prisoners here on Cyprus, the British were choosing 750 people from the Cyprus camp each month and allowing them to enter Palestine. This was reason enough for optimism.

The sunset was a watercolor blanket of fuchsia and purple. The colors remained bright and vivid until the stars filled the sky like tiny diamonds on a bed of black velvet. Shlomie leaned back to gaze up for just a moment before going underground to begin his nights' work. He was tired and wanted to linger, laying on the cool sand, but he knew that the work must be done, the tunnel must be built.

As he lay gazing up at the sky, his back aching from the heavy shovel, from the digging, he heard a woman's laughter. It sounded crisp and clear, like tiny bells ringing in the night. Her voice traveled all the way through him, from the top of his head to the tips of his toes. Shlomie was no longer tired. He felt a burst of energy. He was compelled to sit up and look. He had to see the woman who possessed the laughter that sounded like music.

Chapter 38

On May 14th, 1948, the British Mandate over Palestine expired. Later that day, in the Hall of Independence, Palestine was established as a Jewish state. It was then renamed Israel.

Eretz-Israel, the land of Israel

That same night, the United States recognized the state of Israel. A roaring thunder of elation came soaring out of Jewish communities worldwide. Finally, the Jews would have a homeland. This land would protect them should another dictator like Hitler (God Forbid) ever find his way to power. Unlike in the past, when the Jews had sought refuge from the Third Reich only to find every nation had closed their doors to them, they now had a place to go, a homeland. Here they could live as Jews. Openly. Unafraid. Here they would always be wanted. A prayer sent to God by a broken people had been answered.

Israel. The Promised Land.

But . . .

The Jewish struggle was not over yet . . .

Later that very same night, the Arab League, consisting of four Arab armies—Syria, Egypt, Transjordan, and Iraq—attacked and invaded Israel, threatening to annihilate the Jews.

Chapter 39

Whenever he made his trips to Brazil, Konrad Klausen made them under the guise of a visit to his coworker, Dr. Joseph Mengele. After all, Konrad's job was to assure that the other members of the Nazi Party who had migrated to South America were comfortable. He was to see to it that their requirements were met. Konrad lived in Argentina; he'd been there since the end of the war. But, when the need to do the shameful things came upon him, he preferred to go far away from home to satisfy those wretched desires. And he found that it was most convenient in Brazil. After all, the favela was large and overflowing with poverty-stricken young men who were willing to perform any act that Konrad desired for a few coins.

He took a quick flight early one morning and then spent the afternoon with Dr. Mengele. Whenever Konrad went to Brazil, Mengele was always a wonderful host. He knew all of the important people in Brazil and was highly regarded by the ladies for his good looks. Recently Dr. Mengele had received his driver's license, and he was proud to show Konrad his brand new car. It was a shiny, black Borgward Isabella. Konrad could not help but admire the doctor's taste and envy his dapper good looks.

"I know a wonderful café; we'll sit outside and enjoy the view. Would you like that?" Mengele asked. He had a charming smile and his dark hair was slicked back from his face.

"Yes, that would be very nice." Konrad thought that he should be the one taking the doctor around, but it had turned out that Mengele didn't need Konrad's help to adjust to the move to South America; he had already made more friends than Konrad had ever had.

When they arrived at the café the maître d' greeted Dr. Mengele, using the alias name that Dr. Mengele was living under. "Good afternoon, Mr. Gerhard. Follow me, please; I have your regular table open."

"Charming little place, isn't it?" Mengele smiled, after they were seated. "So, what would you like to eat?"

As they ate and enjoyed several glasses of wine, people passing by greeted Dr. Mengele as Wolfgang. It amazed Konrad that so many people of the higher classes had already befriended Mengele. The other Nazis were far more reclusive.

After lunch Konrad and Mengele drove back to the house where Mengele was living. When they got out of the car, all of the children who had been playing in the park across the street came running across the street to greet them.

"Hello, Uncle," they said. "How are you, Uncle? Did you bring us candy?"

Mengele pulled a handful of hard candies from the pocket of his white linen suit and handed them out to the children. He bent down as they each gave him a hug.

"I love children, especially twins. Twins fascinate me," Dr. Mengele said smiling. "Especially identical twins."

Konrad had heard about Mengele's experiments on children, especially twins and this behavior of friendship toward the children here in Brazil surprised him, but he said nothing. Konrad found Mengele to be very strange, difficult to understand.

"You know the gypsies loved me. They said I looked like one of them," Mengele said. "Do you think so?"

"No, I think you look pure Aryan." Konrad shifted uncomfortably, unsure of what Mengele wanted him to say.

Mengele laughed. "I did a lot of work on gypsies. Such beautiful people, they are."

Konrad was not sure he understood this man at all, and because he didn't, Mengele made him nervous. He'd heard about the sadistic experiments that Mengele had performed, but perhaps what he'd heard was not true.

"Come in and let me show you what I am working on," Joseph Mengele said.

Konrad followed him inside to a makeshift lab. Here he had two small boys chained to a bed. It was obvious to Konrad that they boys were poor, probably beggars. Their skin was dark brown and their small bodies were painfully thin. In fact, it seemed as if their thighs were the size of Konrad's wrists. Mengele had taped their mouths so they could not scream. Their terrified eyes followed Konrad around the room. He tried not to look at them.

Konrad stayed for a few more minutes while Mengele explained what he was doing with the boys. He was itching to run, to escape this strange laboratory. Mengele was explaining something about injecting the dark eyes of the two children with dyes to turn them blue. Konrad didn't want to hear any more. The thought of needles puncturing eyes made his stomach queasy.

"It looks to me as if you are very well adjusted here," Konrad said.

"I am, very much so. As you can see, I've begun to work and experiment on creating a master race once again and that helps me to feel productive. However, in between, I still have plenty of mundane work that must be done. I must spend time removing the tattoos that the SS have under their arms. It's necessary, of course. Just in case the men are captured. Without the tattoos there is nothing to define them as SS officers."

"Yes, the tattoos." Konrad couldn't wait to leave.

"Would you like a cigar?" Mengele asked.

Konrad shook his head. "No, thank you."

"I've acquired quite a fancy for Cuban cigars. Wonderful tobacco."

Konrad nodded and took out a cigarette. Mengele flicked the corner of his gold lighter, which had his name engraved on the side in mother of pearl, and then he lit Konrad's cigarette and his cigar. "I don't know if you've heard, but I am planning to purchase a share in the Fardo Farm Pharmaceutical Company. I think it will be a good investment."

"It should be a very good investment," Konrad said, trying to hide how anxious he was to be on his way.

"I think so. My father came to visit and he gave me quite a bit of cash. So I've decided that it's time to make an investment. Why not make that cash pay off?"

"Yes . . . I think it's a wonderful idea."

Mengele took a puff of the thick cigar. "Marvelous," he said, looking at the cigar and turning it in his fingers. "You really ought to give these a try sometime. You might find you really enjoy them."

"Perhaps I will," Konrad said. "Well, I best be on my way. If you need anything let me know, and please stay in contact. Now, I must advise you that should you feel that you need to leave here quickly, I can have a sea plane whisk you away within a few hours. So, if you feel you are being followed or that someone has identified you, contact me immediately."

"That's good to know. I will keep it in mind."

"And I will keep in touch. I'll let you know how the experiment is going," Mengele said, smiling as he walked Konrad to the door.

"Good afternoon, then," Mengele said.

"Heil Hitler."

"Heil Hitler."

The doctor was charming, there was no doubt about that, but there was something under the surface of this man, something that always seemed to be watching, judging. As Konrad walked back to the bus station, he felt uneasy. The faces of those children unnerved him. Although he'd never committed murder, he'd ordered it, and he'd walked away unscathed. But he'd never gotten close enough to inject the eyes of a child with a long needle filled with poisons. Something about the idea made his skin crawl. Konrad walked more quickly. He was glad when the bus arrived and took him back to his hotel. He checked in. Then he climbed two flights of stairs up to his room, took off his clothes, and lit a cigarette. He would relax until nightfall.

Konrad called the front desk and ordered a bottle of whiskey to be brought up to his room. Then he sat by the window looking out, lost in thought. No one, not even Dr. Mengele, would admit to this, but Konrad believed that Hitler was still alive and Mengele had changed his face. How strange that even though Konrad was part of the inner circle, there was still so much that he was sure remained hidden from him. He lit a cigarette and poured himself a glass of whiskey.

When he was surrounded by the other escaped Nazis he felt all right, but when he was alone, thoughts of his old friend Detrick would often haunt him. Detrick. He pictured the blond hair falling over

Detrick's left eye, his easy smile. Detrick. Konrad had loved him, loved him as a brother, as a friend, but secretly deep in his heart, Konrad had loved him as a lover. Detrick, the strong athletic boy, who in their youth had defended him when Konrad was a weak and sickly child and the other boys had tormented him. Detrick. He whispered the name aloud shaking his head, wishing everything had turned out differently.

He'd tried to make things better for Detrick and his family by getting Detrick a job working for the party, but Detrick had been a traitor. Konrad had discovered the betrayal and realized that Detrick had never really been a part of the Nazi Party. He'd been deceiving them all. Then, the worst possible thing had happened; Konrad had been forced to choose between his own wellbeing and the life of his best friend. Konrad knew he was a coward, and his choice to protect himself had reinforced that shameful trait. And because he had betrayed his Detrick, Detrick was dead. What a fool Detrick had been; he'd been a Jew-lover, and it had cost him his life. Detrick had helped two Jews escape, the girl, Leah, who Detrick had been in love with, and her father. If Detrick had only listened to Konrad, if he'd not been so stubborn, he would have risen in the party. Detrick would have been alive, he would have been here in South America today. But he had refused to give up on those Jews.

Damn him and damn those Jews! Konrad slammed his fist on the table and the bottle of whiskey trembled, almost toppling over. Detrick had been caught and arrested at the border just as he had been about to enter Switzerland. The girl had not even been with them. It had been just Detrick and the old man. And they shot the old man just as Detrick was about to cross over into safety, but Detrick, the fool, had come running back. Konrad had heard about how Detrick had held the old man as he died. Then they'd taken Detrick to the Nazi headquarters and had beaten him to death.

After it was over, Konrad had received a phone call. He had been asked
to come to the Nazi offices where Detrick's body was being held. Konrad had hung up the phone and vomited before he'd left; but he knew he had to go, he had to follow orders. When he'd arrived, he'd seen Detrick's battered body covered in dried blood. Konrad could not forget how his heart had raced, the guilt that had washed over him, how he had wanted to throw himself on top of his friend and weep.

How strongly he'd wished that he could have changed things, altered the course of events. And for a moment, he even wished he could trade places with Detrick, because he knew that for the rest of his life he would carry the guilt. But as he stood staring at the battered body of his oldest and dearest friend, Konrad knew that if he had really had the chance he would never have traded places with Detrick. He was afraid of pain and terrified of death.

It had been almost impossible to control the trembling of Konrad's limbs as the Nazi officer had walked in circles around him, questioning him with skepticism, making implications about his association with Detrick. The interrogation had continued throughout the night, until finally, in the morning, the SS had been satisfied that Konrad had had nothing to do with Detrick's deceitful and disloyal acts. They'd left him alone in a cell for forty-five minutes, and then a guard had returned and released him. It was a terrible memory, but one that was never far from his thoughts.

Soon it would be dark. Konrad took a deep breath, got up, and washed his face. Then he scrubbed his hands, which were rough and cracked from the constant washings.

Konrad knew he should probably eat something, but he had no appetite, at least not for food. On these occasions, when the compulsion to find a boy came over him, he always found it hard to eat. The sun had set. For Konrad, there was comfort in the knowledge that one could become lost in the darkness.

He checked the briefcase that he would take with him. As always, he'd taken great care in putting his supplies together. There was a roll of the newly invented electrical tape that he really liked because it had proved stronger than any tape he'd used before, a sharp-edged hunting knife, and, of course, the gun.

Shaking off the disturbing thoughts that haunted him from the past, Konrad went down to the lobby of the hotel and rented a dilapidated automobile from a driver who was leaning against the side of the building waiting for a fare. Konrad gave the driver enough money to make it worth his while. In fact, it was enough to pay for the car twice over, giving the driver the reassurance that if Konrad stole his vehicle, the car could be easily replaced.

Konrad smiled to himself as he got behind the wheel. The automobile was a piece of junk. He knew that, but it was important that he make this trip alone. Konrad did not want anyone else to drive him. It was much safer for Konrad if there were no witnesses; better that nobody knew where he went or what he did on these nighttime excursions. That way, at the end of the night, his secrets would remain locked inside him forever.

Each time he came to Brazil, he did the same thing. He rented the car and went off by himself to feed his need. He made it a point to try and stay at different hotels, using a different alias each time, so that nobody became familiar with his face or knew him by his real name. Always best to remain anonymous.

The sky had turned gray and the clouds began to swirl as a bolt of lightning flashed in front of him and thunder roared. Sheets of rain came down in angles, covering his windshield and making visibility impossible. Konrad pulled over to the side of the road and parked the car, waiting for the storm to lessen. And…as he did, those damn memories of Detrick crept back into his mind.

Wasted thoughts, Konrad whispered to himself. Wasted regrets. He shook his head, watching the rain assault the streets. At first he didn't realize it, but then he felt his cheeks were wet with tears. Why the hell did thoughts of Detrick still make him cry? He'd only done what he had to do; Detrick had left him no choice. Damn you, Detrick Haswell, damn you to hell. Only someone who you loved with all of your heart and soul could cause you such anguish. Betraying Detrick had torn out a part of his heart, a part Konrad could never fill again.

The rain let up until it was just a slight drizzle. Konrad knew exactly where he was going. The favela.

The park in the favela was more like an empty lot than an actual park. Male and female prostitutes stood on the streets beckoning. Konrad never picked anyone up on the street. He didn't want any evidence inside of the vehicle. Instead, he went to a stone building that housed the public restrooms. Konrad looked around to see if anyone had followed him. He was alone. Nobody of any importance would see him here. He tucked into one of the bathroom stalls. The sharp odor of urine made his eyes sting. But he waited.

The first two boys that came into the bathroom did not appeal to him. They were dark-skinned, dark-haired, and very skinny; not at all to his liking. He sat on the toilet seat looking out through the opening in the door. It was over an hour before another male entered. This one made his heart race. He had light hair and lighter skin than the other two. This was the one. Konrad came out of the stall and began to wash his hands in the sink. Then he turned and smiled at the boy, who was just finishing at a urinal. Over the last few years, Konrad had learned enough Portuguese to communicate.

"Would you like to earn some money?" Konrad asked with a half smile. His hands were cold and jittery with excitement.

The boy was young, no more than fifteen, wearing threadbare rags. He nodded to Konrad. Konrad knew that the kid needed the money, they always did. That's why Konrad liked to come to this place. Here there were millions of these insignificant, poverty-stricken boys, boys whose lives meant nothing to anyone, boys whom the police would not bother to look for. Here, Konrad could do as he pleased.

Chapter 40

Manfred climbed out of the belly of the submarine. He felt as if he had been buried and had been suddenly unearthed. He bent over at the waist, sucking in deep breaths. Then he stood and shivered, not from the cold, for the weather was warm, but from the realization that he'd arrived in a new land, to a new life; a life that would no longer include Christa. He had been instructed before he left the ship that once he departed, he was to walk a short distance, upon which he would enter a town called San Fernando. He was told that he was now in Argentina.

He began to walk, his legs weak and wobbly from his time at sea. Manfred inhaled the fresh air, so unlike the stale tomb of the boat. It was just before sunrise; he looked forward seeing daylight again. He entered the town. It was far too early for anyone to be out on the streets, so he sat on a bench and waited. Soon his contact would arrive.

It was beautiful here in Argentina; the beach, the crystal blue water. He wished Christa were with him, her hand in his, smiling at him with those soft, celestial blue eyes . . .

Just then, a tall, slender man with thin wavy hair and a bright smile walked over, "You must be Manfred Blau."

"Yes," Manfred answered.

"Good. I'm glad to see that you got here safely."

"Yes, thank you."

"I hope your trip wasn't too difficult. I am assuming that this was your first time in a submarine?"

"Yes, it was."

"Quite the experience, I'd say."

"Yes, quite," Manfred answered.

"By the way, I am Konrad Klausen."

"It's a pleasure to meet you."

"The pleasure is all mine." Konrad smiled, then he uttered the code words. "Well, follow me. Everyone has been expecting you." Manfred got up and followed Konrad to an amphibious floatplane that stood waiting just a few hundred meters away

"Let's get onboard," Konrad invited.

Manfred nodded, following him up a flight of stairs and into the body of the plane where the captain was waiting.

"Manfred Blau?" the captain of the plane asked.

Manfred nodded.

"This is Manfred Blau, alias Dolf Sprecht. You know where he is to be taken?" Konrad asked.

The captain nodded.

"Welcome to my plane." The Captain smiled, his teeth perfect and white. "This is an amphibious floatplane. It can take off on land or on the water; a wonderful little aircraft so convenient."

Manfred sat, sinking down into one of the plush black leather seats while eyeing another man sitting in a seat across the row from him.

"Tonight, you two are not my only passengers," the captain said. "I'd like you to meet Obersturmbannführer Adolf Eichmann. To the outside world, he is known as Richardo Klement, just as you are known to the outside world as Dolf Sprecht. When I asked him if the two of you had ever met before, he said that you had not. I must admit, I was rather surprised."

"A pleasure," Manfred said, as he raised his hand in a Nazi salute to a man with a lazy eye, and a sinister gaze.

"Heil Hitler, Work-Detail Führer Blau," Eichmann said, standing to salute then sitting down again and crossing his legs.

"Heil Hitler," Manfred replied, standing as well to show respect.

"It seems I have been called to attend a dinner meeting in Tucuman, and that is where you are headed. So, here we are, together. And, of course, Strumscharführer Klausen and I are old friends." Eichmann smiled a patronizing smile that indicated that he knew he was far above Klausen.

"Yes, that's true," Konrad said.

"You were in Spandau, is that correct?"

Manfred nodded.

"My old friend was there with you," Eichmann said with a cynical smile. "And how is Rudolf?"

"Hess?"

"Yes, Hess. You were in Spandau, so you were in prison with him, were you not?"

"Yes, I was. He is all right. His stomach bothers him. And, of course, being in a prison is not easy for him."

Eichmann nodded. "He always fancied himself a nobleman." Eichmann shook his head. "What a damn fool. He insisted on serving his time, refused to run away when he had the chance. Now look at him . . ."

Manfred studied Eichmann. Adolf Eichmann had a perpetual smirk, one that seemed to mock the world. It seemed to say "I can do as I please, I can get away with anything. I am smarter than anyone else."

Manfred's intuition told him not to trust Eichmann.

"And Speer?"

"He's doing as well as can be expected. It's not easy to be in a prison."

"I can well imagine. That's why, as soon as things began to look as if Germany might lose the war, I went to some of our generous friends in Italy who helped me get here to South America."

"I didn't come through Italy," Manfred said, making conversation.

"I am aware. That was because there was no need. If you were swept out of the country fast enough nobody would be the wiser. After all, you do look a great deal like Dolf Sprecht. And Dolf had served his time. Besides, Sprecht was such a small-time nothing that no one really cared what happened to him."

"Actually, he did serve all of his time. I mean I did."

"Yes, but you do know that there are myriad Nazi hunters who are seeking us out all the time. They are mostly Jews looking for revenge. So, we had to be sure that none of these Nazi hunters recognized you as Manfred Blau. And believe me, these Jews are smart and devious."

"I had no idea," Manfred said, rubbing his chin.

"I always said that we should have sent all of them to Palestine, the Jews I mean. They wanted to go. We would have had them all in one place at one time. Then . . . we could have bombed the whole thing off the map, and "kaput." We would have been done with the whole mess. No one listened. Instead, it was decided that we would build the death camps. What a dirty business; the smell, the constant ashes from the crematoriums, *ichh*. What a mess."

"Are the Nazi hunters trying to find you?"

"Of course, but they never will. I have far too many connections protecting me in Argentina and Brazil. The government is on our side, and they see to it that we have what we need. As soon as any of those blasted Jews are spotted, and believe me, there are spies always watching, I am whisked away by plane to a safer destination. That's why it's a good idea to always live near water. If you should need to escape, it makes the getaway quick and easy if it can be done by seaplane or an amphibious craft."

"Will I be safe here in South America?"

"There are never any guarantees. Be cautious, but don't worry too much about anything. Everything is as much under control here as it can be. Like I said, the government is behind us. They secure jobs for us and help us to maintain our cover. We just have to be watchful. Never let your guard down. Always be aware of who and what is around you," Eichmann said.

Chapter 41

The meeting took place in a large estate homemade of white stone, set back from the road and surrounded by trees. Two large imposing men dressed in the black uniforms of the SS stood at the door holding rifles. They carefully checked each guest against a list of those who had been invited before they were allowed to enter.

Once inside, it felt to Manfred as if he'd been transported back to Germany before the Fatherland had begun to lose the war. There were crystal chandeliers and tables with white linen tablecloths that were embroidered with black Swastikas. Two large double doors opened onto a long patio that was raised four feet above the ground and surrounded by a white, wrought iron railing. The tables were covered with platters of traditional German food: thick sausages on a bed of sauerkraut, potato dumplings, pork roast, and Jaeger-Schnitzel. There was German potato bread and red cabbage, as well as an entire table just for desserts.

It had been a long time since Manfred had enjoyed such wonderful food, and he felt his mouth water as he looked at the overflowing table.

"Why don't you make up your plate, and then come with me and I'll introduce you to the others," Konrad said.

Manfred nodded and quickly gathered his food, and the two began to walk around the room.

"I know it seems strange to be here in South America, but you'll get used to it. I've even started to like it here," Konrad said.

Manfred smiled. The house had a tropical feel to it, with large open windows and massive wicker fans.

"This is our most esteemed Dr. Mengele. He has done a wonderful job of advancing science and medicine." Konrad introduced Manfred to a handsome, dark-haired man who was wearing a perfectly pressed white linen suit.

"Heil Hitler," Dr. Mengele said.

"Heil Hitler," Manfred answered, just as another man walked over to them.

"Heil Hitler."

"Heil Hitler."

"This is my friend and colleague, Dr. Klaus Barbie," Mengele said, introducing the doctor to Manfred.

"It's a pleasure to meet both of you," Manfred said.

Manfred recognized Franz Stangl from Treblinka when Konrad took him across the room to where Stangl had been standing with his friend Gustav Wagner.

"So you see, there are many of us here," Konrad said. "We are working together to rebuild the Reich."

Manfred nodded. "It's a lot different than Germany."

"It's not really as bad as one might have expected. I mean, the weather is nice, and the food is good. You're right, it is not the Fatherland and will never compare, but for now we must make do," Konrad said. "Would you like to take a walk outside? The grounds are lovely and, quite frankly, you look a little overwhelmed."

"Actually, I would like to take a walk, and you're right, I am just a little overwhelmed. I just arrived this morning and I've been traveling all day. I could use a little time to recuperate."

"Understandable. Come, let's go outside," Konrad said. As they stepped out on to the veranda, Konrad reached over and took two glasses of wine from the tray of a passing waiter. He handed one to Manfred, and they both descended the stairs into the garden. A sweet, fruity smell permeated the air as they walked past the mango and papaya trees.

"You are right. It is quite lovely here, really. Charming," Manfred said.

"Yes, it is. It's peaceful. As I've said before, I have come to enjoy living in South America."

"I am assuming that Brazil and Argentina are very much alike?"

"Yes and no. There is the language difference. In Brazil, they speak Portuguese and here it's Spanish."

"I don't speak either."

"It's fine, we have plenty of interpreters, and most of the people you will come in contact with can speak some German."

"Really?"

"Yes, at least enough to get by. Once the natives discovered that we had plenty of cash, they learned the language well enough to sell us this or that," Konrad laughed.

Manfred smiled at him, studying his companion. Konrad was a lot like him in many ways. Both men were small in stature, neither of them athletic or attractive in a classic sense.

"I've been working with ODESSA to bring Eichmann's family here. He misses them terribly. He asks constantly when they will be coming."

"ODESSA is pretty good at making the arrangements?" Manfred asked.

"Yes and no. They have a lot of connections that help them to secure passage for us and for our families. However, the Jews are never far behind. They're like rats you know; sniffing, smelling, never giving up, and they've caught a lot of our good men," Konrad said.

"You don't have to tell me about Jews. I know how deceitful and underhanded they are. When I was at Treblinka, nasty place, my wife was ill and I needed help in the house. I made the mistake of taking a Jewess in as a housemaid. I was good to her because she took care of my dying wife and our child. But do you know how she repaid me? When I went to trial in Nuremburg, she was the first one to go up as a witness against me. It was that Jewess that insured my conviction. I should have killed her when I had the chance," Manfred growled with the memory.

"Yes, I heard all about your trial. Where are your wife and child? I have not received any instructions about bringing them here."

"My wife is dead," Manfred said, and the words stung his heart anew as he heard them spoken aloud, in his own voice.

"And your child? You had a daughter I believe?"

"Yes, her name was Katja. I don't know where she is. I was in prison when my wife sent her somewhere."

"We should seek her out. Didn't you adopt her through the Lebensborn?"

"Yes. You knew about that?" Manfred asked.

"Yes, I read about it a long time ago in a letter praising Himmler's work with the Lebensborn," Konrad said.

"I would assume that the child is probably living with her birth mother," Manfred said.

"Do you remember the woman's name?"

"I believe it was Helga Haswell. I don't have the papers. Christa had them."

"Helga Haswell," Konrad said, his inner antenna flying up with recognition. Helga Haswell was Detrick's sister. Detrick. Again. My God, Detrick. His one true friend; the man to whom he owed so much. Detrick. He still dreamed of Detrick, of his blond hair, his easy smile, his defense of the weak. Could he never escape from Detrick? Never? Konrad wanted to cry out here and now, standing under the moon thousands of miles away from Germany. He wanted to cry out to Detrick, tell him how a day did not go by that he was not filled with shame and regret for betraying him. Detrick. Would he never be free of the memory of Detrick? Konrad sighed. He took a cigarette out of the breast pocket of his jacket and lit it, inhaling deeply. If only he could quiet his mind.

"Are you all right?" Manfred asked, studying his new friend. Konrad had turned pale, a light shade of gray, as if his life was seeping out of him. Manfred had seen dead bodies, many dead bodies, and this was the color they turned when they died. "Konrad . . ."

"I'm sorry. I was thinking about something," Konrad said, trying to smile as he turned back to face Manfred. "Would you like me to check on what happened to Katja? See what I can find out?"

"Could you do that for me?" Manfred replied. He liked this young man, this Konrad Klausen, who was so helpful and charming.

Konrad sucked the smoke from his cigarette deep into his lungs. *Detrick*, his mind cried out, *Detrick, shut up, shut up, let me be.*

"Do you have another cigarette?" Manfred asked, forcing Konrad back to reality.

Konrad nodded. He tipped the pack and Manfred took one. Konrad lit it for him.

"Do you like cigars? I get the most marvelous cigars from Cuba. I'll get you a box." Konrad said, trying to sound casual and stop the trembling of his hands.

"Yes, I'd love to try them. And thank you for offering to help me find my little girl again."

"Of course, it's my job to see to it that you have everything you need here in South America. And besides, I like you." Konrad smiled, but his mind would not be silent. It kept screaming out to him, crying out *Detrick, Detrick . . . Detrick . . .* He could not search for Helga. If he found her then he would be too close to his memories of Detrick. He must find the child, but how, how?

Manfred nodded, "Thank you, anything at all that you can find out for me would be greatly appreciated." He wanted to know what had happened to Katja. Not that he'd ever loved the child; he'd hardly had the chance to get to know her. She'd come into their lives just as things began to go sour. Oh, if only things had been different. But his little girl was the last thread he had left connecting him to Christa, and Christa had loved Katja dearly.

"We'd best start heading back. The meeting is about to begin," Konrad said.

Manfred and Konrad strolled through the lush gardens back to the house. A full moon lit the pathway. Once they were a few feet away, they heard the strains of a violin.

"That's Wagner's 'Wedding March,'" Manfred said, his chin trembling. That song had played at his wedding. He'd held Christa in his arms as they had danced their first dance together as a man and wife, her sky-blue eyes lit by the chandelier. How optimistic he'd been then. It had seemed as if nothing could ever come between them. Nothing except her father, damn him, for hiding Jews, for ruining everything Manfred had worked so hard to build.

"Yes, it is the 'Wedding March.' That's Eichmann playing. I've heard him several times before. He's quite good," Konrad said.

"What a surprise; Eichmann plays the violin?"

"Yes, and quite well," Konrad smiled. Then he stopped and turned to Manfred. "Ah, I forgot to mention this. Do you have a blood-type tattoo under your arm? It is too dangerous to keep it now. If you are caught, it identifies you as an SS officer. But, don't worry, Mengele will remove it for you."

"I was never tattooed. I wasn't in the Waffen SS," Manfred said. "In fact, to be quite honest, I was lucky to get into the party at all. Dr. Goebbels befriended me and brought me in. He was a dear friend. I miss him," Manfred said. He was hoping that Konrad might tell him that it had all been a lie and that Goebbels had escaped after all.

Konrad said nothing. He just nodded.

When Konrad ushered Manfred into the banquet room, everyone was already seated.

"You will have to excuse me. I must go up and speak. Please make yourself comfortable. I'll come by and check on you again later," Konrad said, leaving Manfred sitting alone. A man who Manfred did not recognize stood at the front of the room with a microphone.

"Heil Hitler," he said, saluting. The others stood and saluted back to him.

"We will begin by reciting our oath; the oath that we swore to keep when we joined the party. Gentleman, are you ready?"

The men responded in the affirmative. They all remained standing as they began to recite the oath they had taken long ago when the Third Reich was still strong.

"What is your oath?" the man at the front began.

"I vow to you, Adolf Hitler, as Führer and chancellor of the German Reich, loyalty and bravery. I vow to you and to the leaders that you set for me, absolute allegiance until death," the group answered.

"Please be seated."

"Tonight we are gathered here to discuss a task that is of great importance to all of us . . . rebuilding our Reich," the leader of the meeting said. "So, without further ado, I would like to welcome our guest of honor. Most of you probably know him already. I give you Sturmscharführer Konrad Klausen."

The others stood again, clapping their hands.

"HEIL HITLER," Konrad yelled above the applause.

"HEIL HITLER . . ."

Standing behind the microphone, Konrad looked small. His thick glasses had slipped down his nose, and he pushed them back up before raising his hands to silence the crowd.

"Thank you for your generous applause," Konrad said. "Please be seated."

Once everyone had quieted down, Konrad began.

"My esteemed colleagues: you have been brought here because I have information for you that is vital. It is for your ears only, and that is why this meeting is by invitation only."

Manfred looked around. The others were hanging on Konrad's every word. He had them on the edge of their seats. After having worked with Goebbels, Manfred could not help but appreciate the staging of this event: the large picture of Hitler that hung on the wall behind the speaker; the Nazi flags strategically placed throughout the room. Everything was arranged to recreate a feeling of camaraderie amongst the guests, a feeling that the Reich would rise again.

For a moment Konrad stood in front of them, silent, drinking in the anticipation of the crowd.

"Gentlemen, the news I am about to share with you was delivered to me by a very reliable source. Therefore, I know it to be factual." He hesitated for effect. The crowd leaned forward, waiting . . . "Our leader, Our Führer, Adolf Hitler is not dead." Many of the guests let out a gasp. "The other people who were with the Führer in the underground bunker perished that day, but ODESSA arrived just in time to spirit our Führer away to safety. Presently he is in hiding. I need to ask several of you to aid me in bringing him here to South America. I have carefully selected a few men to be involved in this very secret mission. If you are one of those who I have already chosen, you will be notified over the next few months. But for now, rejoice; rejoice in the knowledge that the Reich will rise again."

Manfred gasped, a hush fell over the crowd. Could it be true? Hitler was alive.

Chapter 42

Although Israel was attacked only a few hours after she had become a nation, Israel's army was already in place. It was formed from the militant groups that the British had considered terrorists while Palestine was under British rule. But, now that Israel was an independent state, these groups of Jews who had engaged in guerrilla warfare, banded together and, because they were united under one rule, they were strong. A navy was formed. Then Israel purchased three B-17 bombers from the United States. The little strip of land in the desert that the Jews had fought so hard to possess was surrounded by enemies on all sides. However, these Jews had seen evil and they'd lived through hell. In order to survive Hitler, they had had to be the strongest of the strong. Anyone not had already perished. So, the Israelis became a force to be reckoned with.

In July of 1948, David Ben-Gurion, the Prime Minister of Israel, gave the order for Israel to bomb Cairo.

This time the Jews would fight back; they would not go like lambs to the slaughter as they did in Germany. Now they had a country, a home, a land worth fighting for. It had finally come to pass. The Promised Land was theirs. And although the loss of life was substantial, Israel won the war.

Chapter 43

Zofia watched Katja playing with Mendel and Rachel. They were running after each other playing tag; it was nice to hear children laughing in the DP camp. Shana was in the barracks lying down. Since her relationship with the American, she'd turned inward, becoming quiet and depressed. Dark gray circles indented the skin beneath her eyes, and she rarely attended meals. Zofia tried to speak to her, sitting beside her bed, but Shana would just turn away and face the wall without answering.

It was a bright autumn day; the sun cast a golden glow over the fallen leaves. Many of the people who had been living in the DP camp began to make plans, plans to go to their homeland. When Israel became a state, every Jew was granted automatic citizenship. On the day that the declaration that Israel was now a country arrived, tremendous elation had traveled throughout the camp, like a warm golden light. The people cheered, some fell on the ground on their knees giving thanks to God. Women and men were crying, hugging each other, laughing; it had finally happened.

The children's giggles rang out again causing Zofia to turn toward them. Rachel and Katja were laughing and Mendel was frowning; then he began laughing, too.

They had become such good friends.

Zofia went to help prepare dinner in the kitchen. She was slicing cucumbers when Isaac came flying through the door.

"Zofia…Israel is in trouble!" He shouted then he grabbed her hand and pulled her toward the main building where the radio was stationed. Isaac was running so fast that Zofia could hardly keep up with him. His eyebrows were drawn together and his hands were clammy.

Within hours, bliss had turned to fear as the Jews sat together listening to the news that Israel had been attacked and she was now battling for her existence . . . once again.

Isaac and Zofia sat with the others who had gathered on the sofas, on chairs, on the floor, standing in the back of the room, all of them listening to the radio. Zofia's and Isaac's hands were clasped together, white knuckled. They shot glances of terror at each other as they waited for news of the war. The room was in total silence as everyone listened to the radio announcer. Their eyes traveled from one to another, searching for answers, answers no one was able to give. Would Israel survive?

Well, no matter what dangers Israel might face, Zofia knew that she and Isaac wanted to be there. They had discussed the matter and agreed that they would rather die fighting for their country than live anywhere else in the world. But even as they awaited the outcome of the horror of the present situation in Israel, Isaac and Zofia faced another dilemma. They must decide what to do about Shana, Rachel, and Mendel. None of them had any money of their own. Zofia and Isaac had spent half the night sitting under the stars discussing the problem.

As soon as he was able to get into town and find a buyer, Isaac sold all of the jewelry that they had stolen from Koppel; everything except the ring that Zofia wore. She'd tried to convince him to sell that, too, but Isaac had refused. Someday soon he would replace it. During their stay in the DP camp, Isaac had also saved a nice sum of money from his earnings from working at the odd jobs he'd taken in town. The money he'd saved, plus the money from the sale of the jewelry, was just enough to pay the passage for everyone to go to Israel; their own family plus Shana, Rachel, and Mendel. However, Isaac and Zofia had hoped to use the extra money to open a bakery in Tel Aviv. If they paid the passage for everyone, there would be no money left over to start their lives once they arrived. It was a difficult predicament.

As they sat on the floor, holding hands, listening to the voice of the radio describing the current situation in Israel, Zofia flashed back to the night before. Parts of the conversation she'd had with Isaac replayed in her head.

"We can't just leave them behind," Isaac had said, referring to Shana, Rachel, and Mendel. Good-hearted Isaac. He never put himself or his own needs first. Sometimes Zofia wished he were more selfish, more centered on taking care of his own family and not carrying the weight of the world on his shoulders.

Zofia had not answered. She felt guilty. She liked Shana and Rachel, and she thought Mendel was a nice boy, but she wanted the best life for her family, and she was struggling with the sacrifice. If they opened a bakery in the city, they would have a financially secure future. *I am a terrible person; I hate to use up all of our money. If we do, then we have to start over in Israel with nothing. No business, no bakery. What will we do?* she thought, crossing her arms over her chest. *How can I feel this way? I am so selfish. Shana has been like a sister to me, and Katja is so close to Mendel and Rachel.*

What a choice, what a decision. If she left the others behind in the DP camp to fend for themselves, their young faces would haunt her forever, but if she paid their passage, then she and Isaac would arrive in Israel with nothing. Where would they go? What would they do? How would they survive? She had told this to Isaac, and he'd said, "We should trust God. God has brought us this far; he will help us."

She had shaken her head. "I don't know. I just don't know."

"All right, let me talk to some people from the joint commission. Let me find out what kind of work is available, if any, in Israel. If there is something that I can do there, some way that I can provide for us, then I feel we can start over without any money."

If only she could be more like Isaac. With everything that they had been through, somehow he still trusted God. She had a hard time admitting it to him, but sometimes she had doubts. It was hard to understand how God had let all of this happen, and why. The Nazis had burned babies, they'd murdered her friends, and Manfred Blau had abused her and stripped her of her self-esteem. It was hard to comprehend God's plan. Still, even with all that she'd endured, she had to believe there was a God, because God had brought Isaac back to her. Yet, sometimes she had doubts. Why now, after all the Jewish people had suffered, did they have to fight another war? Zofia hated herself for losing faith. If only she could lean on God the way Isaac did. His faith was such a comfort to him. Isaac said that he believed that the Third Reich had happened in order to force Jews to build a state of their own. It had given them the strength, the will, to build the state of Israel.

When Israel was given statehood, she and Isaac had appealed to the Jewish Joint Commission for help to pay for the passage for Shana, Rachel, and Mendel, but they were denied. The commission had paid Shana, Rachel, and Mendel's passage once already; there were not enough funds to pay again. Now it was up to Zofia and Isaac. Still, Isaac would go to the commission and ask about work; perhaps they could offer him that.

Before sunrise, Isaac dressed quietly, as he did every morning, and set out in search of day labor. After he'd left, the small cot that they shared felt so empty. Zofia tried to fall back to sleep, but she couldn't. Quietly, she dressed and went outside to walk and think. The camp was quiet. She let herself see it again as she did the first time. This very same DP camp had once held Nazi officers and Jewish prisoners. People had died and suffered here at the hands of the kapos and guards. And although she'd not been in this particular camp, she shivered with the memories of the camps where she *had* been imprisoned.

The sun was beginning to rise as she sat under a tree watching the sky light up. She was desperate to try to make a decision that would affect the rest of her life. Slowly people began to come out of their barracks and head toward the latrine or the main building. Still unsettled, undecided, she went to the kitchen to help serve breakfast. She watched the children as they came rushing in, carrying their trays. As she spooned the thick porridge into their bowls, she thought of Shana again. What would become of the others if she and Isaac took Katja and left them behind? Her mind drifted back to Fruma and Gitel. How kind they were. They'd helped her when no one else would. They'd even put themselves at risk for her, a young girl they hardly knew. Why was she not as generous? She wanted to run away from the invisible but binding threads that wove her life with those of the others; threads of guilt were wrapping themselves around her neck and strangling her.

All day long Zofia kept her distance from Shana. She wanted to be by herself, to decide without the influence of the others. She did want to be with Katja so she took Katja walking and read her stories. They sat together and Katja taught Zofia the game that Katja and Rachel always played with strings.

"I want to buy some yarn and teach you to knit," Zofia said.

"Would I be able to make sweaters?"

"Yes, eventually, but first let's make a scarf. It's easier."

"I could make a scarf and give it to Papa for Hanukah. He would be so excited, because I made it myself."

Zofia smiled at Katja, and leaned over to kiss her. "I will ask one of the volunteers if she can get us some yarn and two knitting needles."

"Can I make a doll for Rachel, too? She says she hates dolls, but I think she only hates them because she never had one that she loved like I loved Ethel."

"Yes, perhaps. We'll see." Zofia said.

"Do you remember Ethel, Mama? I miss her so much."

"Yes, I remember Ethel."

"Do you think she's all right in France?"

"I think she is doing fine. She is probably living with the royal family."

"Do you really think so? Do you think Ethel is a princess?" Katja asked, her young face so serious.

"Of course I do. After all, she looked very royal."

"She did, didn't she, Mama?"

When mealtime arrived that evening, Zofia did not go to help serve in the kitchen. She stayed in the barracks waiting for Isaac. She had done preparation work and so she'd had the opportunity to bring him a plate. Most nights this was her routine. She would help in the kitchen, then bring a plate back to the room for Isaac, where she would leave it for him on their cot. Although eating in the rooms was discouraged, she wanted to make things as easy for him as possible. He would eat when he returned. However, Zofia usually ate with the others.

Tonight Zofia had no appetite. She'd sent Katja to the dining area with Shana and Rachel. The silence in the barracks was unnerving. In fact, it made her want to scream. A strong smell of perspiration always filled the air, and for the most part, she'd grown so used to it that she no longer smelled it, but tonight it was exceptionally strong and nauseating. Everything about the DP camp—the people, the feeling of desperation that she would never escape this life—had her wound tight. She felt that if Isaac did not arrive soon, she might explode.

Zofia began pacing the room, her body stiff, occasionally looking outside to see if Isaac might be on his way up the walkway. When she finally saw him enter the camp, her shoulders relaxed and she sighed with relief. Something about the familiar sight of his large muscular frame made her feel safe.

Isaac entered the barracks to find Zofia seated on their cot, waiting.

"Why aren't you with the others?" he asked.

"I wanted to see you."

He walked over and kissed her while his hand gently caressed her chin. She could see the concern in his eyes, but he said nothing. Instead, he sat down beside her.

For a moment neither of them spoke.

"I brought you some food," she said, handing him the plate, but not meeting his eyes.

"Thank you." He took the plate and laid it down, still studying her face.

More moments of silence passed.

"Zofia," he whispered. "No matter what you have decided about Shana, Rachel, and Mendel, it is all right with me. I love you and I'll respect your decision. No argument."

She got up and walked over to the window, looking out. "I wanted to run away, just the three of us, you and me and Katja. You know how I feel? You understand?"

He nodded. "Of course, I understand."

"But I can't. I can't do it. We must take them with us. All of them: Shana, Rachel, and Mendel. Somehow we'll find a way to survive. We always do," she said. A single tear fell down her cheek.

"I am glad that you made this choice. We will be all right. I'll find work right away when we get to Israel. I'm strong, there is nothing I can't do, and I am willing to do anything. I am glad we aren't leaving them behind."

She turned from the window, her cheeks glistening with tears. "You're such a good man, Isaac. Your heart is so big."

He laughed. "Yours is just as big Zofia, but you don't want to admit it." Then he got up and took her in his arms, kissing her.

"Aren't you hungry?" She asked, as he gently lay her down on the bed.

"I am. I am hungry for your love."

"You always have my love," she whispered.

He kissed her neck and began to unbutton the top of her dress. She sighed and arched her back. Oh, how she loved this man.

Chapter 44

Israel, 1950

"I knew we would be just fine," Isaac said, smiling at Zofia as they entered the kibbutz. "Only here, here in our homeland could such a wonderful place exist, a place where you don't need money to survive. A paradise. Who could have imagined?"

He took her hand. Shana and the children ran ahead.

"It's beautiful," Zofia said. "Look at those trees. The leaves look like silver drops in the sunshine."

"I wonder what kind of fruit they bear."

"I don't know. I've never seen anything like them. But they are magnificent. "

"Shalom and welcome." A short, slender woman with a pixie haircut, dark skin warmed by the sun, and a big smile, walked over to them. "My name is Noa, and you are?"

"I am Isaac Zuckerman, and this is my wife, Zofia. The children are Katja Zuckerman, Rachel and Shana Perlof, and Mendel Zaltstein."

"A warm welcome to all of you. I suppose you want to know a little about this place, and how we live. Let me explain how things work here. As you already know, we are a kibbutz. Here we are like one big family. We work together, and together we build our lives. Everyone has a job, a job that is suited to his or her abilities. You do what you can do. We find that often people are willing to work extra hours, do extra jobs when they see the necessity, because they are so invested in seeing our home prosper. For work, we have many choices. You can work the land, or cook, or help with the children who live in their own small children's house. On the other side of the kibbutz we have an ostrich farm. As you can imagine, there is plenty to do there. Among us, we are blessed to have teachers, doctors, and rabbis; many of them survivors of the Nazis.

When the children turn eighteen, if they are healthy and capable, they serve for two years in the Israeli Army. It is an honor to serve, and it is everyone's responsibility to help keep Israel safe. I think I can speak for all of us when I say that we would give our lives for this little piece of land in the desert. Our people have come from all over the world, but mostly from Hitler's bowels of hell. This is our home, our land. Finally."

"Were you in a Camp?" Zofia asked.

"Me?" Noa replied. "No, I am a Sephardic Jew. I was born here in Palestine, before we became Israel. But, I know what happened in Europe. I have heard so many stories from the survivors. Terrible stories."

"They are all true," Isaac said.

She nodded. "I know. But we must not dwell on the past. Instead, let's embrace the future; the future of our country, the future of our people. Now come, follow me. Let me show you our little piece of paradise."

They followed her.

"Who owns this place?" Isaac asked.

"Nobody does, and we all do. By that, I mean that it belongs to each and every one of us. It is our home. That is why we don't mind working hard to keep it."

They continued walking.

"Katja, don't go too far. Come back here. Shana, bring the girls and Mendel over here, or can you keep an eye on them?" Zofia called.

"I'll watch them," Shana called back.

"No need to worry. The children are safe here. Every adult is a parent to every child. That is how it is on a kibbutz. Everything we have belongs to all of us." Noa smiled.

Isaac beamed. Zofia could tell by the look on his face that he loved the concept of the kibbutz.

"As a married couple the two of you will have your own room. There is a communal bathroom and kitchen, as well as a general living area. The children have their own house. I know from the outside the main house looks like nothing more than a stone building, however it's ours, it is home. I have a feeling you will find it quite comfortable here."

"May I ask you what kind of trees those are? They are so beautiful. The leaves sparkle like silver in the sun. I have never seen any like them," Zofia said.

"They are olive trees. We make olive oil here. We also grow fruit and vegetables; what we can anyway. Come, let me show you."

They walked for what seemed like miles, through orange groves and wheat fields; fig trees and persimmon trees. Against a fence, Zofia saw trees heavy with golden ripe bananas.

"What are these?" Zofia bent to look at tiny pods growing on the ground. "Beans?"

"Yes, sort of. They are wonderful white peas. We mash them into a sauce mixed with garlic and lemon. It's called hummus. Then we spread it on the bread we bake. You'll like it," Noa smiled.

"You have everything here."

"Yes, we do. On the other side, we have chickens that we use for eggs and three cows for milk. We also grow cucumbers, peppers, and tomatoes. The neighboring kibbutz grows lemons. They trade us for our oranges, and sometimes for tomatoes. The land is very dry. It requires a lot of water, but we have scientists who are working on irrigating it."

"It seems as if you are putting everything that you have here to good use."

"We have many scientists and agriculturists that came out of the camps; they are very knowledgeable. Their knowledge has helped us to develop at a rapid pace."

"Where do you find fabric for clothing?"

"We trade with another kibbutz just a few miles down the road that grows cotton. Inside the main building we have weaving looms where we make our own fabric."

"This is a miraculous place," Zofia said.

"This is Israel." Noa said, spreading her arms wide to encompass the land. The warmth of the sun caressed them. "Welcome home."

Zofia nodded. "Thank you . . ." she breathed, her eyes wet with tears.

Chapter 45

Rachel found an open bunk bed that she and Katja could share.

"How's this one?" Rachel asked.

"It's fine. But I'm sort of afraid of sleeping on top; I might fall when I'm asleep," Katja said.

"I'll take the top. I don't mind," Rachel said. "It makes me feel like I'm flying. One day, I'm gonna fly planes."

"I know. I'll be there when you take off to cheer you on," Katja said.

"What do you want to do with your life?" Rachel said, sitting down on the lower bunk.

Katja, now ten, sat beside her. "I don't know, be a wife and mother, I guess. Work in the kitchen? Maybe teach?"

"I don't. I wanna do something big with my life. Something that people will remember," Rachel said, running her hand over the wool blanket. It was surprisingly soft.

"I think that being a wife and mother is something big," Katja said.

"You'll probably marry Mendel." Rachel said.

"I will not! I'm going to marry a handsome man who looks like a movie star. NOT Mendel!"

"Yes, I think you will marry Mendel," Rachel teased.

"Stop it," Katja said.

Rachel got up and started to run. "Can't catch me . . ." she called out.

Katja began to run after her friend.

The two girls ran through the hallway, out the front door and into the sunshine. The cloudless sky was as blue as sapphire.

In the distance, Rachel laughed. "Come on, Katja. You're going to have to run faster than that, especially if you have children. They'll out-run you and get away with murder." Katja ran faster. Rachel slowed down and the two fell together, laughing, under an olive tree.

"I think I'm going to love living here," Rachel said.

"Me, too."

"I think that finally we are home."

"Rach, Katja, come on. Let's get some food. Everyone is having lunch," Mendel called from across the grass.

The two girls jumped up from the ground and ran towards Mendel.

"Did you get a bunk?" Katja asked as the three headed toward the main eating area.

"I finally found one. Did you two get one?"

"Yes, we did, and we even got one together. Katja's got the bottom, I'm on top."

"I met some of the other boys who live here; fellows around my own age. They seem nice. Lots of them are children of survivors. A couple of them are orphans like me."

"Like I was saying to Katja a few minutes ago, I think we're going to be happy here. I think we finally have a home." Rachel smiled, linking her arms in the arms of her two friends.

Chapter 46

Shana joined the teachers, spending her days working with the children. There were large classrooms set up where the children were taught to read and write. They learned arithmetic and, later, more advanced mathematics. Some of the teachers had once been professors, and they taught the older students physics and philosophy. There were classes in Hebrew and in English.

Isaac felt he would be most useful working on the land. His back was strong and he had endurance, qualities many of the survivors lacked because they had been weakened by lack of food and disease for so many years. Zofia worked with the children. In her spare time, she helped in the kitchen, and occasionally she worked with the seamstresses. As she was growing older, she found that sewing was harder on her eyes and so she could not work at it full time. She learned to use a loom and make fabric. No money ever exchanged hands, but life was comfortable. There was enough to eat, and at night there was singing and rejoicing. *THIS* was the Promised Land.

Chapter 47

Zofia watched from the kitchen window as the children ran outside to play. They had a half hour recess before lunch each day. As she cut the cucumber and diced the tomatoes, she saw Mendel, Rachel, and Katja in the corner playing with a ball. Although they had made new friends since they'd arrived, their union remained tight. The three were always together.

Over the last year, Zofia had put on weight. Her once slender frame was now rounded and full. Where once her breasts had been small they'd now grown ample and her thighs and hips had filled out as well. Isaac was thicker, too, but his body had developed more muscle where Zofia felt she'd gotten fat. This was not uncommon amongst the survivors, those who had known starvation had a tendency to eat more than necessary now that food had become plentiful. Isaac didn't care that Zofia no longer had the shape of a young girl. He loved her just as she was, and she knew it, knew it every minute of every day. Zofia had no cause ever to doubt her husband. At night she sat beside him while the younger people danced; her head on his shoulder, both of them content.

On one such night, Shana was dancing with Rachel as a tall, slender Sephardic man, who lived on the kibbutz with his parents, walked over and introduced himself as Avi. He loved children and offered to teach Rachel some traditional Sephardic dances. In his quiet and gentle way, Avi charmed Shana and Rachel until he and Shana became friends. Zofia noticed that in the evenings Avi and Shana went for long walks. They sat together at the bonfires, sometimes holding hands. Often, when the rest of the group went to bed, Shana and Avi remained awake, sitting under the tree and talking well into the night. In the morning, Zofia noticed that Shana would be tired in the classroom and so Zofia offered to help with the children. Therefore, it came as no surprise when Shana told Zofia that she and Avi planned to marry.

"Will you and Isaac stand in for my parents at the wedding? You two have become like parents to Rachel and me."

"Of course. We would be honored," Zofia said, knowing that Isaac would agree.

As was the custom, the entire population of the kibbutz attended the wedding. Shana glowed like a star in the night sky, and Avi stood beside her, tall, proud, and handsome.

Zofia could not help but shed a tear as she watched the young couple stand beneath the canopy as she and Isaac once had stood. Shana and Avi's life together was just beginning. Isaac shot Zofia a glance; his eyes were glassy with tears.

"I love you with all my heart." Isaac mouthed the words to Zofia without speaking, as the newlyweds took their vows.

"I love you, too," she answered in a whisper.

The American, Lucky, who Shana had once believed was the only man she would ever care for, was now long forgotten.

Chapter 48

When the children were in school, Zofia spent her time helping to prepare the enormous meals for the entire kibbutz. After school, Shana often came to help in the kitchen or work in the laundry. No amount of work was too much. Everyone on the kibbutz contributed everything that they could to keep their community going. In the afternoon, between lunch and dinner, Zofia went to the children's house to help. She played games, helped with homework, and read to them. Often Isaac joined her when he returned from the fields; hot, sweaty, but joyful. Isaac would come into the children's house and all of the youngsters would come running to him. He made them laugh, did simple magic tricks, and told them stories. The little ones loved to watch this massive man; their eyes wide, as he told of Noah and his ark, or of Jonah and the whale.

Katja was proud of Isaac and bragged to the other children that he was the strongest and smartest father anyone could ever have. Often Zofia and Isaac stayed at the children's house late into the night until Katja drifted off to sleep. It was obvious to Zofia that her daughter was thriving; she had friends and a safe place to call home.

While she worked in the kitchen, Zofia looked out the window where she could see Katja play catch or tag with Rachel and Mendel. Zofia sang softly to herself in Yiddish while she heard the children's laughter in the background. Life was good in Israel.

Two years passed in what seemed like months. Katja had just turned twelve and was growing up quickly. Zofia and Isaac were constantly busy working. The work was hard and often the land demanded more water than the people of the kibbutz could supply. It was worrisome because there was often a loss of crops. Finally a group of Jewish scientists came to discuss a possible solution.

Isaac was in the field working on the land when he saw them approach. Everyone had been expecting the scientists, so Isaac knew immediately who they were. There were five of them. He watched them get out of an open truck, their dust-covered button-down shirts blowing in the breeze. As they came closer, Isaac recognized Shlomie.

"Is that you, Isaac?"

"Shlomie?"

"It's me. You are here? You made it to Israel?" Shlomie said, embracing Isaac in spite of the sweat that covered Isaac's body.

"Yes, I am here. Zofia is here, too. We live on this kibbutz. And you, Shlomie? You are working as a scientist?"

"Yes, I have re-found my calling." He smiled. "I missed it terribly."

"Where do you live?"

"I am living and working in Tel Aviv."

"What good news. Will you stay for lunch? Zofia will be so excited to see you."

"I will. I would love to see her."

"Good then. I'll see you when you have finished your work," Isaac said.

After Shlomie finished surveying the kibbutz with the other scientists he went back to find Isaac.

"I'm all done here for today. We have some plans we are working on to help with the water shortage. It is a new invention called drip irrigation. It will enable you to use far less water in order to grow your crops. It is very efficient. And since water is so scarce, it is important for us to utilize every drop."

"I always knew you were a genius," Isaac laughed.

"I'm not a genius," Shlomie said. "There are several of us working on this project. We saw a need, and we acted on it. It's as simple as that."

"Come; let's go to the main house. I want to wash up quickly, then we'll go and eat. Zofia should be working in the kitchen today. She'll be happy to see you."

Shlomie smiled, his mind wandering back to the past at the sound of Zofia's name. His mind drifted back to those days in the forest with Zofia, after Isaac was captured. Then his mind traveled to the years he'd spent with Zofia in the DP camp. Zofia. Once he had loved her beyond life. He thought about the past and his heart skipped a beat, but only for a moment and only due to the memories. He was happy with his beautiful Jewish wife from Morocco. That young girl with the dancing eyes who had brought joy back into his lonely life. He'd met her in the Camp in Cyprus. She had taught him how to laugh again, in spite of all he'd endured. She'd been the first woman he'd ever made love to, and it had been an experience beyond any other in his life.

Shlomie had not told anyone yet, but he knew that his wife was with child and it brought him such comfort to know that his offspring would be born in Israel . . . the Promised Land. Yes, Shlomie had suffered, like Job; God had tested him with the Nazis. He'd lost his family, his friends, his opportunity for education. In anger, he had turned his back on God for a long time. But God had not forgotten him. It took time, but now he knew that, and God had given him so much to live for. Shlomie, the man of science, the man of logic, had become a believer.

Coming back to the present, he patted Isaac's sweat-covered back. "I'd love to see Zofia again," he said.

"She'll be happy to see that you are healthy and doing well."

"I would love to tell you both about my wife." Shlomie said. "She is a wonderful girl."

"You are married?" Isaac said, smiling. Long ago Isaac had had beautiful teeth, but Shlomie noticed that one of Isaac's front teeth had been broken and it was now a chip. Isaac was still handsome, but not as handsome as he had once been. Life had taken its toll. Shlomie took a deep breath. They had all surely suffered. But even so, they were the lucky ones. At least they had survived.

"I am married, yes, and very happy."

"Mazel tov!" Isaac said. "Life is good then?"

"Yes, life is good," Shlomie said, and he meant it.

Shlomie never thought that this day would come; this day when he no longer coveted his friend's wife. For so long, he'd been jealous of Isaac for having Zofia's love. Shlomie had always loved both Isaac and Zofia, but he'd always had that secret envy gnawing at him. Shlomie smiled. All of those feelings had disappeared. It was as if a heavy block of stone had been lifted from his back. Now, finally, Shlomie could sincerely wish his friends happiness in their lives together.

Chapter 49

Saturday was intended to be a day of rest. According to the Jewish religion, Saturday was reserved for prayer and giving thanks to God, but often while the adults rested, Rachel, Katja, and Mendel spent the day exploring. They left the kibbutz after lunch and wandered down to the seashore. Sometimes they searched for shells, treasures that they kept or traded. Other times they sat looking out across the water while Mendel would invent stories of pirate ships sailing the high seas. Mendel loved to read, and sometimes he would tell the girls the tales from the books he read. They would sit together fascinated as the sun warmed their skin. As long as they returned in time for dinner, nobody knew that they had left.

One afternoon while the three friends gazed at an azure sky inventing stories about the shapes of the clouds, they heard a noise. Rachel got up first, and then Mendel. Katja stayed behind and watched. She was afraid.

"Come out, you coward," Rachel said. "Come out and show your face. If you're an Arab, I'll kill you myself."

"Rachel, shhh," Mendel said. "Who is there? Who are you? No one is going to hurt you. Come out."

"What if it's a Nazi who escaped and came to Israel to kill more Jews?" Rachel said.

"Don't be silly. No Nazi would dare come here," Mendel said again.

Katja saw movement in the bushes. She got up and quietly, without saying a word went over toward the sound.

"Be careful," Rachel said. She ran to her friend's side.

"It's all right," Katja said. She picked up a tiny black and white kitten. "Look. Isn't she sweet?"

"It's a cat . . ." Rachel said, laughing. "I thought we were being watched."

"Oh, what a lovely little thing," Mendel said. "Can I hold her?"

"Sure," Katja said, handing Mendel the kitten. He took her carefully. The small animal fit into the palm of his hand.

Katja pet the kitten while Mendel held her.

"Let's have a look at this little cat," Rachel said, walking over. She pet the cat's head a couple of times. "You're right; she IS cute."

"Do you think we can keep her?" Katja said.

"I don't know," Mendel answered. "But it's worth trying."

"I agree with you. Let me ask my mother," Katja said.

They returned to the kibbutz, keeping the cat quiet in the small room Katja and Rachel shared until later that night when the evening meal was finished and the dishes had been cleaned. Then Katja went to her mother, who was sitting with her father in front of the children's house. Her mother was carefully moving a needle as she embroidered a piece of fabric, which looked like a blouse. Katja assumed it was a gift for Shana's birthday.

"Good Sabbath, Mama," Katja said.

"Good Sabbath, my Sunshine. How are you?"

"I'm doing well. I have something to ask you."

"Of course," Zofia said. She put the needlework down on the table, giving Katja her full attention. "Go on."

"I found a kitten. I want to keep her. Please, Mama. Please."

Zofia sighed. "I am not sure of the rules on this. I will have to ask. But for tonight, you can keep her. Let me see if I can get you some food for your little friend. Tomorrow, in the morning, I'll see what I can find out about the rules on pets. Until now, I've never paid much attention to this, but for you, Sunshine, I will look into it."

"Thank you so much, Mama." Katja wrapped her arms around Zofia's neck and kissed her. Then Katja turned to Isaac and wrapped her arms around his neck as the front of her hair fell over her left eye. It seemed that no matter how she styled it, her hair always fell over her left eye.

After school the following day, Zofia found Katja sitting outside with Mendel, Rachel, and the kitten.

"You can keep her," Zofia said," but you are responsible for caring for her. No one else is going to help you. Do you understand? If anyone finds urine or feces in your room, you will have to get rid of her. So you can get some sand and I'll get you a paper box. Then you'll have to train her to use the litter box."

"Yes, Mama. Thank you." Again Katja hugged Zofia, and Zofia felt warmth deep inside her heart. All was right with the world.

Chapter 50

Argentina

It all began with dreams of Christa. Manfred could suppress his feelings while awake, but as he slept, his longing for Christa tormented him. He was not used to the extreme heat in January in Argentina, and the ceiling fans did little more than circulate the hot air. Sometimes the extreme weather gave him headaches, followed by nausea. Then when he closed his eyes, he would see bright flashing lights behind his eyelids followed by terrific shooting pain. For several hours, he would lay in bed in a dark room, debilitated, unable to endure light of any kind. Once these episodes passed, Manfred would find himself spent, relieved to bathe his weary body and then fall into a fitful sleep. It was following one such episode that his usual dream took a dark turn and became a nightmare.

As always, the dream started with Christa smiling at him, just the way she did the first time he saw her. Of course, that was when they were teenagers in school and Manfred had chosen to forget that Christa actually had not smiled at him. In fact, it was not until years later that she even recognized his existence. In his dream, he saw her bright blue eyes sparkle and her golden curls bounce as she ran by him late for a class. How he had wanted her then. How he had planned, plotted, and schemed to make her his own. Every action he took, every minute of every day was aimed at winning Christa over as his wife. Often he doubted that his plan would ever work, but that doubt only caused him to try harder. Nothing could change his mind; he was tireless in his efforts.

And . . . it had worked. She had noticed him. And then . . . the greatest of achievements: a wish granted, a wish he treasured . . . somehow, she had grown to love him. The dream flashed to a scene from their honeymoon in the quaint city of Munich, making love in the little chateau with the picture window that looked out over the Alps. Then they were dancing, Christa moving like a ballerina in his arms. As they sailed across the floor, through the corner of his eye, he could see the other SS officers watching with envy in their eyes.

And then in his nightmare, Manfred's eyes would fall upon Himmler. He always knew Himmler had wanted his wife. In this dream gone wrong, Manfred watched helplessly as Himmler and Christa exchanged smiles. In his mind, the room grew dark and only Christa and Himmler remained in the light. Manfred felt as if he were sinking. He heard his own voice cry out "Christa," but she never turned around. Then he was outside of a window, watching Himmler lay on top of his naked wife, her slender legs wrapped around the other man. *NOOO. Christa, NOOO.* The thought tore at him, as the dream began to grow darker.

Then Christa stood up in his dream, naked, and glared at him through the window. Tears covered her face. "YOU KILLED MY FATHER," she said. "I hate you Manfred, I hate you. And yes, it's true, I fucked Himmler. I did it to hurt you, because you deserve to be spit on."

The dream was so real that he felt as if he were there. "Christa…I did what I had to do to save you, to save your mother." His voice sounded like gravel.

"And what about our child, Manfred? The child you never cared about anyway. We adopted Katja from the Lebensborn together. We both promised to take care of her," Christa said. Her voice began to echo over and over, ringing in his head: "Where is Katja, Manfred? Why are you not taking care of her? Do you know what has become of her? Is she dead? Did you let her die, like you let my father die? You coward, coward! You could have fought for him, but you didn't, you didn't. Instead you shot him dead. Then you expected me to still love you. How can I love you? You're not even a man; you're a despicable piece of dirt. If you were any kind of a man at all you would find Katja and take care of her. It's your responsibility. You owe it to me. Maybe this is the only way that you can make it right. And if not, it is the least you could do for me."

Still dreaming, Manfred watched as Christa's once beautiful face became distorted. Her nose grew large and exaggerated like the pictures he'd drawn for Goebbels of stereotypical Jews. Her lips were blue and her skin was as thin as parchment, the way they had been once she had become ill.

"I don't know where Katja is, Christa. You gave her to someone when I was in prison. How am I ever going to find her?"

"That is up to you Manfred. But don't expect to be at peace until you do what is right." Her eyes rolled around, and then they filled with blood, blood that ran down her cheeks like tears.

He awakened, shivering with sweat in spite of the heat. He got up and went to the bathroom, urinated, then washed his face with cold water. It was only a dream, he whispered aloud. Only a dream. He prepared a cup of tea and sat sipping it in the semi-darkness for almost an hour. Then, once his heartbeat had settled, he lay down and tried to sleep. It took two hours before he drifted off, and once he did the nightmares began again.

Now he and Christa were at the house where they lived outside of Treblinka when he had worked there before the uprising. They were standing in the parlor, her eyes were red and shiny like rubies, and she had a crooked and frightening toothless grin. Outside the window, the trees that were growing along a barbed-wire fence reached their branches out toward him like skinny, arthritic fingers with long, dirty nails. They were clawing him. Manfred felt his body tremble. Then he heard a strange sound. The trees were laughing at him; a wicked high pitched noise that filled the air. He ran outside and Christa slowly followed him. Now she, too, was laughing an evil and horrific laugh. Ashes fell on his face, blinding him until he could not see. All around him it smelled like feces, like blood, like death. "Please Christa…," he whispered. "I loved you."

"Love, Manfred? What you did to me, was that love? And what about that poor Jewess, Zofia? You think I didn't know what you were doing to her? I knew. She never told me that you were abusing her, but I knew. You forced yourself on her, didn't you Manfred? You all-powerful Nazi bastard. All of you sons-of-bitches can go to hell with your superior race."

The trees were reaching out to him, clawing their dirty ragged fingernails through his hair, then down his neck and back. Manfred turned to run away but found that he was surrounded on all sides by walking dead bodies with yellow stars on their striped uniform sleeves. These zombies were emerging from the dark spaces between the trees. Christa stood at the front, leading them all toward him. The woman who he'd loved more than he had ever loved anyone was betraying him. She was showing them where he was and how they could get to him. Manfred squinted into the gray, lined faces of millions of Jews, faces of people whose deaths he had ordered, their shadows growing larger in the moonlight.

"Look Manfred, look at these people. You did it, you killed them." Christa was pointing at him, but her hand had turned into a tree branch, the nail on her finger dripping with blood.

The eyes of the Jews glared at him, yellow stars rotating inside of the pupils. These walking dead were coming toward him, pointing at him, and calling out, "MURDERER, MURDERER, MURDERER."

The stench of the ashes from the crematorium began to fill his nose, and he opened his mouth, trying to breathe. Instead, he began coughing and choking, his throat on fire. The dead Jews were getting closer to him. Their forms were blurry as the ash fell like a snow-storm around them. Run, Manfred thought. I must escape before they get to me; but he could not run. His feet and legs were paralyzed.

"You know what you are? YOU ARE A MURDERER, MANFRED," Christa said.

He felt a shiver travel through him. His body trembled, awakening him. He sat up immediately. The sheets were so wet with perspiration that they felt as if there had been a rain storm in the room where Manfred slept. His heart pounded like a drum solo. He looked around the room, rocking back and forth. Was it real? Had this happened? Manfred shivered as he jumped out of bed and turned on the light, praying that it was only a dream. For several moments he stood looking around him at the familiar bed, the ceiling fan, the night table. Everything was in place. It had all seemed so real, so real, but it had been a dream. He was sure that it had been only a dream. He went to the bathroom and doused his face with cold water, never closing his eyes, just in case those terrible visions returned and came upon him from behind.

"It's all right, it's all right," he whispered, as he wiped his face with a soft towel. I'm fine. I was only having a nightmare. It's over. Then he went into the kitchen and poured himself a drink. Manfred guzzled the whiskey and sighed. He could still see them if he closed his eyes; they were still there waiting. Now, if only the alcohol could drown those faces, that blood.

This dream, or variations of it, reoccurred almost every night from that day forward. Manfred began to find reasons to stay awake as long as possible, and he began to suffer from lack of rest.

Damn it. Manfred certainly didn't want the child, Katja. What would he do with her, here in Argentina? Besides, if he were to risk searching for her, it could cause him to be caught. Yet Christa's voice, her bony finger, and bloody eyes continued to haunt him. He began to think of ways that he could keep the child if he found her. Perhaps he would hire a nanny, someone to take care of Katja. Would that fulfill Christa's demands? Would that free him from the horrors that taunted him? He could ask Konrad to help him find Katja. But still, there was that terrible risk in searching for her. Was he willing to take that risk? Katja should be twelve or thirteen by now. The last thing he wanted was a teenage girl with all sorts of demands on his time, and questions. No, he would not go searching and possibly uncover his disguise. He would just leave Katja wherever she was living. That would be best for everyone. After all, the child was probably adjusted to her new life. Yes, best to leave well enough alone.

But those dreams . . .

Book Two

Chapter 51

As WWII ended and the tumult of the following years began, international crises and the Cold War between the Soviet Union and the United States began. The surrender and capture of Nazi scientists, labs, and military facilities led some in the US to have designs on German advancements and knowledge in aerodynamics, chemical warfare, rocketry, and medicine. With Russia now an enemy, and the Space Race in full force, United States intelligence and military services felt that the scientific knowledge these war criminals offered was worth overlooking their crimes committed against humanity. A secret operation offering a safe haven to Nazi scientists, purportedly done without US State Department knowledge or approval, was codenamed Operation Paperclip.

Meanwhile, in a small office in Linz, Austria, thirty volunteers under the direction of a quiet, unassuming man named Simon Weisenthal, labored tirelessly in their pursuit of the escaped Nazi war criminals. Weisenthal had survived the concentration camps, he knew the horrors of the Third Reich, and he was not about to let the Nazis go free.

With the help of the Jewish Avengers, an elite group of Nazi hunters, and Mossad (Israel's secret service), headed by Isser Harel, Weisenthal worked diligently toward his goal. No matter what it took, even if it took a lifetime, Weisenthal would do whatever possible to bring every sadistic Nazi criminal to justice in Israel.

Israel

Katja ran a brush through her long blond curls, and then tied them back with a ribbon. She had just begun teaching the younger students, and she loved working with them. Her Hebrew was impeccable as was her English. In fact, Katja was fluent in several languages acquired throughout her childhood in Europe and on the kibbutz.

Since Rachel and Mendel were three years older than Katja, they were serving their time in the army, the IDF. Rachel loved the IDF. She applied to flight school, but was disappointed to find that women were no longer allowed to participate in combat. She'd told Katja how angry she was at this change in the IDF. Women, she said, had fought diligently beside the men in the war of independence and now females were being reduced to field instructor positions. Still, Rachel chose to repeatedly apply for flight school and follow the path of her dreams, hoping for a change.

The friendship between Katja, Mendel and Rachel had not diminished as they'd grown older. The trust that the three friends had built over the years only grew stronger with time. After Shana gave birth to her son, Ben, Katja and Shana grew closer. Katja, because she loved children, was more than willing to babysit for little Ben, while Rachel had no interest in such things.

One day, Katja arrived at the school early. She wanted to decorate for the coming holiday as she did for each holiday. The children loved the festivities, and always responded to the decorated classroom with excitement. Katja loved to watch them as they entered, their eyes wide with wonder.

It was spring and Passover would take place in less than a week. Both Mendel and Rachel would be returning to the kibbutz to take part in the celebration. Katja was eagerly anticipating the return of her friends. It had been three months since their last visit, and she missed them terribly.

Chapter 52

The table was set, the food prepared, the prayers would begin at sundown. It was the first night of Passover. Katja went back to her room to get ready. She'd spent the entire day helping in the kitchen and she was hot and sweaty, best to freshen up before dinner. Quickly she washed her face and body. Then she put on the new dress that Zofia had made for her for the Passover holiday. Her mother was still, and always would be, her best friend. Zofia was always doing sweet little things like making Katja dresses, or bringing the ripest and sweetest oranges to the school as treats for her. Katja always felt so fortunate that she had parents who loved her dearly, and she adored them in return. The dress was a pink and white floral, gathered to show off her small waist. Zofia had designed it perfectly to compliment all of Katja's attributes. Katja looked in the mirror and smiled, pleased with her appearance. Then she pulled her blond curls back from her face with the headband Zofia had made from a matching pink ribbon and slipped on the ballet flats Zofia had made for her from the same fabric.

Katja left her room and searched for Isaac and Zofia. Since she did not see her parents anywhere, she assumed they were already in the dining room. Katja picked up the little box that contained the necklace that she had gotten for Rachel as a gift. She'd made a deal with a jeweler who worked in town. She traded tutoring lessons for his son for the gift for Rachel. Even though giving presents on Passover was not customary, she missed her friend so much that she wanted to give her a token of her love.

The sun had begun to set as Katja raced to the dining room. When she got inside she was breathless from running. The flush on her face made her even more beautiful.

"Rachel." Katja saw her friend standing proudly beside a table stacked with plates of cut vegetables and bowls of hummus. Rachel was wearing her army uniform. "I missed you." Katja said. They hugged.

"I missed you, too." Rachel laughed.

"What did you do to your hair?" Katja asked. Rachel's long black curls were gone. Her hair was cut short in a pixie style.

"I cut it, do you like it?"

Katja reached up and touched Rachel's short-cropped hair. "I'm not used to it yet."

"You hate it."

"I don't," Katja said. "But I did love your long hair."

"*Ech*, it is too much work for a soldier."

"Are you in flight school?" Katja asked. She knew how much Rachel wanted to get in, but she secretly hoped that she would not be able to. It was dangerous to fly planes, and she feared for Rachel's safety.

"Not yet. But I'm not going to stop trying."

Just then, a tall man wearing an army uniform walked over to Rachel's side. His skin was darkly tanned, his hair dark and curly, and his eyes were the most arresting blue Katja had ever seen.

"This is Elan Amsel, my boyfriend," Rachel said. "He's been in the IDF forever. How many years have you been with the IDF, Elan?"

"This is my third term." Elan answered

"Nice to meet you," Katja said. "I didn't know you had a boyfriend."

Elan's eyes caught Katja's. She felt as if she were glued to his gaze. Katja was on the brink of womanhood at nearly sixteen, lovely, carefree, and innocent. She could not help but stare. Elan was the most attractive man she'd ever seen. But, he was Rachel's boyfriend. Katja quickly looked away, but when she turned back and stole a second glance, Elan's eyes were still bonded to her.

"Mendel!!!" Rachel called across the room. "Come over here."

Mendel had just arrived, tall and lanky in his IDF uniform.

Mendel walked over. "Kat, it's real good to see you." He hugged Katja. "I missed you," Mendel said.

"I missed you, too," Katja said to Mendel, but she still felt Elan's eyes on her back. When she turned, Elan smiled at her. She did not return his smile.

"Come sit, sit, it's time for the prayers," one of the older women in the kitchen called out. "Sit, please, sit . . ."

Some of the men adjusted their yarmulkes. Finally, everyone was seated. Elan had worked his way to a chair between Rachel and Katja while Mendel sat on Katja's other side. There were platters of matzo placed upon the white tablecloth and it had been embroidered with a blue Star of David. When everyone grew silent, the rabbi stood up at the front of the table and the prayers began.

Although Katja did not look his way, she knew that Elan was watching her. She could feel his stare, and she hoped that Rachel was too engrossed in the prayers to notice. When the time came for the Rabbi to ask the four questions of the youngest participant at the table, he turned to a small boy that looked to be about four years old, and said "Moishe, you are the youngest, can you ask the four questions?"

The child nodded, his face serious. There were smaller children at the dinner, but they were too young to shoulder this responsibility.

"So, Moishe, are you ready?" the young Rabbi asked.

"I am ready," Moishe asserted.

The adults smiled as they watched Moishe undertake the job. They could see by the serious expression on the child's face that he felt that the responsibility was enormous.

Then the Rabbi began the questions . . .

"Why is this night different from every other night?" the rabbi asked.

Moishe began to carefully repeat the answer in the prayer book. But Katja did not hear him, because Elan leaned over whispering in Katja's ear, just loud enough for her to hear. His hot breath shot through her like a bolt of electricity. "This night is different from every other night," he said, his voice deep and hoarse, "because tonight is the night that I met you, Katja, the woman I am going to marry."

Chapter 53

"Can I walk you back to your room?" Mendel asked Katja after the celebration following dinner.

"Yes, I'd like that," she said. "Let me say good night to everyone first and then we'll walk. I want to hear all about the army."

"I'll wait here," Mendel said.

Katja said goodnight and "Good Pasach" to her parents, to Shana and her husband, Avi, and to all of her friends. Then she hugged Rachel and gave her the necklace.

"Happy Pasach," she said, winking, "my blood sister."

"Happy Pasach." Rachel embraced Katja. "You still remember when we did that?"

"Of course, how could I forget? I was so scared to cut myself," Katja said with a short laugh.

"We'll always be blood sisters," Rachel said, hugging Katja again. "You didn't have to get me a present. It's not Hanukah."

"I know. I wanted to give you something so that every time you put it on you would think of me," Katja said.

"I think about you all the time, and Mendel, too. You two are my best friends in the world."

"So, are you and Elan serious? I mean, are you thinking about marriage?"

"Me? Hell no. I want to fly planes, not sit at home and diaper babies."

"Having babies is not such a bad thing."

"No, it's not a bad thing; it's just a paralyzing thing. I mean, it keeps you stuck at home . . . do you know what I mean?" Rachel said.

"Rachel, I know what you mean, but I hope someday you will decide to have children. Of course, I don't know from experience, but I believe it is the most wonderful thing that can ever happen to a woman. At least, that is what my mother told me," Katja said.

"Yep, that sounds like Zofia," Rachel said and they both laughed.

"I'll see you in the morning," Katja said.

"Yes, in the morning," Rachel answered.

"Happy Pasach," Elan called out to Katja as he saw her leaving, but Katja did not turn around; she had already begun walking away quickly.

As they walked through the kibbutz, Katja looked up to see Mendel glance at her.

"You look different than I remember," Mendel said.

"It's only been three months since your last visit. HOW? Different in what way?"

"Don't be alarmed," he laughed. "I mean . . . well, different in a good way. I guess what I'm trying to say is that . . ." He hesitated and cleared his throat "Well, just that . . . you are beautiful, Katja."

"Oh Mendel; you are so silly, you're always teasing me. You just wanted to shake me up and make me wonder what had changed. I thought I'd gotten fat or looked old or something."

"No Kat, I'm not teasing. In fact, I am really very serious," he said this as he stopped walking and looked directly at her. You really are beautiful, Katja. You look like a golden goddess."

"You're embarrassing me, Mendel. What's gotten into you? A golden goddess? What does that mean?"

"I don't know, you have beautiful golden curls and your skin is so light and pale," he said this while looking down, not able to meet her eyes directly.

She laughed. "Well, thank you . . . I think?"

"I mean it as a compliment in every way," Mendel said, still not looking at her.

"So what is it like?"

"What?" Mendel's head tilted to the side as if he didn't understand the question.

"The army."

Mendel let out a short laugh. "Oh that," he said. "I had no idea what you were talking about."

"Yes, the army. I want to know all about it. Soon it will be my time to serve and I'm a little nervous. I've never been away from my parents," she said.

"Lots of exercise; lots of discipline. They are training us for the worst possible scenarios, and the truth is they don't let up. They want us to be the strongest of the strong. Every day we are reminded that we are Israel's only defense against a hostile world. Sometimes they make us wear the same uniform without washing it for a week, so that we can get used to the feeling in case it happens that we are in the field and we can't bathe," he said.

"Ewww. So, it's hard?"

"Yes, very. But it's worth it. This country is built on the blood of our ancestors. And the world is not eager to help us protect it. So every soldier must be willing to die in order to keep possession of our homeland. We are all that stands between our small country and all of her enemies. There is no room for mistakes. If we lose Israel, we will never get a second chance to win her back."

"Are you ever scared?"

"Sure. Of course, I'm terrified. But what can we do, you and I both know that without Israel, it is just a matter of time before some dictator decides to eradicate our people. We're Jews after all, we're the Chosen People, chosen for what I am still not sure, but with God's help we have finally taken possession of our dream. Every day of my life, I heard the words; we must have a homeland, the Promised Land."

She nodded. "Yes, it's true."

They continued to walk until they stood together in front of her room.

"It's good to have you home at the kibbutz, Mendel," She said.

"It's good to be home. This is the only home I have ever known. These people are my family."

"Mine, too," she said.

"Yes, but I can hardly remember my parents. At least both of yours are here."

"Yes, thank God, they are both here. I am one of the lucky ones . . ." Katja said, "one of the few lucky ones."

Chapter 54

School was not in session for the full eight days of Passover, and as long as war did not break out, the soldiers were permitted to stay on leave. Katja was glad that her friends would be with her, but she was concerned about Elan's outward display of attraction to her. He was attractive, there was no denying that, but he was also her best friend's boyfriend. Not just her best friend, but her blood sister. She would rather die than hurt Rachel. Elan's reckless attention, and casual flirtations, bothered Katja. She was afraid that he posed a danger to the friendship Katja held so dear. She would be glad when he returned to his army base.

Katja did not go to breakfast the following morning for fear of seeing Elan, of having to talk to him, of the possibility of his saying something flirtatious and unsuitable where Rachel could overhear him. She waited until everyone had left the dining area, and then decided she would go and find something quick to eat. But as soon as she left her room, she was bombarded by several of her female students. The girls were eleven and they emulated Katja, their pretty teacher. They loved to follow her around and talk about hairstyles and clothing trends that they had seen in magazines. Not that Katja was up on these things; she wasn't for the most part, but she let them talk.

Today one of her students had a pile of pictures of American movie stars that she'd cut out of a magazine, handsome men with sly, seductive smiles. Katja glanced at the photos and laughed. One of the girls asked her if she planned to marry and have children someday. Katja just smiled and said she didn't know. She hoped so.

"It's a mitzvah to get married and have lots and lots of Jewish children to replace all of the Jewish people that the Nazis killed," said one of the young girls, spouting the rhetoric that they were constantly fed.

"So I hear," Katja said.

"Katja will get married when she meets the right fellow," another of the girls offered. "And we will have the biggest wedding. I want to help you do your hair. We could put wild flowers in it; it would look very glamorous. Like a movie star from Hollywood in America."

Katja laughed again, but she found herself glancing at the door to Mendel's room. However, she was not looking for Mendel but for Elan, who was sharing a room with Mendel for the holiday. *What am I doing?* she thought. *I don't want to see him. His flattery does nothing for me but cause me trouble.*

"Well, girls, I am going to the kitchen to see if my mother and the rest of the ladies need any help preparing the food for the Seder tonight."

"Can we help?"

"Sure, you can ask the women in the kitchen. They always need help," Katja said, still distracted with thoughts of Elan and Rachel.

When Katja got to the kitchen, Zofia was chopping apples to make charoset for Passover dinner.

"Good morning, Sunshine. You missed breakfast," Zofia said.

"I know, Mama. I overslept. I'm sorry."

"Oh, it's all right. I suppose with school not being in session, it must have been nice for you to get a little extra rest. Here, have some matzo and an apple."

"Yes, it was nice to get a little extra sleep," Katja said, biting into a crisp, sweet apple. "By the way, do you need any help in the kitchen?" Katja asked.

"Of course, but don't you want to spend a little time with Rachel and Mendel before they have to go back to their base?"

"I'll see them tonight," Katja said. She picked up a red apple and a paring knife and she began peeling it.

Zofia studied her daughter. She knew Katja very well, knew her facial expressions. Something was not right.

"Sunshine, what is it?" Zofia asked, stopping what she was doing. She wiped her hands on her apron and then took Katja's hands in hers. "Come, sit. You'll talk to me, you'll tell me what is causing you distress. Whenever your friends come home from the IDF you always look so worried. I know you have a bit more than two years before you have to go, but is that it? Is that what is frightening you??"

"Yes, Mama. I'm not made for the IDF. I am not like Rachel. I'm scared, I'm not that strong."

"I know, Sunshine. I know how you are. You're sweet and gentle and you're a tender, beautiful soul. But everyone must serve. Our country needs us. Yes?"

"Yes, I know, Mama."

"And besides, don't worry too much. You are a woman; they will give you a job working in an office."

"But I will miss you and papa. I know it sounds childish, but I've never been so far away from both of you. And for two years!"

"We'll miss you, too, more than you could ever know. But you'll come home for holidays and before you know it, your service time will be over," Zofia said.

It was true that Katja had been concerned about her requirement to serve in the IDF, but that was not what was uppermost on her mind right now. Katja was annoyed at herself; she was angry that she felt out of control and was allowing an inexplicable attraction to Elan to dominate her thoughts. The more she tried to push those dangerous thoughts out of her mind, the stronger they became. But how could she ever explain this to her mother? Just these feelings felt like a betrayal to Rachel.

The door to the dining room opened and Rachel came into the kitchen. From where Katja sat at the table with her, Zofia could see the necklace that Katja had given Rachel sparkle against Rachel's sunburned chest. Rachel walked over and kissed Zofia's cheek, then Katja's.

"Thank you, I love it," Rachel said, her hand gently caressing the necklace.

"I'm glad," Katja said. "I can't tell you how lost I've been without you and Mendel. It was always the three of us together, and all of a sudden you two were off to the army and I was all alone here."

"Yes, I've missed you, too. I see you are busy, but if your mother wouldn't mind, I wanted to ask you if you would like to come outside. Elan is playing the guitar and everyone is singing along. I thought you might enjoy it," Rachel said.

"Oh—I should help my mother prepare for tonight," Katja said.

"Nonsense!" Zofia snapped, sounding harsher than she intended. "Since when have I needed you to help me peel a few apples? Go—go outside and be with the other young people. Enjoy your time with your friends."

"But Mama—there is a lot to do—"

"Go. Go now—take her with you, Rachel. She works too hard, and never takes the time to have any fun."

"See, your mother insists. Come on, Katja," Rachel said.

Rachel took Katja's upper arm and pulled her up. Katja shook her head. "Well, I can't fight both of you. If you insist . . ."

"I do," Zofia said.

"And so do I. Come on," Rachel said. "Mendel is outside, too."

The trees were filled with blossoms, and flowers had begun to poke their delicate green stalks through the ground. Spring was on its way.

"Di Di Akezi Einayim V'elvav, Di Di Di, Hey Hey Hey," Elan sang as he strummed the guitar.

A chorus of the children's voices raised in song greeted Katja as she walked over to the tree where Mendel was sitting and waiting.

"Just the girl I want to see," Mendel said. His voice was almost drowned out by the singing. "Sit, here, next to me." He patted the ground.

The shade from the tree blocked the direct sunlight. Only tiny slivers peeked through the branches.

Katja smoothed her skirt and then sat down, turning to smile at Mendel. Then she began to sing along.

"Di Di Di . . ."

The depth of Elan's stare when he saw Katja stopped her cold. Those blue eyes were the color of a bluebird she remembered seeing in a picture book long ago; bright, arresting, and royal. His gaze was bold and direct, filled with desire. Could Rachel see the lust in his eyes? Did Rachel notice Elan looking at Katja? Katja felt a shiver go up her spine. She snapped her head away from Elan's gaze, but before she did, she gave him a look of disdain. Mendel noticed Katja trembling and he put his arm around her.

"Are you chilled?" Mendel asked. The weather was still cool, although each day it grew warmer. "Would you like me to go back to my room and bring a jacket for you?"

"No, I'm all right," Katja said, leaning close to her old friend Mendel, as he gently caressed her arm. She was so close to him that, in spite of the music, she still heard him sigh.

***

The eight days of Passover flew by so quickly it seemed as if Mendel and Rachel had just arrived, and now the time had come for them to leave. Katja loved having her friends back at home. Often, in the late afternoon, she took long walks with Mendel. In the morning, while cleaning up after breakfast, she spent hours talking with Rachel, but most of all she spent a good deal of time during the entire week avoiding Elan.

Time was going by so quickly. Katja knew that the years until she entered the IDF would could come and go in a heartbeat, and then she would be a soldier. She understood that it was her duty. However, she was afraid, afraid a war would break out during her term of service and she would be close to combat, perhaps even in the line of fire. She'd never held a gun, and she had never wanted to. But, besides fear of the army itself, Katja was also uneasy about leaving home. For as long as she could remember, she had been at her mother's side. They were closer than sisters in many ways and that bond had grown even stronger after Rachel and Mendel had been drafted. Being an only child, Katja felt very close to both of her parents. She could talk to her mother about almost anything; they would sit together and talk for hours about Katja's feelings, her hopes and dreams. Sometimes they would laugh about the strange nature of the opposite sex. Katja loved her mother, but her father was her rock, her strength. When she thought about the man she would someday marry, she wanted him to be just like Isaac.

Once in a while Katja would catch her mother studying her with an odd and serious expression. It was a puzzling gaze that Katja found unreadable. She had never questioned her mother about it because she could not explain what she thought she saw, not in concrete terms anyway. It was more of a feeling, something akin to intuition. But still Katja had no idea of the meaning behind the stare.

Many happy years had passed for Katja on this subsistence farm in Israel, enough time to blur the darkness of the past. She'd danced at Shana's wedding, and cried tears of joy as Mendel read his haftorah portion in Hebrew on the day of his bar mitzvah. She'd set the broken wing of a bird with Rachel's assistance, and together they'd cared for the animal until it was ready to fly away. Katja could still remember how both she and Rachel had been sad and happy at the same time as they watched the brightly colored bird take flight. They had stood beneath the tree and watched until the bird became nothing more than a spot in the sky. Then they had looked at each other, knowing that they would never see their feathered friend again but also assured that what they had done was right. The time had come for him to fly away.

With all of the different survivors that had migrated to Israel, Katja had the opportunity to continue speaking all of the languages she'd learned. Her body grew strong and got sustenance from the warm sun, the healthy fresh fruits and vegetables, as well as the joy in the song and dance of her people. Most of all, living in Israel on a kibbutz had given her pride in this wonderful nation that was born from the blood of the Chosen People All of this had miraculously erased every dark memory of the early years of Katja's life, those years when she'd lived as the golden child, bred as a perfect Aryan by the Nazis.

Of course, she could not remember her birth in the home for the Lebensborn, or that she had been created by a racially pure German woman and an SS officer. And how could Katja know that as an infant she had been one of the chosen ones because she had been christened by Himmler himself, given her name, and declared the pride of Hitler's future Germany. Then, still too young to have any recollection, at just one year old Katja had been presented by Heinrick Himmler as a gift to a childless Nazi couple; Katja's new parents had been the feared SS officer Manfred Blau and his ailing wife, Christa. And of course, she could not know that a year later, Manfred's job had been moved to Treblinka concentration camp. He had brought his family, including Katja, with him to live in the house that stood beside the barbed wire of the camp.

For two years, Christa's illness had been getting worse. So when they'd arrived at Treblinka Manfred had decided that they needed a nanny to care for their child. He had gone out to the camp and to search amongst the prisoners, the poor souls who the Nazis had marked for death. And . . . it was there that he made the fateful decision that would change Katja's life forever.

Manfred Blau, had chosen Zofia. He had forced her out of a line of prisoners and had ordered her be brought to his house. Zofia, a Jew, an inferior taken from the barracks of Treblinka, had come to be Manfred's house slave. She'd loved tiny Katja from the first moment she had held the baby in her arms. In fact, for Zofia, Katja had been a godsend. Zofia missed her daughter Eidel, terribly, and so she loved and cared for Katja as if she had been her own child.

Then, following Manfred's trial, Christa had given Katja into Zofia's care because she had known she was dying. But even then, Katja had been only six, very nearly seven years old, and so, it seemed to Zofia that much of what had happened in those early years had faded into a distant memory for Katja. Sometimes Zofia wondered if Katja remembered anything at all about the months she and Katja had spent in England before boarding *Exodus*, but since the child never mentioned anything, Zofia assumed that she'd forgotten.

Many times Zofia felt guilty, as if she owed Katja an honest synopsis of her early life, but the need to tell Katja was overshadowed by the suffering Zofia knew that the truth would cause her daughter. Growing up as Katja did, Zofia realized that Katja would be shocked and horrified to know that she was not really born Jewish, but born to the worst of all people, to Nazis. So, Zofia swallowed her guilt, closed her eyes to the truth, and remained silent. Zofia watched as Katja grew up. Katja laughed, played, studied, and lived with her cherished Jewish friends. She carried her father's name, Katja Zuckerman, and around her neck she wore a gold mezuzah with a tiny Hebrew prayer written on parchment inside. This mezuzah was her most cherished possession. It was a gift that her parents had given her when she turned thirteen.

Chapter 55

On the morning before the soldiers of the IDF were to return to their posts, Mendel got up very early and walked alone for several hours. He was debating with himself, he wanted to tell Katja how he felt about her, but he could not find the words. If he told her that he thought he was in love with her, it might make her uncomfortable and it could ruin the beautiful friendship they had, and she was still so young. There was no doubt in his mind that their friendship was a true gift from God, and he cherished that gift. But Mendel wanted more. In fact, he had wanted more from Katja for many years. He'd always had a soft spot in his heart for her. But he'd been too shy to ever tell her how he felt.

But now, they were old enough to have a serious relationship. And Mendel wanted that with Katja. In fact, after they had both served their time in the army, he wanted to marry Katja and have a family of their own. He'd never had a family, not one he could remember, and he longed for a wife and children. Someone in this world he could call his own. But he had no idea how to approach the subject, and what the consequences would be. It could either be wonderful, the most wonderful moment of his life . . . or it could be hell. He could lose everything, everything he held dear.

When Katja came out of her room that morning to go to the main dining area, she saw Mendel waiting for her, leaning against a tree. She rushed over to him. Knowing it was his last day, she brought out a nicely wrapped package with a scarf she'd knitted for him. It was thick brown and beige wool. Those were good colors for Mendel.

"I made this for you, for the winter." She smiled and handed him the gift.

He smiled and took it. "Thank you, it's really nice." He rubbed the wool through his fingers absentmindedly.

"Don't you like it?" she asked.

"Of course I do." He smiled at her.

"Well then, try it on." She put the scarf around his neck. As she did their eyes locked. He wanted to tell her, yearned to tell her, but he could not speak the words. Mendel wanted to pull her close to him, to kiss her, and for a moment, just a single instant, he almost did. Then Rachel and Elan came walking up the walkway.

"You ready to head out?" Rachel asked Mendel.

"As ready as I'll ever be." Mendel said, the courage he had felt just a moment earlier . . . gone.

Katja reached up and planted a kiss on Mendel's cheek. "Be safe," she whispered.

Then Katja hugged Rachel, "Be safe."

"I will," Rachel said.

"Goodbye, Elan; it was nice meeting you."

"You're not going to wish me to be safe?" Elan asked, with an expression of mock hurt.

"Of course I am. Be safe, Elan."

"I will, and I will be back to visit this lovely kibbutz very soon," he said with a crooked smile.

Damn, Katja thought. He certainly is handsome. Katja watched as the army truck pulled away. School would start tomorrow, and so it was time to go back to her daily life.

Chapter 56

Manfred had settled into the small cottage that Konrad had rented for him and had just begun working at a factory where Konrad had placed him when he received a wire from Konrad.

The boy who delivered the message waited until Manfred tipped him, and then he left.

Manfred took a deep breath; perhaps this letter contained information about Katja. Did he want to know, did he really want to find her? He tore the envelope open and sat down to read the contents.

"I will come to your home this Friday evening. Please do not invite anyone else as this is an important, top secret meeting that will take place just between the two of us. I look forward to seeing you then. Konrad."

Manfred wondered what Konrad had to tell him. He reread the note several times. What could be top secret? Perhaps he'd found Katja, and was unable to disclose her whereabouts in a wire. Or it could have something to do with the Nazi hunters that Konrad had told him about. Perhaps it was a job change—that would be something he would relish. However, there was no telling what top secret information Konrad was about to deliver. Manfred would just have to wait until Friday night.

Manfred hated his job. He was not physically strong and had never done menial labor. All day long he worked on an assembly line and his feet and back were aching while he waited for the clock to say he could punch his card and leave. Manfred found the work degrading. After all, he was an artist. The men he worked with spoke Spanish, laughing and carrying on with each other, leaving him feeling alone and alienated.

The week passed slowly, but finally Friday arrived. Manfred was glad to have the company, but a little worried about what Konrad had to tell him.

It was early evening when Konrad arrived. He came to Manfred's door carrying a package filled with food and a bottle of schnapps.

"Come in, Konrad, Manfred said. The last time they had seen each other they'd agreed to be on a first name basis.

Once inside with the door closed, Konrad saluted. "Heil Hitler."

"Heil Hitler. It's good to see you. How have you been?" Manfred asked.

"I'm doing well, thank you, and you?"

"I'm doing well. But I was wondering if you'd found another position for me," Manfred said.

"I brought some food for dinner." Konrad placed the package of food on the table. "A new position is what I've come to discuss, but first let's have something to eat."

Manfred nodded in agreement.

"The place looks wonderful," Konrad said, indicating the cottage.

"I had the maid come this morning to ensure everything would be in order when you arrived."

"I do appreciate the gesture," Konrad said.

They sat down to dinner. The entire time Konrad only made small talk. Talk of the weather, talk of the food, but nothing of what had brought him to see Manfred.

After they finished, Manfred opened the schnapps and poured them each a glass.

As they settled into the wicker sofa, Konrad turned to Manfred.

"To the Reich," he said and lifted his glass.

Manfred clinked glasses, "To the Reich."

"Manfred," Konrad said, and he cleared his throat.

"Yes . . ."

"I've come to see you, because you've been chosen for a very special mission," Konrad said, taking a swig of his schnapps. "Let me explain. As you know, this is all top secret. I will begin at the beginning. When our Führer went down into the underground bunker with Goebbels and his family and his new wife Eva Braun, there was already a top secret plan in place. This was a plan that was known only to ODESSA. The rest of us were unaware of what was taking place. Hitler felt it best to keep it as secret as possible. What was planned was this: everyone except the Führer was to commit suicide in the underground bunker. Then ODESSA would bring a body double for Hitler and leave it there with the others. Then, to make it even more difficult to identify the bodies, ODESSA planned to start a fire. Then they would take our Führer, safe and alive, but presumed dead by the world, to Argentina.

This would have been all well and good except there were Jewish militant forces at work. They had spies that had infiltrated ODESSA, and these sneaky Jews knew the plot. When the ODESSA agents were on their way to the bunker, the Jews laid in wait and attacked them. They killed all of the agents and then dressed in their clothing. When these Jews posing as ODESSA arrived, Hitler was waiting. They told him that the body double would be placed in the bunker and the fire started once Hitler was safely far away from Germany. Our Führer was then taken to a plane that he believed was waiting to take him to safety in South America. Instead, once the aircraft was in the air, Hitler found that he had been captured and was on his way to Holland.

As we speak, our leader, the most important man to the rebirth of our Reich, Adolf Hitler, is being held and tortured. Now it is our turn. We must infiltrate this group of Jews in order to rescue Adolf Hitler. Manfred, we need your help to carry out this mission. It won't be easy and it is no doubt, very dangerous. But it must be done. Are you willing to go to these measures to save our leader and rebuild our Reich?"

"Why me?"

"You are not the only one. There are several others. But it is an honor, Manfred Blau . . . an honor to be chosen as one of the men who will be instrumental in the resurrection of the Third Reich."

"But won't they recognize me?" Manfred was nervous. He didn't want any part of anything having to do with Jews. The nightmares came flooding back to him as he listened to the rest of the plan.

"No, nobody will recognize you. Dr. Mengele will reconstruct your face; no one will know who you are except us. And to insure that you do not lose your identity in the party, photographs will be taken before and after the surgery. We will keep those records so that your Nazi brothers will know you."

Manfred scratched his chin. This was some news, and quite the request. "You mean to tell me they've had him for almost fifteen years? Where?"

"In a secret prison in Israel. Once Israel became a nation, they took him from Holland and brought him there. Some of our highest men in ODESSA had heard rumors, but these things had to be checked out before we began a rescue mission. In fact, we are still unsure, and that is why we are sending you."

"Again? Why me?"

"You would dare to ask? This is an important opportunity to show your loyalty."

Again, loyalty. Manfred took a deep breath. Would he ever be truly forgiven for what his father-in-law had done? Would he spend the rest of his life proving his devotion to the party? "Of course, I will do it. By the way . . ."

"Yes, go on?" Konrad asked.

"Was Dr. Goebbels really dead?"

"Hard to say. We believe he was, but we cannot be sure. You will be the one to clarify everything."

"Me alone?"

"No. Two others will accompany you. You will pose as Jews; you will be attempting to join Mossad."

"The Israeli secret service?"

"Yes, the militant groups I mentioned earlier are now a part of Mossad."

"Why would they allow us to join? Aren't they a very difficult organization to infiltrate?"

"Yes, you are right, they are. But I will brief you with a story. You will be a survivor from a concentration camp with a mission to find and destroy Nazis."

"But how will I have knowledge of their operations in Israel?"

"You won't. You will pretend not to know anything about the imprisonment of our Führer. Your story will be that you were trying to go to work for that famous Nazi hunter in Austria, but when you arrived at his office you discovered that his office had been closed. So you came to Mossad to carry out your mission, which you feel is your life's purpose."

"ISRAEL?" Manfred coughed. "BUT, I CANNOT BELIEVE THAT YOU WANT ME TO GO TO ISRAEL?"

"Yes, of course. Where else would these Jews take our Fürher to punish him? And perhaps even Dr. Goebbels. Even though Goebbels and his family's bodies were found, they could have been body doubles."

"Then why not Hitler, too? Why would they not have left a body double for Hitler?"

"That's what we need you to find out," Konrad said.

Manfred nodded. He didn't want this job. The last thing he wanted was to have the face of a Jew and to live among them. The thought sickened him. It reminded him of that Jewess, Zofia, and how close she had been to his wife and daughter. Then, of course, there were always those terrible recurring nightmares of Christa and Katja. He shivered slightly.

"Are you all right?" Konrad asked, pouring himself another glass of schnapps.

"Yes, I'm fine."

"Then you will do it?"

"Of course; I would do anything for the Reich."

Konrad poured another glass and handed it to Manfred.

"I knew that you would. Heil Hitler," Konrad said.

"Heil Hitler," Manfred answered. They raised their glasses, and Manfred felt sweat under his arms. His mind was drifting to those terrifying dreams.

"I have only one request . . ." Manfred said.

"Go on."

"I will wear any disguise that you want me to wear, but I cannot bear to have my face redone as a Jew. I could not bear to look in the mirror and live with a face that repulsed me. If you are willing to allow me to wear a disguise and not have a permanent reconstruction, I will be honored to do anything you ask of me."

"I understand. And we will honor your wishes," Konrad said, thinking that it would be easier this way. No need to involve Josef until it was absolutely necessary.

Chapter 57

Katja's concerns about serving in the IDF had proved unwarranted. In fact, she loved being in the army. It was wonderful to be an adult, away from home, yet still surrounded by young people who shared her love for Israel. She was stationed in Tel Aviv, a newly developing city. Katja had never seen so many people and all of them busy running here and there. The University of Tel Aviv had opened only a few years prior and already it was becoming a respected place to study, with lots of students from other countries in attendance. Katja lived in the barracks with over fifty girls her own age. They talked about everything from boyfriends to how to clean a gun.

In many ways, except for being on the outskirts of a big city, this was not too different than the kibbutz where she had grown up, except for the intensive IDF training. In boot camp it became apparent almost immediately that Katja would best serve the Israeli army by doing office work. She was hardly strong enough to carry out the maneuvers, and the sound of gunshots unnerved her. But it was not a problem. The officers teased her and told her that she would be a great person to make the coffee for everyone else. However, there was no malice in their words. It was a good-natured teasing, and Katja never felt out of place. She learned to type and take dictation. Her boss, a six-feet-five, overbearing, strong-willed, Sephardic Jew, learned to love her because of her easygoing personality. He loved that she was always respectful and never argued. It seemed to everyone who knew her that Katja could not be driven to anger. She laughed easily and often, giving the office a pleasant atmosphere. When other soldiers were called in for meetings, Katja eagerly made coffee and then went to the kitchen and brought out a brick of halvah or a small sponge cake. She cut these in slices and placed them on a tray. When she left the room, her boss made a point of bragging about the efficiency of his secretary.

One afternoon Katja was alone in the office. She was finishing up a typing and filing project for her boss. Once she was done, she was told that she could have the remainder of the day off. So she was rushing to finish. As she put the files in alphabetical order, she thought about how nice it would be to take some time and visit the old city. If she left early enough she could take a bus. Perhaps, since the following day was Friday, she could leave a note that she was taking the day off and spend the night in Jerusalem. For several months Katja had been meaning to do that. However, she'd been too busy and had not yet had the chance. Perhaps Mendel would want to join her.

First, she rolled the paper through the typewriter, and then she carefully arranged it to be sure it was straight before she began to work on the final page. She checked to be sure that everything was in order. She had only one more report to finish. Her fingers found the keys and she began to type. Click, click, click . . . When the typewriter was in motion, it seemed to have a rhythm of its own; it was almost musical. Sometimes when Katja was alone in the office, she hummed tunes while she plugged along.

There was a knock at the door.

Katja was not expecting anyone. She got up and opened it. Her mouth flew open in surprise.

"Elan? What are you doing here?"

"I'm on leave. I had a little time and I knew where you were stationed so I came to see you."

"How did you know where to find me?"

"I've got my ways," he said, winking, and then laughing. "I happened to see your enlistment papers on a desk when I was called in for a meeting. As soon as I saw them and knew where you were stationed, I knew I had to come and see you."

"Where is Rachel?"

"I don't know. We haven't been seeing each other. I guess you could say that she and I don't see eye-to-eye."

"What does that mean?"

"It means that I want a wife, not a fighter pilot. I want a woman in my life who is happy to be a woman. Do you understand?"

She understood. But she would not acknowledge the fact. To do so would be to betray her best friend. "I don't know what you mean."

"Rachel doesn't want a home and family. I mean, she loves kids, but what she really wants is to get into flight school. I want a wife who will give me children and be willing to devote her life to raising them."

"I'm sorry to hear that you two broke up," Katja said.

"Yes, well . . ." He shrugged. "Sometimes it is for the best to break up early. Do you know what I mean? Better now, then later when there are children to worry about."

Katja looked away and began walking back to her desk.

"That's enough about the past," Elan said. "So . . . like shawarma? I know a restaurant around the corner from here that makes a delicious shawarma. So, how about you have dinner with me?"

"I don't know. I have a lot of work to do."

"Ehh, the work will be here tomorrow. You can't work all night."

Katja was almost done with her work, but she was thinking about Rachel. Would having dinner with Elan be a betrayal? Besides, this was not her plan.

"I really don't think so, Elan," she said.

"Do you want me to beg? Please, please, lovely Katja, will you allow me to buy you dinner?" He was joking and she knew it.

"Stop teasing me." She shook her head and turned away to file a handful of newly typed papers. Damn, he was handsome, rugged and tan. Also, incredibly sexy in that uniform.

"I don't mean to be teasing you. I just came all this way to ask you to have dinner with me. The least you could do is humor me. What is a dinner? It's not a life commitment. I'm not asking you to come home with me and meet my parents or to marry me tomorrow. I'm asking you to accompany me for a quick bite to eat. You are making it all so serious. Come on, I hate to eat alone . . . say yes."

She took a moment and studied him, frowning.

"What? . . . you don't like how I look? Maybe I'll go and change into a suit and tie. Would you go out with me then?

There wasn't a woman in the world that would not grow weak at the knees just looking at him in that IDF uniform, Katja thought.

"It's Rachel. I don't want to do anything that could hurt Rachel."

"Rachel wouldn't care. She would be glad that we both had someone to eat with. That's all, just to go to dinner . . . just having something to eat. Nothing more. So you'll go?"

He was so damn insistent, too.

"All right. Yes, I'll go." Why am I doing this?

"When should I come back here to get you? Or would you rather I picked you up at your barracks?"

"Here is better. I'll be ready in an hour," she said.

"I'll be here and I'll be on time. Maybe I'll even be early," he said, winking at her as he left.

What the heck was she doing?

After Elan left, Katja sat gazing out the window with unseeing eyes. She felt uncomfortable, as if she were about to do something she would surely regret. Rachel was far too close a friend for Katja to not consider how this might affect their friendship. Quickly Katja finished her work and packed up her things. Then she left the office before Elan returned to pick her up for dinner. Looking around her to be sure he was not outside waiting, she exited the building and went back to hide in her barracks.

Chapter 58

All night, Katja felt strange, as if any minute Elan would appear at her door. In an odd way, she almost wished he would. She liked him. It was undeniable. But then again, there was Rachel. She loved Rachel, the only sister she'd ever had. Although they were not related by blood, they grew up as close as twins. Katja did not sleep well that night. She considered contacting Rachel and asking her how she felt about Elan, asking Rachel if she would mind if Katja had dinner with him. However, even as close as the two girls were, Katja wondered if Rachel would tell her the truth. By the time morning arrived and Katja left for work, she was glad that she had decided to leave before Elan arrived. It would be best for everyone if her rude behavior had discouraged Elan and he did not come looking for her again.

The morning was slow. Her boss had telephoned to say he would be late and asked her to straighten up a few folders and then arrange them alphabetically on his desk before he arrived. She did as he asked, then prepared a pot of steaming coffee. When Katja had first come to the army she'd not really liked coffee, but as time went by she'd found that the rich flavor and hearty aroma soothed her. The last time she'd seen Rachel, Katja noticed that Rachel had begun smoking cigarettes. Katja had tried a puff of Rachel's cigarette only to feel as if she were suffocating; she then had an uncontrollable coughing spell. "It's awful. Why would you ever smoke?" Katja had asked Rachel.

Rachel had just laughed. It had been several months since Katja had seen Rachel and she missed her terribly.

Katja was still thinking about Rachel when her boss called again, right before lunch, telling her that he would be in a meeting all day, and if she were finished with all of her work she could take the rest of the afternoon off. He was so good to her. Katja smiled as she hung up the phone. Although Elan's visit had interrupted her plans for the trip to Jerusalem, Katja had other ideas for the day. She would take the afternoon and do some shopping. Hanukah was right around the corner and she wanted to purchase some gifts to bring home. Mendel and Rachel would be there and so would her parents. The holidays were always something she anticipated with delight. Ah yes, and a gift for her boss and his wife, something special.

The long awaited holiday finally arrived. Katja took a bus home with a suitcase filled with gifts for her parents and friends.

As always, Hanukah was a splendid time on the kibbutz. Every evening, for eight nights, the menorah candles were lit while everyone stood in a circle, their faces alight with the joy of the season. Then one of the elders told the story of the Maccabees. The children sat cross-legged on the floor, their eyes wide with wonder, as the story of the rebel army who took Judea began to unfold.

Mendel, Katja, and Rachel all arrived within hours of each other. It was wonderful for Katja to see her friends again. That night they ate crisp potato latkes with applesauce and sour cream. Then, after the prayers were said and the candles lit, they exchanged gifts. Mendel brought both girls pieces of jewelry. For Rachel he brought a silver eagle to wear around her neck.

"When I saw this I thought it would be perfect for you because you want to fly planes. You want to soar through the sky like an eagle," Mendel said as he helped her fasten the chain.

For Katja he brought a white gold ring with a fiery opal stone. She opened it and gasped. "This is beautiful Mendel."

"It is beautiful, just like you." He winked.

He took the ring from the box and as he slid it on her finger she had to turn away. The emotions that she saw in his face confused her. Had he ever looked at her that way before? Perhaps she was just imagining it all.

"Thank you, you should not have gotten me anything so extravagant," Katja said.

"I wanted to," Mendel smiled.

The girls exchanged gifts with each other and gave Mendel the presents that they had brought for him. Then they all went to sit under the stars and sing along with the guitar player. The three of them sat together on a blanket singing the old familiar songs that they had been singing on Hanukah since they were little children.

"Dreidel, Dreidel, Dreidel, I made you out of clay. And when you're dry and ready, oh dreidel I will play." The group sang in an off-tune chorus while the children sat spinning their driedels playing the same games that Katja, Mendel, and Rachel had grown up playing.

As they sang, Katja glanced through an opening between the heads of the people singing to see her parents. Isaac and Zofia sat together, her head on his shoulder their hands locked together. A pain shot through Katja's heart as she watched them. Her father had begun to look older. She knew he was only in his mid forties, but to Katja the aging of her parents was her greatest fear. Isaac's once thick, curly golden locks were now thin and streaked with gray. On his face, he had the stubble of a grey beard. Her mother, once slender as a reed with heavy black, wavy hair, was now thick at the waist with silver running through her locks and reminding Katja that Zofia was forty. Katja had somehow believed that they would never age. That they would always be young and always there for her no matter what. As she watched them, their mortality dawned on her. Someday they would be gone and she would never see them again.

The night was cool. Even though she wore a thick sweater, she felt a chill run down her back. Katja shivered and almost broke into tears. "I'll be right back, I want to go and see my parents," Katja said to Mendel and Rachel.

She got up and walked over to her parents, reached down and hugged them both.

"Happy Hanukah, my precious Sunshine," Zofia said, hugging her daughter.

"Happy Hanukah," Isaac said, reaching over to kiss Katja's forehead. "We've missed you. After the singing is over, you'll come back to our room. We have a little present for you."

She looked at them, her heart overflowing with love. Someday she would not be able to sit beside them to hug them, to hear their laughter. Why did people have to die and leave you? Why did God make us all so vulnerable? Tears began to form in her eyes, but the night and the crowd and the singing helped her hide her feelings from those she loved.

That night Katja found it difficult to sleep. For the first time she wondered what life would be like when her parents died. She had no husband, no family of her own, only Rachel and Mendel. Katja began to feel she would like to marry soon, to have children, to redirect some of the overwhelming love she felt for her aging parents.

In the morning, on the day after the holiday was over, Rachel and Katja packed their things at the same time. Rachel had taken up whistling and it made Katja smile to hear her.

"You whistle like a man," Katja said.

"What, you think only men whistle?"

"I don't know."

Rachel smiled at her friend and then began to whistle again. Katja laughed, and then Rachel laughed, too.

"Rach, do you ever think about getting married?"

"Sure. Every girl thinks about it, but I can tell you this, I'm not ready. I don't know if I'll ever be ready," Rachel said. Then she glanced over at Katja who sat down on the edge of her bed. "What's the matter? You look like you've just been to a funeral."

"I don't know. I've been thinking crazy thoughts."

"Well, stop it! We only have a few more hours together. Let's go and get Mendel and play a game of kickball" Rachel gently punched Katja's shoulder.

"What are you going to do when you get out of the army?"

"Reenlist," Rachel said.

"I should have guessed as much."

Rachel laughed, "You know me so well. What are you going to do?"

"I don't know. I feel so lost. I guess I could come back here and teach again."

"That's an idea. You were really good at teaching."

"Thanks. But I'm not sure what I want to do."

"Mendel wants to go to the University. He says he wants to be a journalist or a lawyer. Nu? So what else would he want to do? What do you think about that?" Rachel said. "Going to school, I mean. Maybe you want to go to the University, too?"

"Perhaps. I don't know," Katja said. She got up and walked to the window to watch the children playing red rover. They sang as they held hands. "Do you remember when we used to play that?"

"Of course I remember. You could never break through the line." Rachel laughed.

"I know," Katja said. "You always loosened your grip to let me through.

"YOU KNEW THAT?"

"Of course I knew. You've always taken care of me in your way," Katja said.

"Well, you've taken care of me, too."

"Rachel, can I ask you something?"

"Of course."

"Do you promise to tell me the truth?"

"Sure, I'd never lie to you. What is it Kat?"

"Remember that guy Elan; the one who you brought home a few years ago for Passover?"

"Vaguely; why?"

"Do you have any feelings for him?"

"I barely remember him," Rachel said.

"Are you sure?"

"Yes, I'm sure. Why?"

"Would you be hurt if I went out with him?"

"Have you seen him? I don't even know where he is."

"He came by my office a few months ago."

"Is he still enlisted?"

"I think so," Katja said.

"Then you should have no trouble finding him. Sure, go out with him. I don't mind at all."

Katja gave Rachel a hug. She wondered if Rachel really felt a little stiff or if it was her imagination.

"Come on; let's get in a game of kickball before we have to head out. I'll go and get Mendel. Meet me out in the field," Rachel said.

"All right; I'll be out in a few minutes," Katja said, shutting her suitcase. She felt a strange, lonely feeling as she watched Rachel walk by the window on her way to Mendel's room.

Chapter 59

After Katja returned to her army base she wondered why she'd ever asked Rachel about Elan. She was not bold like Rachel. Katja would never contact him, she was far too shy. And after the way she had treated him, it was doubtful Katja ever see him again. Katja continued her weekly correspondence with her parents, Mendel, and Rachel. Each week she wrote a letter and each week she received one. Rachel never once mentioned Elan, and neither did Katja.

Mendel was the oldest and he was done with his military service first. He surprised Katja with a visit to her base. She had just finished work and walked outside the building. There, on the steps stood Mendel. He was smiling and leaning against the railing. Katja was so happy to see him that she ran into his arms. He lifted her high in the air.

"Kat, how are you?" He said, after twirling her around.

"I'm doing well. How are you?"

"I'm fine. How do you like the IDF?"

"It's all right. I'll bet you're glad you're done."

. "Yes, I'm glad I served, but I'm glad I'm finished. Unless there is a war and I am called back up, my life now belongs to me," he said.

Katja asked, "Will you go to school now?"

"Yes, I think I will. But I was thinking maybe I would attend the University of Tel Aviv so that I could be near you." Mendel smiled as he turned to Katja

"That would be lots of fun. We could spend our free time together."

"I was thinking that," he said.

"It sounds like a wonderful idea."

"Are you done working for today?" Mendel asked, taking the books and work she was carrying. "I'll take these for you."

"I just finished."

"Nu, so let's have dinner?" he said.

"I'd love to."

They walked to a small restaurant down the street that had tables and chairs arranged outside under umbrellas.

"You think it's still too cool to sit outside?" Katja asked.

"Whatever you want. I am fine outside; I'm fine inside," Mendel smiled.

They got a table away from the street. Mendel ordered two glasses of wine and a plate of hummus with warm pita bread was spread with garlic butter.

"I was thinking I would study photography and journalism. But I'm not sure. If I get a job in that field I'll always be right in the middle of the fighting if there is another war."

"That's true. But what else would you want to do?"

"I'm not sure. I want to do so many things. But of course I must choose something that I will be able to work at once I'm finished. "

"Yes, that's very true. So what else do you have in mind?"

"Law . . . I think I would make a good lawyer."

"I think you could do whatever you set your mind to, Mendel. You're very smart."

"Now you're embarrassing me."

They both laughed.

"Let's get some food. I'm famished. What else would you like to order?" he asked.

Chapter 60

It became a ritual. On Friday nights, Mendel and Katja shared Shabbat dinner. Because they were homesick, they tried as best they could to recreate the Shabbat dinners of their youth. Mendel had a small apartment and it was easier to cook there than in the barracks. Together they prepared a suitable Sabbath dinner. Then Katja placed a lace shawl over her head, lit the candles, and said the prayers. After dinner, they often reminisced about the antics of their youth. They spoke with affection of Rachel. They both missed their blood sister.

On Sundays, they enjoyed the crystal blue water and the sparkling white sand of the beach. Mendel paid for the food and Katja prepared it and packed a picnic basket. Katja enjoyed having Mendel so close by. Often, after a difficult day at work, she would call him and they would meet for a quick dinner at one of the cafés near her office. He told her about school, she told him about work, and her time in the service seemed to fly by.

A big celebration in honor of Israeli Independence day was to take place in the center of town in Tel Aviv. There would be an abundance of food and drink, a parade, and music. All public offices were closed, including the university. Mendel and Katja agreed to meet at the site of the event at noon. Katja hated to be late and she wanted to be sure that she and Mendel would have good spots for the parade, so she left twenty minutes early.

When she arrived, the streets were already filled with people. The flag of Israel, bearing the blue Star of David, hung proudly from a post stuck in the middle of the square. Musicians had already begun playing and couples were dancing. Katja found two spots near the front. She sat down and placed her handbag on the ground next to her, saving it until Mendel arrived. Then she absentmindedly began to sing along with the music.

It was old familiar Yiddish folk music and it made her think of her parents. She missed them. Only one more year and she would be finished with her military service. Then she could return home. Perhaps she would return home permanently and teach, spend as much time with her parents as she could. As Katja sang softly to herself, lost in thought, she felt the warmth of the presence of someone come up behind her. Then she heard a deep male voice begin to sing along with the music.

Katja turned quickly, a little frightened at first.

"Hello, Katja."

She was stunned. She could hardly find her voice.

"Elan, how are you?" Katja asked.

Chapter 61

Konrad walked through the over-populated streets of Buenos Aires, looking around frantically. He was light-headed— his heart beat was elevated and he felt beads of sweat forming on his brow. What if he were being followed? What if they knew everything he was doing? His fellow Nazis would have no sympathy for him. There was never to be any sympathy for the weak, the weak must be weeded out, eliminated. There is no other way to build a master race. He could hear Hitler's speeches ringing in his head.

But the dream of the Third Reich had evaporated, the master race was dead. He must not allow himself to be choked up with fear. That was how mistakes were made. None of his fellow Nazis suspected him. Why would they? He had never shown any form of disloyalty to the party. And if he could find a way out, he would not be going to this meeting. However, when he was captured several months earlier by Mossad, he had been given the choice: Either he would betray his fellow Nazis, or the Israelis would kill him; quite simple. They'd tortured him, hurt him, and terrified him. Konrad had never realized that he had such a low tolerance for pain. It shamed him to remember, but he'd given up within a few minutes. He had made a promise to do whatever they asked if only they would stop the pain.

"Lie to us," the huge hulk of an Israeli said, "and we will find you again, but this time we will have no pity. We know where you live, and we know the places you go. I promise you, we will come for you. If you do not keep your promise to us you will be sorry." He did not doubt them for a moment. The Nazi party was going to hell, and he secretly doubted that the Third Reich would ever rise again. Konrad was not one to remain devoted to a hopeless cause, a political party that could no longer offer him anything. At that moment, staring into the endless black pool of the Israeli's eyes, Konrad had decided to do whatever he had to do in order to save himself.

Konrad took another quick look around. He was pretty sure he was alone, not followed. Then he rapidly slipped into the hallway of the run down high-rise and rang the bell for apartment #3, as the directions he'd received had instructed him to do.

Chapter 62

Mendel had made inquiries all around campus. He wanted to find a skilled and reputable jeweler. He was given some names and told that some of the finest diamond cutters had set up shop in Tel Aviv. He'd never had cause to consider making such an elaborate purchase before, and he wanted to be sure that he made a solid investment. Since Mendel's arrival in Tel Aviv, he'd been working between classes as a waiter at one of the more posh restaurants, saving as much money as he could. He wanted to buy the nicest diamond he could possibly afford.

On a silver-blue, cloudless day, Mendel strolled up and down the avenue gazing into the windows of the jewelry stores. He felt giddy and excited, but also a little crazy. How does one buy a diamond engagement ring for a girl he has never even kissed? It was not as if Mendel didn't know Katja. He felt that he knew her, and she knew him, better than anyone else in the world. Except maybe Rachel, but Rachel was different; Rachel was more like a boy. Katja had always been his special princess. When they were children, Katja had often come to talk to Mendel when she was upset about something. Rachel refused to acknowledge weakness and was always acting as if her spine was made of iron and she didn't understand emotional traumas. When Katja was distraught when her cat died, it was Mendel who had comforted her. He had held her in his arms, running his hand over her hair as she curled up into him. He'd soothed her with as much wisdom as he could muster, hoping to lighten her pain.

Although they had never kissed or dated, Mendel felt as if he and Katja were closer to each other than to anyone else in the world. Rachel had not told him when she began to menstruate, but Katja had. Well, she had not exactly come out and told him, but she was moody and out of sorts, and when he guessed she had admitted to him what was wrong. He'd gone to the kitchen and gotten her hot tea, bringing it back to her room; sitting with her while she had sipped even though boys were not allowed in the girls' rooms. He'd taken a chance of getting into serious trouble. But for Mendel, Katja was worth the risk. He'd tried to make her laugh, but she had been feeling so under the weather that he had coaxed her to rest. Then when she'd fallen asleep, he had covered her with a blanket and had watched her sleep.

Mendel knew how much Katja loved pretty things so he'd bought her a beaded sweater for Hanukah one year. She'd screamed with delight, hugging him tightly. For Mendel it had been one of the happiest moments of his life. So, he'd come to Tel Aviv for school, yes, but even more for Katja. Mendel was in love. He wanted to marry his best childhood friend, and he was going to buy a ring so that he had something to give her when he proposed.

Mendel Zaltstein opened the heavy door to the jewelry shop. A tall, thick man with a long dark beard, side burns that hung in spiral curls over his ears, and a black and silver yarmulke greeted him.

"Welcome. How can I help you?"

"I want to buy an engagement ring," Mendel said. His own voice sounded foreign to him, but the idea of marrying Katja felt so right.

Chapter 63

"So, how do you do it? You look even more beautiful than I remember," Elan said, smiling. His teeth were white and sparkling in the sunlight, against his olive skin. "You hurt my feelings, you know, when you disappeared that night we were supposed to have dinner." He wore his army uniform shirt open. His chest was filled with well-defined muscles, tan, and hairless.

"I know it was rude of me, I'm sorry. I couldn't meet you," Katja said. "I should have left a note."

"Yes, you should have told me. I think I deserved some sort of an explanation. After all, I did come all the way back to the office looking for you, and boom . . . the office is closed and Katja is gone." He looked at her with mock anger.

She shrugged. "I don't know what to say, except that I am sorry."

He laughed. "It's all right. I've already forgotten about it. In fact, I am glad to see you. May I sit?" he asked, indicating the chair Katja had saved for Mendel.

"I suppose so, until Mendel arrives."

Elan sat down.

"I didn't know you spoke Yiddish, yet you were singing the Yiddish song," she said. "I thought you were Sephardic, born and raised here in Israel."

"You're right. I don't speak Yiddish, but with the arrival of so many survivors from the camps in Europe, I can speak a little of lots of languages, and I can understand most of them fluently."

"Very impressive," she said, smiling.

"You are multi-lingual, too?"

"Yes, I am," she said, not knowing what to say. The conversation dragged, she was uncomfortable. He was handsome enough, probably the most handsome man she'd ever seen, but she didn't know what to say to him. It would be best if he just left and went on his way.

The band started another song, this one in Hebrew. "You know this song?" he asked her.

"No, I've heard it before, but I don't know the words."

Elan began to sing. Then he got up taking both of her hands and began to lead her in an Israeli folk dance. Katja laughed, trying to break away and sit back down although she had no reason to be embarrassed. Other people were dancing in the street. But she was embarrassed.

"Come on; dance this one dance with me? I promise if you do, I will go away."

She danced but as they danced, as she looked into his laughing eyes, she realized that she didn't want him to go away. By the time the music stopped they were both out of breath.

"Can I get you something to drink?" he asked.

"No, thank you. I'm going to wait for Mendel."

"I know I'm sticking my neck out and you're probably going to chop off my head, but can we maybe try this again?"

"The dance?" Katja asked.

"No, the dinner. One night this coming week, maybe you'll agree to have dinner with me?"

"Elan . . ."

"All right, so I should not have asked," he said, getting up to leave.

He looked so sad and dejected.

"Wait." She felt something stir inside of her. Katja was afraid that if she let him walk away this time he would never return.

He turned around. "Yes?"

Damn why was he so handsome?

"I'll have dinner with you."

"Tomorrow?"

"Yes, all right, tomorrow."

"How about I sit here with you during the parade?" Elan asked.

"Mendel is coming."

"I know; you told me. I know Mendel. It will be good to see him again."

Across the street someone had set up a game whereby the player took a ball and threw it at shelves that had been lined with stuffed animals; if the player successfully knocked one of the stuffed animals off a shelf, he or she won the toy that had been knocked off. Katja watched as the players paid their coins, only to leave without the stuffed bears or lions. Elan watched in silence as well.

"These boys don't have such good throwing arms," he said.

"No, they don't."

"Would you like to see how it's done?" Elan asked.

He was so damn arrogant, too.

"Sure." She almost hoped he would miss.

Elan leapt over the bleachers and down to the street. He took a coin out of his pocket and paid. The carnival barker gave him two balls. The first one he threw, he missed. Katja was watching, but he did not turn back to see her response. Instead, he took better aim. The second time he threw the ball he knocked over a bear. Then he paid again and this time he knocked over an animal with each of the two balls he threw. Elan took his prizes and made his way back up the bleachers to Katja.

"These are for you."

She laughed. "NOW YOU have quite an arm!"

"I suppose I do."

"How about this? I'll keep one and we can give the other two to some children walking by?"

"They're yours. Do with them what you will." He smiled. "Which one do you like best?"

She chose the tan lion with his thick mane and gave the two teddy bears to two sisters sitting a few feet away.

"I hope this is all right with you," She said.

"Of course it is. It reaffirms to me that you have a generous heart. Of course I've always known that you did . . ."

Just then Mendel walked over.

"Hello, Katja," Mendel said. "Sorry I'm late. I had something come up."

"Hello. I saved you a seat for the parade. Do you remember Elan?"

"Sure. You were dating Rachel, weren't you?" he asked. Katja thought she detected a slightly sarcastic tone in Mendel's voice as he looked at Elan, then at her and the stuffed lion.

"Yes, that was a few years ago."

"And now are you living here in Tel Aviv?"

"I'm stationed here; still in the service."

"You signed on for a fifth term?"

"Yes, I love this country of ours. I want to serve."

Mendel became quiet and more withdrawn while Elan dominated the conversation. All during the parade, instead of standing and cheering with the crowd, Mendel seemed distracted. Katja thought he had something on his mind, but Elan kept her engrossed in conversation, not giving her a chance to ask what was wrong. By the time the sun set and everyone gathered to watch the fireworks, Mendel had left, claiming he had a test the following day. Katja knew how hard he'd been working to gain acceptance into the law program, therefore she thought nothing of his leaving early.

Mendel walked back towards the university. Had he been naïve, believing that Katja was developing feelings for him? Before today everything seemed so right. They'd spent all of their spare time together. Today Elan had shown up from out of nowhere and Katja was different. She was laughing more, giggling almost. Elan had demanded all of her attention with his ridiculous stories about his platoon. He'd imitated voices of people walking by, and Katja had laughed. She'd laughed more than she'd ever laughed with Mendel.

Mendel felt alone, dejected, and foolish. His heart was heavy as he entered his dorm room and slammed the door behind him. Then he sat down on his small bed. Right next to the bed, on the nightstand, was the little box with the ring inside. He spotted it and felt the tears well up in his eyes. Fool, he thought. Picking up the box, he flung it at the wall. "Why, God? Why did you do this to me? You took my family, you took our home, then I finally found a little happiness, and you took that, too. Either you hate me and want me to be miserable or you don't exist at all," Mendel said aloud.

***

Katja felt the heat of Elan's thigh against hers as they sat on the bleachers. It sent shockwaves through her that unnerved her. She tried to move away slowly so that he would not notice, but he turned his head and looked directly into her eyes. The sky lit up with color as a multitude of fireworks exploded overhead in celebration of the day.

"It's beautiful, no?" Elan said, his eyes reflecting the lights.

"Yes very," Katja answered.

A thunderous sound roared as a million blue stars of David exploded across the sky. They both looked up.

"This country of ours fills me with such pride," Elan said.

"I know; me, too."

Elan turned to Katja. She was looking up in awe as another round of blue stars filled the sky. Then he took her into his arms. Katja felt her entire body go weak, melting into the strength of his muscles against her chest. When Elan kissed her, she felt a round of fireworks exploding inside her heart.

The following day, Elan and Katja went to a restaurant that Elan had suggested for dinner. They were escorted to a private table in the back that had a crisp linen table cloth. Elan pulled out the chair for Katja. The waiter handed them both menus. Katja felt awkward, not sure what to do, so she studied the menu quietly for a few moments.

"So what looks good?" Elan asked.

"I don't know. You've been here before? What's good?" She felt foolish, but she'd never been on a real date before. It was understood that Elan would pay the check, and she was uncomfortable as she went over the prices.

"Why don't I order for both of us? Is there anything that you don't like?"

"No, whatever you decide is fine." She smiled, feeling stupid.

"I promise you will enjoy your dinner," Elan said. He had such confidence.

For Katja, the times that she and Mendel had gone out for dinner had been like spending time with a brother. She'd never considered their evenings to be dates. It was easy for her to order, sometimes she offered to pay, but most times, Mendel refused. However, she never felt uncomfortable, it all just seemed natural. Perhaps it was because they'd grown up together.

Elan ordered far more food than she was used to eating. Besides, she was nervous, her stomach was a flutter and she felt as if she could hardly eat anything at all. Katja wiped her lips with the napkin several times, afraid that she had food on her face. Elan ate with gusto; he was not at all self-conscious.

"I'm glad you decided to finally have dinner with me," he said.

She smiled.

"You like the food here? I think it's the best in the city."

"It's very good."

"So tell me a little bit about you, Katja. You are such a mystery . . ."

"ME? A mystery? How? I am just a girl who grew up on a kibbutz, nothing more. No mystery."

"I think you have deep thoughts; tell me some of them. I would like to hear all of your secret inner feelings and thoughts," Elan said, leaning on his hand with his elbow on the table. Even as crude and outspoken as he was, Katja could not help but find him terribly sexy.

She laughed. "I don't know what you mean."

"I mean, what do you think about when you are alone? What are your dreams?"

"I don't know. I think this is rather personal," she said, clearing her throat.

"I'm sorry. I didn't mean to pry. It's just that I want to know everything there is to know about the beautiful Katja."

"Like I said, there isn't much to know."

"You and your family were survivors. Were you in the camps?"

"Yes, we were survivors. But I don't remember much. I don't know if we were in the camps. My parents don't talk about it, and I know it upsets them, so I don't ask. I was very young and it was so terrible that I guess I must have put it out of my mind because I don't remember anything at all. Except that we spent some time in a DP camp waiting to go to Israel. But it wasn't a concentration camp. Those are my first memories."

"I can understand."

"I often feel as if the Nazis stole my youth. I don't know if that makes sense."

"It does, they stole a lot from our people."

"Yes. That is for sure."

"All right, enough about the Germans. Let's talk about your bright future. So what do you want to do when you are done serving in the IDF?"

She shrugged. Gosh, she felt so boring. She'd not made any decisions about the future. She had nothing exciting to say. He was probably quite ready to drop her off back at her barracks. The very idea that he was losing interest was upsetting to her. But she had no idea of what to do or say. *I'm so clumsy, so inexperienced.*

"How about hunt Nazis?" Elan took a sip of wine.

"Me? You've got me mixed up with Rachel. I'm not much of a fighter. I wish I were, but when I tried to fire a rifle, I couldn't aim accurately and the sound was very loud," she said.

"I would love to do that, hunt Nazis I mean. In fact, I know of people who I would love for you to meet."

"Nazi hunters?"

"Not exactly. Can I take you somewhere exceptional this coming Sunday? There is something I want you to see."

"Where?"

"You'll have to trust me. Will you go?"

"All right; yes, I'll go."

"So, for now, let's put the past behind us. I have a real surprise for you, something we can do tonight . . ."

"You are full of surprises."

"This is going to be fun. It's something I think you will enjoy."

When they finished dinner Elan paid the check and helped Katja with her sweater. Then he took her elbow and they walked out into the night.

"It seems cooler then it was earlier. The temperature must have dropped," he said. "Are you cold?"

"A little," she said.

He took off his jacket and draped it over her shoulders.

They walked silently for a moment. The only sound was the click of Katja's high heels on the pavement.

"So where are we going?" she asked.

"You'll see."

They walked two blocks, and then turned left. Elan opened the door and led Katja inside. It was dark and smoky. He helped her down the stairs into a room that was filled with people. Very loud American music blasted from a jukebox, a machine with records that spun on a turntable inside.

"Do you know who this is?" he asked.

"Who *what* is?"

"The singer on the record that is playing."

"No idea. I've heard some music like this before, but not very often, and I don't know the musicians by name. "

"His name is Elvis Presley. How do you like the music?"

"I do," she said, watching a couple whirl and spin on the dance floor. "It has a great beat."

"Would you like to learn to dance like that?" Elan asked. "It's called the jitterbug."

"Yes, I've seen people do that dance, but I've never tried it myself." she said. Her heart was pounding to the beat of the music.

"Elan, come on over here," said a man wearing an IDF uniform who was sitting with a group of people.

"Shalom," Elan said. "Katja, this is my friend Seth."

"Shalom, Seth," Katja said.

"Well, isn't she a beauty?" Seth said. "Why don't you kids sit down?"

"Thank you," Katja said, glad it was dark so that no one could see her blush.

"So, who are all the others?" Elan asked.

"Let me introduce you . . ."

It would have been impossible to remember all of their names, especially along with trying to hear them above the music. A song came on the jukebox that Elan recognized. Without any warning he stood up and pretended to have a microphone in his hand as he did an imitation of Elvis Presley.

Love me tender, love me sweet, never let me go…" He sang along with the record in his heavily-accented English, making his way to the front of the room.

Everyone at their table and the surrounding tables roared with laughter as Elan's hips gyrated. Katja laughed, too. When the record was finished, Elan burst out laughing. As he headed back to his seat, the other guys patted him on the back.

"Great performance, Elvis," one of them teased.

"Thank you, thank you very much." Elan said, imitating Elvis Presley, his Israeli accent making the words even funnier.

It was plain to see that Elan was well-known and well-liked. How could such a strong man be so serious one minute, and so funny and lighthearted the next?

The beers that Elan ordered for Katja and himself arrived. He took a swig, and when the next song came on Elan took Katja's hand and led her to the dance floor where he began to teach her to dance. Elan was light on his feet, a true athlete. He spun her around, singing in her ear while she giggled.

Katja was not as graceful as she would have wished to be, so it took her a while to learn to jitterbug. However, Elan didn't mind. They danced until late into the night. When she returned to her room just as the sun was coming up, Katja decided that she loved American music, and . . . she loved Elan.

The following day Katja's boss laid a pile of work on her desk. She had never stayed out so late on a work night and her head ached with exhaustion. She began to sort through the papers when the phone rang. Her heart jumped in spite of how tired she was. It could be Elan.

She took a deep breath, calmed her voice, then picked up the phone and answered.

"Sergeant Greenberg's office, this is Katja speaking, how can I help you?"

"It's me. How are you?" It was Mendel.

Katja felt her heart sink with disappointment. "I'm all right. I was out late last night. I'm a little tired."

"Out with whom?" He tried to sound causal but it came out jealous and overbearing.

"Elan."

"Really? Elan again? You just saw him on Sunday."

"Yes, I know, we had dinner last night."

"And you were out late having dinner?" Mendel said.

This was not like Mendel. He was sounding like an old biddy, full of questions.

"We went dancing."

"You don't dance."

"He taught me. We went to a club to listen to American music."

"American music?"

"Yes, Elvis Presley, Chuck Berry, it's a lot of fun." She said, apologizing but not knowing why she was sorry.

"I see," Mendel said; his voice cold.

"Mendel, what's wrong with you?"

"Nothing. Nothing at all."

"You want to meet me for lunch today?"

"I can't. I have a class," he said, his voice distant.

"How about dinner?"

"I don't know. Aren't you having dinner with your brave soldier?"

"Elan?"

"Who else?"

"No, Mendel. I'm not. If you would like, I would love to have dinner with you."

"All right, let's have dinner." His voice was softer; she thought it almost sounded sad.

"Mendel, what's wrong?"

"Nothing; I'm just studying."

"Then we'll meet for dinner?"

"Yes, is six o'clock good for you?" he asked.

"It should be. I have a lot of work, but I'll manage," she said.

"Six o'clock then. I'll come by your office."

"See you then," she said.

He hung up.

Katja sat looking at the phone and listening to the dial tone. Perhaps Mendel was feeling left out now that Elan was in the picture. She shook her head. Men.

All morning Katja drank coffee on an empty stomach until her mouth tasted like spoiled milk. At lunch she forced herself to have a square of pita with hummus, but she was too tired to eat. And worse, she had not heard from Elan yet today. How silly of me, she thought. Why would Elan call me today? We have plans for Sunday, and it's only Tuesday. There is no reason for him to call. Yet she felt nervous, afraid that she'd done something wrong. Perhaps he'd lost interest. *How odd for me to feel this way*, Katja thought. *I'm hanging on to a man whom I hardly know. I need to stop this right now.*

But she couldn't.

She forced herself to get through the day. When Mendel arrived at ten to six, she smiled at him and tried to appear casual, but inside she was twisted up like a ball of yarn after a kitten had spent an hour playing with it. Katja thought that Elan would at least have telephoned sometime during the day, if only to say hello. *Stop . . . stop thinking about this! Why am I so crazy about this fellow? I don't even know him really.*

At first Mendel was cold towards her, but he warmed up after an hour or so. Katja tried to keep the conversation going with Mendel, regardless of the inner conflict about Elan that was tearing her up.

"How was your test?" she asked.

"I did well, I think."

"I know you did, Mendel. You've always been very smart."

"There is a lot of competition to get into law school. I hope I make it."

"You will. I have confidence in you," she said. She thought she saw his eyes grow moist.

"Thanks, Kat," he said, his voice cracking ever so slightly.

When she got back to her room, Katja took a hot bath. She was beyond tired, yet when she lay down to sleep, she couldn't rest. How could she have such strong feelings for Elan, having just met him? Why was she so upset that he had not called? She stared out the window at the top of the tree that was moving gently in the night breeze. *This is ridiculous.* She turned over, forcing her eyes shut. *I need to sleep. I have to work tomorrow and I don't want to be as drained as I was today.* After an hour of tossing and turning, she finally drifted off to sleep.

Elan did not call the following day or the one following that.

Katja was distraught.

Katja only worked a half day on Friday because of Shabbat. True to form, on the day of the Sabbath, Mendel called in the morning, asking what he could pick up from the store for their dinner. Katja went through the motions of planning with him. If she did not hear from Elan by the end of the day, he would not be able to reach her until Sunday morning. She thought he would have been more careful to secure their plans if he intended to keep them. Maybe he didn't intend to keep the plans at all. Maybe he was punishing her for the time she stood him up for dinner. By noon, she was almost in tears. *Why do I care so much? A week ago I didn't even think about Elan. He is nobody to me; nobody at all.* Her hands were cold as ice as she straightened up the office, getting ready to close for the weekend.

The office door opened. "Delivery for Katja Zuckerman," said a jittery teenage boy who had a face full of pimples. He entered with a long white box.

"I'm Katja Zuckerman," Katja said.

"Sign here."

She did.

Katja knew she should have her boss inspect the box before opening it; there was always the chance that it could contain a bomb. That was protocol. But her boss had left and she couldn't wait until Monday, so she took a chance and opened it anyway. Inside were a dozen red roses. Her hands trembled so much she could hardly open the card.

I just wanted to let you know that I'm thinking about you and looking forward to seeing you on Sunday. I will be at the barracks to pick you up at 1 p.m. We'll have lunch first, and then I'll take you to a very special place. See you then, Elan

She held the card to her chest and a tear fell on her cheek.

Chapter 64

Konrad felt a chill snake up the back of his neck as he looked into the unyielding eyes of the Mossad agent, eyes so black that Konrad could not distinguish the pupil. There was no doubt in Konrad's mind that the Israeli would kill him and not think twice.

"So, tell me . . . what have you arranged?" The agent held a rifle, which was not pointed at Konrad, but just the presence of the gun reminded Konrad of the threat.

Three other agents surrounded Konrad. As he looked from one to the other, he felt his throat close as if he were being smothered. Konrad coughed in an effort to gain his voice, cleared his throat, and tried to speak, but no sound came from his lips.

The Mossad agent laughed. "You see how you feel right now? This is how all of the Jews you executed must have felt. Did you ever have any pity? Ever, Klausen? Ever when you looked into the eyes of the old women? Or how about the little children; so young, so helpless?"

Konrad was choking. His eyes were red and water ran from them and from his nose. He knew he was staring directly into the face of death. He knew it now and he knew if before, when Mossad had captured him and given him this deal. That was why Konrad Klausen had agreed to the terms without a fight.

"Listen Klausen, it's as simple as this. I want your Nazi friends and you want to live. So, you give me what I want and I give you what you want. You don't deliver, and well . . . then you die. Quite simple, really."

Konrad watched the agent move around him like a panther. He'd never been so afraid, never felt so vulnerable. And the worst part of it all was that he knew how much this Israeli hated him. If he looked into those onyx eyes deeply enough, he could see the faces of the Jews he'd killed.

"Speak, you bastard." The agent was becoming impatient. "I don't have all the time in the world to sit here and wait for you."

"I have Blau for you." Konrad strangled the words out of his closed throat. "Perhaps I can get Mengele and Eichmann too, maybe more. I'll get as many as I can . . . please . . . don't hurt me." Konrad thought he must sound like a dying bird.

"Not bad work, Klausen. I have to give you that much. I'd heard that you were an easy mark, a coward. That's good for our cause; it makes you willing to betray anyone to save your own hide." The Mossad agent looked at one of the other agents. "I knew Manfred Blau was not dead. He is posing as Dolf Sprecht."

The other Mossad agent, a short, muscle-bound man with a bald head, spoke from behind Konrad's chair. "What about Heim, you slimy bastard?"

"I don't know about Heim, but I'll try."

"Try hard, Klausen. Your worthless life depends upon it."

Konrad wondered how they knew that Manfred was living under another name. He wondered if they already knew the alias for Mengele and Eichmann as well. He assumed that they did. They somehow seemed to know everything.

"How soon can you bring Blau to us?" the one with black eyes spoke.

"I don't know. I have to arrange things."

The Mossad agent nudged Konrad hard in the ribs with the butt of his rifle. "I said how soon?"

"How soon do you want him?"

"Next month. I'll give you one month. That's all you get."

"Next month then," Konrad said. "I'll have him for you by next month."

"You better."

"I will," Konrad said, rubbing his ribs where the soldier had bruised him.

"You told Blau what we told you to tell him, right? You said that Hitler was alive and that he was to help you aid the son of a bitch in an escape?"

"Yes, I told him what you told me to tell him." Konrad felt the sweat beading on his brow.

"We want them all, but we'll take Blau for now. Work on the others. I expect a lot more from you. I'll be in contact with you to give you your instructions."

Konrad nodded. "How will you find me?"

"We know where you live. We'll find you. And if you don't come through . . . well, like I said, we'll find you."

Konrad shivered. Just how much did they know about the places he went and the things he did? The favela? Did they know about the favela? Did they know about his having sexual relations with other men? Would they ever reveal that? The thought sent a pang of fear up his spine. Maybe they were just toying with him, and they already knew how to find the others, because if they were following him that would lead them right to the other Nazis. Or maybe they were just faking; maybe they didn't know where he was living. Konrad was afraid to ask any questions, he couldn't wait to leave, to run out of this terrible place; to escape from the feelings of weakness that were squeezing his heart. Maybe, just maybe, they knew where all of the Nazis were and they just wanted Konrad to betray his loyalty to the party, to show how pathetic he was. There were so many different possibilities, but no answers.

"Get out of here you snail, you can go now. If we find out that this plan has been compromised in any way, you can consider yourself a dead man. So don't try anything foolish. Understand, Nazi boy?"

"Yes," Konrad panted.

"Go."

Konrad ran out the door of the building. Once outside he leaned against the brick wall trying to catch his breath. He liked Blau, but he had no choice; it was Blau or him. A stream of urine ran down the leg of his pants, pooling on the sidewalk. Konrad hated himself for what he must do.

Chapter 65

Sunday morning came and the sun burned in the sky like a golden fire. Katja bathed and then put on her prettiest dress. It was white with a pattern of red roses gathered to accent her tiny waist. Even though her hair had natural curls, she'd set it in pin curls the night before to make them even more defined. She took two tortoiseshell hair combs that her mother had given her as a gift and pulled her hair back on each side securing it with the combs. Then she looked in the mirror and applied a light coat of red lipstick, which she then put into her handbag. Satisfied with her appearance, she brewed a pot of coffee and waited for Elan to arrive.

He was on time, one o'clock exactly.

"You look wonderful," he said.

"Thank you."

"Are you hungry?"

"I am, in fact." Katja had been so excited that she'd forgotten to eat breakfast.

"Good. I have a great place for lunch."

Elan opened the car door and helped Katja inside. Then they rode up the coast. The sea met the sky like a bed of sapphires against a softly waving blanket of blue topaz. Rising up behind the water were golden mountains as strong and as old as the holy land itself. Elan reached for Katja's hand and gently squeezed it.

"Our home is a beautiful place."

"It is," she said.

They stopped at a small café right on the water. The host sat them at a table outside with a large red and white umbrella and matching tablecloth.

"Do you know what you would like?" Elan asked, after Katja had a few minutes to look at the menu.

She shrugged. "You've been here before?"

"Yes, would you like me to order?" he asked.

"I would," she said. Katja liked it when Elan took charge.

They ate salad made from large chunks of ruby red tomatoes and crisp cucumbers that tasted as fresh and cool as the breeze off the water. Then they had falafel and hummus rolled in pita bread. Elan ordered so much food that Katja felt as if she would burst.

"I can't possibly eat another bite."

He laughed. "You hardly ate at all."

"But I did."

He laughed again. His appetite was hearty.

When they finished, Elan opened the car door and Katja slid back into the passenger seat. As he went around to hop in on the driver's side, she quickly reapplied her lipstick. It was so strange for her to be this concerned about her appearance.

Elan turned on the radio and he sang along with the American tunes that Katja had heard the other night. She loved the rhythm.

"I wish I could take you to see some of these singers when they play live," he said.

"Do they come to Israel?"

"I don't know, but I am going to keep my eyes open. And if they do, then we'll go."

She smiled at him. He had an easy baritone voice, with lots of beat. She'd never slept with a man, but Elan ignited a desire inside of her that made her think of things she'd never tried.

"We're here," Elan said, pulling the car up to a building in the middle of the desert. "It's a kibbutz."

"I can see that," she said. "So, why are we here?"

"You'll see," he said, getting out of the car. He opened her door and reached for her hand. "Come…let me show you something."

Katja walked beside him, the heels of her shoes sinking into the earth. He helped her up a hill and they entered the white stone building.

"Elan!" a male voice called out. "Shalom."

"Shalom," Elan answered. "I brought a friend."

"I can see that, and a pretty one."

Elan laughed. "That she is. This is Katja. She shares your last name."

"Zuckerman?"

"Yes, I am Katja Zuckerman," Katja said.

"This is Yitzhak Zuckerman, any relation?" Elan asked.

"I don't think so," Katja said. "But, shalom, it's nice to meet you."

"Follow me; I'd like you to meet my wife," Yitzhak said.

They walked through a long hall and out the back door.

"Zivia," Yitzhak called. "Elan's here and he has brought with him a friend."

A woman, prematurely aged but still beautiful—with wavy dark hair sprinkled with threads as silver as the leaves of the olive trees—came walking over. Her eyes were gently mapped with spiderweb lines and when she focused her gaze on Katja it felt as if Zivia could see into her soul.

"This is my wife, Zivia," Yitzhak said. "This is Elan's friend, Katja."

"Shalom."

"Shalom and welcome to our humble home," Zivia said, tilting her head.

Just then an attractive man came over and hugged Elan. "Shalom, my brother," he said.

"Katja, this is Tuvia. Watch out for him, he's a flirt."

Tuvia laughed. "Shalom, Katja. Welcome."

"Shalom," she said.

"Let me get you something to eat," Zivia said.

"We just ate, but thank you," Elan answered.

"But you must eat. Come, at least you'll have some fruit. I insist," Yitzhak said.

They followed him into the kitchen.

Katja felt the immediate welcome of a warm embrace from Elan's friends.

They all sat down at a handmade wooden table while behind them a big fan circulated the air. In a few minutes, Zivia brought out a platter of oranges, persimmons, and bananas, all ripe, fresh, and appealing.

"I brought Katja here because I wanted you to tell her your stories. It's important to me that she understands why I feel I must stay in the army and defend this country, even if I ever take a wife," Elan said.

Katja shot him a glance. A wife?

"Our stories." Yitzhak nodded his head and sighed. He knew that he must keep telling the world what had happened so that it was never forgotten. "Hmm . . . all right. Katja would you like to hear a story?"

She smiled. "Of course." She had no idea what Elan had in mind, but she could see him out of the corner of her eye and his face was grave and serious.

"Then I am going to tell you," Yitzhak said.

"You know what this place, this kibbutz, is called?" Yitzhak spread his arms, indicating the land that they were on.

She shook her head.

"This is the Kibbutz of the Ghetto Fighters. You know what the Warsaw Ghetto was?"

"No," Katja said.

"When the Nazis came and took us from our homes, they put us all in a ghetto. My wife, Zivia, Tuvia, and I were in the Warsaw Ghetto uprising."

Katja sat glued to his every word.

"Let me start at the beginning. So, the Gestapo would come to the house of a Jew and force everyone to leave. Then the Nazis would steal everything that the Jews had in their house. But more importantly, they sent the Jews to ghettos. These were small areas enclosed by walls and barbed wire. The three of us, Zivia, Tuvia, and I, met in the ghetto in Warsaw, Poland. It was a terrible place, dirty, full of disease with no way to escape . . . but the worst part about it was the "quotas." What *are* quotas you ask?"

She shrugged her shoulders.

"Well, you see, the Nazis had plans for us. Plans we knew nothing about. We only knew that every day, the trains were loaded with people. The Judenrats, these were Jews who worked with the Nazis, had to make lists of the names of people who they chose to send on the trains. Every day they had to meet a quota. The Judenrats were bastards who were willing to sell out their own people to save themselves. They were dangerous; we had to watch out for them. In many ways, they were worse than the Nazis.

Anyway, so back to the story . . . These people, the ones that were chosen to be sent on the trains, they were being sent to extermination camps. At first, we didn't know. But later, we did. You know what is an extermination camp?"

Katja had heard a little about the camps from the survivors. They didn't like to talk about it very much. "I know a little."

"Well, the Nazis had decided that we Jews had no right to live. So they were going to annihilate our entire race. In fact, they were very systematic about it."

She had heard bits and pieces. Katja nodded her head.

"They built camps, concentration camps. Some of the camps were work camps and some were strictly death camps. Now, not that you couldn't die in a work camp, because even if you were valuable to the Nazis they might kill you anyway, but if you had a skill that they needed, you had a better chance of surviving. We, in the ghetto, still didn't know about these camps yet." He shrugged, throwing his hands up.

"Anyway, so, every day the box cars were loaded, so full that the people had to stand crushed together without air, food, or water. In the summer, I was told it was so hot that all the babies would die well before the trains arrived at the camp. All of us in the Ghetto were seeing these trains, but still we didn't know where they were going until escapees from the camps came to tell us. At first, we didn't believe them. We didn't want to believe them. They said that there were mass executions in gas chambers; hundreds of people killed at a time, then the bodies burned in crematoriums right in the camps. This news terrified us, but at the same time, it empowered us. We knew we were doomed, whether we were chosen to go on the train that day or the next, we would all eventually be killed. Having this knowledge helped us make a decision.

"We had secret meetings, meetings we had to keep from the Judenrats. But a lot of people joined; at one of these meetings, we all decided that if we were to die, then we were going to die fighting. We had to make a plan; yes? So, we all met in an apartment in one of the buildings. We discussed how we would kill as many Nazis as possible before they did us all in. But how? Where and how could we get guns? When should we rebel?

"Passover was coming and most of us were trying to make plans for a small celebration, but when we understood that the Nazis were planning to kill all the Jews, we decided to put our holiday plans on hold. Instead, we chose Passover as the date of our uprising. We learned that the Nazis were going to liquidate the ghetto, send in their troops, and take all of us to camps where we would surely die.

"As fate would have it, they planned to do this on the eve of Hitler's birthday, April 19, 1943. Ahh . . . we knew this was the perfect day for a fight. We decided to give Hitler a real surprise, a birthday present he would never forget. There were seven hundred and fifty of us. We would be going against a well-trained, well-armed troop of at least twice as many Germans," Yitzhak said.

"Now, for me, this was a hard thing to do, not because I was afraid to die, but because for the first time in my life, I had found love and I was afraid for the life of the woman I loved. I didn't want to see her hurt; I couldn't bear the thought of her suffering. Zivia was all I had; she had become my whole world. If I it became necessary or had been possible, I would have died to save her from our bleak future in the ghetto or the camps. But, of course, this was not an option. In the Warsaw Ghetto, my life was worth less than the trash in the streets, so I had no bargaining power. I talked to Zivia after the meeting, I held her hands, and I looked into her eyes. I told her of my fears; I told her that I was powerless to save her. I cried. I could do nothing else. So, I cried. She held me. She was and is a strong woman, my Zivia.

"Then she insisted that we had to fight. 'If we don't go down fighting, she said, than the Nazis will have won.' I knew that there was no other option so I nodded in agreement and said a quiet prayer to God in hopes that Zivia would not be killed. I didn't sleep well that night or the nights that followed. But we, all of us Jews, began to prepare for what was to be the biggest uprising against Hitler that the Nazis had ever known.

"We started to buy guns and ammunition on the black market, most of them from the Polish underground; they hated the Nazis almost as much as we did. We stored the guns and ammunition. In order to make the Nazi guards think there were more of us than there really were, we decided to set up shooting posts all over the ghetto. Many of these posts were to be manned by just one person, a man or a woman, but because the gunfire would come from all over the place, the sons of bitches would think there were lots of us, yes? It was our plan.

"Everything was set to go. We dug underground escape routes that led into the forest. We were prepared to leave the ghetto or die trying. Either way, we would not go into the train cars willingly.

"On the day that the fighting began, the soldiers came strutting through the ghetto, clicking their heels. I can still see them, so proud and arrogant; Hitler's superior race at work. I remember turning to Zivia and taking her hand, kissing her palm, then kissing her lips gently, cherishing the moment and holding her close to me. I said, and I can still remember the words 'Zivia, I love you, and if we are to die today, then I pray that God will let us die together.'

"She held me close. When I finally let go, I saw that her face was wet with tears. I kissed those tears one by one. Still, I can taste the salt on my tongue. You see, we did not know if we would be alive the next day. My biggest fear was that I would survive and she would not. And I was so afraid, because life without her would have been unbearable.

We made it through the first day. You should have seen the faces on those Nazis when they were walking through the ghetto as they always did, unaware, unafraid, and then the shooting began. At first they just stood there, they couldn't believe we were fighting back. Then, you know what they did, they ran . . ." He laughed. "They ran."

He laughed again. "You should have seen the cowards in their uniforms, running down the street."

He slammed his fist on the table. "It was such a gratifying sight to see. But they came back and the fighting escalated. We fought with everything we had; men, women, and even children fought side by side. We fought so hard that they couldn't beat us. In fact, Hitler called out his army. Would you believe it? He needed his army to fight against a small group of starving, poorly-armed Jews. He set them on us, but still we continued, with homemade bombs, with whatever ammunition we had gathered. We rained down on them like the fires of hell. For a month we held them off. It was a tremendous victory. There were dead Nazis in the streets.

"But then they bombed the synagogue. The blast and the fire lit up the sky like it was the end of the world, the buildings shook from the blast. The Nazis took torches and ran through the streets, starting fires that sent black smoke swirling through the tiny apartments where we huddled. Our ammunition was almost gone. We knew we were close to being finished. So . . . with one last ditch effort we blasted them with all we had. Then, those of us who could get out, escaped through the underground tunnel into the forest. The smoke from the fires was so thick that you could not see in front of you. I remember I grabbed Zivia's hand and we ran coughing and choking, our faces blackened with smoke, through the underground tunnel. Zivia fell and I lifted her into my arms and carried her the rest of the way. I don't know how we made it out. There was no air to breathe.

"Once we entered the forest, I coughed and vomited. Zivia was not conscious so I continued to carry her. It seemed as if I ran for hours, but I cannot tell you how long it was before I finally stopped, falling over into the cool grass, hidden by the trees of the forest. For a few minutes, we both lay there. I thought she was dead. I didn't want to know if she was. I wanted to believe that she was alive. I prayed, I cried. And then suddenly, from out of nowhere, the hand of God reached down and blessed us, and Zivia began gasping for air. I held her in my arms and patted her back until she vomited black mucus. Then Zivia began to laugh between coughing, and I, too, began to laugh. We kissed, mixing the sweat and ash on our faces. Both of us were filled with joy. We were alive, and with the help of God, we were together."

"For the next two years, Zivia and I joined with a group of partisans living off the fat of the land. It was there that we found my dear friend, Tuvia again. We were so happy to see that he, too, had survived. We all stole what food we could find from local farms, fished in streams when we could, ate lots of raw potatoes, but most of all we kept moving. The winters were hard, but we made it, and when the war was over Zivia and I wanted no part of Europe any more. It had been our dream to come to Palestine, and so once Palestine became Israel, we came here, to our homeland, and built this kibbutz in honor of the uprising and to remember those who died in the battle."

Katja could not speak. The story had moved her to tears. She looked over at Zivia who was smiling at her.

"I know it's a sad story," Zivia said, "But it is a happy one, too. We are here, here in Israel. Home at last. And, we are the lucky ones. We didn't end up in the camps like lots of others did."

Katja bent her head; she had no words for the emotions that were running through her.

"Is this your first time on a kibbutz?" Zivia asked.

"I was raised on one."

"So you must have met lots of survivors, yes?"

"My parents are survivors. But I don't know their story; they don't like to talk about it. And most of the others don't want to discuss what happened either."

Zivia nodded. "Yes, that is quite common. Do you want to know more, do you want to know what happened to the others?"

"Yes and no. I feel like I should know, but it frightens me," Katja said. "I have heard bits and pieces of stories on the Kibbutz, but my mother always tried to protect me. She would discourage people from talking about their experiences in front of me."

"It is frightening, but so that this never happens again, it is important that the young people know and that they tell their children and their children tell their children, and so on and so on. You understand. Only through knowledge can we prevent this from ever happening again . . . and, of course, most importantly we are protected because we have a homeland, we have Israel."

Katja felt her heart swell with pride, tears came to her eyes. These were her people. This was her legacy.

"Come with me. I have others who will tell you their stories, too."

Katja turned to Elan. "You want to go? You want to know?" he asked.

She nodded. "Yes."

He nodded. "Go then. I'll stay here with Yitzhak. I've already heard all the stories."

Zivia wrapped her arm in Katja's and took her outside. They walked across the land until they came upon a man picking apples.

"Anshel, Shalom," Zivia said.

"Shalom," he answered. He was sun browned and, except for his honey brown hair, he reminded Katja a little of her father.

"Come down from that ladder. I have someone I want you to meet," Zivia said.

Anshel climbed down. Although he was probably in his mid thirties his face was deeply lined, giving him the appearance of a much older man.

"This is Katja. Katja this is Anshel."

"Shalom."

"Shalom."

"I know that you are busy, but I've brought Katja to see you so that you could tell her what happened when you were in Auschwitz."

His face that only a moment ago had seemed alight with joy, now turned dark with memories.

"Auschwitz," he said, his shoulders slumped. Shaking his head, he repeated "Auschwitz."

Chapter 66

A black rotary phone with large-print numbers sat on an old desk made of wood that had long ago lost its luster. It began to ring. It was the office of Mossad.

"I believe that I have some credible information about Eichmann's whereabouts." It was Simon Wiesenthal. "The source is reliable. From what I understand, he is living in Argentina."

"How do you know this?"

"His son was dating a girl. The boy bragged about his father being the famous Nazi who murdered Jews. It just so happened that the girl was Jewish. She told her father and he came to me. He said that Eichmann is living under the alias Richard Klement and working in a factory in Buenos Aries."

"Very interesting. Do you have any information about Blau or Mengele?"

"Nothing on either one."

"We'll check this all out. Then we'll take care of it," the Mossad agent said.

"Good."

Chapter 67

"So you want to hear my story?" The man did not look at Katja; instead he stared out across the land.

"Only if you want to tell me. I understand if it is too hard for you."

"Hard for me? Yes, it is hard for me to talk about it. The truth is that my time in Auschwitz is never far from my mind."

"My parents are survivors, but they have never told me their story. I've always assumed it was too hard to talk about."

"Yes, yes . . ." he said, "Auschwitz."

Anshel sat still and gazed across the fields. It was afternoon and the brightness of the day had begun to fade. For a long time he said nothing. Katja could smell the faint scent of apples.

"Sit down." Anshel motioned to the ground as he sat in the shade of an apple tree. Katja and Zivia sat beside him. "So, maybe you have heard of the Angel of Death?"

Katja shook her head. "No."

"His real name was Dr. Joseph Mengele, but we called him the Angel of Death; he was the most sadistic person I have ever met. I saw him for the first time, when I got out of the boxcar with my mother and my twin sisters Charna and Zusa. My father had been blessed to have passed away in the influenza epidemic a few years earlier. At least he never saw what happened to his family. Alava Shalom, he should rest in peace. After my father died, I at age fourteen had become the man of the house. This was quite a responsibility for a young boy, yes?"

Katja nodded.

Before the war, we lived in small village in Poland. My mother did housekeeping and cared for a wealthy woman who lived a few miles away from our little cottage. This woman lived in a big fancy house. I remember her; she was a nice lady who was very sick and she couldn't walk. She gave us extra money, clothes, things, you know, especially when she celebrated Christmas. I can't say anything bad about that woman. A good heart, she had. When my father died, my mother was so brokenhearted that she couldn't work anymore. In fact, she had a hard time getting out of bed, so I left school and went to work in a factory, a textile factory. My twin sisters were eight years old, beautiful girls." He sighed. "Oy."

Katja heard the pain in his sigh and almost wanted to ask him to stop, but he began to speak again. "So, anyway, we didn't have much, but we managed. It was not a year later that the Nazis invaded Poland. They came and they made us register, they took us from our homes, and then we were sent to a ghetto right in the center of town in the city of Lodz. The ghetto life was rough. The Nazis gave us rations that were not nearly enough to feed us, but I was young and strong so I worked with the black market bringing in food and necessities from the outside. Some of what I brought I sold and the rest my family used to survive. At night, I climbed over the rooftops and was back inside the walls by morning. Because I did this we had a little extra; it made things easier.

"Then the Nazis began to liquidate the ghetto. Little by little, the people were sent away. When our turn came to go, I was afraid to fight back. They told us lies. They said they were relocating us to work camps. I wanted to believe. I thought to myself that we would be of more use to them as workers than we were in the ghetto. Who would ever think that they planned to murder all of us? Who could believe such a thing? "

He pulled a piece of grass from the ground and studied it for a moment, rolling it in his fingers, and then he continued.

"Like I said, my mother, my sisters, and I were loaded into a boxcar filled with people. The stink was so bad from the excrement, the urine, the vomiting, and the sweat that I could not stop gagging for the entire first day. The car was made of wood slats and only tiny pinpoints of light came through. We had no windows so we could not see anything and we had no idea where we were headed. It was summer and the heat was smothering. For eight days, we rode in that filthy train car. Amongst us were the bodies of those who'd died along the way, and the bodies of those who were dying. There were buckets filled with excrement that splattered as the train jolted along.

"But most of all, I remember the distinct smell of fear. Fear has a smell, you know. If you have never smelled it, you would not understand. But once you have, you will never forget it. The ride was terrible, but when the train rolled to a stop, the anticipation and then the reality of the horror of what came next was even worse. Outside we heard the harsh German guards hollering commands at the people who'd been taken out of the boxcar in front of ours. My mother squeezed my hand. 'Stay with your sisters Anshel; don't let them take the girls away from you.'"

"'You'll be with us, Mama,' I said.

"'Perhaps, but if not, you stay with your sisters. Promise me, Anshel . . .' my mother said. I don't know what she was expecting, or what she felt instinctively, but her eyes were glowing with tears. More than anything, I wished there were something I could do to stop what was happening to us. I hated to see her in such distress, my poor mother. She had suffered so much when she lost my father.

"But before I could say another word, the rickety wooden door of our boxcar rolled open. 'Mach schnell; schnell. Schnell,' one of the guards yelled. 'Come on you swine; get out of this stinking car. Only a pig could live like this. There were guards with guns everywhere. They prodded us out into the sunlight. After having spent so much time in the dark, it was hard for my eyes to adjust. I was squinting and could barely keep my balance.

"When my eyes finally focused, I saw a big sign in front of me. It said: "Work Makes You Free." This sign was in German, of course. My mother grabbed my hand and I held the hand of my sister who held the hand of her twin. One of the guards pushed us forward and we were forced into a line of people.

"'Men over here; women over here.' One of the guards indicted two lines. 'He is only a boy,' my mother said, as the guard tried to push me into the other line. 'Please let him stay with us.' The guard ignored her, pushing me with the butt of his rifle. 'Get into the other line, schnell,' he roared.

"I released my mother's hand. I was about to go to the other side and then . . . he walked over, Dr. Mengele, wearing a perfectly pressed, crisp white lab coat. Not a wrinkle, in spite of the heat. On his hands he wore clean, white cotton gloves. 'I'll take this from here,' he said to the guard, waving him off with a flick of his hand. What a handsome man. He was tall with thick dark hair, deep penetrating eyes that were a mixture of hazel and green, and such a winning smile. At the time, I didn't know who he was but I was to learn soon enough. This was the Angel of Death, Dr. Joseph Mengele. Nu?

"So you would think that evil would be ugly, isn't that right? You would expect a monster. I know Jews don't believe in the devil, but I have my own thoughts on that. I believe that the devil is real, and he comes in many forms. Rarely is he ugly. Instead, he is handsome and winning, so as to confuse the world. When you look at Mengele, you say to yourself, how could such a good-looking, refined person be a demon? Ahh…but he was, Mengele was a demon of the worst kind; an evil spirit, a dybbuk, who got pleasure from torturing children and invalids. He loved to lord over the weak and helpless, giving them pain, while at the same time pretending to save them. Of all the Nazi criminals, I think maybe he was the worst. Or maybe I just think so because of what he did to my family and me.

"'Twins?' He said. I can still hear him, his voice was calm and gentle, but his eyes became excited, bright and flashing. 'Such beautiful twins. You can call me uncle. Uncle Mengele.'"

"Mengele touched my sister Charna's cheek and she cringed. 'No need to be afraid of me,' Mengele said. 'Here.' He reached into his pocket and took out two pieces of candy, one for each of my sisters. Then he looked over at me. 'How inconsiderate of me,' he said and he took out another piece of candy and gave it to me. I took it, skeptical, but I dared not ask any questions.

'You three come with me,' he said, indicating my sisters and me. Then he called over the guard. 'Send her to the left,' he said, pointing to my mother. At the time, I didn't understand, but later I learned that he had just sent my mother to the gas chamber. She died that day."

Katja put her hand to her throat. "My God," she whispered.

"Yes, all day long Mengele stood with his white gloves, pointing to the left for this one, to the right for that one. It was he, this Angel of Death, who would decide who should live and who should die."

Katja thought about her parents. Had they gone through this? Had they met this terrible doctor?

"Mengele separated us, the boys and the girls. My sisters went one way and I went the other. You see, I have this hump in my back, and it attracted him. He loved deformities, so he decided that I was a worthy subject. He would let me live so that he could use me for his experiments. I went to the boys' special barracks, a place where he kept what he called 'his children.' These were his special ones, his favorites. First of all, he loved his twins, but he also liked the deformed, hunchbacks, cripples, dwarfs, you understand?

"Outside the window of the boys' barracks was a large stone building, and from the top of it foul-smelling, thick, black smoke poured out into the air. I asked one of the other boys about it; he was a twin. I said, 'What is that building?' I had never seen such a thing. To me it looked like it was on fire inside. I will never forget the boy's answer to my question: 'It's the crematorium where they burn the bodies of the Jews they murder. When Mengele is done with us, he'll kill us, too, and that is where they will burn our remains.' The boy paused, then went on, 'You see me?' the boy said. 'I can't walk anymore. I used to walk, but one day Mengele did an operation on me, and now my spine is twisted. Soon he will finish me off.' I had no idea what this all meant. Still, even now, I can remember the icy fear that crept up the back of my neck; it felt like a frozen fingernail scratching ever so slightly; I shivered.

"A few weeks later, I met one of the Sonderkommandos; this was what they called the Jews that were forced to work in the crematorium. He told me that my mother's body had probably been burned that very first day, perhaps even as I sat looking out the window at the angry red smoke filling the sky.

"Every day I tried to get a glimpse of Carna or Zusa, but I could never see them. Meanwhile, Mengele began to take an interest in me. I had no idea at the time what he had planned, only that he came every day and brought us candy, and asked us to hug him. He seemed so kind, I began to trust him. Then one day, he took me to what he called his operating theater. There he did something to me that I will never forget." Tears began to form in Anshel's eyes. "He took a thin tube of glass and inserted it in my (you'll excuse my being so graphic) penis while I was fully awake. I was crying and begging him to stop, the pain was terrible. Then he broke the glass. I cannot begin to tell you what that felt like. I remember hearing someone scream. It took a few minutes to realize that the sound was coming from my own throat.

Next, I felt a needle enter my testicles. It was unbearable. Mengele was smiling. I can still see his face. He was enjoying my suffering.

"After that horrifying experience, I was taken to the hospital. There I was given something to calm me down. I passed out. When I awoke, I had trouble urinating. I've had trouble since. And of course, I cannot produce children. That should be the end of my story, no? But it isn't. My sisters, my dear sisters," he sighed.

"Do you want to go on?" Zivia asked.

Anshel nodded. "I was still in the hospital when I saw Charna. She was sick, filled with blisters. She was so weak that she could not speak. Charna, happy, cheerful Charna. I couldn't believe it was her. Charna, who had always been the one to sing and dance. She lay there motionless. That night Zusa snuck into the hospital. I saw her. I was weak, too, but I called out 'Zusa, it's me, Anshel.'

She came over with tears in her eyes. 'He, Mengele, gave Charna a shot that gave her this disease. He is giving it to one twin of each of the sets of twins. He says he is trying to find a cure. All I know is my sister is dying. And now you, too, Anshel.' She began to cry. I couldn't believe how thin she'd gotten. We, Mengele's special children, got better food than anyone in the camp, but I figured that she had stopped eating. I tried to reach up and take her hand, but I was too weak. She leaned down and kissed my forehead. 'If Charna is going to die, I want to die with her,' she explained. I tried to protest, but she wouldn't listen.

"Zusa climbed into the tiny bed beside Charna and she cuddled into her. From where I lay, I remember thinking that was how they must have been together when they were in the womb. I did not hear them speak, but I knew that they had a special way of communicating with each other. They had always had it, from the time they were babies. By morning, Zusa was sick. I heard her coughing, hacking. When Mengele saw what she had done, he pulled Zusa out of the bed and threw her on the floor. Then he began kicking her, in the face, in the stomach. Blood was everywhere. I cannot forgive myself for being, too, weak to stand up and kill him. But I couldn't move. By nightfall, both of my sisters were dead.

"As you can see, I survived, in body, but my spirit is dead. I can never forget what happened and I can never forgive myself for not saving my family. So I live, but I am only half of a person. I will never find happiness in life."

"I'm so sorry," Katja said.

He nodded. Tears covered his face. "Yes, but I am here, I am in Israel. And for that reason alone, I am blessed. Besides, compared to so many others, my story is nothing. I met two boys, twins, in the camp. Nice boys. I remember they were so close that they seemed to know what the other was thinking. One day Mengele decided to hook them both up to electric wires. Then he gave one a shock. I saw it because I was cleaning up the operating theater. Mengele often chose one of us to clean the area for him. So, anyway, he shocked the boy so hard that the boy cried out. It was such a high pitched cry. I can still hear it. Then Mengele said to the boy, 'You choose. Either I will shock you again or I will shock your brother.' When the boy refused to choose, Mengele shocked them both. Yes, he was that cruel.

"It ended with the boy shocking his brother to death. The pain was so severe that he couldn't take it again; even though he clearly agonized as he shocked his brother. This was the kind of thing Mengele enjoyed. These two twins, they were only ten years old. The one boy who lived, he would have to live with the knowledge of what he had done for the rest of his life. His conscience would surely haunt him. Mengele made sure that he survived. He wanted to ensure that the boy would never get over being responsible for the death of his beloved brother. So, you see, my story is not so bad. At least I was not forced to cause the death of anyone else, especially anyone I loved. "

***

On the way home from the kibbutz Katja was silent, starring out the window as the countryside rolled by.

"Do you know why I brought you here?" Elan said.

She shook her head. "No, but it was horrible. It was the most horrible thing I've ever been through. Those poor souls, and there must have been so many more."

"Yes," he nodded. "There were, and those were the ones who survived the Nazis. When the camps were liberated, there were millions of dead bodies in piles. They killed a lot of Jews."

"Please Elan . . . enough . . . I don't want to hear anymore."

He touched the top of her head. He saw that she was crying.

"I am sorry you had to hear all of this. But, I brought you to this kibbutz so that you would understand why I must stay in the army. When my tour is over, I must re-enlist. I must defend this country with my life. If I ever marry, my wife will have to understand that this country will come before anything, even my family." His eyes glazed over with pain. Could he have lost Katja for bringing her to this kibbutz, and for what he had told her? He shivered. He'd taken a big chance, but he had to, she had to know.

"You have come to mean a great deal to me, Katja, and I knew that someday, if Israel called me to war and you and I were serious, even maybe married, you might ask me to quit the army. After all, it is a dangerous life, especially for a family man. I may leave the army and live a civilian life, but if Israel is ever attacked, no matter how old I am, I will go to serve. I wanted you to see what was done to our people. It was the only way that I could make you understand the importance of our Jewish homeland. You see, no matter where I am or what I am doing, if Israel needs me, I must go. So, I must be sure that I have made myself clear. Any woman who becomes my wife must know this in advance."

Elan had not turned on the radio when they got into the car, so the only sound was the sound of the wind coming through the open windows. They drove in silence for a few minutes. Katja could see that Elan was anxious; he was tapping the steering wheel with his fingers, but he said nothing.

"Pull the car to the side of the road," she said.

He glanced over at her quickly, then pulled the automobile out of traffic and parked. Looking down at the steering wheel, he waited.

Katja did not say a word as she moved over closer to Elan. Then she put her arms around his neck and kissed him softly. She gazed deeply up into his eyes and said, "I would not want you to be any other way, Elan. It is your courage, your sense of right and wrong, and your incredible devotion to your purpose that makes me feel the way I do about you."

"And how is that? How do you feel about me, Katja?" His voice was small, cracking, and vulnerable.

"I care a lot about you," she said, reaching up and pushing the hair out of his eyes.

"Katja," he said, "I love you."

Chapter 68

From that day forward, Elan and Katja spent every free moment together. When time permitted, they met for an hour for lunch. In the evenings, they either went to dinner or brought food in from a local restaurant to Elan's apartment. Elan was not religious, but he enjoyed the Shabbat dinners that Katja and he shared. On Saturday, they rested together; sometimes they even went to services at the synagogue, Temple Beth Ami, down the street from the army base where Katja worked. Sundays were special days; they had picnics, or rode horses bareback along the beach. They watched the sunset in each other's arms.

One such Sunday, after they'd taken a long drive out of town and hiked through the mountains, they stopped by a crisp, clear brook with a waterfall. Night had begun to descend and the stars came out, sparkling like diamonds in a bed of black velvet. The couple sat on the rocks, Katja with her head on Elan's shoulder.

"You have become my life," he whispered into her golden hair. "I love you so much."

She wanted to tell him that she loved him, but she was afraid. Love.

He touched her hair so gently that she barely felt his hand. Carefully he held her chin and turned her face towards him. Then he kissed her. She felt her body respond in ways she'd never felt before. He continued to kiss her, slowly; her eyes, her neck, her bosom. She did not want him to stop, but she must tell him. "Elan."

"Yes, love . . ."

"I'm a virgin."

"Do you want me to stop?" He looked into her eyes, steady, kind, loving. He waited for her answer.

"No."

"Are you sure?"

"I am sure."

He looked at her as if he was seeing her for the first time, the admiration in his eyes stirring her blood to passion. "You are a goddess," he said. Then tenderly, slowly, softly, Elan, this man of power, of strength, this giant of a warrior, made love to Katja with a gentleness she never knew was inside him.

Chapter 69

Mendel telephoned every day, but it always seemed that Katja was too busy to talk. She put him off gently, not meaning to hurt his feelings. Finally, after several weeks, he came to see her at her office.

"What's wrong, Kat? Did I do something to upset you?" Mendel asked, sitting in the chair opposite her desk.

"No Mendel. I am so sorry. I've been incredibly overwhelmed with work."

"It's all right. How about this weekend? Let's go to a film on Sunday."

"I can't, I have plans with Elan."

So that was it, it was Elan. He should have known. Looking at Katja he realized that she was glowing, she was in love. He'd lost her forever. He should have known. But, he'd hoped he had been wrong. Now he knew for sure.

"Maybe some other time . . ." Mendel said, knowing that the time would never come.

"Yes, soon . . ." she said. He nodded, not turning to look back at her as he walked out the door. He didn't want her to see the tears in his eyes. She never even knew how he felt about her.

Chapter 70

"I would like for you to meet my family," Elan said on a Sunday afternoon, as they lay in bed alternating between reading, eating, making love, and napping.

"I would love to meet them."

"Good, then I will arrange it. When can you take a few days off from work?"

"I don't know. Let me find out."

"The High Holidays are coming up. How would you like to spend Rosh Hashanah and Yom Kippur in Jerusalem?"

"In the Old City?"

"My family lives right outside the Old City. It is a beautiful place. Have you ever been there?"

"Never, but I know it is holy to all religions. I have been wanting to go there for years, but I never had the time."

"So, you'll try to take a week and a half off from work, then?"

"Yes, I will try. We will be closed for the holidays so that would be the best time to go."

"As soon as you're sure that you can go, I will talk to my mother and tell her we are coming. She'll be very excited. She loves to have company, and when she sees how skinny you are she'll take it on as her personal mission to fatten you up."

"That's all I need!" She said, laughing.

He started laughing, too. "More of you to love," he said. Then he buried his face in her neck and began kissing her and tickling her at the same time.

"Stop . . ." she said, still laughing.

"I love to see you laugh. You are so beautiful when you laugh."

She shook her head in mock anger.

He stopped and took her in his arms, looking deeply into her eyes. She felt herself melt like a chocolate bar in the hot sun. Elan pressed his lips to hers slowly, gently. She sighed. "I love you, Katja," he whispered. "I love you. And I cherish our Sundays. . ."

"I love you too, Elan . . ."

"Katja?"

"Yes? . . ."

"Will you be my wife?"

She sat up on her elbow and looked at him lying across the bed. His chest and arms were hard with muscles built through years of army training, his eyes were deep pools of dark mystery. Elan. She loved him.

"Yes...yes, I will marry you."

Chapter 71

There was only one telephone at the kibbutz, and it was rare that anyone called. It was a big black desk phone with a heavy, curved receiver sitting on a table in the main living area of the big house. One of the women had been passing by, carrying a basket of laundry, when she heard it ring.

"Who is this?" She said, picking up the receiver incorrectly and talking into the mouthpiece.

"Turn the phone around and put this side up to your ear," the caller said.

The woman did as she was told.

"Yeah....who is this?"

"It's Katja Zuckerman. Can you please get one of my parents for me?"

"Katja, Katja." The old woman laughed. "Katja, you called on the telephone."

"Yes, I did. I need to speak to one of my parents. Please, can you get either one for me?"

"This is Thelma Rosenfield. You remember me? Yes? I used to give you hamantaschen when you were little. Yeah? You remember how you loved my cookies?"

"Yes, Mrs. Rosenfield, of course I remember. How are you?"

"I'm fine. I'm very good. You are in the army, aren't you?"

"Yes, I am. I am so sorry to cut you short, but I don't have much time. Can you please find one of my parents?"

"You know what we got here? We got a television set," Thelma Rosenfield said. "How have you been? I hope you're not sick? You should be getting out of the army pretty soon?"

"Yes, I'll be out in a few months. I am fine, thank you for asking. But, Mrs. Rosenfield, I don't mean to be rude, but I don't have much time. Can you please get one of my parents?"

"Oy, yes, I'm sorry . . . of course. I start talking and I lose track of time. Wait, don't hang up the telephone. I'll go and get one of them right away."

It was 1960. Everyone, except the people on the kibbutz had a phone. Katja smiled to herself. Poor Thelma; this was probably the first time she'd ever talked on a telephone.

There was silence for several minutes and Katja became concerned that she'd been disconnected. Then . . .

"Katja? . . ." It was Zofia. "Sunshine, how are you? Is everything all right?"

"Yes, Mama, everything is fine. I am fine. How are you and papa?"

"We are doing well. We miss you, of course."

"I know. I miss you both very much." Katja felt the tears well up in her eyes.

"Mama, I won't be home for the holidays this year."

"Why, you have to work? Don't tell me that there is trouble in the country. Dear God, not that," Zofia said. Everyone knew that in Israel war could break out at any time.

"No, Mama. Everything is all right. I have something I want to tell you, but I want to tell you in person."

"Katja, tell me . . . please. I will worry."

"Don't worry. It's something good."

"I can't let you off the phone until you tell me." Zofia was becoming more nervous and worried as she grew older. The memories of what she had been through during the war and before having settled in Israel haunted her; the happier she was, the more the threat hung over her head of losing everything in an instant.

"All right, Mama. I will tell you, but try and keep the secret from Papa. I want to tell him myself when I come there."

"I'll try. Nu? So what is it already?"

"I'm getting married."

"OY, Married? Katja, who is the boy? You never mentioned anyone. Who is it?"

"His name is Elan and he is wonderful. We are going to see his family for the holidays and then we will come to see you for Hanukah."

"Elan . . . he is a Sephardic? That's an Israeli name."

"Yes, he was born just outside of Jerusalem."

"My baby is getting married." Zofia sighed.

"I know you will love him."

"So, if he makes you happy I'm sure we will love him. You will live here on the kibbutz?"

"I'm not sure. We haven't decided," Katja said.

Zofia wanted to cry. She'd been counting the days until Katja would finish her time in the army and return to her family. Now, Katja may never return to live on the kibbutz, only to visit. "Well, you'll decide later. The most important thing is that you should be happy," Zofia said. She was trying her best to sound cheerful, but the words caught in her throat.

"You sound upset Mama . . ."

"No, I'm shocked is all. I wasn't expecting this; it came a little bit unexpectedly, you know? How could I be upset if my Sunshine, my precious little girl, is so happy? How silly you are. Of course I am happy . . . I can't wait to meet your future husband."

"You will meet him very soon. He will be the son you never had. I love you, Mama. Tell Papa I love him, and I miss you both," Katja said.

"We both love you. And we miss you, too. Be safe, and be well. And I will count the days until Hanukah," Zofia said.

"Bye, Mama."

"Bye, Sunshine." Zofia hung up the phone. Then she sank into a chair and put her head in her hands. Then she whispered softly, "Dear God, please watch over my child and protect her."

Chapter 72

Katja took the day off before the first day of Rosh Hashana, and she and Elan drove toward the Old City. They wanted to be there before sundown on the day of the holiday. It was a lazy, golden September afternoon. The sky was deep blue and the trees were beginning to shed their leaves.

"You never told me much about your family. Do you have brothers and sisters?" she asked. "I'm an only child."

He laughed. "You know, it never came up. With other girls there was always this lag in conversation, you know. I mean we were always searching for something to say, so we would talk about family and things like that to fill the silence. But with you, love, it wasn't like that. We never need to fill the empty space. It was always filled with our feelings for each other."

She giggled. "You are certainly philosophical today."

"I feel philosophical. I am getting married," he joked.

"Okay, and about your family? Do you have siblings?"

"Yes, I do, actually. I have a brother and a sister. My brother, Aryeh is the oldest, then me, then my baby sister, Aleana."

"And your parents, will they like me?"

"You're nervous?" he said, taking her hand, suddenly serious.

"Yes," she nodded. "I guess I am."

"Well don't be. They are going to adore you. How could they not? Huh? I do."

She shrugged. "I've never done anything like this before."

"Don't feel bad, neither have I," he said smiling, his dark eyes a-light and dancing. Then he squeezed her hand. "It's going to be just fine. You'll see."

They arrived at the entrance of the Old City just as the sun was about to set. The stone buildings seemed to rise out of the earth against the orange and purple background of the sunset, like an ancient testimony to the wonder of Israel. In the center of town, Katja could see a large golden ball.

"What is that?" Katja asked.

"It is the dome of the rock, an ancient Muslim temple."

"It looks beautiful."

"Yes. The Old City is magnificent. Maybe tomorrow we will take a little tour."

The Amsel family home was in Jerusalem, on the outskirts of the Old City. It was a single story stone building bleached white by the sun.

Elan took Katja's hand and smiled at her. Then he winked and opened the door to the house where he'd grown up.

"Hello," Elan called out.

His mother rushed out of the kitchen.

"Elan . . ." She grabbed him and kissed both of his cheeks. The she called out "Come Aryeh, Aleana; Elan is here." Elan's mother was a short, stocky woman. Elan resembled his father; a tall well-built man who got up from the sofa and walked over and hugged him.

"It's good to see you, son," his father said.

Then others came rushing in to greet Elan. Behind his brother and sister was a short girl with bleached blond hair, false eyelashes, and a very short haircut. Her young face was filled with freckles.

"Elan." His brother hugged him, then his sister hugged him, too.

"I want you to meet Katja," Elan said.

"Welcome, Katja," said Aryeh, Elan's brother.

"Welcome," Aleana, his sister said, less sure.

Aryeh introduced the girl with the short blond hair. "This is Brenda. She is from America. She came to stay at one of the kibbutzim where I work and we met there."

"Hello, Brenda," Elan said. Then he turned to Katja, "My brother is a mechanic. He goes to the different kibbutzim and fixes things."

"Well, this should be an interesting holiday," his mother said, wiping her hands on her apron. "Both of my sons have brought girls home. And neither of the girls are Sephardic. So, to me that means that you don't want a girlfriend who looks like your mother?" She laughed, but her face said that she was not joking.

"Mom, please be nice," Elan said, giving her a look of warning.

"Elan, please, don't misjudge. I am only making a joke. Katja understands. Don't you, Katja?"

Katja nodded, uncomfortable, not knowing what to say.

"It's just . . . well . . . two blonds? Oh well, at least you're both Jewish."

"Of course, she is Jewish, mother. I wouldn't bring a girl to meet you who was not Jewish. Especially one I plan to marry," Elan said.

"MARRY?!" His mother's face went pale. "You're going to get married?"

"I guess now is as good a time as any to tell you. Yes, Katja and I came to tell you that we are getting married."

"Mazel tov," Aryeh said, grabbing his brother and patting his back. Then, turning to Katja and hugging her, "Welcome to the family."

"Yes, mazel tov," Aleana, his sister said, crossing her arms in front of her chest and stealing a glance at their mother.

"It's late. Why don't we settle in for the night and we can all get to know each other tomorrow?" Elan said.

He and Katja walked to the back of the house. "This is my room. This is where I grew up."

His mother was close behind. "I don't think it is proper for you two to share a room in our house until you are married. So, I fixed it so that you and your brother can sleep in your room, and the girls can sleep in Aleana's room."

Elan shrugged. "Are you all right with this?" he asked Katja. "We can always get a hotel room if you would rather."

"No, I am fine," she said, not wanting to start off on the wrong foot with her new family.

Preparing food at the Amsel household was much different from the way it was done at the kibbutz. Katja offered her help, but Elan's mother was not open to anyone else working in her kitchen. She would not accept Brenda's help either. Only her daughter was allowed to help. Mrs. Amsel hardly spoke to Katja and Katja felt very out of place. But on the second day of their visit, Katja and Elan went with his brother and Brenda to tour the Old City. They invited Aleana but she declined. Brenda was open and friendly. She told Katja about life in America and how much she'd come to love Israel. They became fast friends.

Later in the week, the two couples went to the market on Ben Yehuda Street where Elan's father owned and operated a fruit stand. They shopped for a few hours and then returned to the house. Had it not been for Brenda, Katja would have felt alone and alienated.

On Yom Kippur, the family went to temple. "I am not religious, said Elan. I know it sounds hypocritical, but this is the only day of the year that I actually go to Shul. I fast, too. Just in case. You know, just in case all this religious stuff is true."

Katja laughed. "You are such a strange man, Elan." She teased him. She had always fasted on Yom Kippur. Everyone did on the kibbutz. At the end of the day, they broke the fast with a feast, welcoming in the New Year. Katja was glad that they were leaving Elan's parents' home in the morning.

"She's not as bad as she seems," Elan said about his mother, as they rode back toward Tel Aviv. "She's just really protective of her children. You'll get used to her, and as she gets to know you better, she'll come to love you. Besides, we won't be around my family that often."

Katja nodded.

"Come on, beautiful, give me a smile," he said. "When you smile you light up the world."

She laughed "Elan . . ."

"And when you laugh I know why I chose you to be the mother of my children. I want to make a thousand Jewish babies with you. I want us to single-handedly rebuild the Jewish race that rulers, like Pharaoh and Hitler, have been trying to destroy since the beginning of time."

"A thousand children—won't I be tired?"

"Well, at least two."

"Two sounds much better." She laughed again.

Chapter 73

As Konrad was strolling to the small café where he had breakfast each morning, a boy of about seven years old approached him and handed him a note. Before Konrad could ask the boy who the message was from, the child disappeared down an alleyway. Konrad opened the envelope. As he had guessed, it was from Mossad. Konrad had his orders. Mossad was giving him until the end of January to arrange the capture of Manfred Blau. Konrad felt guilty. He'd grown to like Blau. He was a good friend whose company Konrad enjoyed.

But Konrad also hated Blau because he saw a lot of himself in the man. He saw many characteristics of which he was ashamed. They were both weak, both unattractive, not the strong Aryan athletes they yearned to be. Back in Germany when Konrad had worn his uniform, it made him feel important, special, even handsome. But without it, he had slowly reverted back to the ugly boy he'd once been, the child who had endured mocking at the hands of his peers. He knew just by looking at Blau that Blau had also been, like himself, the clumsy boy who didn't fit in.

Now, Konrad must betray Blau. He had no choice. However, Konrad didn't feel as bad as he'd felt when he betrayed Detrick. Nothing in his entire life had been as bad as that. But it certainly didn't feel good. Perhaps he could do with a trip to Brazil to the favela. That always gave him the release he needed. For a long time he'd tried to be sexually active with women, he'd even tried violent and sadistic sex with prostitutes. For a while it almost satisfied him. But once he'd engaged in sex with a boy, his body never responded to women again. He hated the boys who had sexual encounters with him. They reminded him of his perverse desires.

He'd become so disgusted with himself that he'd even killed a few of them, stabbing them numerous times, then leaving their mutilated bodies in the public bathrooms where the acts had taken place. He'd never planned on murder, but the rage would come over him, and before the boy knew what had happened, Konrad began stabbing him. Sometimes he would see the boy's face turn into Detrick's, other times it would turn into his own. When he saw himself, he would turn the most violent, stabbing and cutting until the reflection of his own face disappeared. Whenever he left the favela he promised himself that he would never return. He would tell himself that this was the last time. And then . . . he would feel that need stir, causing his heart to race and the blood to rush to his ears, and he would return to look for another boy.

Chapter 74

When two people are in love, they rarely pay much attention to anything surrounding them. Katja quickly forgot about her mother-in-law's difficult personality, and she seemed to forget about her friendship with Mendel. As close as she and Rachel had been all of their lives, she still could not bring herself to call Rachel and give her the news. But December 10 was coming up fast and that was the first day of Hanukah. She and Elan planned to arrive at the kibbutz on the second day. They'd shopped for gifts for both her family and his; mailing the ones they'd purchased for his family and packing the ones they had for hers. It should have been an exciting time. But, secretly Katja was worried. Had Rachel been honest when she said that she had no romantic feelings left for Elan?

The temperature had dropped during the night and it was unusually cold the morning that they left Tel Aviv. Katja watched the city fade away as they drove towards the kibbutz where she had spent her childhood.

As expected, the main house was decorated with menorahs. Katja knew her mother would be either in the kitchen or in the children's house. She directed Elan to the guesthouse and then went off to find her mother. Zofia was sitting on a bench with a little boy beside her. He was writing numbers in a workbook with a red crayon. Katja watched her mother for a moment, and her heart ached with love. Zofia was so patient. She wore a heavy sweater that tied at the waist and slivers of gray had begun to appear in her hair, which was caught up in a soft bun at the back of her neck. Katja felt a shiver of sadness come over her as she realized that her mother would not live forever, someday she would be gone. Even as a little girl, Katja had had nightmares of losing her mother. And now as she watched Zofia, she realized that the hard life her mother had lived had taken a toll, and although Katja was not sure of her mother's exact age, she knew that Zofia was in her early forties, but she had begun to look weathered.

"All right now. Recite the numbers for me," Zofia said, closing the book.

"One, two, three, four . . ." the child said in Hebrew.

"That's very good, now in English."

The boy began to count in English when Zofia turned around and saw Katja. Her face lit up. "My Sunshine, come here. Let me look at you." Zofia stood up. Katja ran to her mother.

Zofia took Katja in her arms and hugged her. Katja buried her head in Zofia's hair and for a moment, Katja allowed herself to linger in that safe, familiar fragrance that was her mother.

"I'm so glad you're here," Zofia said.

"I brought Elan with me. He's at the guesthouse."

"I can't wait to meet him. Come, let's go out into the field, and see your father. He will be so happy to see you."

When Isaac saw Katja approaching with Zofia he climbed down the ladder he was standing on. Katja could not help but remember that when he was a young man he'd jumped off ladders much taller than this one. Katja knew that her parents had lived a hard life, and it had taken its toll on their bodies. They both seemed so much older than they were. The stabbing pain shot through her heart again. Her parents were aging and one day they would be gone. One day she would not be able to hug them or talk to them.

"Papa . . ." Katja said, running to him.

He hugged her tightly. "Katja, Shalom sweetheart, welcome home . . . welcome home."

She couldn't help it; she was crying.

"Don't cry, sweetheart, this is a happy time," Isaac said. "Come on, Mama; let's go and get Katja something to eat."

"I brought a friend. Someone I want you to meet, Papa."

"OH? NU? So who is your friend?"

"His name is Elan."

"Ahhhh, a boyfriend"

"Yes, Papa, a boyfriend."

"Well, so come on. Let's go and meet this boyfriend who thinks he is good enough for my little girl," Isaac said, joking.

"I think you'll like him. At least I hope so."

"Does he make you happy?" Isaac said, wrapping his arms around Katja's neck on one side and Zofia's on the other.

"He does, Papa; he is very good to me."

"You love him?"

"Yes, very much."

Isaac glanced at Zofia and nodded. "Then I am sure we will love him, too."

They found Elan in the guesthouse with Mendel and Rachel.

"Katja, it's been a long time since I've heard from you," Rachel said.

"I know. I'm sorry." Katja looked away. She couldn't meet Rachel's eyes.

"I see you've brought Elan here for the holidays," Rachel said, her face calm and unreadable.

Katja nodded, stealing a glance at Rachel. She wasn't sure how to proceed. She loved Elan, but she was terrified of losing her lifelong friend.

Everyone was standing around waiting for Katja to speak. She could not look at Rachel, so she turned to her parents.

"Mama, Papa, this is Elan."

"Welcome," Isaac said and he gave Elan a bear hug. "Happy Hanukah. Come on, let's go and get you two something to eat. I'm sure you're both hungry."

Elan laughed. "What is it with us Jews? Why is it food is always on our minds?"

Isaac put his arm around Elan. "I can't wait to get to know you better."

"I feel the same way. I have been eager to meet Katja's family," Elan said.

They all walked toward the main house. Rachel caught up with Katja.

"You go on ahead. I want to talk to Katja," Rachel said, taking Katja's arm and slowing her down.

Katja had been worried about this conversation. That was why she had not been in contact with Rachel since she and Elan had begun seeing each other.

"Why haven't you called me or answered any of my calls?" Rachel said.

Katja shrugged.

"It's Elan?"

Katja nodded.

"You think I feel bad because I dated him a long time ago?" Rachel asked.

"Yes, and I'm sorry. The last thing I would ever want to do is hurt you."

"You did hurt me, but not by dating Elan. By avoiding me. You are my sister, my blood sister. I don't care about you and Elan. I told you that before. But I don't want to lose you because of him."

"And what about you, Rachel? I haven't known you to date anyone since Elan. That's why I was so concerned, so guilty. I was afraid that you might still care for him."

"Sit down, Katja, I have something to tell you," Rachel said, as they passed a wooden picnic bench.

Katja was worried about leaving Elan alone so long with Mendel and her family, but this was important. She sat down. Rachel sat down beside her.

"I haven't dated anyone else because after dating Elan I knew what I was. I knew what I wanted and what I didn't want. I just didn't know how to tell you. I wasn't sure what you would think."

"I don't understand."

"I'm a lesbian, Kat. I have a girlfriend; she and I live up in Golan Heights. Because we don't think that our families would be able to cope with the situation, we don't spend holidays together. She goes to her family for the holidays and I come here to mine. No one knows about us but you and Mendel."

"Oh . . ." Katja said. "Oh . . ."

"Are you upset? Disgusted?"

"Neither," Katja said and she turned to look at Rachel. Then Katja hugged her dear friend. "Oh Rachel, I'm relieved. I never wanted to hurt you. I was so afraid that this relationship between Elan and I would cost us our friendship. I am going to marry him, Rachel. I love him."

"God bless you both. I am more than happy for you," Rachel said. "But I guess you don't know," Rachel cleared her throat, " or you don't realize . . ."

Katja's eyes met Rachel's. "Realize what?"

"Kat are you blind? Can't you see it? Mendel is in love with you. He has been for years," Rachel said.

"Are you sure?"

"Yes, I am positive."

"He told you?" Katja asked.

"Many times. He was hoping to marry you."

"Oh, poor Mendel. What am I going to do?" Katja bit the side of her nail.

"I don't know Kat. What can you do? You and Elan are in love. Mendel will just have to accept your marriage," Rachel said. "In time he will find someone of his own. But now that you know how he feels about you, be gentle with him. It's going to be hard for him. By the way, now that you know the truth about me maybe someday you and Elan will come up to Golan. I would love for you to meet my girlfriend. She's an American. Her name is Sandy."

After Katja and Elan announced their engagement, the entire kibbutz was buzzing with excitement and wedding plans. The wedding would take place on the kibbutz. Elan's family would be welcomed there. Rooms would be set up in the guesthouse where they could stay and be comfortable. Since Katja would be finished with the army by March, the couple set a wedding date in June. This would give Katja and Zofia enough time to make a dress and plan. Katja noticed that Mendel was sitting alone, staring out the window, not participating in the planning. Now she knew why. Her heart ached for her childhood friend. She went over to sit beside him as he arranged and rearranged the pile of white candles beside one of the menorahs.

"I'm sorry I've been so busy and unavailable lately," she said, softly touching his arm.

"It's all right. You're busy with Elan. I understand."

"Still, that's no excuse for not being there to talk to a good friend," Katja said. "We will have to spend more time together."

"I can't. I'm busy with school. But, I want you to know that I am happy for you Kat. I want you to be happy more than anything else in the world, and Elan seems to make you happy."

"Thanks Mendel," she said, squeezing his arm.

He nodded. His eyes were glassy and she hoped he wouldn't cry.

"You'll be here for the wedding, won't you?" she asked.

"Of course; for you Katja, I would do anything," Mendel said. He smiled at her, but she saw the sadness in his eyes.

Chapter 75

Three days before they were to begin the mission, Manfred received a package with instructions from Konrad. Inside it was a bottle of peroxide that Manfred was to mix with another bottle that contained a dark hair color. Then he was to cover his hair with it and leave it on for a half hour; after that he was to shampoo the mixture out of his hair. A fake mustache and sideburns were also inside the box, with a small bottle of spirit gum to attach them, and a passport for "Michael Morgenstern." There was also a plane ticket and instructions to meet Konrad at the airport at nine in the morning that Wednesday.

Manfred was careful to follow the directions exactly, without making any mistakes. The picture on the passport looked a great deal like Manfred after he'd finished with the hair dye. He boarded the plane and was led to his seat by the stewardess. He was sitting next to a man with curly red hair. Looking more closely, he saw that it was Konrad wearing a wig and thick black glasses that almost covered his entire face.

Manfred nodded to Konrad as he sat down. Konrad returned the nod. Anyone watching would have thought the two men were strangers.

The plane flight to Holland was turbulent. Several times Manfred found himself glancing at Konrad to see if the plane was in trouble. Konrad seemed unfazed by the shaking so Manfred assumed all was well. The stewardess brought their food, but Manfred had no appetite. He was worried about the mission they were undertaking.

"Are you sure that this will be as easy as you say?" Manfred whispered, as inconspicuously as possible.

"Yes, I'm positive. We've paid off the guard at the prison where they are keeping our Führer. ODESSA paid him very well, I might add," Konrad said. "All we have to do is go to the hotel and wait. They will bring Hitler to us."

"What if they don't?"

"They will."

"If it is so easy, then why did you need me?"

"I need you to help me distract the people at the airport when we are on our way back to South America. It isn't as if Hitler does not have a very distinctive face. Of course, he will be wearing a disguise; I have everything to change his hair color and his facial features in my bag. Still, it will help if you flirt and engage the airline personnel making you memorable, while making Hitler and me less so. Keep everyone busy. I have some magic tricks that I brought. They are silly sleight-of-hand tricks, but they will keep everyone laughing and entertained. Meanwhile, I will attend to our Führer's needs. He might be ill or weak and need help. Still, we don't want to draw any attention to him, so I will see to it that his disguise is effective, while you take care of the distraction aspect."

Manfred took a deep breath. He really didn't want this job. He'd have preferred to stay in Argentina. But how could he refuse? The party had done so much for him and now it asked that he pay back. Perhaps once this was over, he might finally be restored to the favor that he had enjoyed before his father-in-law had so carelessly thrown everything away. So, here Manfred was, sailing through the sky, watching the clouds fade through the window of the aircraft, on his way to save the Führer. If the mission failed, they would all end up in prison, or worse.

Konrad and Manfred checked into the hotel as Michael and Joseph Morgenstern, brothers. Jews. It was a less-than-standard hotel, and no one seemed to pay much attention. Their room could have used a good cleaning. The sheets on the bed should have been white but were gray with dirt. The vents had pockets of dust stuck to them. Manfred set his suitcase on the bed, and sat down on a chair next to a table. Konrad got a bottle of schnapps out of his suitcase and offered Manfred a swig. "Have some. It will help relax you," Konrad said.

Manfred drank deeply. Konrad watched. The liquor had been drugged. Although Manfred didn't realize it, he'd been drugged the same way that he had drugged Dolf Sprecht before he'd killed him. Manfred yawned and handed the bottle to Konrad. "Have a swig," he said, his words already beginning to slur.

"I will join you in just a moment. I have to use the bathroom," Konrad said. He left the room but did not head to the end of the hall to use the facilities. Instead he stood outside the room and waited. It would not be long before Manfred was passed out. Konrad walked the length of the hall twice. He went into the bathroom and stood in a stall for several minutes. Then he walked slowly back to the door of the room he shared with Manfred. An older man walked past Konrad. The man had his arm around a very young woman, wearing a tight skirt and low cut blouse. Konrad nodded to them, assuming she was a prostitute. Then he checked his watch again. It had been five minutes. Time enough.

Manfred was passed out on the bed with his feet on top of his suitcase when Konrad entered the room.

"Manfred . . ." Konrad said, to be sure that he was not awake.

No answer. "Manfred . . ."

Konrad checked Manfred's pulse. He was alive, but he was out cold. Konrad picked up the phone and gave the operator the number that he'd been given by the Mossad agents. Konrad knew that they were waiting to hear from him.

"Blau is here with me at the hotel, and he's passed out," Konrad said.

"Leave the room with the door unlocked," the Mossad agent said. "We'll take it from here. By the way, Klausen, Blau had better be there, and he'd better not have a gun. No funny stuff. If there are any problems with this mission, it's you who will pay."

"Everything is just the way you wanted it. I did what you asked me to do," Konrad said.

"Good, it had better be. And, by the way, you'll be hearing from us within the next week. We want Mengele next."

"I told you I will bring him to you."

"You'd better, if you want to live," the Mossad agent said.

Konrad looked at Manfred one last time before he left the room. Then the old wooden door creaked as he closed it. Konrad wrapped his arms across his chest; shivering, he walked down the hall. This reminded him too much of what he'd done to Detrick, and made him sick with guilt. Now they wanted Mengele. Blau was a small player next to Mengele. Konrad was afraid to bring the doctor to Mossad. If he did, he was sure ODESSA would find out, and they would kill him.

All Konrad wanted was to escape Mossad. That would mean that he had to leave the Nazi party behind, he must never return to Argentina. If he did not go back, there was a good chance that they would never find him or any of the others for that matter. He could not go through this again with Mengele or Eichmann. They were too important. ODESSA would find out. He had to get away. When he got to the airport, he tore up his return ticket to Argentina. The next plane to South America was going to Chile. He would be on board. He had plenty of money to start over. So, when he arrived in Chile, he would find an apartment and a job. Then he would change his name and disappear from everyone—from the Nazi party and from the terrible Israelis who were constantly hunting him.

Chapter 76

Manfred's head pounded and his back ached when he awoke. It took a few minutes for his eyes to focus. Either this was a nightmare or he was inside of a jail cell. Perhaps things had gone awry. Where was Konrad? Probably in the cell next to his.

"Konrad . . ." Manfred called out, his head aching even as he tried to speak. "Klaussen, where are you, where are we?"

A tall man who looked like a giant walked over to him wearing an Israeli army uniform. On the lapel Manfred saw a pin. It was a golden Star of David.

"Welcome to Israel," the man said. "You're here to be tried for your crimes against humanity, Manfred Blau."

ISRAEL! This was surely a nightmare. "Where is Konrad Klaussen?"

"He betrayed you. He gave you over to us to save his own hide, Blau. That's the kind of people you Nazis are. NO real loyalties."

Manfred stood up and stumbled over to the bars of his cell. "KONRAD," he yelled in panic, hurling his body against the metal. "KONRAD."

"Holler all you want; there is nobody here to hear you." The Israeli took a cigarette out of his breast pocket and smiled at Manfred as he lit it, leaning against the wall. "There's just you and me and a whole bunch of Jewish soldiers who hate your guts. And by the way, Blau, you sadistic bastard, maybe we'll make soap out of you or a lampshade out of your skin. Isn't that what you did to the Jews? Shit, Blau, you killed little children, women. Now you want sympathy. Come on, be serious. You and your sick Nazi friends can all go to hell. I'd like to break your nose, but I don't want you to go on television, especially in America, looking like you've been beaten. You are our guest now and we wouldn't want people to think that Israel was an ungracious host, now would we? God forbid anyone should feel sorry for you. But believe me, you could use a good beating."

Chapter 77

Everything seemed to be working out for Konrad. It had been over a month since that day in Holland. He had escaped them all; he was living in a small village in Chile, and working as a clerk at a dry goods store. He had no papers, but he was using the name Fredrick. He'd always admired Fredrick the Great. It was a simple life. In the morning, he walked to work carrying his lunch. The work was mindless, easy. He stocked the shelves, smiled at the customers, and then headed home. In the evening, he prepared a simple dinner, sometimes a can of beans with a crust of bread, other times a hunk of cheese. Then he'd spend the rest of the night alone. Sometimes he read, other times he took to making small objects out of wood. He'd learned to whittle as a boy and now he whittled tiny figures.

Since Manfred's arrest Konrad had had no contact with any of the other Nazis. But more importantly, he breathed a sigh of relief that Mossad had been unable to find him. When he could get newspapers that had international news, he read them with guilt as he watched what had become of Manfred. The trial was to begin for Manfred the following week in, of all places, the homeland of the Jews, Israel. Even the word, Israel, gave Konrad the chills. That was one place he never wanted to see. There was no doubt that Manfred would be convicted and hanged.

Konrad knew that he should stop watching the events unfold to preserve his sanity, but he couldn't. Every time he saw Manfred's face on the television screen, he felt like vomiting. At night, dreams of Detrick became more frequent, but now they included visions of Manfred as well, horrible visions. In Konrad's dreams he sometimes saw Detrick and Manfred in a gas chamber, both of them reaching, trying to climb out of the piles of dead bodies—the way the Jews had done when he watched the gassings. In his dreams, both Detrick and Manfred were reaching desperately, the fingernails on their hands had turned to a bloody mass of shredded flesh, and they were both bleeding from the nose, mouth, and eyes. Once again, Konrad could smell that distinct and terrible odor of death, of feces, and of urine that he'd smelled when he visited the camps. The guilt at having betrayed his friends followed him like a dark shadow, haunting him every moment of every day.

So far, since he'd come to Chile, Konrad had resisted his need to fulfill his sexual anger with a boy that resembled Detrick. But his urges were growing strong. Perhaps the only thing that would relieve his feelings of anger, guilt, and frustration would be a visit to the campamentos, the slums of Chile. Konrad didn't want to go there; he'd promised himself that he would stop. He'd tried to stop . . .

Konrad already knew where to find the nearest shanty town and how to get there by taxi. He'd heard a lot about the place during his time in Chile. People warned of the dangers of the poverty-stricken campamento. Konrad took heed of their words, but he'd gone to the favela in Brazil and he had managed to stay safe there. He was smart enough to get by. Konrad loaded and packed a small pistol in one pants pocket and a switchblade knife in the other. Then he went out on to the street to catch a cab. Yes, a night with a young boy would help calm his rattled nerves.

Konrad spoke enough Spanish to make himself understood, so when he requested to be taken to the campamento, he could tell by the driver's reaction that it was rare for anyone from the better areas of town to ask to be driven there. But the cabbie didn't protest. The driver stopped just as Konrad requested, right across the street from an empty lot. As soon as Konrad paid him and got out, the taxi sped away as if the cabbie wanted to get out of the slums before he got robbed.

It was only about nine at night, but there was no one around. When Konrad had gone to the favela, the park would be buzzing with prostitutes by now. He lit a cigarette and ran his hand over the cool steel of the gun in his pocket. Insurance. Perhaps he needed to walk further into a wooded and deserted area just a few feet away to find what he was looking for, but first he would check the public men's room that he noticed was in a small building just outside the park area. The male prostitutes in the favela had used a similar place to perform their acts.

Konrad entered the bathroom and flipped the light switch. A dim single bulb lit the room. He was struck by the strong odor of urine.

There were stains of it on the tile wall over the urinal and on the floor beneath. But there was not a soul in sight.

He began to walk along the trail through the park. It was just a thin, muddy walkway carved through the trees. Perhaps he would not find what he was looking for here. Perhaps he would be forced to return to the favela and risk either being caught by Mossad or exposing the other Nazis and then be in danger with the party. He stopped to take another cigarette out of his breast pocket. The trees cast shadows all around him, their black arms reaching into the night. Konrad shivered. There was no use going any further. Konrad turned and began walking back towards the street.

"*Pssssst* . . ." A male voice came from behind the trees. "Are you looking for a date?"

Konrad knew what that meant . . . he'd found a male prostitute. "Yes, I am . . ."

"How much you pay?" the man asked.

"What do you want?"

"2,000 pesos. But I do whatever you want. No questions."

"Come out here where I can see you," Konrad said.

A young man of about nineteen, with blond hair and an athletic build, stepped out from the darkness. Konrad's heart skipped a beat. This one was perfect. His first thought was 'Detrick.' Konrad felt a smile wash over his face. What luck he was having today. It usually took him a long time before he found a man with blond hair in the slums of South America.

"Fine, 2,000 pesos." He would have paid more.

"What you want?"

"I want you to suck me."

The boy nodded. "Give me the money first."

Konrad took out a wad of pesos and handed them to the boy, who stuffed them into his pocket.

"Take off your pants," the boy said. "And lie down."

"Why don't we go into the trees a little, in case someone comes by?"

The boy followed Konrad into the trees. Konrad undid his belt and took off his pants. He kept them beside him, the gun still cool and reassuring inside the pocket. The boy began to take Konrad's penis into his mouth. Konrad sighed deeply. The boy increased the pressure and moved more quickly in response to Konrad's moans of pleasure. Then, just as Konrad was about to ejaculate, his eyes half closed and his body in complete surrender, the boy pulled a knife out of his back pocket and with the flip of his wrist it was opened. The silver steel shined in the moonlight.

Konrad saw only a glimpse of the knife before it found its way beneath his ribs. The boy twisted the knife several times. Still kneeling over Konrad, the boy checked to be sure that the half-naked man was dead. Once the boy felt no breath or heartbeat coming from Konrad's body, he got up and cleaned the knife on Konrad's shirt. Next, he rummaged through Konrad's pockets, taking his lighter, his watch, and his money. He took the gun that bulged in Konrad's back pocket and the knife that lay tucked beside it, and shoved them both into his belt. Then the blond boy stood up, shook down his clothes and left. Once he'd gotten far away from the body, he wiped the gun and the knife clean with the tail of his cotton shirt and tossed them far into the dense woods where they would be difficult, if not impossible, to find. Then, after a quick glance in all directions, he walked rapidly away from the murder scene.

Once he left the park, the boy slowed down his pace, so as not to draw any attention to himself, but the streets were deserted. There was no traffic, and he kept walking until he heard a bus coming down the street. He jogged across the street just as a bus pulled to the stop. With the agility of a leopard, he hopped on board, paid his fare, and curled into a corner seat. Only a few people were aboard the bus that night, people who worked the late shift. Some of them had drifted off to sleep with the motion of the vehicle. The bus let out a belch of smoke as it pulled away from the curb and turned the corner. Then it picked up speed on its way out of the campamento. The boy rode for a long while after the bus left the slums, then he walked to the front and asked the driver to stop. When the bus came to a complete stop, the boy hopped down the stairs and onto the sidewalk. Then he strolled for several blocks until he ducked into a phone booth. He inserted several quarters into the payphone and once he got a dial tone, he placed a call.

"Shalom," a man answered.

"Shalom," the blond boy said.

"Avraham, are you all right. We've been worried."

"Yes, I am fine," Avraham, the blond Mossad agent, answered.

"Were you able to complete the mission?" the Mossad agent on the other end of the phone asked.

"It's done." There was no question in Avraham's mind that he would do anything for his country. Nothing was too difficult.

"He's dead?"

"Yes."

"Did you make it look like a robbery?"

"Of course," Avraham said.

"Good work. Get on the first plane and come home to Israel. We have a trial beginning for the son of a bitch, Manfred Blau."

"I will be home as soon as I can," Avraham said. "I can't wait to be back on Israeli soil, back with my wife and my son."

"God bless you and keep you safe, my brother."

"Shalom."

"Shalom."

Chapter 78

Katja took the day off on Friday. Aryeh and Brenda were coming to Elan's apartment for Shabbat dinner that night and she wanted everything to be perfect. This was their first visit, and she'd planned a special menu, purchased a white tablecloth, and a set of four white china dishes. Aryeh had called Elan to say that he and Brenda were getting married. That was when Elan had invited them to come for Shabbat to celebrate their engagement. Katja didn't mind. Having grown up on a kibbutz, she loved to have a lot of people around.

She was mashing sesame seeds for tahini while the radio played in the background. Her English was good, and she had really come to enjoy American music. Ever since Elan had introduced her to rock and roll, she couldn't get enough. The station she was tuned into had a mixture of Israeli and American artists. On occasion, when she knew the words, she sang along. Just a little more lemon and the tahini would be perfect! She began cutting thin pieces of eggplant to fry.

"We interrupt this program to bring you, firsthand, the trial of Manfred Blau, the sadistic Nazi who was captured and is now standing trial in Israel," the voice on the radio said.

A Nazi? Katja hadn't heard anything about this, but she could not help but remember her visit to the Kibbutz of the Ghetto Fighters and the stories of the horrors that the Nazis inflicted upon people. She listened more closely.

"State your name for the court."

"My name?"

"Your name."

"Dolf Sprecht."

"Your given name, sir."

"Oh, yes. Manfred Blau."

"Were you or were you not responsible for the torture and death of thousands of Jewish people at the Treblinka concentration camp?" the prosecutor asked.

"I only did what I was told. I am a soldier; a soldier must follow orders."

"We have a list of Jews who testified against you at Nuremburg before you escaped. Do you remember your trial?"

"No, I don't remember anything at all," Manfred said.

"Well then, let me remind you of their names."

The man began to read off a list. Katja shook her head. What a terrible man, she thought, beating an egg to soak the eggplant in before breading it.

The prosecutor read . . . "Samuel Goldstein, Rivka Jacobson, Martha Greenberg, Leon Blumberg, Joseph Saltzman . . .

Then she heard it . . .

"Zofia Weiss," the prosecutor said.

My mother? That's my mother's maiden name.

Katja dropped the slice of eggplant on the floor and ran into the living room. She turned up the volume on the radio.

The prosecutor continued reading names. Suddenly, Manfred began laughing loud, hysterical laughter. Katja felt a shiver as she listened.

"You don't understand how it was. You can't know the weight I carried on my shoulders. The responsibility we had in order to build a superior race . . ." Manfred said. "You only know what you see."

"Where is your family, Manfred Blau?"

"My family?" Manfred said, his voice suddenly broken and small. "My wife is dead. My Christa, is dead. You see, that was a sacrifice that I had to make for the party. That's what I mean, you don't understand."

Katja thought Manfred sounded insane. Did he kill his wife?

"Did you murder your wife, Manfred Blau?"

"She died when I was in prison. But the party took her away from me. First it gave her to me and then it took her away . . ." Manfred said.

"I see," the prosecutor said.

"You see nothing," Manfred answered, his voice raised.

"When you were younger, didn't you and your wife adopt a child from Himmler's Lebensborn organization? What happened to that child, Manfred Blau?"

"I don't know what happened to Katja. Poor Katja. My wife loved that little girl."

"And you, did you love the child?"

"I don't know. Love. I was so busy with my work that I didn't have time for a child, so I brought in a Jewess to take care of her. Christa, my wife, was very ill. She could not care for the child. That person that I took into my home was Zofia Weiss, the Jewess you just mentioned. My wife and I always treated her well. I still don't know why she testified against me. Ungrateful, good-for-nothing Jew. That's what she was, an ingrate. I could have killed her, but instead I took her into our house, under my roof where my family lived. We fed her, protected her, and gave her shelter. And then, look at what she did to me. She turned on me, testified against me. Stood in the courtroom and told them lies that would condemn me to death. Hitler was right, Goebbels was right; Jews are deceitful, dangerous. You can't trust them."

"The child, Mr. Blau. What happened to the child?"

Katja forgot to breathe. She was cold and shaking. She'd heard the prosecutor say that the child's name was Katja.

"When I went to jail, my wife took the child away. It was the last I saw of them—the little girl or my wife."

"Did you kill the child so that she would not be raised outside of the Nazi party? The way that Goebbels and his wife murdered their six children? Did you Mr. Blau?" The prosecutor's voice came booming through the radio.

"I swear I did not . . ."

The questioning continued, but Katja was no longer listening. Katja's hand went to her throat; she couldn't catch her breath. She was hyperventilating. What was all of this about? This Nazi, this Manfred Blau, had mentioned her mother, and he'd mentioned her name, too. Katja.

Katja put her head in her hands and bent forward. She was afraid she might faint. *I must go to my mother. I have to know the truth.*

When Elan arrived at the apartment, he found the kitchen a mess. It seemed as if Katja had stopped right in the middle of preparing dinner. How strange. Perhaps she'd run out to the market for something she'd forgotten. Then Elan saw a note on the table. He picked it up and read:

Dear Elan,

I'm sorry to have left so abruptly. An emergency arose. I had to go home. Please don't follow me. I will explain when I talk to you. I will be in contact as soon as I can.

Kat

Elan re-read the note. This was not like Katja. He wondered if one of her parents had taken ill. She would never have run off for no reason. Aryeh and Brenda would be there in a half hour. He would wait for them and explain. Then he would get in the car and go right to the kibbutz. Whatever Katja was going through, he wanted to be there with her, to support her in any way that he could.

Chapter 79

The kibbutz was buzzing with people, as it always was on Shabbat. Katja entered the main house to find several of the adults gathered in groups, talking, clearing the dishes. As she walked through the crowd, in search of her mother, several of the women hugged and greeted her, but she could not respond. Her heart felt as if it had turned to stone. Her eyes scanned the room until she saw Zofia and Isaac sitting with another couple. Her parents were holding hands. Katja felt a shiver come over her as she slowly walked over to them. Each step was bringing her closer to words that she dreaded but knew she must hear.

"Sunshine, what a wonderful surprise," Isaac said. "What brings you here on this Sabbath night?"

Zofia got up to hug her daughter, but Katja pulled away.

"Mother, I have to talk to you. Alone."

Zofia's head tilted to one side. A deep furrow formed between her eyes.

"I'll be back," Zofia said, turning to Isaac and the others.

Then Zofia and Katja walked, without speaking, to the room Zofia and Isaac shared. Zofia sat on the bed and patted the area next to her for Katja to sit. Katja remained standing with her arms crossed over her chest. She could not meet her mother's eyes.

"Mama, have you been listening to the radio?" Katja asked, but she knew that Zofia, like the others on the kibbutz, had little interest in the outside world.

"You know I don't listen to the radio very often. The only radio we have is in the main house and I'm usually with the children. Why? Katja, what is it? What's wrong?"

"Manfred Blau. Do you know that name, Mama?" Katja had been turned away, looking out the window, but when she spoke the name, she whirled around to look at her mother. Zofia turned white. She looked into Katja's eyes and then looked away. The intensity was too much to bear.

There was silence for what seemed like hours but, in actuality, was only seconds.

"Yes. I know that name."

"He is on trial here in Israel. It's all over the news."

"Manfred Blau was convicted and sentenced to death long ago in Nuremburg," Zofia said, her voice barely a whisper.

"You testified," Katja said.

Zofia nodded.

"You knew him."

Zofia nodded again, biting her lower lip.

"Am I the child that he and his wife adopted from something called the Lebensborn?" Katja asked, her voice cracking. "Please say no, please let it be a mistake . . ."

Zofia shrugged, shaking her head. Her trembling hands open.

"Answer me, Mother. Please, answer me. I have to know the truth. Who am I, Mother? Who am I?" Katja was yelling. Tears were spilling down her face. Her face was crimson and her body was shaking violently.

Zofia felt the tears well up in her eyes. She threw her hands in the air in a gesture that seemed to be asking God why?

"Yes, Katja. Yes, you are that child."

"I am not your daughter?"

"You are my daughter. I raised you. I love you. But I did not give birth to you. I am not your birth mother."

Katja turned away. She felt as if her body was covered in ice. Her trembling grew even more powerful. "Who is my mother? What is the Lebensborn? And why was I adopted by an SS officer?"

"Oh, my God," Zofia whispered. "I tried to shield you. I never wanted to tell you. You were raised here in Israel. You are as Jewish as anyone here."

"Except for my blood. Who am I, Mother? Who am I?" Katja walked over and shook Zofia shoulders. "Tell me now."

Zofia stood up. Her legs and back ached. She squatted down and pulled the old cardboard valise from under her bed where she had kept the papers hidden since she, Isaac, and Katja had come to Israel. She knelt in front of the suitcase and pulled the lock open. Her hands were shaking so badly she could hardly move them. Zofia glanced at Katja, then she took the envelope out from beneath the lining where she'd hidden it so long ago. Turning away from her daughter, she handed her the envelope.

Katja opened the envelope and sat down on the bed.

ADOPTION PAPERS FROM STEINHÖRING, INSTITUTE FOR THE LEBENSBORN.

Mother: Helga Haswell - verified to have no tainted blood. Pure Aryan.

Father: SS Officer (Married, not wishing to disclose his identity) However, acceptability verified.

Born: January 30, 1941, in Steinhöring, the home for the Lebensborn, Munich, Germany.

Christened by Reichsführer Heinrick Himmler, and given the name Katja.

Adopted: March - by Christa and Manfred Blau. Wife, pure Aryan, Husband, SS Officer. Adoption request granted by Reichsführer Himmler and Minister of Propaganda Dr. Josef Goebbels.

When she finished reading the paper, Katja looked at Zofia, dazed. She still held the paper in her hands.

"How is this possible?" she said under her breath. "I am the offspring of everything I hate. I have Nazi blood running through my veins."

"I'm sorry," Zofia said.

"Sorry for not telling me, or sorry for taking me in?"

"For not telling you. I would never be sorry for taking you in. You have been my child, the light of my life. I love you. Your father loves you. Whatever it was that brought you to us doesn't matter. We can just fold this paper up and put it away forever. We can forget about all of this."

"No, mother, we can't. It's all over the news—and besides, I can't marry Elan now. My blood is contaminated. It wouldn't be fair to him." She was weeping with heart-wrenching sobs. "He wants to have Jewish children, not babies with Nazi roots."

"Don't be foolish. He will understand. You are not a Nazi. You were an innocent child. None of this was ever your fault. A bunch of sick men tried to create a world where every child was blond with blue eyes."

"And I am . . . blond and blue-eyed." She was shaking so hard that Zofia went to her and tried to embrace her, but Katja shook her off.

"You are beautiful. There is nothing Nazi about you. You grew up here in our homeland, you grew up Jewish. You are one of us."

"I need to tell Rachel and Mendel before they hear it on the news. And, God help me, I have to tell Elan." Katja straightened up and wiped the tears from her face with the back of her hand.

Katja called Rachel first, but there was no answer. Then she called Mendel. As soon as she heard his voice, she started to cry again. She told him everything. She read him the papers from the Lebensborn Institute. He listened in his patient, quiet way.

Then he said, "Where are you?"

"I'm here, at the kibbutz. I don't know what to do, Mendel. I'm scared. I don't know who I am, where I came from. And God help me, my real parents are Nazis. She was sobbing so hard that she was choking.

"*Shhh*, listen to me, Kat. I'll be there in the morning. Then you and I will go and find this woman, this Helga Haswell. If she is your birth mother, then that is a good place to start. She will probably have a lot of answers for you."

"I'm not a Jew, Mendel. The people who I love, my mama and papa, are not my parents. I'm a Nazi. I want to die. I don't want to go on living this way."

"Stop it! No, you are not a Nazi. And they *are* your parents. They raised you and took care of you. Anyone can have a child, but not everyone can be a parent. Now listen to me, Katja. You are as Jewish as I am. Please don't do anything foolish; just wait for me. You hear me, Kat? I mean it. I'm getting in the car as soon as we hang up. I'll be there as soon as I can," he said.

Elan arrived first. It was two o'clock in the morning. Katja was staying in the guesthouse, but she was not asleep. Elan didn't know where to find her so he knocked on her parent's door.

"I'm sorry to wake you," he said, when Isaac opened the door. "Is Katja here?"

"We weren't asleep. Yes, she's in the guesthouse."

"What is it? What's wrong? She ran out of the house like a lunatic, without telling me anything. She left me a crazy note. I was worried sick all the way here. Is someone ill? Is someone dead?"

Zofia walked over to the door. She wore a bathrobe and her hair was undone. By the redness of her eyes and her tear-stained cheeks it was clear that she had been crying. "I think Katja should tell you herself."

"Then take me to her. PLEASE."

They knocked on the door of the room where Katja was staying. She opened it, thinking it was Mendel.

"Elan, you shouldn't have come. I asked you not to come," Katja said.

"You've been crying," he said, trying to wipe the tears from her cheeks. She backed away as if his touch was fire.

"We cannot get married."

"You're talking crazy, Katja, what is it? Another man?"

"I am not who you think I am. I am someone dark and horrible."

He looked at her, confused. "Katja, what are you talking about?"

Then she told him.

He listened without speaking. By the time she had finished, his face was ashen.

"We can't marry," she said.

He looked away. He could not bear to see the pain in her face when he told her what he must tell her. "You're right, Katja. We cannot marry. I love you. I will go to my grave loving you. But, as I told you once before, this country means more to me than my own life. I must not pollute the bloodline."

Zofia was standing there, looking at him. "Pollute the blood, Elan? You're beginning to sound like a Nazi yourself. How can you say these things? Katja is Jewish; she was raised to be Jewish."

"I could accept everything if she were just gentile, and I would marry her if that were all there was to it. But it's so much more, so much more. She has Nazi blood. The blood of our enemies. Not only our enemies but the worst of the worst—the blood of the SS, for God's sake. We have no idea how many of our people's deaths her parents are responsible for. That would be our children's ancestry; that is the blood that would run through our children's veins. I can't do that."

"Elan!" Zofia said.

"I'm sorry, Kat." Elan shook his head. Then he turned and left.

Katja threw herself on the bed and began weeping hard again. Isaac sat down beside her, putting his arm around her shoulder. "Let him go Kat. Any man who would leave you for something that is not your fault is a man that you would be better off without." Katja sat up and buried her face in Isaac's shoulder. Then Isaac rocked her like he did when she was little. "It's going to be all right, Kat . . ." he whispered.

Zofia and Isaac stayed for several hours, until Zofia finally asked the kibbutz doctor for something to help Katja get to sleep. When Katja finally fell asleep, Zofia breathed a sigh of relief. Then she took Isaac's arm and they went back to their own room.

Mendel arrived at five thirty in the morning. He went to the guesthouse and looked up the room number where Katja was staying. Then he went to the room and knocked on the door. No one answered and he began to knock harder. He was about to go for help, to find someone to help him knock down the door. What if she had killed herself? He started down the hall, running towards the big house, when the door to Katja's room opened.

"Mendel," she said, her voice soft and broken.

"Katja. My God, Katja," he said. He ran back. "Are you all right?"

"No, I'm not."

He followed her into the room. When he flipped the light switch, she squinted.

"You look dazed. Your eyes are really glassy. Did you take something?" he asked.

"Yes, but it's not what you're thinking. My mother got me a sleeping pill from the doctor, to help me sleep."

"Kat," Mendel said, sitting down beside her on the bed.

"I told Elan."

"And . . ."

"He agrees with me. We called off the wedding."

Mendel nodded, saying nothing.

"I want to find her, Mendel."

"Find who."

"My birth mother. Helga Haswell."

He nodded. "I figured you would."

"I have to. I don't want to see or talk to that horrible Manfred Blau, but I have to find my birth mother."

"I know."

"Will you help me?"

"Of course, I'll help you. But I'm not sure we'll be able to find her. And Kat . . . if we do find her . . . well . . ."

"I have to do it, no matter what the consequences, so that I can go on with my life," Katja said.

"I'll do what I can to pull up any records. We'll search Germany, Poland, France, Switzerland, Austria, Norway, Denmark, everywhere, for a Helga Haswell. Now, remember, so many of the Nazis fled Europe and are living under assumed names. So, there might not be any listings for a Helga Haswell. But it's all we have to go on."

Chapter 80

Manfred Blau was tried and convicted in 1964. His execution date was set and Israel made sure that he was heavily guarded for every moment that remained of his life.

The morning of the day that Manfred would face the noose, he wept. After all the years that he had denied the existence of a God, now he called out in desperation for God to help. He was afraid— alone and afraid. Would it be painful? Would it be quick? Was there an afterlife? What would happen once this world, the only world he knew, turned dark to him forever? Would he see Christa again? Would he have the opportunity to tell her how sorry he was for everything? Would Dr. Goebbels be there? Was there a hell? Or was there nothing at all? Was it all over, everything over?

Manfred swallowed hard and put his hand up to feel the tender skin on his neck. He felt panic rising inside him, but no matter how loud he screamed or how hard he cried, no one would come, no one would listen. Manfred Blau would die today. These moments would be the last moments of his life on earth.

Several survivors of the camps who had suffered by Manfred's hand watched the execution. Zofia was not among them.

Chapter 81

Katja knew she must return to the army and serve the remainder of her time. But since she'd come upon this knowledge of her birth, everything had changed for her. Even before she had met Elan she'd enjoyed her job. Then, once Elan had come into her life, every day was filled with joy. Now, however, she counted the days, the hours, the minutes, until her tour of duty would be over and she could leave Tel Aviv and all of the memories of Elan behind. Although they lived in the same neighborhood, Katja never saw Elan; not when she was shopping for things she needed, or picking up her boss's laundry. Not ever. Mendel, however, was a constant in her life again. He went to the library and returned with stacks of journals, then he kept her company while he quietly researched her past, looking for answers. The answers she needed so desperately.

Mendel could see that the light had gone out of Katja's eyes. She was kind and friendly, and always made him feel welcome. But she never laughed anymore. She no longer sang while she folded laundry. He saw the overwhelming sadness in her and knew there was nothing he could do to ease her pain. Of course, he knew that she must miss Elan, although she never mentioned his name. All of the pictures that she kept beside her bed of her and Elan were gone, and Mendel never asked what she'd done with them. Yes, he'd always loved her, and he wanted her for his own, but not like this, not because she was hurt and lonely. Mendel would rather have suffered all the pain in the world than to see Katja miserable. And, he would never take advantage of her desperation. Instead, he would be the same as he was when he was just a childhood friend; ever constant in her life. He would help her get through this. And he would pray that whatever information awaited them about her birth parents was not as terrible as his speculations.

Zofia and Isaac called every week, and she spoke to them, but she could not help but feel that they had betrayed her by keeping the important information about her adoption from her. Zofia tried to explain. She begged Katja to understand, but Katja refused to listen.

Finally, her time in the army was done. Katja made the necessary arrangements, and she returned to the kibbutz. Mendel took a leave from school and returned with her.

Mendel and Isaac were alone one afternoon, outside in the orchard.

"So, what have you found out about Katja's past?" Isaac asked.

"I cannot find anyone by the name of Helga Haswell anywhere in Europe."

Isaac shrugged "I was doubtful about you finding her birth mother with everything that happened during the war. People just disappeared."

"I know. But I did find something. I mean, it could be nothing, but I haven't told Kat yet. I wanted her to finish her time in the army before I told her."

"What did you find?"

"Well, I found a listing for a woman in Switzerland, her name is Leah Haswell. Maybe she is Helga's sister."

"*Hmmm*, perhaps, but Leah is a Jewish name."

"Yes, I know. It's very strange."

"There could be no connection at all."

"That is possible, but for Kat's sake, I want to go to Switzerland and see what we can find."

"What about Zofia? She would want to go with you. Her heart is broken over this situation with Katja. Katja has pushed her away. We call Kat every week and she is very cold to her mother. Zofia raised her as if she were her own child. Regardless of how Katja came to live with Zofia, Zofia is everything you could ever want from a mother."

"Where did Zofia find Katja in the first place?"

"Well, Zofia was a prisoner in Treblinka. That Nazi who was on trial, that Manfred Blau, was an official at Treblinka. He needed a housekeeper and nanny for his daughter. He decided on Zofia. From what Zofia has told me, Blau's wife was very kind but very ill. Zofia took care of Katja from the time she was just a baby. Then the prisoners in Treblinka staged an uprising and Blau's wife helped Zofia escape. She escaped into the forest. That was where we met. We were in hiding. After the war was over, Manfred Blau was captured and he went to trial in Nuremberg. Zofia was living in a DP camp. A lawyer came to see her and asked her to testify. In exchange for testifying, the lawyer promised Zofia that he would help her to start her life over in London. She did. Zofia said it was very hard for her, but she knew that it must be done. When Zofia was in the courtroom, she saw Blau's wife sitting in the audience.

That night, the wife went to see Zofia at her hotel room. She told Zofia that she was dying, and she asked Zofia if she would take Katja and care for her and raise her. Zofia said that Blau's wife did not trust Manfred to care for the child even if he were somehow not convicted; although it was quite apparent that he would be. Of course, Blau was convicted and sentenced to death. Zofia never knew that he had escaped. So, she tried to shelter Katja by never telling her the truth. I always told Zofia that she should tell Katja, but she couldn't. Zofia and I love Katja as if she were our own offspring. Zofia couldn't bear to tell her; she didn't want to see her hurt. Zofia thought that Manfred was dead and his wife, too. She believed that the secret died with them."

"And I suppose Blau has never told anyone where his wife sent Katja?"

"From what Blau has said at the trial, I have come to understand that the wife was dead by the time Blau escaped from prison. She never had a chance to tell him that she sent Katja to live with Zofia."

"So, Blau has no idea what happened to Katja."

"Exactly right. And Zofia wants to keep it that way, for Katja's sake."

"I can understand, but if Katja wants to talk to Blau, we have to try to arrange for her to meet with him."

"I hope she doesn't want to see him. According to Zofia, he was a depraved, sadistic son of a bitch," Isaac said.

"I don't doubt that he was," Mendel nodded. "Even though I can remember a little of what it was like in Germany during the war, I still find it hard to believe that most of the Nazis were even human."

Chapter 82

Zofia made herself available to Katja, but she did not force her daughter to communicate with her. Instead, she just waited, praying that Katja would realize that Zofia had done what she believed was best for Katja. And that Katja would forgive her for not telling her the truth.

It was several days that Katja remained in her old room without coming out. Zofia and Isaac were worried. Mendel brought Katja food and went in to sit with her, but she hardly ate. She told him that she could not forgive her mother. Many times he explained how Zofia only meant to protect Katja because she loved her. For hours, Katja lay with her head on Mendel's lap while he stroked her hair in silence.

Then finally, one morning, Katja got up. She splashed cold water on her red, tear-stained face, and went to find Zofia where she was working in the children's house. She entered quietly. Zofia's back was to the door so she did not see Katja enter. Zofia was surrounded by a circle of children to whom she was reading a story.

Katja watched Zofia. She remembered how her mother had read to her. She remembered how Zofia had taken old worn-out socks and given them to her, along with buttons, pom-poms, paper, and paste (that she'd made from flour and water) to make puppets, so that Katja could use the puppets to act out the stories in the books Zofia read to her. Isaac had cut a hole into a large cardboard box. Then Katja and her parents had painted the box to make it into a puppet theater. Katja, Rachel and Mendel had spent many Sunday afternoons putting on puppet shows while Zofia and Isaac had watched patiently, laughing when it was appropriate, and always clapping and cheering. They were good parents. She could not have asked for better.

No matter what had happened; no matter who had given birth to her, or who the man was that spawned her, Isaac was her father and Zofia was her mother.

She had tears in her eyes as she heard Zofia ask one of the little girls, "So Chana, what do you think happened to the glass slipper?"

"I don't know Mrs. Zuckerman . . ."

"Does anyone know?" Zofia asked.

One of the children raised his hand, "Yes, Ari?" Zofia said.

"Maybe it got broken, or maybe the fairy made it disappear."

"Perhaps," Zofia said. "But you'll all have to listen very closely while I finish the story if you want to find out."

"Will the prince marry her?" another little girl asked. "How will he ever be able to find her?"

"Listen," Zofia said, in an inviting whisper. "I will tell you . . ." Then she began to read.

Katja stood there for several minutes, the tears welling up in her eyes. She covered her mouth with her hand. Zofia was still so patient. Katja took a deep breath. Then she walked over and touched Zofia's shoulder. Zofia jumped a little because she hadn't been expecting anyone. Then she turned and saw Katja.

"I love you, Mama." Katja said.

Zofia studied Katja. For a few seconds she couldn't move. Then she stood up and hugged her daughter, patting Katja's back the way she did when Katja was little. "I love you, my Sunshine."

"I'm sorry, Mama. Can you forgive me?"

"I've already forgotten anything you ever did that would need forgiving. I love you, Katja. You are my child, my heart and my life." Tears rolled down Zofia's cheeks.

"If Mendel can find any information, he and I are going to go and meet Helga Haswell. I want you to be with me. Will you go?"

"Of course. You know that I will."

"Yes, Mama, I knew you would."

The temperature was in the low sixties when Mendel asked Katja to come for a walk through the orchards. "I want to talk to you," he said.

"You have news about my birth mother?"

"Take a heavy sweater," Mendel said. "You know how cool it can get out there."

She nodded, grabbing a thick, navy-blue, wrap-around sweater with a thick belt. He helped her put it on. "There, now you'll be nice and warm."

"Mendel, please, talk to me. Tell me what you know."

"I'm going to tell you everything. Let's walk."

They walked for several minutes. People from the kibbutz who were working in the fields waved and Katja and Mendel waved back. Katja's heart was beating so hard that she felt she might vomit or faint.

"Mendel . . ." she said. "Please." She knew he dreaded this, but it had to be done. She had to know.

"I searched everywhere. I can't find anyone by the name of Helga Haswell."

She sighed. "I thought that might happen."

"But I did find something strange. I found a Leah Haswell. It could be nothing. This woman may not be connected in any way."

"Leah? Leah is her name?"

"Yes."

"Maybe Helga changed her name?"

"But why? Leah is a Jewish name. If she is posing as a Jew she would have changed her surname as well."

"That's right. So, I have no idea if any of this information is even related to Helga," he said.

"I have to know for sure. I have to meet her. Where is she?"

"Switzerland. I figured that you would want to go there and find out whatever we can. So, I've already arranged a flight."

"But my mother wants to come with us," Katja said.

"I know. I talked to her. I got a plane ticket for her, too."

"For the three of us?" Katja asked. "And my father?"

"We ran out of money. He said that he understood. He said that it was best that the three of us go together. He said that he will stay close to the phone in case you need him."

"Papa . . ."

"You're parents love you very much, Katja." Mendel said.

"It must have been expensive," she said.

"I had a little money saved and your father gave me what he could."

She nodded. "Oh Mendel, I'm so scared."

"I know. I'll be right here beside you."

"Thank you. Oh Mendel, you have always been right beside me, throughout my entire life. What a good friend you are. I am so blessed to have you."

"You'd do the same for me or for Rachel."

"You're right, I would."

"We are blood sisters and brothers, right?" He smiled and winked at her.

She mustered a smile for him. "Yes, we are. You still remember that? When Rachel made us all cut ourselves?"

"Of course, how could I forget? It bound us together forever . . ."

She smiled. "I am so grateful to you, Mendel, for everything."

He smiled. "We leave in three days. Can you be ready?"

"Yes, but we should tell my mother; to make sure she is ready."

"I'll take care of everything," he said. "Don't worry about anything at all."

Chapter 83

Leah Haswell had just finished giving her fourth piano lesson of the day and she was worn out. For a woman alone, it was difficult to make ends meet. However, she still loved her deceased husband and although she'd had many offers, she could not bring herself to remarry. Her son, Daniel, was staying late at school to participate in an athletic event. He was so like his father. His father had been a contender to enter the Olympics if not for Hitler.

If Hitler had not come into power, everything would have been different. The Nazis had taken her home, her father, and the man whom she loved, the father of her son, Daniel. Leah gathered the sheet music together and placed it neatly inside the seat of the piano bench. It would be at least a few hours before Daniel returned. Since he would be home late they would have a light dinner. An omelet, perhaps.

On the nights when Daniel was not participating in soccer or some other sport, he had recently begun working. He insisted on helping his mother with the finances, and it broke her heart that he could not put full concentration into his schooling. She'd protested his getting a job, but he would not hear her. He worked at the loading dock of a nearby factory, bringing home enough money to make things a little more comfortable.

She filled her teapot and put it on a low flame to boil, and then she took the book she was reading down from the shelf and sat down for a few hours of escape into her novel. She had hardly begun reading when the phone rang. It was probably another piano student needing to schedule a lesson. Leah stretched and stood up to pick up the receiver. Then she took the pen and appointment book she kept by the phone.

"Hello."

"Is this Leah Haswell?"

It was a man's voice. Her heart began to beat quickly. Was it the school? Was something wrong with Daniel? "Yes, this is Mrs. Haswell."

"My name is Mendel Zaltstein. I am so sorry to bother you. And . . . I know that this call might seem strange. But, it is very important that I ask you this . . . do you know a Helga Haswell?"

It had been years since anyone had mentioned Detrick's sister's name. Years since she'd heard of Helga. In fact, the last time was when Detrick had gone to see his sister at the farm, leaving her and her father alone in Berlin. She'd told Detrick to go and see his sister, begged him in fact. But it was while he was gone that Leah and her father, Jacob, had been taken by the Gestapo. Leah sunk down on the sofa, the cord to the phone stretching taut, as her hands trembled. The appointment book dropped to the floor and she almost dropped the receiver.

"She is my late husband's sister." Leah cleared her throat. "Why do you ask? Why do you want to know?"

"Let me explain," Mendel said. And then he told her everything.

Chapter 84

A week later Zofia, Katja, and Mendel arrived at Leah's apartment. It was the same apartment where Detrick had left Leah so many years ago when he went on his mission to rescue her father. It was a small flat, and although it was sparsely furnished, there was an air of dignity about it.

"Please, come in and sit down," Leah said.

"I'm sorry that we are intruding on you," Zofia said, "but you were one of the only Haswells that Mendel was able to find in all of Europe."

"Yes, that would probably be right," Leah said. "My husband's parents were older and have probably passed on. And Helga, well, she got married. So, her last name would be different."

"Do you have any idea of her married name?" Mendel asked.

Katja sat at the edge of the corner of the sofa.

"I'm not sure. But if my memory serves me, she married a farmer. His name was Kurt and they lived somewhere on a farm in the outskirts of Munich. That much I do remember."

"Was Kurt an SS officer, or a Nazi?" Katja asked, her voice small, almost a whisper.

"No, at least I don't think so. My husband, Detrick, never mentioned anything like that." Leah looked at Katja. She resembled Detrick and Daniel so much that Leah thought she might cry. The blond hair, the way it fell over her left eye. *Detrick, my Detrick. This is your sister's lost child. I can see it in everything about her.*

Katja looked around. She saw a menorah up on a shelf, and pictures of a young, blond boy who looked a great deal like her, who was wearing a yarmulke and tafillin. He stood beside a Rabbi in what appeared to be a bar mitzvah picture. "Are you Jewish?" Katja asked.

"Yes."

"So Helga is Jewish? How can that be if I was born in the Lebensborn? The man who impregnated her was an SS officer. I don't understand at all."

"Helga is not Jewish. My husband was not born Jewish. He converted."

"The picture is your son?" Katja asked.

"Yes, it's my Daniel. He's my life. He looks a lot like you. You, Katja, look a lot like my husband. Detrick was a wonderful man; his heart was so good."

"Was Helga like him?"

"I never met her. But she had to be somewhat like him. They were brother and sister."

"That doesn't mean anything," Katja said, crossing her arms over her chest. "She got pregnant by an SS officer. How could she do that?"

"I don't know. I don't know what happened," Leah said.

"And then she gave me up, as if I were nothing. How can I ever forgive her?" Katja said. Zofia walked over to Katja and sat down next to her, putting her arm around her daughter's shoulder.

"This is none of my business, but I am going to say something. If I am out of line, please say so." Leah looked at Katja. "I know that the man who fathered you was not the ideal father, but my husband also posed as an SS officer in order to protect my father and me. So, your father may not have been what he seemed. During the war, things were different. People did strange things to survive. It is hard to explain. If you were not there, you could never understand."

Zofia nodded. "I was there, I understand."

"Also, please, remember this . . . you and your mother seem to be very close. If Helga had not given you up, you would never have met your mother. So sometimes, maybe things happen for a reason."

Katja looked at Zofia. She loved her mother. Zofia had given her everything, everything but life. Katja reached up and touched Zofia's hand on her shoulder. Then she smiled at Zofia. Zofia was crying.

"Sometimes things happen and we think that they are bad things, but if we look at them more closely we realize that God has given us a gift in return for all we have lost. I loved my husband more than anything in the world. And I lost him. But, at least before God took him, he gave me a son, my Daniel—my precious Daniel. So, you came into the world in a way that you find unacceptable, I understand this. However, if you look more closely, you will see that God has given you a mother who loves you. Perhaps a father, too? And a dear friend who is standing beside you even now." Leah indicated Mendel. "Things are not so bad, Katja."

Katja nodded. "I do have a dear father, as well. And in many ways, I am blessed. I live in Israel, the land of our people . . ."

Leah smiled and nodded.

"Do you have any family in Israel?" Katja asked.

"I don't know. I had a brother. A brother I loved very much. He ran away when he was young, and he always had wanted to go to Israel. I've tried to find him, but I never could. So, I've always prayed that he made it to Israel."

"Perhaps we know him, what was his name?" Katja asked

"Karl Abdenstern. Do you know him?"

Zofia's head snapped as she turned to look at Leah. "Karl Abdenstern. That is your brother?"

"You know him?"

"OH, MY GOD. I know him. I had a child. A little girl. We were in the Warsaw Ghetto. The Nazis were liquidating the ghetto. Your brother, Karl, was involved in the underground. He was also involved in the black market. He saved my daughter's life. One night," Zofia took a deep breath, "He took Eidel, my daughter, she was a baby at the time, and he carried her over the ghetto wall and into the arms of a wonderful friend of mine who was not Jewish. This woman raised Eidel as her own daughter. If it were not for Karl, my daughter would have been dead."

Katja looked at Zofia, shocked. "Where is Eidel? You never told me about her. I never knew anything about you having another child. Was she Isaac's?"

"No, Isaac was not her father. And you're right, I should have told you. I should have told you so many things. After the war, I went to find Eidel. I was going to take her away to live with me. But when I saw her relationship with Helen, the woman who I'd given her to, I knew that I must leave her where she was. Eidel and Helen had grown very close. Helen raised her as her own."

"Does she know that you are her mother?" Katja said.

"I don't know. I never told her. She was so happy with Helen, so content. She had her friends and her life. I couldn't rip her away from all of that."

"So you took me?"

"It wasn't like that at all. You were not a substitute for Eidel. I loved you. I love you for being who you are. You are my daughter, Katja. But I will explain further. When you were a little girl I was in the Treblinka concentration camp and that man, Manfred Blau, took me in as his housekeeper. He and his wife had adopted you a couple of years earlier. You were so little and so sweet. Manfred's wife was a good, kind woman. She treated me well. I took care of you because she was sick. So, I raised you since you were a baby. It was like you were mine from the beginning.

When the camp was dismantled and the Nazis ran away, Manfred and Christa took you with them. I missed you terribly every day. Every day I thought about you, praying that you would be all right. I never thought I would see you again," Zofia said. "Then, I testified against Manfred and Christa was there in the courtroom. She came to my hotel room that night and said she was dying. I knew it was true. She was very sick when you were young, and she looked even sicker at the trial. She asked me to take you, to raise you. There was no question in my mind. I wanted you. I loved you, and to me you were like a gift from God. The next day I met her outside the courtroom. She had you with her. From the moment I took your tiny hand in mine, I knew that I would give my life to keep you safe. And since that day, you have been my daughter, Katja. I love you."

Katja listened. Then she began to cry. Zofia took her into her arms and patted her back. "*Shhhh*, Sunshine. *Shhhh*, it's all right."

"Have you seen my brother again in Israel?" Leah asked Zofia.

"No, I never saw him again after I was taken to the camp. I am so sorry, Leah. I don't know what happened to him."

"I like to believe that he made it to Israel, to the Promised Land," Leah said, a sad smile on her face. "He always dreamed of a Jewish homeland."

The room was uncomfortably silent for a few minutes.

"Do you know what kind of farm it was where Helga was living, dairy? Or what kind of crops they grew?" Mendel asked Leah.

"I can remember Detrick saying something about strawberries and asparagus. Sometimes, in the small villages, the people know each other. You might explore the little towns in the outskirts of Munich," Leah said.

"Yes, that's a good idea," Mendel said.

"Did you know about anything about the Lebensborn?" Katja asked. "I had never even heard of it before I found out that I was born there.

"A little, not much. The Nazis were crazy. They wanted to create a master race. The Lebensborn was a place where they were handpicking women to breed with SS officers in hopes of creating a master race."

"My God, that is unbelievable. So I was basically bred," Katja said.

"Does it matter, Katja? You are a beautiful, wonderful girl, with a good family and good friends. What's past is past," Leah said. "If you dwell on the past, it will kill you for sure. You must move forward with your life now."

Katja considered this. "You're right, I know you are. I'd still like to meet her, though. I mean, after all, I would like to ask her a few questions . . . Helga, I mean. I wonder if I have any siblings."

"When Detrick went to visit Helga on the farm, I know that Helga was pregnant," Leah said.

"*Hmmm*," Mendel rubbed his chin. "So, either Katja was born on the farm and then sent to the Lebensborn, which I highly doubt, or she has a brother or sister."

"I would guess she had a brother or sister," Leah said. "Would any of you like some tea?" Leah asked.

Zofia, Mendel, and Katja shook their heads.

"No, thank you," Zofia said. "We've taken up enough of your time. I think we have to go to Munich. That's the next stop on our journey."

Leah nodded. "Good luck to you. I hope that you find the answers that you are looking for, and God bless you."

They left. Leah closed the door. Suddenly the silence felt heavy around her. She sat starring out the window, lost in memories of Detrick from many years ago. Detrick had looked so handsome when he went to see his sister in Munich. She could still remember the day. His aqua blue eyes shining with love for her. Regardless of the fact that he was wearing that horrible Nazi uniform, he was incredibly handsome. Even now, so many years later, she could still feel her heart skip when she thought about him.

Detrick . . . they had loved each other so much. She knew how hard it was for Detrick to live a lie, to pretend to be a Nazi when he was secretly married to her, a Jew. But he'd done what he had to do to protect Leah and her father. Then, while Detrick was in Munich visiting his sister, the real nightmare began. The Gestapo broke into their house, taking Leah and her father by force. She could still see her father's face bleeding from where the Gestapo agent had struck him. That was the last time she ever saw her father—the last time.

She and her father rode in the back of the automobile, not knowing what the Nazis had in store. Her heart was beating so hard she thought it would explode. Jacob had patted her arm, reassuring her, telling her that everything would be all right. That was the last time she'd seen his kind face. They were sent to separate camps. Papa, oh papa.

Then Detrick by some miracle, had come to the camp and rescued her. He'd stayed with her for only a short time and then he'd insisted that he must go and try to rescue her father. When he did not return within a few weeks, she felt sure that they both had to be dead. If Detrick were alive he'd have come back to her. But even though she knew the truth, she still hoped against all odds that somehow he had been arrested and was not dead but detained in a camp somewhere. How much she had loved her father, and how much she'd loved Detrick. Dear Detrick, he had risked everything for her. Then he'd put his life on the line a second time to try to save her father, Jacob. However, the second time he had not been as lucky.

Outside of her window the sun began to set. The sky was a watercolor painting of pinks and purples, but Leah hardly noticed. She forgot to prepare dinner. In fact, she did not get up from the sofa until Daniel came through the door.

Chapter 85

The small farming village where Kurt's family had lived for generations was a friendly town where everyone knew their neighbors. It was the fourth village that Zofia, Mendel, and Katja came to during their search. Finding Helga was surprisingly easy. They went to the general store and asked about Kurt and Helga. The old woman who ran the shop knew them well. She bought strawberries and asparagus from their farm when they were in season.

"Are you friends of Helga and Kurt?" The old woman winked and smiled as she revealed a mouth missing several teeth. She had a giant wart on her cheek that looked like a small flesh-colored golf ball. She had small, beady, dark eyes.

"Yes, we are," Mendel said. "Do you know where they live?"

"Of course, right up the road. There is a wire-fenced pen on the right-hand side of the road that will be filled with goats. When you see it, turn left. The farm you are looking for, where Kurt and Helga live, will be on the south side of the road. It's a big white house set back from the road. You can't miss it."

Katja nodded her head. "Thank you," she said, feeling unsteady. She pulled on Mendel's sleeve. "Can we go, please?"

"Of course, Kat," Mendel said. Then he thanked the old woman and they left.

Mendel began driving toward the farm. Katja held on to her handbag that was lying on her lap. She had two white-knuckled fists. The automobile rolled and stumbled across the dirt road.

After several moments of silence, Katja turned to Mendel.

"I can't go through with this," Katja said. "Please, Mendel. Take me back to the hotel. I want to go home, home to Israel."

"Are you sure?" Zofia said. "For the rest of your life, Sunshine, you will wonder who your mother and father were. We are here, just a few miles away. The woman who has the answer to all of your questions is just beyond that bend in the road. Now, for me, you have always been my daughter. Sharing you with your birth mother will be hard at first and if you want to turn back, I won't stop you. But I think that you should know the truth."

"Mama, I'm so scared," Katja said. Her voice sounded like a little girl, and it touched Zofia so deeply that she felt a pain deep in her heart.

"It's going to be all right. Nothing will change. I am your mother. I will always be your mother. And, you are Jewish. You were raised by Jewish parents to be Jewish. But now that you know the past, you won't be able to go forward with your life until you know everything."

Mendel reached over and took Katja's hand. "No matter what happens, I'm here for you Kat."

She nodded. "I know; you've always been here for me, Mendel."

"You decide now. The decision is yours. I will support you in whatever you choose," Mendel said, pulling the car over to the side of the road. Then he put the vehicle in park and waited. "What do you want me to do? Should I turn the car around, and go back to the hotel?" Mendel asked.

"No. Go to the farm," Katja said.

Helga was sitting outside peeling potatoes when the automobile came slowly up the drive. She squinted from the sun to see if she could recognize the automobile. It must be tourists who had made a wrong turn. It seemed that every couple of weeks a car filled with folks who were lost came up to the farm asking for directions.

Mendel pulled the car over to the side of the driveway and parked.

"Stay here for a minute," Katja said to Mendel and Zofia. Then she got out of the vehicle alone. Mendel stole a quick glance at Zofia, who shrugged in disbelief. Zofia's eyebrows were drawn together and the color left her face.

"Helga Haswell?" Katja said.

"I used to be Helga Haswell." Helga leaned forward as Katja walked closer so that Helga would be able to see her better.

"Do I know you?" Helga asked, tilting her head to one side. "You look very familiar."

"My name is Katja. I was born at Steinhöring, the home for the Lebensborn. According to my papers, my birth mother was Helga Haswell."

Helga grasped her throat. Her eyes flew open wide. Then she fainted.

Zofia and Mendel came rushing out of the car. Zofia went to Katja and Mendel went to see about Helga.

Kurt had heard the automobile and he came walking out of the fields to see who had come to the farm. When he saw Helga lying on the ground surrounded by strangers he rushed over to her. Then he bent at his wife's side. "Sweetheart, wake up. What is it? HELGA!!!"

Helga lay still.

Kurt ran to the kitchen and got a bottle of smelling salts. As soon as he put the open bottle under Helga's nose, her body jerked and she regained consciousness. Kurt helped Helga to sit up. "Are you all right? What happened? Let me get you some water," Kurt said.

"No, no water. Stay here, Kurt. I need you."

"What's going on here? Who are you?" He turned to Katja and asked.

It was Helga who answered; her voice a soft, raspy whisper. "That is my daughter, Kurt. The child I gave birth to, who was taken from me at the Lebensborn." Helga was shaken, but she studied Katja. For what seemed like a long time neither of them spoke. Then Helga stared into Katja's eyes and said, "A day never passed that I didn't think of you. Every year since the day you were born, I've remembered you on your birthday. I would say to myself, 'What is my daughter doing now? This year she will be two, she must be starting to walk, and to talk, too. This year she is five, she will start school.' I would pray to God that someone was holding you when you cried. All I could do was hope and pray that someone was caring for you . . . loving you as I would have if I could have."

"My father was an SS officer?" Katja cleared her throat.

"Yes. I am ashamed to tell you that he was. But you should know the truth. You deserve to know. I was young and so foolish. I didn't realize what the Nazis were all about. To me they were just men in uniforms that seemed handsome and powerful. I was taken in. And then you paid the price. Dear God, Katja, I am so sorry. So sorry. I had no idea when I signed into the Lebensborn that they would take you away from me."

"You didn't give me up willingly?"

"Oh, God, no. I wanted to keep you. I begged to keep you. But I was a single mother. The man who was your father was long gone, and they would not let me have you without him. I could not adopt you unless I married an SS officer. Dear God, I begged Himmler to let me keep you, but he refused. You have no idea how much I wanted you, how much I did not want to lose you. I had no choice. I held you for only one minute after you were born, and then they took you away. I watched the nurse carry you out of the delivery room, and I tried to will myself to die right then and there. But I didn't die. I was young and strong, and I lived.

A week later I left Steinhöring. Alone. Without you. I cried for a very long time, on and off for many years. Then I finally got pregnant, and although I never forgot you, my pain was eased a little when Jana was born."

"I have a sister?"

"You did. You had a sister. She died a week after her fifth birthday. I always felt that it was God's punishment to me for what I did, for getting pregnant out of wedlock, and then going to the Lebensborn . . ."

Kurt put his arm around his wife. Then Kurt said "It was terrible. I was afraid Helga was going to lose her mind. She kept talking about you, rambling on about the child that was taken from her at the Lebensborn, and then she would talk about Jana, our daughter who died. She couldn't eat or sleep. Finally, I had no choice; I allowed the doctor to put her into a sanitarium for a few months. Since then she's been a little better. But she has fainting spells and I would rather that you would all leave, and let her be. I'm not sure she can take this," Kurt said.

"It's all right, Kurt. I need to do this. I owe it to my daughter," Helga said to Kurt. Then she turned to Katja, "Please sit down. Don't leave. We need to talk this out."

Katja nodded.

"Come inside," Kurt said to Katja, Zofia, and Mendel. Then he helped Helga to her feet. Katja noticed that Helga's feet were swollen and when she walked, she seemed to be in pain.

They sat at the kitchen table. "Can I get you anything, something to eat or drink?" Kurt said, his voice cracking, not knowing what to do or say.

"No, thank you," Katja said. Mendel and Zofia shook their heads.

Helga took a breath and sighed. "Katja, can you ever forgive me? I know what I did was wrong, but your forgiveness would mean the world to me." Helga's face crinkled and she began to cry again. Kurt stood beside her, his hand on her shoulder. The once-glamorous and beautiful Helga was now an aged and weather-worn farmers' wife. Her waist was thick and deep lines, caused by years of sorrow, covered her face. Still, her sky-blue eyes were as mesmerizing as they had been when she was just a young girl. Those eyes remained as lovely as they had been that first time that Helga had met Eric, the handsome SS officer who had impregnated her with Katja and then left her without ever looking back. Helga's hands reached out and she seemed to be imploring Katja to understand. Her eyes were glossy with tears but she caught Katja's gaze and held it. "Please, Katja. Please, I am begging for your forgiveness."

Katja shook her head, took a deep breath and looked away. "I forgive you," she said, and she did. What other choice did she have? This woman who had given birth to her had been just a child at the time—just a young, foolish child.

Helga got up slowly and tried to put her arms around Katja. Katja could not return the embrace, but Katja did not push Helga away. She stood very still with her arms at her sides.

"The last time I held you, they were ripping you out of my arms. It was right after you were born. I remember screaming, screaming so loud that I can still hear the echo of my own voice, the way it sounded as they carried you away from me . . ." Helga said.

When Katja began this journey she thought she would hate this woman. She was expecting to find Helga and curse at her, hit her, take all of her anger out on her, but she didn't. She couldn't. However,

Katja didn't love her, either. Helga was nothing more than a stranger and all Katja could feel for her was pity—pity for a teenage girl who got wrapped up in something far too big for her to understand. Even though when Katja looked at Helga, Katja could faintly see her own features in Helga's face, she felt no attachment to her at all.

"There are things I need to know," Katja said.

"Go ahead. I will tell you anything that I can."

"Are there illnesses in my family, things that I might be prone to?"

"None that I know of."

Katja nodded. Mendel had suggested she ask that.

"I am Jewish. The man who fathered me was an SS officer. Did he kill many Jews? Did he? Tell me. I need to know the answer to that question, even though it horrifies me, and it makes me sick to think that his blood runs through my veins," Katja said.

"I won't lie to you. I can't. I don't know what he did, Katja. I hardly knew him. And I knew nothing of his actions with the Nazi party. I hate what the Nazis did to the Jews. I hate everything that the Nazis did. None of it should ever have happened. I am ashamed to be German. But please, you must know, not all Germans were Nazis. Kurt hated the Nazis and everything they stood for, and once I found out what they were doing, I hated them, too. I am ashamed of what the Nazi party and of what I did to you. And God knows I am sorry."

"You hardly knew my father?"

"I was young. I thought I was in love. He was handsome. A good-looking man in a uniform. I was just a girl. I had never even thought that anyone could be as cruel and heartless as the Nazis turned out to be. I know that it is no excuse, Katja. There is no explanation that could justify what I did."

"What made you decide to go to the Lebensborn?

"He left me. I was pregnant. I was alone. I couldn't tell my parents. I couldn't bring the shame of having a child out of wedlock down on their heads. My family doctor suggested the Lebensborn. I jumped at the opportunity. I didn't think ahead. It all seemed so easy. But then, from the first moment when I felt you stir inside of me, I knew I'd made a terrible mistake. I wanted to keep you. I begged them. But they would not listen. Katja, Katja. All I can say is I am sorry. From the bottom of my heart, I am sorry. I met Kurt in the Lebensborn. His sister was my roommate. Kurt and I fell in love, and I realized that I wanted nothing to do with any Nazis any more. As soon as I got out of Steinhöring, I came to the farm and we got married. I've led a simple life since then."

"Did you ever try to find me?" Katja asked.

"Of course. When the war was over, Kurt and I searched. We discovered that you were adopted by Manfred and Christa Blau. We heard that Manfred died in prison, which of course we now know is not true. But at the time Kurt and I believed it. Then we looked for Christa and found her obituary. There was no mention of you. We had reached a dead end. I was distraught. I thought you were dead . . ."

"There was nothing she could do, Katja. Believe me, she tried. She even looked for Eric. We thought he might have taken you. We looked all over Europe, exhausted all of our funds, but we couldn't find him," Kurt said.

"In my heart I am a Jew. I was raised a Jew. I don't know how you feel about Jews, and I don't care. You may have given birth to me, but you are not my mother," Katja said. "This is Zofia Zuckerman; she is my mother."

Helga nodded as the tears ran down her cheeks and her nose was running. She coughed. Kurt sat down beside her and pulled her close to him.

"I know you don't believe me, Katja, but I've always loved you. I dreamed of this day for so many years. I prayed that you would come to find me. I hoped, I prayed, that you were alive, and that you would someday forgive me for what I had done. I don't expect instant understanding but please, Katja, over time, try to understand. You probably won't believe this either, but I have nothing against Jews. I am glad that this woman, Zofia, raised and took care of you," Helga said. "I am grateful to her." "I am grateful to you," Helga said to Zofia.

"I believe you." Katja gently touched Helga's arm. It was a difficult gesture for Katja. She felt only pity, no ties to this strange woman at all. "I think we should go," Katja said.

"Katja . . ." Helga said.

"Yes?"

"I know right now that your head must be spinning. You are hurt and confused, but please consider coming back to see me. I don't expect you to love me, and I know that I am not like a mother to you, but maybe we can be friends. Maybe, please, maybe, sometime in the future," Helga said.

Katja shrugged. "I don't know. I don't know what to say," Katja answered.

"It's all right. Just think it over, please." Helga said.

"I will," Katja answered, and then she turned to Mendel. "Take me back to the hotel, please."

"Are you staying in Germany for a while?" Helga asked.

"No, I'm going home. I want to go home," Katja said.

"Home?" Helga asked.

"I want to go home to Israel . . . to the Promised Land."

Chapter 86

When they returned to the hotel, Katja took a long, hot shower. Then she lay on the bed. Zofia left her alone in the hotel room, giving her time to think. Katja closed her eyes in the dark room. Her journey was over; now she knew. She'd seen her birth mother, heard the reasons why Helga didn't raise her. Katja believed Helga when she said that she had wanted to keep her child. What really constitutes a mother? Was it the woman who raised you, who held you when you cried, or the one who carried you in her body for nine months? Was it the one who pushed you into the world and breathed the breath of life into your tiny lungs? Did bloodlines really matter? So, her father had been an SS officer. Despicable. But how much of him was really inside of her? She had never felt any evidence of hatred or cruelty within herself, nothing that attached her to this man from the SS. Whoever Eric was, to Katja, he was only a stranger. Isaac was her father. It was Isaac who taught her right from wrong. His values had shaped her life. The only ties she had to this Nazi was a few minutes of pleasure that he'd taken with the woman she'd met today, another stranger, a woman she would not claim as her own mother.

Katja sat up and leaned back against the headboard of the bed. She put her hand over her forehead. There was no doubt that the tension of the day had caused her to have the beginning of a nasty headache. Today was the first time she'd heard of Eidel. Zofia had so many secrets. She wondered if the day would come when Eidel would come searching for Zofia, asking questions. It was all so complicated. In a way Eidel was her sister, but not by blood. Her mind felt like it was a merry-go-round going at breakneck speed; so many questions without answers. Katja decided that soon she must confront Zofia and ask to know every secret that her mother kept. It was the only way that things could be as they were before . . .

There was a knock at the door. "Katja, it's me, Mendel."

Katja got up and opened the door. She was wearing a fuzzy, pink bathrobe that had begun to pill with age. The room was dark except for the light shining through the slatted blinds over the window. Her hair was still wet from the shower. "Come in," she said. Then she sat down on the bed.

"How are you doing?" Mendel asked, sitting down beside Katja and rubbing her shoulder.

"I don't know. I'm just trying to make sense of everything."

"I understand. But I don't think you *can* make sense of it really. I think you just have to accept it and then go forward with your life."

"You're right. I can't change what happened."

"And you know what? I wouldn't want to. Everything that has happened to you has made you who you are, and you are a wonderful girl, Kat. I have wanted to tell you this for a long time." He lifted her chin so that he could look into her eyes. "I love you."

She gazed at his face. He was so genuine.

Mendel.

He'd been her best friend, always there for her, for as long as she could remember.

Mendel.

When she was ten years old, he'd climbed a tree, almost breaking his neck, to retrieve her cat.

Mendel.

When she was sixteen and sick with whooping cough, he'd sat by her bed and read to her. Everyone else, except her parents had stayed far away. They were afraid to catch her illness, but not Mendel.

Not Mendel.

Then, a few years later, he'd gone to work in town at night so that he could buy his first car. When he brought it home, she was the first one he took for a ride. And, even though he treasured that vehicle, he let her use it as he taught her to drive. But, most importantly, when her life exploded, and all of this horrifying information came to light, Elan ran away, but not Mendel. Mendel stayed and Mendel comforted her. He'd found Leah and then Helga, because he knew that she must know the truth so that she could release it. He'd made all of the arrangements to bring her to Europe.

Mendel.

She was still looking into his eyes. Mendel . . . he was funny, gentle, sincere, and easy to talk to, warm, understanding, and intelligent. She smiled at him and squeezed his hand. Mendel, with his tussled hair, his eyes the color of a field of green grass after a sun shower, sprinkled with golden dandelions.

Katja reached up and touched his face. "Mendel" she whispered, shaking her head.

"Do you think that you could ever love me, Kat?" he said. "I would marry you in an instant. I'd make you a good husband."

His eyes were locked on hers and glassed-over with emotion.

"I do love you, Mendel. I just don't know if it's in the way that you want me to love you. Maybe it is. Perhaps someday I could marry you. It is just that, right now, I am so perplexed. This has all been a great deal for me to absorb. I need time. I need time to sort out my feelings. I'm not saying no. I'm just saying please, give me time."

He gently ran his fingers over the curve of her face. "You can have as much time as you need. I've always been here. I'll always be here. And I'll always love you . . ."

Chapter 87

Aryeh, Elan's brother, was the only one who knew how badly Elan felt about his break-up with Katja. Elan didn't tell Aryeh, but he knew his brother. They were close in age and they grew up as the best of friends. Aryeh knew that Elan was not one to express his feelings in words, but Aryeh could see the sadness that seemed to have overtaken Elan.

When Brenda and Aryeh got married, Elan drank to excess at the wedding, and then he got into a fistfight with another guest, busting the man's lower lip. Then, after Aryeh had spent a half hour on his wedding day, settling his brother down; Elan had decided to leave. As he stumbled out of the reception hall, he took a turn and fell down the stairs, embarrassing his mother. Aryeh refused to allow Elan to drive, and Elan got angry, punching his brother in the stomach. Then he turned and walked out, leaving his family to worry about him until the following morning.

A year later Brenda announced that she was pregnant. Elan sent flowers to his sister-in-law, but he did not make a trip out to see the couple. Nor did he call. The last conversation that they had had was the morning after the wedding when Aryeh telephoned to be sure that Elan had made it home safely. Then, Elan and Aryeh had not spoken in over a year. Elan's parents were still angry with Elan for his behavior at the wedding, but Aryeh recognized what Elan was going through and he forgave him.

When the time came to re-enlist in the IDF, Elan declined. Instead, he left the army and began to wander. He spent a few months backpacking through the Golan Heights, alone and lost in thought. When he returned from the wilderness he spent a couple of weeks at a kibbutz. He kept to himself and when anyone tried to befriend him, he was cold and distant.

One morning before sunrise, Elan left the kibbutz without ever saying good-bye to anyone. Then he checked into a cheap motel and lay soaking in the Dead Sea for several days, letting the water draw the impurities out of his body. He lay staring up at the blue sky, thinking how the color matched Katja's eyes. At night, Elan drank far too much and then he slept until late in the afternoon. The money he'd saved while he had been in the army was dwindling fast. He had tried to leave his old life behind, tried to run away from anything that made him think about Katja. But, Elan could not overcome feeling guilty for how he had treated his brother. So finally, over a year and a half after Aryeh and Brenda's wedding, Elan picked up the phone and called Aryeh.

"Aryeh, it's Elan."

"How are you? Where are you?" Aryeh's voice went a few octaves higher than normal.

"In a motel."

"Are you all right?"

"I'm fine. I'm just doing a little traveling," Elan said, trying to sound casual.

"I miss you. Mama and Papa are worried about you."

"There's nothing to worry about. I'm doing fine. I just wanted to call and say hello. See how Brenda was doing."

"She's doing all right. We're excited. The baby will be here before you know it, just a couple more months. You'll be an uncle."

"Yes, can you just imagine? I'm happy for you both," Elan said.

"Why don't you come and stay here with us for a while?" Aryeh said.

"I might just do that someday. Who knows? We'll see."

"Elan, listen to me. I don't know where you are, and I have no idea where you're going, but please try to keep in touch, will you? I don't like not hearing from you for a long time. It makes me worry."

"Oh, come on! How can you worry about me? You know I can take care of myself."

"Yes, I know that."

There was an uncomfortable silence.

"Aryeh, I'm sorry for ruining your wedding." Elan said.

"You didn't ruin my wedding. You're my brother, my blood. Just having you at the wedding helped to make it perfect. So, forget it, whatever happened is the past. Come now, and stay with us, please. Brenda and I would love to have you."

"We'll see. I'm checked into this motel right by the Dead Sea. I'm paid up for a month. When the month is over, maybe I'll come," Elan said, knowing he would never go stay with his brother and his brother's wife.

"I'm glad you called, Elan. Give me the number at the hotel so I can call you once in a while, just to say hello."

Elan felt wretched. He didn't want to give Aryeh the number. He wanted to crawl underground and rot there.

"Elan, please, just give me the number. I would like to try and stay in touch. It would mean a lot to me if I could hear your voice at least once a week. Besides, I sometimes need a friend. With Brenda pregnant she acts crazy a lot of the time. It would be good to be able to call my brother when she gets nuts. You know?"

Elan laughed. "I have heard that women get crazy when they're pregnant."

"It's true. Sometimes she's happy, the next minute she's sad. Sometimes she's mad at me for no reason. It all makes no sense. But I try to be as patient as possible."

"All right, got a pen?" Elan said.

"Yes, what's the number?"

Elan gave Aryeh the number to the hotel, then the extension number to his room. It felt good to be back on speaking terms with his brother.

After a few drinks from a bottle, that he kept beside his bed, Elan fell asleep, forgetting to eat. He was losing weight. His clothes were loose and he had begun avoiding looking in the mirror.

The days turned into weeks. Elan lost track of time. He was terribly lonely, but so tied up inside of himself that he couldn't express his feelings to anyone. Each week, when Aryeh would call, Elan would act as if he were doing great. He'd tell Aryeh, how much he was enjoying his travels. But, Elan knew that his brother didn't believe him.

Then, one evening at eight o'clock, the phone in his room rang. For no logical reason, Elan immediately thought of Katja. Perhaps she'd gotten the number from Aryeh. When he thought of Katja, Elan's heart beat a little faster, even though he knew it was just a fantasy. He'd been lying in bed watching television, drinking. He put the glass of whiskey on the nightstand and turned to lift the telephone receiver.

"Hello."

"Elan." It was Aryeh. This call would be his second call this week.

"How are you?"

"Not so good, Elan. Papa had an accident."

"What kind of accident?" Elan sat up in his bed.

"Well, Papa was driving the truck. He was going to pick up oranges. It was a long ride. If he had called me, I would have gone for him. But he didn't call me."

"So? Where is he? Is he all right? Talk Aryeh . . . Tell me . . ."

"He fell asleep at the wheel, Elan. He's dead."

"Oh MY GOD . . ." Elan said, his hand trembling as he held the receiver.

"You have to come home for the shivah. Mama needs you."

"I'll be there," Elan said.

Elan hung up the phone, his mind still hazy from the alcohol. Then, without folding his clothes, he threw all of his things into his backpack, got into the car, and began driving toward his parent's home. He stopped a few miles down the road and got a cup of black coffee and a glass of ice water. He drank the coffee quickly although it burned his tongue. Then he poured the water over his head. His hair and his shirt were soaked, and it was cold outside, mid-January. But, at least he was awake and alert. Now he could go home.

Chapter 88

Elan stood at the gravesite, holding his mother's arm. The way that she swayed in the wind, it felt as if she wanted to fall into the grave beside his father.

They returned to the house where Elan and Aryeh had grown up. Outside the neighbors had left a bottle of water and a box of paper napkins. It was a tradition that when Jewish people returned from a funeral at the cemetery, they poured the water over their hands before entering the house. This is what they did.

Inside the house, all of the mirrors had been covered and the immediate family removed their shoes. The Amsels were in mourning, and this was the shivah period. During the shivah, which would last for the next seven days, all of their friends and relatives would come to the house bringing food, to pay their respects. And, before the visitors departed, they would eat something sweet so as not to take the bitterness of death with them when they left. Traditions.

For seven days Elan sat on one side of his mother, while his sister, his brother, and Brenda sat on the other as people came and went. Brenda looked as if she might go into labor at any given moment. Some of the visitors tried to distract Elan's mother with good memories of his father, others just offered condolences. On the seventh day, after everyone had gone, Elan's mother poured herself a cup of coffee and came to sit down between her sons.

"Elan, I would like to talk to you," she said. He looked at her. His mother, always so strong, so in control, now looked weak and lost.

"Yes, mother?"

"I want you to take over your father's business. It would be good for you. Aryeh is working as an accountant. He is doing well and he should not change jobs. But I think this would be good for you."

"No, mother, I don't want to spend my life like a fool, working at a fruit stand in the market," Elan said.

His mother's eyes, already red from crying, flashed with anger. She slapped him hard across the face. "It was good enough for your father. What makes you so high and mighty?"

"I'm sorry, mother. I didn't mean it that way."

"There is no way to mean it. You will come home and stay here with me until you get on your feet. And you will take over your father's business."

This was a twofold operation on her part, Elan thought. His mother was worried about him. She knew he had no direction and she was trying to straighten him out. But, at the same time, she needed him to support her. She needed him to work the business. He didn't want this, but how could he leave her alone without anyone to help her. She could never lift the boxes of produce herself. If he left, she would have to try and sell the business. And then what? If she moved in with Aryeh and Brenda their marriage would suffer greatly. He knew how demanding his mother could be, and two women in one household? Not a good situation at all. So, what other choice did he have?

"All right mother. I'll do it."

"Don't look so pained, Elan. It's not a bad business. You'll earn a living and make some friends, too."

"Yes, mother . . ." he said. "I'm tired. I'm going to bed."

While they were sitting shivah, the boys had each slept in the rooms where they slept as children. Tonight, Aryeh and Brenda left to go home.

Elan went to his room and took off his clothes. His life had not turned out the way he'd planned.

Chapter 89

At first Elan hated working at the busy market on Ben Yehuda Street. Around every corner and down every aisle, buyers and sellers bargained for everything, from jewelry to spices. The noise level took some getting used to, and most days ended with Elan closing his stand to return home, his head pounding with a terrific headache.

But, as the weeks went by, Elan made friends with the owners of the neighboring stands. He got used to Amand, the jeweler, calling out to the tourists walking by. "I have the finest gold. My gold is 24-karat. Look, come on, just take a look."

Or the old man who came every Wednesday morning to buy his food for the week. "I'll give you fifty shekels for those olives," the old man could be heard saying to the vendors.

"Fifty shekels? That's not even enough for half of this. Look at the size of the bottle."

"Fifty-five shekels and that's my final offer."

"Sixty. Sixty shekels. Look at these olives. Beautiful, beautiful I tell you."

"Done."

And the sale was made.

His friend Gad often brought him pita stuffed with falafel, and in exchange Elan gave him apples, ripe persimmons, and lettuce.

Elan was too tired to go out at night, and he didn't drink nearly as much as he had before his father's death. The market forced him to be awake at 4:00 a.m. in order to set up, and so he was usually in bed by nine.

Work consumed him, and he was glad that he had very little time to think or to reminisce. Still, when he saw a girl with long golden curls walking through the stalls in the marketplace, his heart ached for a moment with the memory.

Brenda gave birth to a little girl three weeks after the shivah ended. Elan was there with

Aryeh to celebrate.

And so it was that the years crawled by. Elan's mother grew older and more dependent upon him. Without her husband, she was lost. She leaned on her son for everything. Elan didn't care. He wasn't looking for a wife, or a life of his own. He'd given up. It had been a long while since his breakup with Katja and he'd decided that he was done with women. Meanwhile, Elan's relationship with his brother grew stronger. He became a wonderful uncle to his niece, bringing clever gifts for her birthday and Hanukah. It began to seem as if Elan would grow old as a lonely bachelor.

But . . . then, it happened.

On a day like any other, Elan was sitting at his stall in the market, waiting for customers to arrive. He was eating an apple. "Do you want an apple?" he asked Gad, who was just across the aisle.

"Yeah, sure," Gad said.

Elan tossed him a shiny, red apple.

It was then that a petite young woman with long, straight hair the color of red clay, walked up and began bargaining with Gad for a silver necklace. The fire-haired woman was accompanied by a girlfriend with short, curly brown hair. He watched them. The little one had spunk. He laughed to himself.

"You would think it was diamonds instead of silver and opals," she said, tossing her red hair just as a ray of sunlight fell upon it, making it look like a flame. "I'll give you two hundred shekels. That's it, that's all it's worth."

She was American. Even though she spoke Hebrew, he could hear it in her accent.

"Two hundred shekels? I'd give it away first," Gad said.

"Then give it away. See if I care. There are plenty of other sellers here," the little redhead said. Her curly-haired friend had gone a few feet away to look at some cloth handbags.

"Gad . . . come on . . . give it to her for two hundred; she's a friend of mine," Elan called to Gad.

"You know her, Elan?"

"Yeah, I know her."

"All right, then. You're a friend of Elan's? For you . . . 200 shekels, it is."

After she made the purchase, the redhead came over to Elan's stand.

"Hey, thanks," she said.

"Of course," Elan smiled. "I'm Elan." She was not beautiful, but she had a warm smile and a cute sprinkle of freckles across her nose.

"I'm Janice, and that's my friend, Bonnie." The girl pointed to her friend, who was a few stalls away, deciding on which handbag to purchase.

"Nice to meet you."

"Same here."

"So you are visiting Israel?" Elan said.

"Yes, Bonnie and I are staying on a kibbutz."

"Ahhh, so you are our Jewish-American cousins. May I ask how you like Israel so far?"

"I love it. I've only been here a few weeks, but it's a wonderful country. When I told my friends I was coming they said that when I got off the plane I would feel like kissing the ground because this is the Jewish homeland."

"And did you?"

"Did I what?"

"Kiss the ground?"

"Well, no, but I did feel at home." She smiled.

"I'm glad. Welcome to our home." He smiled

"Listen, I owe you for helping me with that negotiation over there. How about if I take you to lunch?" she said. She was so open, so American. He had never known a woman to be so forward. The boldness made him smile.

"Well, I never leave my stand for lunch. But how about if I take you to dinner?" he said, surprising himself. Elan had not been out with another woman since his break up with Katja.

"I'd love that," she said, picking up one of the apples on his stand and taking a bite.

Gosh, she was bold. But he liked it.

"Good. Where can I pick you up?" Elan asked.

"I'll meet you here at the market. What time do you finish?" she asked.

"Five," he said.

"I'll be here at five-thirty. How is that?"

"I look forward to it."

Chapter 90

Elan and Janice went to a small café a few miles from the market, inside of the old city. She asked a million questions about the menu. Elan finally suggested that he order for the two of them. Janice laughed, and then she agreed. "You can order for me this time, but I'll study more about the food here and next time *I'll* be able to order for *you*."

Elan laughed.

They sat for several hours at an outside table, under an umbrella, with a candle illuminating the night.

"So you were born here in Israel?" Janice asked.

"Yes, I'm Sephardic. This country means everything to me," he said.

"I have noticed that all of the Israeli's I meet seem to feel that way."

"It's because we have to fight constantly to keep this little piece of land."

"You know, in America, when you meet someone, you never talk about America. But in Israel, when you meet someone, it seems that Israel is the first thing that you talk about."

"This country is different than any other place in the world. It was built on the blood of our people," Elan said.

She nodded. He watched her, wondering if she realized how serious he was about that statement.

"So tell me more about you . . . what do you like to do?"

"I love American music. I love comedians. Have you heard Menachem Zilberman, the comedian? He's on the radio all the time."

"Yes, I love him. He's hilarious."

"You can understand him?"

"Most of it, yes," she said. "My Hebrew is not too bad."

"He does a live show in Tel Aviv. We should go sometime," he said.

"I would love to."

"So tell me a little about you, Janice."

"I live in a primarily Jewish suburb of Chicago, which is a big city. I love to paint, and someday I want to be a famous artist. Like Dali."

"Have you done any paintings since you've been here?"

"Not yet. But I know I will. It's so beautiful here that I can't help but be inspired."

"Yes, it is beautiful," he said. "Do you have any siblings?"

"A sister, and a dog, who is like another sister."

He smiled.

"You want to see a picture of my dog?" Janice said, taking a picture out of her wallet of a beautiful golden retriever. It was sitting beside a young girl who had hair the same color as Janice's.

"She's pretty."

"Who, my sister or the dog?"

He laughed. "Both.

"So what about you? Do your parents live near here?" she asked.

"My father passed away, and I've been living with my mother. She needs me to support her and she's getting old. I wouldn't want to leave her alone. She could fall or something else could happen. Losing my father was very hard on her. She depended on him for everything."

"That must be tough. I mean you're still young and I'm sure you go out all the time," Janice said.

"No, not really. Believe it or not, this is the first date I have been on in years," he said.

"Because of your mother?"

"No, I had a bad break-up. It happened before my father passed away."

"Do you want to talk about it?" she asked.

He shook his head, "No, I'd rather not. It's in the past."

"I had a bad break-up, too. I'd been dating this boy for two years and one day he just said that he met someone else."

"How old are you?" he asked.

"Eighteen."

"Do you know how old I am?"

"No idea." She shrugged.

"Let's just say that I'm closer to thirty than I am to twenty. Do you think I'm too old for you?"

"Not at all. You're older and more mature than the boys I knew at home in the states."

He smiled. "I have an idea. Let's both forget the past. We can start fresh from today. I'd like to make a toast to the future." He poured them each a glass of wine and they clinked their glasses.

"To the future."

"To the future."

The following night Elan picked Janice up at the kibbutz where she was staying and they dined together again. By the end of the week, Elan took Janice to meet Brenda and Aryeh. They went to Brenda and Aryeh's home, where the four of them had cake and coffee and sat on the floor playing with Elan's niece, Aviva.

Elan watched Janice with the baby. It had been a long time since he'd considered that he might want to have a family of his own. Aviva took to Janice right away. Janice played with the toddler, making her laugh. And for the first time in a very long time, Elan's heart was touched—touched by this warm and gentle American girl.

When she met Elan's mother, Janice was respectful. Of course, as Elan predicted, his mother was critical and negative, but Janice was Jewish and because she was Jewish, Elan knew that his mother would get used to Janice. And, besides that, Janice was smart. The second time she came to see Elan's mother; she brought her a gift, a lovely silk scarf. Slowly, with patience, Janice began to win the affections of her boyfriend's cantankerous mother.

Although he considered taking Janice to the Ghetto Fighter's kibbutz, he could not bear to go back there. It would only rekindle memories of Katja. And, of course, he could not forget Katja's background. Yes, it was best to stay away. So instead, Elan took Janice walking along the beach at night. He kissed her under the stars and, ever so slowly, Elan began to feel alive again.

Janice was not the kind of girl to sit back and allow Elan to wallow in self-pity. She was full of life, and her exuberance was contagious. When Elan was not working, Janice taught him to play tennis. At night they went to the theater. On Sundays, they swam in the Mediterranean and took hikes into the mountains. Before Elan met Janice, he had lost his zest for life. Now he felt that, in many ways, she'd saved him.

Aryeh and Brenda wanted to take a vacation, so they asked Aryeh's mother to stay with Aviva for a long weekend. She agreed. It would be easier on the child if Grandma came to Aryeh and Brenda's house. After all, Aviva's toys and things were already set up there.

Elan's mother left on a Thursday morning.

That night, after work, Elan picked Janice up at the kibbutz. For the first time since they met, Elan and Janice were totally alone in Elan's house. Janice insisted upon preparing an authentic American dinner for Elan. She peeled and cut potatoes, which she planned to mash with butter and salt. Then she breaded chicken breasts to fry. As the potatoes began to boil on the stove, Elan walked into the kitchen. He came up behind Janice and then he turned Janice toward him. He kissed her softly at first. Then she put her arms around him and kissed him long and deep. He reached over and turned off the burner on the stove. Then he lifted her in his strong arms and carried her to his bed.

It had been a long time since Elan had been intimate with a woman. Although his physical needs were overpowering, he forced himself to be slow and tender. Gentle, gentle with this wonderful girl who had breathed life back into his broken heart.

After they made love, she took his hand and kissed his palm.

"I love you, Elan," she said.

"I love you too, Janice. You have done so much for me. So much more than you could ever know," he said. "Do you think that you could live in Israel? Do you think you could make this place your home?"

"I do. I love it here."

"You know that this land means a lot to me. Because of how important Israel is to our people, it will always be a priority in my life. It's important to me that you understand that."

"Yes, I understand. I feel the same way."

"You do?"

"I do. I understand perfectly."

"Will you marry me?"

"Really?" she said, her face lighting up.

"You don't want to?"

"I do, I do want to . . ."

"Then, will you marry me?"

"Yes," she said, turning over and kissing him, then laughing, "YES . . ."

Chapter 91

Frances Lichtenstein woke up to the ringing of the telephone. Her heartbeat increased to a rapid pace. Her daughter was in Israel. They had agreed that Janice would telephone once a week, on Sunday. If it was her, then something must be wrong.

"Hello."

"Mom?"

"Who is it? Is it Janice?" Mr. Lichtenstein asked, awakened by the phone.

"Yes, Ron, it's Janice," Frances said to her husband. Then she spoke into the receiver. "Are you all right? Is everything ok?"

"Yes, Mom, it's better than okay. I've met someone. I am getting married. He's an Israeli, and the most wonderful man I've ever met."

"What, Janice? Who is this man? You are far too young; you have to come home and go to college. You hardly know this boy, you haven't even been in Israel for a year and you're going to marry someone you just met? You promised if we would let you go for a couple of years, you would come home and go to college. Now this?"

"I can't leave him. I love him. I am going to stay here and live in Israel."

"This is ridiculous. You can't do this. You've only been gone a few months. You hardly know this boy," Frances said. "Please Janice, don't do anything crazy."

"What's going on?" Ronald asked.

"She met some boy in Israel. Now she wants to marry him, and to stay there."

"Give me the phone," Janice's father said.

"Here, you talk to her. I don't know what to do."

"Janice, it's your father."

"Hi, Daddy."

"Your mother told me you want to get married and stay in Israel?"

"Yes, I do. I am going to get married and stay in Israel."

"Who is this boy? What does he do? Is he in college?"

"His name is Elan, he is an Israeli, he owns a fruit-stand in the market, and he's a little older so no, he's not in college."

"A fruit stand? Come on Janice." Her father's voice was raised. "And . . . older, how much older?"

"About ten years."

"Listen to me. You come home and then you spend a year apart from him. You go to college and then in a year, if you still feel the same way, I'll make you a beautiful wedding," her father said.

"I'm sorry, Dad, I know you mean well. But I've made up my mind. I am going to marry him. Now, the only decision is whether we get married here in Israel and have a small ceremony or whether we come to Chicago and have a wedding."

"Janice!" her father yelled.

"You and Mom can decide."

Chapter 92

Once her parents agreed to the marriage, Janice went home to put things together for the wedding. She would need a gown, something that did not require much alteration, which was difficult because she was short. However, her figure was slim and, therefore, the only necessary alterations were the length. Then, there was a problem with the rabbi. Rabbi Shultz, who she had known her entire life, was booked every weekend for the next six months. This substantiated her mother's argument, that she needed more time to plan a wedding. But Janice took control. She found another rabbi to officiate the ceremony, and although the hotel where the wedding would take place was not her first choice, it was available for a Saturday night and so Janice booked it. The florist Janice chose was a little known flower shop that was eager to please. So, with a lot of effort, and Janice's strong will, the entire event was put together and would take place in three months. Barbara, Janice's sister, tried to convince Janice to change her mind, to give herself more time. Barbara felt that Janice was rushing things, but it was no use. Janice had made up her mind.

While she was in Chicago, busy with the wedding plans, Janice called Elan every evening, charging the calls to her parents. Elan protested, because of the cost. But she insisted that her father would not mind and that money had never been an issue. So, Elan gave in, and quite frankly, he was glad to hear her voice. He missed her. He missed their evenings together. Janice was wonderful company. Elan enjoyed having someone to share meals with other than his mother. He relished the time they spent making love, teasing, and laughing. He missed their afternoons at the beach, and her witty jokes. She was well-read and kept him abreast of world events with interesting insight and lively conversation. Yes, he missed her very much.

Once the wedding was planned and the date set, Elan and his family made plans to travel to Chicago. Elan closed his fruit stand for two weeks. Then he, his mother, his brother, his brother's wife, and his niece, all flew to Chicago for the wedding. Although Janice's parents were upset that she was moving to Israel, they knew their daughter. Janice was stubborn. She had made a decision, and she would not be swayed. So, rather than lose their daughter entirely, their only alternative was to welcome her husband and accept their new family of in-laws.

Elan and his family were excited about the trip to America. They arrived several days before the wedding. Between parties and dress fittings, Janice drove them around, showing them the Field Museum of Natural History and the Art Institute of Chicago. She took Brenda shopping at her favorite store, Marshall Field's while the boys stayed at home with Aviva.

The wedding was scheduled for a Saturday evening. On that afternoon, Janice and Elan did not see each other. It was tradition that the bride and groom be separated until the moment the bride walked down the aisle in her dazzling white gown and veil.

The chuppah was made of large cabbage roses in pink and white, and the bridesmaids wore pink dresses of the exact same shade of pink. A harpist played as each of the bridesmaids walked down the aisle. Elan's brother, in a black tuxedo, accompanied Janice's sister and then Janice's best friend, Bonnie, was escorted by a close cousin.

Next came Elan. He was handsome in the black tuxedo that fit his broad shoulders and slender waist. Then the music stopped. After a moment of silence the harpist began playing "Here Comes the Bride." Janice entered. She looked elegant in her white lace gown inlaid with pearls. Elan watched Janice approach. He smiled as she winked at him from beneath her veil. Yes, he'd made the right decision.

Janice joined Elan under the chuppah, and then they turned to face the rabbi. As they took their vows, Janice's mother wiped a tear from her eye. Then the rabbi handed the glass of wine to Janice. She took a sip of the wine and handed it to Elan. He finished the wine and then returned the glass to the rabbi, who wrapped it in a white napkin and placed it on the floor. Elan stomped on the glass, and the sound of the shattering filled the room. Then the entire crowd of guests yelled "Mazel tov."

In honor of their Israeli guests, Janice's parents served all Israeli foods during the cocktail hour. The bar was open all night, and only the best liquor was served. Then the dinner was served. Plates overflowing with food were carried to the tables by white-gloved waiters. The band played and the couple had their first dance as man and wife. Then, after dinner, there was a long, extensive sweet table with an ice sculpture and every imaginable dessert.

Elan and his family had never seen such opulence.

On a lovely spring evening, Janice Lichtenstein became Janice Amsel.

The Amsel's stayed in Chicago for a week. Janice took her new family sightseeing. They went to the Museum of Science and Industry, where they saw a futuristic telephone. The phone had a screen attached to it, and the parties who were talking could see each other on that screen as they talked. Amazing! It was mind-boggling to think about what wonderful inventions the future could hold. They took an elevator down through an actual coal mine. Then they left the museum and had lunch at a kosher deli on State Street, with sandwiches so thick that none of them could finish.

America, the land of plenty.

Chapter 93

The newlyweds moved into the house where Elan lived with his mother.

There was some tension between Janice and her mother-in-law. Both were strong-willed women, secretly competing for dominance of the home. Elan was at work during the day, and that was when the competition was in full swing. But, because she was afraid that her son and his wife would move out, at night his mother made an effort to be as well-behaved as possible.

Elan found that his wife was a wonderful help with his business. She had a good mind, and she was a wonderful artist who painted signs that attracted customers. She didn't mind hard work, and many days she came to help him at the market. They shared the same sense of humor and, as time went by, Janice grew to be more and more beautiful in Elan's eyes.

And so a year passed.

One night, as they lay in bed, she turned to him, "I have a special surprise for you."

"Oh?" He put his arm around her.

"I got tickets to see Menachem Zilberman in Tel Aviv. He's coming next month. I got us a hotel room. Why don't you take off for a couple of days, we can make a little get away of it?"

"I hate to leave the business . . ."

"ELAN!" she said, disappointed.

He laughed. "Of course, I'll take off. You silly girl. I wouldn't miss it for anything."

She laughed and reached up to kiss him. He turned her over and began kissing her neck.

"I love you so much," she whispered.

"I know you do, and I love you, too."

Chapter 94

On the way to the comedy show Janice turned to Elan, "Honey, please, pull over. I'm sick to my stomach."

He looked at her, his eyes filled with concern. Then he swerved the car to the side of the road. She got out and vomited.

"You're sick. Let's go home," he said.

"No, I'm fine."

"Janice. You just threw up. You're sick. I insist that we go back to the hotel."

"No, we've been looking forward to this evening for a month. I want to go."

"I don't care how long we've been looking forward to it. You're more important to me than a show. Now, let's go back home, so that you can lie down," he said.

"I feel better."

"I'm worried. Maybe it was food poisoning from the restaurant where we had dinner."

"Elan"

"Yes?"

"I was going to wait to tell you. I wanted to surprise you after the show tonight. But I guess I'll tell you now." She smiled at him and rubbed her belly. "I'm not sick . . . I'm pregnant."

"Janice! Oh MY GOD! I am going to be a father!" He reached across the seat and took her into his arms. "How long have you known?"

"Only a few weeks. I wanted to wait until tonight to tell you."

"OH, JANICE."

"You're happy?"

"Elated, I am on top of the world." He laughed and kissed her.

She laughed. "I am happy, too. We'll have to think of names."

"I'd like to use my father's name. I thought Aryeh would have named their daughter for him, but before my father had passed away, Aryeh had already promised Brenda to name the child for her mother, who died a year earlier. So, I would be so grateful to you if you would agree to name the baby for my father. His name was Gidon."

"Then if it's a boy, the baby's name will be Gidon."

"You would do that for me?" Elan asked.

"Yes, of course. I love you," she said.

"And if it's a girl?"

"I don't know, we'll have to figure it out," she said. "What is the female form of Gidon?"

"It doesn't need to be the same name, only the first letter."

"So her name will begin with a *G*?"

"If it's all right with you?"

"Of course it is. Do you like the name Gabby?"

"An American name? Yes, I like it very much," he said. "We'll have to give her a Hebrew name, too."

She reached over and squeezed his hand. "We'll figure it out together."

"Well, since it is June, the baby should come in February."

"Yes, the doctor gave me a due date of February 15th."

"February 15th," he said, and smiled.

The theater was filled with people. There were lines to get inside, and then more lines to the seats.

Once they were inside, Janice turned to Elan.

"Elan, I have to go to the bathroom," Janice said.

"Are you sick again?"

"A little. I guess it's to be expected." She smiled.

"All right. I don't want to get separated with all these people, so I'll wait right here outside of the bathroom until you come out. Then when you come out, we'll go and find our seats together."

"All right. I'll be right back."

She turned and walked through the door with the sign above it that said WOMEN.

Elan waited just outside the bathroom door. It seemed to be taking a long time. He watched the door open and close, women coming out and more going in. The lines into the theater were growing. He was worried about Janice; perhaps she was really ill.

Then the bathroom door opened. Elan saw a flash of honey-colored curls dripping down slender bare shoulders, eyes as blue as the Mediterranean Sea. The blond woman turned and her eyes locked with his. Those eyes, those celestial blue eyes, they brought back memories of making love, of looking down and getting lost in their depth, as they shined back up at him like stars, leading his way through the darkness. Those eyes had never stopped haunting him.

"Katja?" Elan said, his mouth was suddenly dry.

"Elan?" her voice cracked. They had not seen each other since the break-up.

He stood staring at her, stunned; he could not move. He wanted to speak, but no sound would come out of his mouth. Katja. She was more beautiful than he remembered. He had to say something, anything, before the moment passed and she was gone forever. Just as Elan was about to speak, Janice walked out of the bathroom. Janice took Elan's arm, "I'm sorry it took so long, there was a heck of a line in there. Let's hurry. The show is about to start," Janice said.

Elan nodded as Janice led him away. As they were walking towards the auditorium, Elan could not help himself, he had to turn back, he had to see her again, even if only for a second. Their eyes met. Katja, he thought . . . Katja.

Katja entered the stairway to the expensive box seats she shared with her husband, Mendel. Her muscles felt tense as she sat down beside him. He took her hand in his own, and kissed it gently. The four-carat emerald cut diamond caught the light and sparkled in a rainbow on the wall. She turned to him, smiled, and thought "Mendel, God bless Mendel."

On the other side of the auditorium at the entrance to the balcony, Janice handed the tickets to the usher. "You're up in row R, straight up the stairs, and then to the left," the usher said.

"Come on, Elan; why are you in a daze? I want to get to our seats before the lights are dimmed."

Elan nodded, forcing his head to turn back to his wife. Then he followed Janice up the stairs of the theater to their seats, right on the aisle. Janice slid into her chair. Elan sat down beside her.

"This is going to be fun. I just love Zilberman. I listen to him on the radio all the time." Janice reached over and patted Elan's hand. "What a perfect night this is, isn't it?" she said.

Elan felt his breath catch in his throat, a bead of sweat trickled down his cheek.

Before Elan had a chance to respond, the lights in the auditorium flickered twice, and then the room went dark. Zilberman took the stage. The crowd roared with applause and the show began.

Chapter 95

On the following day, which was June 5, 1967, Israel surprised her Arab neighbors who had been threatening to attack her. Instead of waiting for their assault, Israel took the reins. She turned around and seized the Gaza Strip. And so, the Six-Day War began . . .

Coming soon: To Be An Israeli

Afterword

On May 23, 1960, the Prime Minister of Israel, David Ben-Gurion, made an important announcement to the world . . .

With the assistance of Simon Weisenthal, Mossad had found Adolf Eichmann. They had kidnapped Eichmann and brought him to Israel, where he would stand trial.

The world watched as Eichmann's crimes were revealed. Eichmann took the stand on his own behalf, pleading for forgiveness. The trial ended on August 14, 1961, and on December 12 at 9:00 a.m. of the same year, he was convicted and sentenced to death for crimes against humanity. Then, on May 31, 1962, a noose was placed around his neck and Adolf Eichmann was executed by hanging.

Mengele, the Angel of Death, was never caught. Right after the war, he had several close calls; he was even imprisoned and escaped. Later, while he was hunted by the Avengers, whenever Mossad came close to capturing him, he disappeared. In 1979, he was living in Brazil. One morning, he went out for a swim and drowned. It is speculated that he had a stroke. But, there is no definitve evidence. Perhaps a Mossad agent finally caught up with him.

Please visit *www.RobertaKagan.com* for news and upcoming releases by Roberta Kagan. Join the email list, and have a free short story emailed to you!

A note from the author:

"I always enjoy hearing from my readers. Your feelings about my work are very important to me. Please contact me via Facebook or at www.RobertaKagan.com. All emails are answered personally, and I would love to hear from you."

Continue on to next page to discover more works by Roberta Kagan

Acknowledgements

Thank you, Thank you, Thank you.

First, I'd like to thank Ellen Sunshine, my editor. She took my messy manuscript and worked on it tirelessly, even through the holiday season, and now it is a novel that I am proud to have written. Ellen's meticulous attention to all of the details, not only the grammatical errors, which were plentiful, but also the historical details and the consistency made this novel a credible work. She has been my special angel on this project and I cannot thank her enough.

Then I would like to thank my dear friend who is the president of my book club and the director of all of my social media campaigns, Leigh Ann Lochtfeld. Her incredible technical savvy has helped me to gain an audience for my books. She has been with me for a year now, and she has been an ever-constant source of true inspiration.

And although she would not want to be mentioned, I want to thank the light of my life, my daughter, who formats all of my books and overseas the final copies making sure everything is organized and in order. I've seen her sit at the computer for hours at a time working on my novels. She is a no-holds-barred critic, and her honesty is sometimes painful but always insightful and (I hate to admit it) usually right.

Also, a great big hug and thank you to my husband, who reads every one of my novels and has always been my biggest supporter and fan. It's always a comfort to know he is behind me in everything I do.

I want to take a moment to thank God for sending me this difficult but rewarding life's purpose. It is always an honor to serve you in any way that you see fit to use me.

Blessings to all of my readers. YOU are the reason that I research. You are the reason I write. Without you, there is no purpose, and so I thank you from the bottom of my heart for your support. Every one of your letters means the world to me. And although I don't know all of you individually, I personally read and answer every one of your emails. I wish all of you the best that life has to offer, and may each of you always find that flicker of light that gives you joy.

Manufactured by Amazon.ca
Bolton, ON